ANGEL
OF THE
OUTBACK

Land of the Far Horizon

Voyage of the Exiles
Angel of the Outback

LAND OF THE FAR HORIZON ⚓ 2

ANGEL OF THE OUTBACK

PATRICIA
HICKMAN

BETHANY HOUSE PUBLISHERS
MINNEAPOLIS, MINNESOTA 55438

Cover by Patricia Keay

Published by Bethany House Publishers
A Ministry of Bethany Fellowship, Inc.
11300 Hampshire Avenue South
Minneapolis, Minnesota 55438

Printed in the United States of America.

Library of Congress Cataloging-in-Publication Data

Hickman, Patricia
Angel of the Outback / Patricia Hickman.
p. cm.

1. Australia—History—1788–1851—Fiction. 2. Frontier and pioneer life—Australia—Fiction. 3. Women pioneers—Australia—Fiction. I. Title. II. Series: Hickman, Patricia. Land of the far horizons ; 2.
PS3558.I2296A54 1995
813'.54—dc20 95–466
ISBN 1–55661–542–6 CIP

To my parents,
Lemond and Jeanie Davis,
avid garderners whose simple trust and faith in God
taught me to simply trust and have faith.
Every time I see a flower bloom
I will always remember
the garden of my childhood.

PATRICIA HICKMAN is a full-time writer and the wife of a pastor. She is the author of three books. She lives with her husband, Randy, and their three children, Joshua, Jessica, and Jared, in Louisiana.

Contents

1
Song of the Bush

January 1793

A small iron-barred window allowed in the early rays of dawn that bathed Sydney Cove in a watercolor wash of pale yellows and rosy pinks. The glory of the pure morning light streamed into the cold, dark room of the stone prison, outlining the cadaverous forms in a crimson mantle.

"It's a long time until forever." Rachel Langley smoothed the amber locks of the eleven-year-old Irish boy lying curled up on a frowzy cot. The rickety and brittle wooden bed threatened to collapse with the boy's labored breathing. A solicitous frown creased Rachel's brow. The sallow, clammy skin of the boy gave her good reason to worry. She stroked his cheek as she had done earlier, hoping to detect a dwindling fever instead of a rising one. She pressed the thin wisps of hair to the side of his pale face, and the strands clung to her fingertips like seaweed.

Coughing racked the boy's body as he tried to speak. A victim of the fever and famine that had swept through the colony at Sydney Cove, he was very weak and his voice faltered, "That's how l-long I'll be here, Miss Rachel—forever."

Walking over to gaze out the small window, Rachel saw the morning song of the bush had begun. Appearing almost rabbitlike, a kangaroo lifted her soft, brown head above a eucalyptus branch. The sun on her fur gave a warm, amber glow as she nibbled on gray-green leaves. Surrounding the kangaroo, a swarm of insects strummed out a herald for the dawn of day.

Rachel glanced around the dank stone cell, hand-hewn and built by convict labor. The frail forms, wedged closely about the room, scarcely stirred beneath their thin blankets, oblivious to the day that dawned so brilliantly around them. All of these boys were known by the military guards as "little depraved felons."

A model prisoner, Rachel had found a measure of freedom in being allowed to visit the juvenile sectors of the convict colony and to care for the sick and dying. Entering the dismal cells with a basket of ointments, Rachel was often greeted with grateful smiles from the young, ailing prisoners.

Rachel was taller than most of the women in the settlement. She had a firm, determined chin and a rosy complexion that glowed with feminine elegance. With her fiery locks draping around her shoulders and cascading about her shapely frame, she had become a welcome sight to the young felons, who affectionately called her "Sydney's Angel."

"Let me pray for you, love," Rachel's voice whispered above the sound of the lyrebirds calling from the few remaining wattle trees surrounding the stone structure. The boy nodded carefully, lest the movement cause another fitful bout of coughing. Rachel closed her eyes, holding back the tears that threatened to betray her confidence in the boy's future. "Please, Lord," she entreated, as much for her own faith as for the lad's. "Give him comfort and take the pain from him. Give him hope and peace. Jesus, be merciful to these your lambs."

The boy smiled wanly at Rachel and whispered, "Thank you."

"Hurry it up in there, convict!" A short-tempered guard ordered Rachel to bring an end to her labors. "You're wastin' time, y'are."

Her face bowed in forced servility, Rachel mustered enough courage to ask, "Have me papers come yet, Corporal Sykes?"

"No! An' ye may as well quit inquirin'! You'll be a convict until the militia decides otherwise. Now there's cells to swab, so hurry along or you'll take your next stop at the cat!"

Standing next to Sykes, a burly, stringy-haired mariner grinned lasciviously at Rachel, exposing his yellowed teeth. "You come an' visit me quarters next, wench. I'll take the wind out o' yer sails!"

Rachel felt a chill touch her nerves but kept her eyes bonded to the hard floor. In the last five years, her adroitness at keeping her distance from the loathsome men assigned to Sydney Cove had all but become an art.

"Get on wif ye!" Sykes shoved the mariner toward the door. "Nothin' but dogs sniffin' round for trouble, that's wot!" Turning to Rachel, he warned, "I can't keep 'em offa ye all day. Now out wif ye, wench!"

"Comin'. I'm almost finished with this lad, I am." Rachel answered quietly, subduing the angry retaliation that quickly sprang to mind. *Hold your tongue, girl!* she warned herself. *Not Christian, those thoughts*. She drew a bottle of foul-tasting laudanum from the basket and pulled the tiny cork from the top. "Here, now, love." Drawing the boy's face close to her own, she tilted the brown bottle and dribbled the contents into his mouth.

The boy winced, swallowed the medicine, and coughed hoarsely again while Rachel rested his head gently against the bed. "Thankin' you kindly, Miss Rachel. You've the best heart in this whole world, you do at that."

A mischievous grin crossed Rachel's face, and her green eyes gleamed down at the boy. "Hush up, now. No need to tire yourself worse, young man. I've just nothing better to do with me time, that's all."

"Sure you do. Like that other lot, you could be tradin' your favors for comforts and rum and such. I think the other boys are right, Miss Rachel. I believe you're really an angel," the lad whispered cautiously, keeping one eye trained on the guards.

Turning her head, Rachel coughed, then raised herself from the boy's side. A pain twisted sharply through her chest. The prison surgeon had warned her of the contagiousness of the diseases she had been tending. But no one else seemed willing to assist these young wards of England's harsh transportation system. Rachel pitied the children and remembered the cruelties that had been inflicted upon her and had robbed her of her own childhood innocence. *I must help them.* Her mind was set.

To the unskilled transportees, the land upon which the convict colony had been settled in Sydney Cove was unforgiving and cruel. The convicts transported from England had been forced to hack into the unplowed soil of New South Wales with rudimentary tools and bare hands. The inexperienced and poorly equipped slave labor had yielded little in the way of sustenance. Many convicts soon found the threat of the whip more welcome than the fruitless hours spent pounding away at the rocks. But the famine had shown no partiality to its subjects, and due to their meager allotments, even the cruel military guards found themselves haplessly added to the lists of the starving. As their hunger grew, so did their resentment against the convicts.

Rachel tugged at her ragged, coarse prison gown. The canary yellow and gray tunic had clearly marked her, as well as the other convicts in the settlement, the colony riffraff. Transportees, considered by the settlers to be worthless and fit-for-nothing, created an immediate footstool for the free Australians.

Once a prisoner fulfilled the seven-year transportation sentence, his or her life in the colony was no simpler. When granted freedom from the stone jails, the ex-convict was given another burdensome label—*emancipist.* The emancipists carried their own brand of stigma and an embittered cloak of prejudice which followed them throughout their days in Sydney Cove.

Stepping through the threshold of the prison door, Rachel

pretended to straighten the ointments, but her eyes were cast obliquely toward the feverish forms. "Forever *is* a long time, lads," she whispered to herself, remembering the thousands who had already perished. As the guard slammed the door behind her and the sound echoed through the cramped wing like a bound spirit, she reminded herself, "But the Lord is the timekeeper."

The morning rose in silent splendor beyond the fern-lined ledges and gorges surrounding the government square. The yellow beams of sunlight appeared to alert the spiked banksias that day was awakening, and their starburst designs stretched toward the heavens and awarded the morn with their exotic fragrance. But beside the beauty of nature lay also the ugliness of man. For the hopes of England did not swell quite so gloriously as did the day.

The putrid aroma of mud, animal waste, and human blood wafted through the bottom floor window of the government building. John Macarthur, his trim and tall frame erect, winced at the foul smell and turned his face from the window, where he sat outside the lieutenant-governor's office. A Scottish officer, Macarthur proudly wore the military's royal red coat, cut away at the hips with tails reaching to the back of his knees. He had arrived in New South Wales on the Second Fleet, accompanied by his wife and infant son. Although his military record was clean, he was prone to impetuous fits of anger, which provoked his fellow officers and left him unpopular among his peers. But his choleric disposition had served him well in the harsh surroundings of the convict colony, and his unbending attributes had not escaped the attention of the newly appointed lieutenant-governor, Francis Grose.

Macarthur's eyes, small and dark and the color of gunpowder, darted again toward the open window, where the light of the cloudless morning illumined the dingy town square. From his position, he could see a convict receiving no less than two hundred lashes at the flogging post. Knowing the punishment would most likely leave the victim an invalid and his back skinless, he mused inwardly, *I hope ye live, ye beggar. Death would serve ye more poorly than agony*. An enigmatic smile curved his ruddy face, setting off a gleam of gratification in his eyes.

The simple wooden door that led to Grose's office opened quickly, and a small-framed man bustled through, adjusting the spectacles on his face. He stopped briefly to acknowledge the lieutenant. "You Lieutenant Macarthur?"

Macarthur nodded, his eyes peering intently toward the open door as he reached to adjust the uncomfortable shirt frill protruding from the curve in his waistcoat.

"Good. Lieutenant-Governor Grose is anxious to meet with you. You may enter now." The man continued on his way down the hallway, his feet pounding the wooden floor in quick, determined succession.

Lifting himself from the chair, the lieutenant entered the doorway and found Francis Grose pouring himself a cup of tea. "Lieutenant Macarthur reporting, sir," Macarthur called politely.

"Come in, Macarthur." Grose seated himself while placing the teacup to the side of his desk. "Take a seat. We've much to discuss."

The sound of the flogging drifted through the window. Pain-filled wails of the victim punctuated the stillness of the day, a sound on the compound as common as that of birds in the trees.

Grose scowled as his hand stopped midway to his lips with the teacup. "Let's take a walk, shall we? I need some fresh air. It will do you good, as well."

"Certainly, sir."

Grose ambled tardily, assisted by a gold-topped cane. "Walk ahead of me, will you? This leg o' mine gives me trouble from time to time. Got wounded badly in the American rebels' War of Independence. Least I'm still alive!" His ashen face showed signs of stress. Deep lines gravitated from graying brows and pale blue eyes.

Macarthur nodded politely but sighed inwardly. He had little patience with those who were physically inferior.

The two departed through the rear of the government

building, giving little notice to the convict laborers digging lethargically in the sandstone quarry nearby. The lot of the felons had been reduced to nothing short of slavery. Under the first governor's command, the officers and convicts had been meted out equal rations, much to the military personnels' indignation. Desperately wanting a separatist class, the military guards had resorted to physical abuse to put the convicts in their rightful place. Resentfully, they referred to the felons as "crawlers."

Walking past the plebeian shacks of mud and twigs, Grose surveyed his surroundings. Extending his hand ceremoniously, he said with pontifical simplicity, "Here's our oyster."

"Beggin' yer pardon, sir?" Macarthur was taken aback by the leader's comment.

"New South Wales, man. We're sitting in the center of a gold mine that everyone has overlooked." Grose gazed outwardly toward the sea, his eyes looking beyond the lapping waves of the beach. "Take our Governor Phillip for example. The man was blinded by the obstacles; he couldn't see beyond them. That's why he's departed for England."

"How long until a new governor's appointed?"

Grose crossed his arms speculatively and with a coarse hand stroked his chin. "Months . . . maybe years. At any rate, Phillip's system may have worked for jolly old England. But these felons are not your typical citizenry. Just look at them! They're useless to themselves, and to anyone else for that matter. I'm reversing Phillip's benevolent and useless measures. I'm replacing all the magistrates with military men."

"It's a very bold move, sir, and I might add a relief to all our men." Macarthur saw opportunity rising before him. "And where kin I be servin' you, sir?"

"I'm appointing you regimental paymaster and inspector of public works. You will be in charge of delegating convict labor to the settlers. You will also oversee all the consumer goods that enter our port."

A light gleamed in Macarthur's eyes. Power was finally and rightfully granted him. "Thank you, Lieutenant-Governor, sir."

"That's not all. I'm immediately offering one-hundred-acre

land grants to all corps officers, as well as ten convicts at no charge. We will maintain their cost at government expense."

"Again I thank ye, sir!" Macarthur began mentally choosing the most gifted of the inmates to serve him. "I kin select my plot o' land this afternoon?"

"Absolutely. It won't be long until we'll have these miserable convicts where they belong—right under our thumbs."

Macarthur glanced toward the government building. An animalistic shriek caught his ear. He shrugged indifferently, estimating that the two-hundredth stroke had been laid upon the convict's back, leaving the victim suspended from the post like a bug in a web.

"They're all like beasts—might as well make use of them. The *crawlers* will earn our fortunes for us." Justification rose in Grose's tone.

Yes, and so will the blasted emancipists! Macarthur assessed.

While Grose rambled on about the details, Macarthur sensed a delight swelling within his breast, and it smelled of wealth. His lovely Elizabeth, expecting their second child, would soon be living in the surroundings she deserved if he seized the future Grose just offered him. The resentment John Macarthur had harbored against the government quickly dissolved into glee as he began formulating his plan for a military monopoly.

Patting the enfeebled lieutenant-governor across the back, Macarthur chuckled darkly, "I believe you've made a decision you'll not regret, sir. I'm yer man." Clasping together sinewy hands, he pursed his lips while intrigue filled his thoughts. The two reentered the hushed confines of the government building while the wind from a distant rain began stirring the wattle trees.

Beyond the trees, a group of convicts scattered, making way for a settler's wagon. The exiles returned at once to their toil, their demeanor suggesting that the day had passed without incident. They had paid no heed to the robust Scottish lieutenant when he had meandered unceremoniously through their chain gang. Ambition was an invisible predator.

Within moments John Macarthur emerged from the brick

building that, like the prison compound, had arisen from the ground by the sweat and toil of the inmates of New South Wales. A calculated plan smoldered in his mind, and within his grasp lay the future and the authority to alter the fate of every life in New South Wales—bond or free.

"I wouldn't think such a ridiculously small creature could cause so much harm." Katy Prentice, a young woman of eighteen, stared at the wilted vegetable leaves in her garden patch. "Why do you waste your time planting food only to have this happen?" Crouched at the garden's edge, her blue eyes smoldered in disgust as she lifted and examined a dead leaf.

"It's the soil, I tell you." Her father, George, middle-aged and favoring his right leg, stared over her shoulder.

"It's cursed!"

"Posh, it's nothing of the sort! But it *is* too sandy." His retort carried a ring of defensiveness, although the fondness that shone from his eyes betrayed his adoration of his daughter. Twisting his trowel into the root of the plant, George lifted a white worm from the soil. "Cutworms are everywhere! Blasted creatures are eating everything."

Katy pushed a blond strand of hair from her oval face and pulled up her russet-colored muslin frock. She had grown accustomed to the comfortable life she had found while serving as a clerical assistant to Governor Phillip. She dusted the soil from her skirt hem impatiently.

"I suppose it's back to the gov'ment stores again. Drat! Jake Fields says the military's tryin' to ruin everyone. That junta'll be the death o' all of us, I vow."

Katy took the trowel from her father's grasp and plunged it into the dirt again. "Papa, the Corps has been formed for our help—not our harm!"

George studied his daughter's face. Even with the smudge of dirt on her upturned nose, she was the loveliest young woman in the settlement. But after shunning several proposals of marriage, tenacious Katy had forged into her parents' farming problems once her position with the governor had come to an end. She had all but taken over the management of the small farm since Governor Phillip had departed for England. "Katy . . ." George spoke quietly.

Katy reached to crush the worm with the edge of her thumb. "Yes, Papa?" Her brows grew slightly pensive upon seeing her father's serious frown. She often worried about his health, and her concern marked her conversations with constrained gentility.

"You shouldn't put so much stock in the Corps. They could be the cause o' our ruin."

"So we're discussing this topic again? I thought the matter was settled—you and I shouldn't discuss politics." Stooped at the garden's edge, Katy placed tanned fingers upon her knee and gazed at him forlornly. Sometimes Papa was so out of step with the rest of the world—and too suspicious. "You worry unduly."

George's eyes narrowed; his brow pinched with disdain. "Katy, you could've gone back to England with Governor Phillip. You were his favorite employee, you know. He taught you about the finer things of life—and now you're spoiled. Your only choices here are workin' for the junta or farmin' with us." Resolve marked his gaze as he crossed his arms. "I can't see you stayin' with us, Katy. Our life's too simple. You'll grow restless. I know you—"

"The finest place to be, Papa, is with my family—and don't be so hard on us Prentices!" she scolded. "We're a tough lot and hard to keep down. But I must respect the Corps and what they're trying to accomplish."

George shook his head. "Then how can you call yourself one o' us?"

"I'm not an emancipist—I know that. But there are two I would die for." Katy crossed her arms at her waist, her eyes set with determination.

"Your loyalties are divided—you'll be forced to make a choice one day."

"Posh!"

"The corpsmen are ruthless, Katy. They're the worst kind of Australians I know of. Entanglin' your life with them'll only put more pressure on us. Can't you see what you'd be doin' to your family?"

"Papa, I would never bring harm to you. Didn't I speak on your behalf to have you pardoned early with Mum?"

George surveyed his modest plot of land. "An' I don't mean to sound ungrateful. But there's a storm brewin' over this colony—an' it smacks o' corrupt politics!"

Pensively, Katy gazed into the morning sunrise reflecting apple gold in their small pond. "Maybe so, Papa. Until a new governor is appointed, things will be a bit out of sorts. But we still have our lieutenant-governor—"

"*A little out o' sorts?* Grose is going to favor the military—hands down! The emancipists are like dogs to the man. We may have to take matters into our own hands." His brows knit together as a thought struck his mind.

"Oh, dear, you shan't oppose the military, Papa. They'll ruin you for certain."

"What then? Sit here and starve?"

Standing abruptly, Katy dusted her plaid apron with her hands as her ribboned sash blew around her frame. "There's always the stores."

"The stores are more full o' rats than larder! I'm writin' a letter to Parliament and that's final! There's a ship leavin' in a few days fer England. I'll see that me letter leaves with it and is hand-delivered to Lord Sydney 'isself!" George Prentice sighed, for he knew his daughter was a strong and determined woman. Even as a child she had found her way into the life of the one man who would first rule Australia—Captain Arthur Phillip. It was by Phillip's hand that George and his wife, Amelia, had been pardoned after three years as convicts and given a plot of land to develop. But what with her every need being met for the past five years, Katy's fidelity had been distorted. "Katy, I owe me life to you, child, but remember it is God who keeps us in His hand. He's always in control even when wickedness reigns. Don't put your trust in the Corps."

"Oh, Papa, you act as though I have some sort of sacred allegiance to them. I'm only saying that the Corps is all we have for the time. Perhaps they're a godsend."

"A plague more like, if you asks me! We 'ave to pray that

a new governor be sent—an' soon. Or else the whole colony'll turn into a haunt for demons!"

Katy squeezed her father's arm and gazed toward her parents' small shack. She hated having words with Papa, but he was determined to see a miracle, and waiting for miracles was not her gift. Perhaps a visit to John Macarthur himself *was* now in order. The man was surely more reasonable than Papa had imagined. *I'll just give the Lord a little help,* she decided. "You write the letter," she said resignedly. "I'll see that it's delivered myself."

"No! You can't put those healthy boys in with the sick ones! I won't stand for it!" Rachel stood blocking the cell door.

The block structure had been designated as a contagion ward, but the overcrowded conditions had forced the militia to take ruthless measures. A sentry stood guarding a group of young boys, the most recent transport arrivals. They were gaunt from starvation. But they had arrived free of illness, and their bony limbs hung limply at their sides. "Out o' the way, wench, or I'll beat yer hide raw!" The guard shoved Rachel roughly. "Thar's no other place for the waifs. Move yerself, now!"

But Rachel persisted, stepping back as quickly as he had shoved her away. "Move them into the tents, then." She tried to sound reasonable. "At least they'll not be exposed to the fever. If you put them in the contagion ward, the epidemic will spread through the prison again, and we'll all be sick!"

"The surgeon 'isself 'as signed off this block as bein' well enough." The sentry wagged the paper in front of Rachel's face.

Studying the paper quickly, Rachel's brow furrowed. "I don't give a *snap* for what that surgeon's done! The boys in this block are still contagious. I know—I've seen the effects, Private. Can you at least go and bring the surgeon to me?" She stood firmly in the doorway, blocking the man's way.

"Surgeon White ain't got no time to deal wif the likes o' you." Pulling the whip from his belt, the marine private drew back his arm. "Step aside!" His tone was definitive.

"I won't!"

"Blamed if you won't!" The guard drew back his arm, the whip snapping over his head, and the young felons behind him cowered against the wall.

Her face rigid, Rachel prepared for the blow. "I want to see Surgeon White." Her tone was calm, her eyes unflinching.

"What goes here, Private?" Attired in a red tunic, a tall, gray-haired man stepped from under the portico of the military building. His shadow stretched in front of him like a thin walking stick.

"Dr. White, sir." The sentry snapped to attention. "Little trouble 'ere with the wench. I'm ready to ship 'er off to Norfolk, I vow."

"Perish the thought, Private." White's gaze grew sympathetic for the girl. "What is your complaint today, Miss Langley?" His tone was steady, but resignation clouded his face.

"The sentry says you declared this cell of sick boys well. But they aren't, sir. They can't hold down water."

White held out a gloved hand to the sentry. "I signed the papers?" Perusing the document, he shook his head. "They slip these under my nose so quickly, I daresay I have little chance to read them." He lifted his face and his eyes softened apologetically. Gripping the paper in front of his face, he ripped it in two and shot out an order. "Take your overflow of prisoners and erect some tents! This cell is still quarantined!"

Cutting his eyes bitterly toward Rachel, the sentry grew defensive. "But we got every square inch o' cleared land taken up by stone buildin's an' tents now."

"Then clear away more trees, Private! Is that understood?"

Grinding his teeth and clenching his fists, the guard glared at Rachel. "Aye, aye, Captain." He saluted and swaggered away with the pale-faced boys lagging close behind.

"My apologies, Miss Langley, but I caution you. These soldiers can be vicious when an officer's back is turned. I'll warn you not to be crossing them so often." White's voice was firm.

"If I hadn't stopped them, those healthier boys would've been exposed to the fever."

White clasped his hands below his waist, his face astute.

"I agree you do what you do for all the right reasons. But you're putting your own life at risk." His tone was grave. "Please—for your own sake—don't interfere again. Do I make myself understood?"

Rachel indicated her agreement with a slight nod, her eyes cast sideways. As White turned to walk away, she shook the chastisement from her mind. *I'll be out soon enough—and when I am, England will know of these abuses!* She pulled the ragged shawl about her shoulders and gathered up the small basket of medicinals. She could hear the sentry bark cruelly to the weakened boys, forcing them to pound the parched ground with worn-out tools and bare hands. Watching the surgeon pull away in his fine carriage, she shrugged as the shroud of her solitary plight weighed heavily on her mind. "But when will England hear. . . ?"

2
LIGHT ON THE COVE

Two guards in black bicorn hats carried a limp form into the room. Dragging the young woman to a cot, they rolled her onto it with an air of little concern. Behind them, a figure quietly waited in the shadows until the shuffling sound of their boots faded down the hallway.

Her face peering first from the corner, Rachel stepped forward cautiously. Fear of the fever inhibited her movement. Her face reflected a gravid emotion, held back by the sheer force of her will. In her grasp was an old clay container, misshapen in form and compounded from Australian soil.

The woman on the cot stirred and turned her face toward the blurred figure in the shadows. "I . . . I must get up. . . ." Her voice faded.

"You'll do as you're told, Betsy Brady, or I'll . . . I'll tie you down if I must!" Rachel emerged fully from the dark corner and stood over the cot, her green eyes pleading for her dearest friend's cooperation.

"I have to get up, Rachel. The boys in the contagion ward will be looking for me." Betsy began to lift her head but then fell back onto her cot as dizziness overtook her. Pulling the blanket to her breast with chilled and trembling hands, she seemed oblivious to the Australian heat.

"I've seen to the boys. Don't I always do what I say?" Rachel poured out the fresh water she had just drawn, knowing instinctively that her friend would benefit greatly from it. She feared Betsy's symptoms were much akin to the plague that had swept through the colony like a ghostly scythe, taking all the unfortunates in its baleful path.

Betsy moaned. "I can't just lie here, Rachel. There is so much to do, and I feel useless."

Rachel smiled. "You *are* useless, so lie still." She pulled a strip of cloth from her frayed pocket, dipped the fabric into the cool water, and wrung it over the clay vessel, being heedful not to spill a single drop. "I'll just place this on your forehead." Her tone was overly cheerful. When the smallest finger of her right hand contacted Betsy's skin, the sick woman flinched in alarm. *She's burning up!*

Stepping cautiously to the window, Rachel pulled back the tattered cloth that a prisoner had hung over it. Her titian hair glistened at her shoulders as the light of day streamed into the room. "You need sunshine, not darkness," she scolded. She punctured the fabric with a nail on the wall and suspended it permanently.

Squinting with a pained expression, Betsy whispered hoarsely, "Will you please draw those closed? I much prefer the darkness."

Frustration rose in Rachel's tone. "For once in your life, please listen to me."

An older gentleman entered the cell and Rachel recognized Surgeon White at once. "Bring the rest of them in here," he ordered the guards.

Wearing the customary bandanna wrapped around their noses and mouths to prevent contagion, the guards carried in six more women, all with the same familiar symptoms.

"Bubonic plague," the doctor sighed as he gave the diagnosis.

Rachel forced back the tears. "Betsy, too, Dr. White?"

"Pity. It's her own fault—she has exposed herself. As a matter of fact, you'd best be quickly on your way. Just being in this room has exposed you to the threat of contagion." The doctor stepped behind the guards, who were quickly filing out, and called, "I want this area maintained strictly for the victims of the plague, men. Is that clear?" He muttered worriedly to himself, and then was gone with the rest.

Rachel stepped from the room for a moment. Then gathering the clay water jar and Betsy's medicine basket, which she had placed outside the doorway, she tied a ragged scarf around her mouth and reentered the contagion cell. Standing over the first young woman, she sighed, pulled some laudanum from the basket, and began administering her limited supply of medicinals. Embracing death had become an old waltz at Sydney Cove, and Rachel had learned all the steps by observing Betsy.

The prow of the *Lady Juliana* split the final green waves of open sea and nosed into the bottle-shaped cove of Sydney. A blanket of drizzle had settled on the harbor, casting a gray shroud around the frigate. Sea-weary, her occupants had departed eleven months prior from the city of Plymouth on the English Channel.

The ship carried some good news from home by way of long-awaited mail and meager provisions. But from the holds below, more female transportees filed out and stared over the railings, their eyes hollow and orphanlike. To the militia, their presence only represented more mouths to feed.

"Letters! Letters from England!" The shouts went up from those who stood around the small shacks dotting the settlement. Eager for news from England, the women grabbed their children and infants and followed the men to the harbor.

A tall figure positioned himself at the bow of the ship and with blue-gray eyes surveyed the commotion on shore. The Reverend Heath Whitley, an Anglican minister from Devonshire, pulled a black cape about his neck and face to block the drizzle. A wind tore at his flat-crowned hat, ruffling his glossy black hair across a tanned, wide forehead.

"We'll be goin' to shore shortly, Reverend, sir," a shipsmate called to the minister.

"Thank you. I'll be more than ready," Whitley replied, his tone laden with relief and tinged with sarcasm. He had enjoyed a good trip on the sea, but the laborious voyage from England had churned his insides sour.

Observing the landscape, the minister's gaze followed the white shoreline to the mud huts, some of which appeared ready to collapse under a good wind. The minister had been warned of the bleak surroundings at Sydney Cove, but no amount of description could have prepared him for what his eyes now beheld.

The rain had quickly turned the settlement into a muddy mire. Clay-filled rivulets broke through the undisciplined earth like pulsing arteries, carrying along a smelly compilation of everything the settlers had chosen to discard. Wild dingoes gathered around the gullies, fighting over kangaroo bones and rotting fish heads. White man had made his first impression on Australia's shores, and the earth had begun to groan under the burden of it.

Whitley cast his eyes from the settlement to the sky. "You know what you're doing, Lord, but I'm not so certain I do." His broad jaw was set hard with a perfect row of white clenched teeth. A slight feeling of disappointment invaded his thoughts. This run-down colony seemed an unlikely site for founding a new church.

The glowing lanterns along the stern cast a dusklike pall over the vessel as it rode against the backdrop of the storm-darkened sky.

Marshaling the mates around the deck, the captain shouted, "Tie 'er up, men!"

Whitley strode casually to the captain's side, pressing his boots cautiously against the green slippery wood of the deck. "You've been to Sydney Cove before?"

The captain had grown to like the pleasant minister. Most clergymen he knew were pale, indoor, bookish types. But Heath Whitley's words had often penetrated deep into his conscience. The minister's rugged, work-toiled hands, and his knowledge of the hunt reflected his love of the outdoors—the mark of a man, in the sea captain's estimation. "Aye, an' vowed to not return, I did at that. But the last supply vessel sent out was lost at sea. I've brought some victuals like flour an' such. It'll be a long time a'for they'll see England's beef at Sydney Cove."

Whitley sighed heavily upon hearing the news. Not as much for himself as for the colonists and convicts. He had suffered hunger during the American Revolution and still retained a curving bayonet scar beside his left ear that reminded him of his own mortality. Long-suffering had become one of his few virtues, but watching others suffer or seeing another man's blood sometimes caused him to be seized with anxiety.

"You're certain you want to stay behind, Reverend?" The captain squeezed the amber tip on his roll of tobacco, now dimmed by the drizzle.

"Certainly. Why not?" Whitley assured; his eyes seemed to kindle at the question. "It's God's work. This colony needs God no less than England—true, Captain?"

Snapping his fingers at the jacktars lumbering carelessly by with their burden of barrels, the captain chuckled. "What makes you think this worthless lot'll listen to what God 'as to say?"

"They don't care, I'm sure. But I can't worry about their reaction. I just go forward in what I believe is God's will. The results are up to Him."

A group of female convicts whistled from the gangplank, scratching at their coarse gowns. The marines had been informed they could select their servants and even their wives from the convict newcomers aboard the transport, and so they stood eagerly on the dock, handpicking the most attractive—a difficult task considering the hardships the convict women had endured. The eager females called to the officers through the foggy drizzle, calling attention to themselves in hope of being selected. A cloudburst sent them screaming back onto the ship.

The minister and the captain dashed toward the forecastle for cover.

"Thar's your church ladies, Reverend! Put 'em in a new dress an' they'll still be a bunch o'—"

"Sinners like us, Captain?" Whitley shook the rain from his hat. "I won't be changing their outsides, and our eyes can't see into their hearts. That's where the Holy Spirit's work begins."

"Lofty words, Reverend. But I still say yer wastin' yer time."

The marines shoved the women past the forecastle. One female whirled around to slap the face of a bristly marine who jostled her too roughly. The denigrated marine retaliated with a blow to the woman's ear and sent her tumbling across the rain-soaked surface. Her eyes smoldering with hatred and hostility toward her keepers, the convict pulled herself up from the deck and spewed bitter expletives at the seaman.

Two marines grabbed the young woman and dragged her past the captain and the minister, dropping her next to them. She spat at their feet contemptuously.

Whitley stepped back instinctively, but his eyes remained stationed on the convict girl. Compassion rose from within as he spoke. "Handle the girl more gently, men. She's still a woman."

Hearing the minister's words, the convict turned quickly. Her face softened, although her eyes remained hardened with skepticism. "Why do *you* care?"

"Only because of Christ who lives within me." Whitley stepped out from the forecastle to stand closer to the girl. He extended a muscular hand in a gesture of good will.

"A bloomin' church boy in this place?" The girl began to laugh almost giddily. "Now what will they do wif *you*?" Amid the rude guffaws of the marines, she scrambled to her feet, refusing to acknowledge Whitley's extended hand.

Whitley grew rigid, like a stone pillar standing in the rain. His mind was seized with weakness, and no words would emanate to form a fitting reply. His rain-soaked woolen cloak hung heavily on him, as did the burden that cloaked his spirit. Saddened, he watched as the convict women were shoved uncaringly toward the gangplank.

Taking his place beside the lost-looking clergyman, the captain adjusted the oilskin, which had kept him dry during the stormy onslaught. "I guess I should wish you a great deal of good luck, Reverend Whitley. You'll need all the 'elp you can muster." With that, the sea captain strode toward the gangway, barking out orders to his crew to prepare the merchant ship for its return to England. Settling in the wilds of Sydney Cove would never be a consideration for the English sea captain. *Only a madman would consider such a venture!*

The convict girl's words still rang in the ears of the young minister. That he was under orders from no man had crossed Heath's mind more than once. He could easily remain on board the *Lady Juliana* and return to England, dismissing the voyage as another bad experience. But his heart was rent upon seeing the discouraged faces of those who waited upon the shore. He could no more head back to England than he could carve out his own heart.

Turning to retrieve the small bag of personal belongings that waited beneath the covering of the ship, Heath Whitley stepped almost ceremoniously toward the exit plank. Destiny seemed to beckon from the mud and squalor on shore. In his heart, he carried the unwavering belief that the future of the colony's faith lay within the pages of the tattered Writ tucked in his bag. He was certain that somehow, with God's help, a church would arise from the agony of this new, foundering nation.

Amber rays of sunlight streamed through the iron blue clouds scattering the final drops of rain onto the land. The sun was taking its rightful place in the sky again, clothing the cove with midday heat. Sticky clay, now partly dried, collected around the horses' hooves and tinged their whited fetlocks the color of rust. The paymaster's driver clucked his tongue and reined the bay mares to a halt in front of the guards' post—a common edifice of Australian "wattle-and-daub." Rain had washed through the mud structure, exposing the framework's skeleton of myrtle twigs.

His arms crossed in a patronly fashion, John Macarthur gazed from the wooden seat of his wagon at the group of prisoners assembled before him. These were the stronger and healthier convicts from the prison compound, although their wan appearance suggested anything but health. The men and women alike stood with slovenly stances, their clothes hanging ragged about their frames, their faces downcast.

Macarthur gripped the seat and pushed himself to his feet. Dismounting the weathered buckboard, he recalled the words of his bonny wife, Elizabeth. They had enjoyed fresh biscuits with eggs and fried kangaroo meat earlier that morning in their simple home.

"Please try to find us a political offender or a forger. They're not as frightenin' as a highwayman or a violent robber." Elizabeth had placed her reddened hands upon her pregnant stomach for emphasis. "I'll be mad as a meat axe if you fetch back a robber. We canna have robbers teachin' our bairn their ill habits, can we?" Her small, prim face carried a firm look of authority.

Kissing John affectionately on the forehead, Elizabeth had set about her morning chores, washing and starching the infant clothing she had bundled over from England for their firstborn son. Her pale violet eyes, small and set closely together, sparkled with expectancy. Compared to the last few dreary months, her steps had seemed more energetic today. John could almost read her mind. An anxious gaze revealed her thoughts—plans for a new house brimming with servants.

Returning to the task at hand, John Macarthur's tone carried a fervency, his peppery disposition plowing into the convicts without burden. "I'm needin' to choose a few o' you to work in my fields plooin' and some of you to help my guid wife with her chores. Elizabeth is due any day to deliver our next bairn." He paced in front of the prisoners. The land he had selected to build upon was prime farmland in Parrametta, and he wanted the soil plowed and tended to with meticulous care.

Several of the prisoners whispered among themselves,

their faces newly animated. Most were encouraged at the thought of better surroundings and perhaps a lighter load of work. But one of the women took several steps back from the front line, concealing her slender frame behind the taller convicts.

Handing the lieutenant a roster, a young marine commented dryly, "This is the best we got, Lieutenant. Not a lot to choose from, if you asks me."

Macarthur moved instinctively into the wide shade of a wattle tree. The heat collected under his gold-laced black hat with the torridity of an oven. Perusing the list, he ran his sinewy finger the length of the roster and sighed. Then his eye caught sight of a particular offense listed by a feminine name. Lifting his face, he let his eyes speculatively run the length of the row of convicts.

The marine stepped into the shade beside him, his hawk-like nose drawing near to the roster. "Find any that interest you, sir?"

"Just this one for now." Macarthur pointed to the name. "She was transported for stealin'. What's been told you aboot her?"

"She's a fair choice, sir. Kind o' cocky, I vow, but she does 'er work better'n most."

"Guid enough. Call her for'ard please."

"Aye, sir." The marine strode casually out into the heat once again and positioned himself in front of the convicts. His face scowled quizzically when he was unable to locate the female. "Whar's Rachel Langley?" he shouted over the heads of the felons.

Muttering to one another, the prisoners gazed around their ranks, shrugging indifferently.

Rachel, who remained hidden behind the others, clenched her fists at her sides. *Of all the names he could have chosen. . . .* With a resigned sigh, she stepped out from among the prisoners. "I'm Rachel Langley." Her eyes locked with the marine's, resistive, and then were cast back to the ground.

A cloud seemed to lift from Macarthur's countenance. He observed the girl's attractive face. *With a new set o' clothes, she'd be a first-class maid for Elizabeth.* Approaching her guardedly, he decided to question the female. "Have you ever helped a lady in birthin'?"

Rachel recalled with great dread the births in which she had assisted aboard the First Fleet. Many of the babies born to convict women had died either aboard ship or within the confines of the prison colony. Her greatest horror had been to break the news to a fifteen-year-old transportee that her baby, a tiny premature daughter, was stillborn. The young, grieving mother, a mere child herself, had cradled her doll-like infant, anguish aging her colorless face beyond her years.

Nodding slowly, Rachel answered the paymaster in a tone barely audible. "I have, sir. I've helped some mothers."

"Weel enough, then!" Macarthur bustled past, waving a sinewy hand. "You'll do weel enough." He turned with an official air back to the marine. "Select ten convict men for my fields, will you? And five more females for the hoose chores. That should satisfy Elizabeth."

"Aye, sir." The marine saluted and retrieved the roster from Macarthur.

Before Macarthur could mount the wagon, Rachel mustered the courage to approach the official. "Excuse me, sir." She stepped toward the tall man with her head slightly bowed.

Wheeling around, Macarthur's brow was pressed in a scowl. Agitation punctuated his retort. "What now?"

"May I speak with you, sir? I can assure you it will only take a moment," Rachel asked, hopeful. Something in the girl's manner deluded Macarthur's choleric temperament. "Go on, tell me then." His voice carried a marked change, almost losing its rigidity.

"I've been tending a sick friend. She could die, sir. Would you please select another to take me place? I feel I should be at her side."

Impatience surfaced once again. *The lassie's impertinent!* Macarthur steeled his gaze and stared beyond the Langley girl's gentle, pleading face, choosing instead to address the marine guard. "Have these convicts loaded up an' ready to depart in half an hour!" he barked, his unseasoned authority intoxicating his senses.

The paymaster's icy response touched a nerve in Rachel's sensitivities, giving her the courage to speak once again. "May I go with you then, sir, and return later to tend Betsy Brady?"

Rushing toward the girl with his fingers curling into a fist, the marine guard said, "I'll take the fight out o' the wench, I will!"

Macarthur raised his palm calmly toward the marine. "No need to beat her—just yet." Most of the convict women were bold and surly, but the gentility of this woman brought out a paternal quality in the paymaster that surprised even himself. Besides, he didn't wish to present Elizabeth with a freshly battered lady's maid. "Young lady, might I remind you that yer new circumstances will greatly improve yer rankin' in this dreary colony. Once we move onto our new estate, servin' Elizabeth Macarthur will elevate you to a better way o' livin', no doubt. Surely you don't wish to jeopardize yer own future?"

Although Rachel yearned to leave behind the convict colony, her compassion prevailed. "Betsy Brady has saved more lives than I could ever count, sir. In my estimation, saving her life could improve the future of the entire settlement."

A wave of reactions rippled through the prison ranks. Heads nodded and favorable words were exchanged in regard to the dying convict girl lying in the contagion ward.

Refusing to acknowledge convict opinion, Macarthur shook his head. "Ye'll accompany the other convicts today. My decision's not changin'. Elizabeth's needs are a far cry above some rabble convict woman's."

A second driver and wagon approached from the muddy road behind them. It was void of occupants, and the marine guard hailed it heartily. "Over here! We're to load up these prisoners and deliver them to the paymaster's farm." Macarthur's driver dismounted to convey instructions and directions to the other driver. Rachel felt a cloud of disappointment envelop her. As she was shoved into line with the others, disillusionment tormented her thoughts; her sense of right and wrong lay trampled within her wounded spirit. When truth should have prevailed, it was merely cast aside like a worn-out shoe.

Staring bleakly toward the stone building which stood isolated from the others on a barren slope, Rachel whispered softly against the still, arid heat of the day, "I'm sorry, Betsy. I've failed you again."

3

Mission of Mercy

Sitting amidst a pile of limbs and scattered leaves, a young Scottish boy twirled a slender, bare tree branch. Behind him rose a wild glade, dark with trees that encircled the land his family had built upon several miles north of the harbor.

"Me spear you!" he squealed at an invisible adversary.

Hefting the sharpened myrtle limb over his shoulder, the tyke tossed it clumsily. His father had taken him hunting on occasion, and often the two had encountered aborigine hunters spearfishing or stalking Australian prey. The boy found great delight in mimicking the black-skinned natives, who seldom missed their mark.

His upturned nose wiggled, and he rubbed the itch soundly, streaking red clay across his tanned skin. Shiny auburn locks curled around the lad's wide forehead and ears, framing roundish eyes the color of cocoa and giving him the look of an African bush baby. He stared at the make-believe spear quivering in its resting place. Sometimes his imagination simulated trees into soldiers, and war became a capricious game. Today his battle was with nature. "Kill you, kanga-woo!" His thick brows scowled in mock fierceness.

A shrill cry rose within a few yards from where the youngster had seated himself. His head jerked toward the sound, a queer anxiousness seizing his guileless mind. "Mither?" he called. When no reply came, a soft whimper emanated from the boy.

"John-John!" A call sounded from near his house. "Where are you?"

Arising quickly from his nest of leaves, the boy froze, his joints immovable when the shrill cry resounded again, alarming him further. His eyes grew moist and his throat grew tight. "Mith—" was all he could choke out.

The shrubbery, encircling him like a maze, rustled near his toy spear and drew his eyes to the chiseled limb and then toward the dark leaves that threatened his small sanctuary with their whispered stirrings.

Reaching with trembling fingers, the lad stretched toward the myrtle branch while his heart drummed against his heaving chest. His make-believe world had disintegrated. Fear loomed invisibly beyond him with the sound of the dark glade pulsing toward his vulnerable soul. As the leaves parted in one violent swish, the child screamed as hysteria replaced his will to fight.

"John-John!" A young woman scooped the frenzied youngster into her arms. "Whatever is wrong?"

His eyes still seized with panic, the child examined the intruder. Recognizing her, he collapsed against the woman's breast and sobbed.

"It's all right, lad. I didn't mean to frighten you so," the housemaid apologized. "Your father wanted me to see to you. Your mother's havin' her baby, she is, and your papa's out o' his bloomin' mind!" She stooped to retrieve his heelless, latchet-ribboned shoes.

Another cry rose from the direction of the house. John-John recognized the voice as that of his mother. "Mither!" His anxious cry was quickly soothed by the maid.

"Don't worry, lad. Your mum's havin' a hard time of it, but

she'll be fine soon. It's your father who needs a good stiff drink." She shook her head, seeing his muslin English sailor attire had been soiled.

Carrying John-John to the rear porch, the housemaid settled him into a chair and presented him with his noonday meal. Pushing his chair under a small cedar table, the maid sighed heavily. The mistress's labor had set the whole cramped household into a state of distress. While a field hand ran for the doctor, the lady's maid, Rachel Langley, had set to work delegating chores to all the household domestics.

Rachel's soothing voice came as a distant murmuring from the mistress's bedroom in the rear of the house.

"How long, Rachel?" Elizabeth Macarthur opened her eyelids slightly, too weakened to speak above a whisper.

Rachel shook her head. "It's going to be a while, Mrs. Macarthur. Rest yourself if you can, but try not to fall asleep." *God help me! Where is that doctor?* Rachel squeezed a cloth over the blue floral wash basin.

Elizabeth Macarthur had been a difficult woman to serve. The new paymaster's wife wasn't accustomed to having servants at her disposal and viewed the matter as a luxury associated with status. Today, however, she clung to Rachel like a stray kitten. Ordering her meddlesome husband from the bedroom, she had insisted that no one be allowed in her room except Rachel and Dr. White.

After laying the cloth across Elizabeth's perspiring forehead, Rachel seated herself on a stool and picked up the small cap she had been knitting for the new arrival. "What do you want this time, Mrs. Macarthur?"

"Sleep."

A humorous light crossed Rachel's face. "No, I mean, would you prefer a girl this time, or do you want another son?"

"What difference does it make? I canna change anythin' by wishin', now kin I?" Elizabeth shifted her weight against the feather bed, preparing for another hard labor pain.

"No, but it's always jolly fun to take a guess." Rachel was determined to keep her mistress preoccupied.

"I suppose Mr. Macarthur would wish for another wee laddie."

"And you?"

The corners of Elizabeth's mouth turned up faintly. Her eyes, a muted violet, seemed to light up at the thought. Growing slightly wistful, she answered, "A daughter would be wonderful, now wouldn't it—all those bonny dresses an' laced ribbons?"

Nodding without looking up from her handiwork, Rachel smiled. "I agree, ma'am. Little girls are so sweet, aren't they?"

Elizabeth's eyes followed Rachel's movements. Her brow furrowed slightly while her eyes rested for a moment on Rachel. "You ever had any children?"

Rachel shook her head. "No. Never married." Staring at her work, she resumed the handiwork task, the needles clicking more rapidly than before.

"No men in your life—ever?"

An uncomfortable silence hung in the air between them.

"You can trust me, Rachel. Tell me—I want to know." Elizabeth pried most successfully sometimes; she possessed an unusual talent for unearthing information, often surprising even herself.

Sighing, Rachel bit her lip and glanced up at her mistress, shame etching her countenance. "I've told you of me past?"

"Aye."

"I met a man aboard the First Fleet who I thought was wonderful. He was a handsome corporal—Brock Chaney was his name. I thought I was in love with him."

"But you weren't?"

Rachel sighed. "It's difficult to say, ma'am. But my faith in God was stronger. I turned down his advances, and I'm glad of it now."

"Why is that?"

"I believe the good Lord spared me much hurt. For I found out later that Corporal Chaney was engaged to another in England. His only intent was to use me."

"Scoundrels come by the boatloads these days, it seems." Elizabeth closed her eyes again, wrapping her arms around her stomach. "What of your family?" Her voice was strained.

"I don't know. I could never bear to tell them of me sentencing."

"Oo-oh!" Elizabeth's face grew ashen as another labor pain began to build. "I . . . I . . . it's much harder, Rachel . . . will you *do* something?" Her tone grew tense.

Rachel's knitting needles scattered to the rug. Reaching for Elizabeth's trembling hands, she gripped them firmly while her mistress shook violently and the spasm of pain intensified.

"Don't push yet, Mrs. Macarthur! Wait just a bit longer!"

"I can't wait!"

Rachel held Elizabeth's eyes with her own, authority sweeping through her. Control was a must. "I can't help you if you won't listen!" Her words were forceful and exacting. "You must!"

Elizabeth's pain was too intense for her to be angered at the servant girl's boldness. She focused on Rachel's expectant face and nodded, succumbing to her demand. The servant had become the mistress.

The large Australian moon hovered above the hilly pastures like a new planet about to collide with earth. Twilight overtook the sky, and evening descended into the landscape with an ebony opaqueness much like the inside of a crypt. To the unprepared traveler, the sudden darkness meant blindness.

"Cursed night! Bugs are eatin' on me like a tribe o' pygmies, they is!"

"Where're the torches? I asked you to light them an hour ago, Moses."

"Sorry, Reverend. I kept tyin' these here reeds together tryin' to make a wall. I wanted walls on this hut b'fore nightfall, I did."

"You're *sure* you know how to build?"

"Anybody kin build a hut. Takes no brains fer that kind o' rubbish." Moses waved his hand slovenly and seated himself in the dirt. "Could use some rum 'bout now, I could at that," he muttered to himself.

Reverend Whitley shook his head and rolled his eyes. Entrusting the building of his makeshift parsonage to two convicts, he found himself wishing for a good, skilled carpenter from England. He recalled the scene of his arrival at port.

Requesting laborers, Whitley had waited for hours in the dusty hallway of the government building. He soon realized he would receive little cooperation from the government, and his frustration gave way to resignation. Here, in Australia, the military controlled everything.

John Macarthur, the paymaster, had been away from the government building, so a sleepy corporal had volunteered two half-starved felons as a meager human offering. His workers in tow, the minister left the convict camp and set out to find a suitable location upon which to build a church and a parsonage.

"I found the torches, Reverend!" The second convict, Felix, sounded jubilant.

"Good." Heath Whitley sighed and pulled a blanket around himself to fend off the insects.

A spark kindled in the campfire. Felix tilted the torch toward the glow and then held it outward while the flame grew to a yellow-and-orange blaze. His eyes narrowed as the blackness beside him took on the outline of a man. "Look out, Reverend!" Felix shrieked.

Moses dropped face-to-the-ground while Whitley, stiffening at the sight of the large male aborigine who glowered down at them, stared in fascination.

"Whar's your gun, Reverend?" Moses squeaked, his voice trembling.

Whitley stood slowly, hoping not to excite the native. "I can't hand *you* a rifle, Moses! You're a convict." His lips scarcely parted. The aborigine laughed in a low guttural way. He wore no clothing and his hair, woven into thick braids, stood out from his head. In the firelight, he resembled a maddened Medusa.

"Speak English?" Whitley edged toward the savage, keeping his voice moderate.

"*Barramundi!*"

The minister stopped abruptly. He had never beheld a man with skin so dark. "By Jove, he's the color of coal!" With keen interest, he studied the primitive, his eyes entranced by the visitor.

"H-he's goin' to finish us off, that's wot!" Terror rose in Moses' throat.

"Perhaps not." Whitley saw beyond the difference of skin color and language. He felt drawn to the man, and their eyes interlocked as both searched for a mutual link.

At once, the native lifted his spear and held it above his shoulder. "*Barramundi!*"

"Look out, Reverend!" Moses shouted, scrambling with Felix for cover in the bush.

Aiming the spear into the fire, the savage held the tip over the flames, revealing two large fish. Making friendly gestures with his other hand, he appeared to be inviting Whitley to join in his evening meal.

"Ah! Yes! *Barramundi!*" Understanding broke through Whitley's thinking. "Fish!"

"Ah—yes!" The native uttered his first English words. "Ah—yes, fish!"

Sudden laughter echoed beneath the galaxy of stars. Reverend Heath Whitley had not come to Australia—Australia had come to him.

"Let me drive the wagon, Katy! I'm the man when Papa's not here!" Caleb Prentice, an imperious five-year-old, tried to pull the reins from his elder sister's grasp. Tall for his age and with eyes the color of robin eggs, the towhead possessed a stubborn nature, a customary Prentice trait, which chafed the impatient spirit of any adult who attempted to rout him.

"No, Caleb, it's black as pitch out here!" Katy yanked the reins, inciting a nervous nicker from the aging plow horse. Apprehensively noting the unattended campfire smoldering off the roadway, she shook her finger at her headstrong brother. "There's bushrangers running loose." She often had to correct the lad, becoming more of a mother than a sister to him. "You'll get extra chores tomorrow if you defy me!" she scolded in a low tone.

"Blast it all!" The boy's temper ignited. "Labor's for convicts! I'm not a convict, am I?"

Katy cringed. The lad was too young to remember much about their first three years in the convict colony. It hadn't been easy for Mum, caring for a baby in prison. Their mother, Amelia, freed after a letter from her accuser proved her innocence, lived resignedly with the "ex-con" stigma hanging like a black cloud over her life.

Returning her thoughts to the task at hand, Katy admonished, "Hard work is expected of any decent person, Caleb George Prentice! Don't be brazen with me or I'll tweak your ears, I will!"

Caleb waited to see if Katy's threatening gaze would result in any serious action on her part. The rules in his mind warranted that he wait until the opponent blinked. If he could win the staring side of the contest, he proclaimed himself the victor. Seeing Katy had settled into the squeaky seat and had focused her gaze on the road again, he relaxed.

Caleb grinned an impish, one-sided grin and an irresistible dimple appeared. "Katy, Katy is quite the lady!" His eyes sparkled like a cherub's, melting Katy's sternness. Her face softened and she laughed quietly.

"You should be ashamed, young man, tormenting your own sister."

Caleb's brows arched, a hopeful gaze lighting his face. "Can I drive, then? Please?"

Katy felt her will crumble and she yielded to the boy. "Oh . . . here!" she relinquished the reins. "Look yonder. There's the government building straight ahead. Pull up front and I'll go place the letter on Macarthur's door. It'll be the first thing he sees in the morning."

Caleb whistled shrilly to the nag and flicked his wrists expertly. "Hup, Nellie, you ol' fleabag, you!" he commanded.

The wagon quickened its pace and Caleb grinned confidently. "She can put some road behind us with the right driver at the helm." Mustering the wagon in front of the government building, he said jauntily, "You may step down, your highness."

With apprehension, Katy eyed the leering, bleary-eyed mariner who stood leaning against a white portico pillar in front of the government building. "I'll just be a moment, Caleb—stay in the wagon." Warning tinged her voice.

Stepping cautiously from the buckboard, Katy took several rigid steps toward the front entrance. Curling the letter in her hand, she slid it beneath the brass door handle. Breathing a relief-filled sigh upon accomplishing her chore, she turned at once to make haste for the wagon. *Mum was right again. We dawdled too long at the farm*. They were two hours from home. The sun had sparked its final pink glow behind the Blue Mountains, pulling down the evening shade of night upon the traveling duo.

Katy stopped abruptly, a sudden, nauseating stench of rum reaching her nostrils. Whipping around, she looked up to find her pathway blocked. "What do you want?" she snapped indignantly, glaring at the odious offender.

The mariner stood interposing his bulk between Katy and the wagon. A tricorn hat cocked forward, shading his face. He studied the girl with malicious intent. "Little company's all, wench."

Fearing more for Caleb than herself, Katy eyed the man threateningly. "Move or I'll—"

Stumbling drunkenly, he turned and looked up and down the length of the portico, then grinned lecherously. "No one 'round but us an' the moon, pretty lass."

Katy swallowed hard, feeling the beating of her heart inside her ears. She gasped when the mariner reached for her trembling arms.

"Hold it, skunk!" A young voice, sharp and commanding, shot from the wagon.

The mariner jerked his head toward the threatener, giving Katy the opportunity needed to duck from his grasp. "Caleb, don't!" she shouted to the lad, who stood towering from his perch upon the wagon seat.

"Don't be a fool, waif!" the mariner snarled.

"I'll blow your head off, beggar! Back away or you're dead!"

"Heh!" The lout chuckled, then widened his eyes as he toyed with the lad. "Wouldn't want to hurt your fellow man, now laddie. I gots a mum at 'ome just like you does."

"I'll shoot *you* and your mother too! Now, get away from my sister!" Cocking the rifle with confidence, five-year-old Caleb prepared unflinchingly for the kill.

Katy leaped to the side of the bewildered drunk and dashed for the wagon. Throwing herself into the seat, she motioned for Caleb to lower himself, and he responded with proficient speed. While Caleb kept his sights aimed at the intoxicated seaman, knees braced against the bench, Katie shouted to the horse, "Y'hah, Nellie!"

The fury in Katy's tone set a fire in the old nag and she lunged forward, the muscular frame snapping forth the wagon like an apple cart. Hooves beating the dirt road, the travelers fled through the borough, seeking the friendly glow of a neighbor's candle. Spying a lit window ahead, Katy yanked the reins to the left. "We'll see if the Muncys'll take us in for the night. They know us well enough."

"You should've let me blow his lights out, Katy." Caleb perched himself against the bench, staring behind them into the blackness. "He'd be deader'n a hammer if you hadn't stopped me!"

Katy shuddered at her little brother's words. "What're you learning in this Godforsaken land, Caleb George Prentice?"

"Kill or be killed, your highness," he said forthrightly.

Katy shook her head. *How do we teach him otherwise, Lord?*

Rachel threw a cloak about herself while dashing into the stables. "Quickly, Harris! I need a horse!"

The startled farmhand responded slowly, unaccustomed to taking orders from a housemaid. "What's wrong, Rachel? Is Mrs. Macarthur in trouble with the delivery?"

"No, Harris! You must listen to me! Mrs. Macarthur's

child's been born—both are fine. But she's allowing me to tend to my friend Betsy. I must go quickly! A life's at stake! Do you understand?"

Harris studied the urgency in the young woman's face. "I do at that, miss. I'll hitch up the team for you right quick like."

"No time for a wagon, Harris! Saddle the stallion for me. He's as fast as lightning, that one!"

"Mr. Macarthur won't like that at all, miss—you takin' Prince George. And I don't like it a smidgen neither—a lady ridin' alone into the convict colony, what with it bein' so dark out there an' all!"

"Regretfully, Mr. Macarthur has passed out in his living room. The cook loaded him up on rum while the missus was in labor. I'll return home long before he awakens."

Shaking his head, Harris lamented, "The things you women talk me into. . . ."

"Here's the saddle!" Rachel lifted the leather English saddle from the paddock posts. "I have Prince George's saddle blanket."

Harris reluctantly complied. "Not fittin' for a lady to straddle a man's steed. Not proper at all!" After tightening the girth, he held out his roughened hand to offer Rachel a leg up.

Rachel placed her left boot firmly in his grasp while gripping the saddle horn with her right hand. Swinging gracefully up into the saddle, she sat firmly astride the stallion, her black-checked skirts draping the flanks like a robe. Her time spent assisting at the Macarthurs' barn had served her well. "Thank you, Harris."

"You sit well, lass." Harris handed a riding whip to Rachel.

Securing the whip beneath her arm, Rachel felt for the handwritten note in her pocket that would assure her passage. "I've chased many a fox in my day, Harris."

"I wouldn't doubt you, lass."

Reining Prince George to the left, Rachel rode out from the covering of the stable. Her arm whipped around, snapping the crop against the stallion's flank. From beneath the creature's hooves, pebbles exploded through the air, spanging against some milk pails. Rachel scarcely noticed the small wallaby that sprang behind her, startled by the clamor.

The moon offered little light along the pathway that led from the Macarthur farm. Riding furiously, Rachel had but one thought—*Help Betsy!*

Miles from the convict colony, Rachel tried to push worry from her mind. The highways that snaked from the prison offered dangerous territory for armed men, let alone for a woman. Lax security commonly sent escaped convicts roaming the bush at night, pilfering and robbing. "Fly, Prince George! Take me to Betsy!" Rachel leaned into the mane. Gnarled trees loomed along the narrow roadway like dark sentries, their rocking branches luring travelers in a hushed siren's song. Glistening through the narrow trunks, the river's end—a billabong—mirrored the sky, silvery stars reflecting gemlike on the water's surface. The night had awakened river creatures that slithered to the bank in pursuit of quarry. Her eyes searching for open road, Rachel fought to keep the stallion from galloping into the bush. The woods fell silent, enclosing her like a coffin without ends.

Surely the prison colony is closer than this! She wondered if she had missed the turn, the blackness veiling the road—a cruel trickster. Rachel felt the stallion's muscles tense beneath her, hooves grinding into the packed earth. Halting suddenly, the horse whinnied shrilly and threw back its head, bruising her chin. Panic seizing her, Rachel sensed dark figures surrounding her on the road.

"Go!" Rachel swung the whip around again. She gasped when the stallion failed to respond. "Lord, help me!" she prayed. She felt the horse jolt when invisible hands seized the bridle. "Who are you?" Her temper stirred, she demanded fearfully, "What do you want?"

Voices muttered in the darkness, but no one replied. Listening intently, she discerned the sounds were not English. *Natives!* she realized. *Aborigines!* "No!" she shrieked, feeling the blood pulsing through her head. "God, make them leave me. . . ."

Large hands clamped hard against Rachel's lips, silencing her protests.

Loud cheers and gleeful chants pierced the stillness of the night, sending a pack of dingoes scurrying for cover. Satisfied with their newly snatched quarry, the dark-skinned men held the torch close to Rachel's face, delighted with the terror in her eyes.

Rachel closed her eyes. She could no longer bear the eager grimaces of the natives. A tear trickled down from her eye to the stranger's broad hand. *Dear Lord, I'm without strength—send your angels!*

4
One Dim Flame

England

On the other side of the earth, the first blush of morning dawned warm, with rays of golden light playing through a circle of soaring fowls. Falling into formation, the gulls flew silhouetted against a cerulean sky. A distant horn sounded, followed by another brief call that rolled across the hills, announcing an early ride to the eager hounds. Sitting atop a stomping black thoroughbred, a stout magistrate adjusted his flat cap and turned to wink at his riding companion, naval contractor Duncan Campbell.

"Off they go, Campbell! Men who feign a love for the hunt." His crisp English dialect, refined and authoritative, intruded on the morning silence.

"Some do feign and some truly burn to see the flash of red fur." Campbell, a middle-aged fellow of medium build, shifted slightly, the leather squeaking beneath him. "You're no master of hounds yourself, Judge Fortner. Why do you punish yourself twice weekly?" An acerbic smile curved his wide jaw.

Fortner winced at the comment and, choosing to ignore the insult, retorted coldly, "The smell of blood, perhaps."

The two men watched the horses' flanks disappear into the woods as the Duke of Beaufort and his young son played out their strategy.

"Shall we go, then?" Fortner offered.

"After you, sir." Campbell gestured with a gloved hand.

Cornelius Fortner gazed speculatively into the brush, pondering the preferability of following the roadway and fence lines as opposed to jumping the fences. "Shall we follow the gate lines instead? Young Beaufort rides too wildly, to my liking at any rate."

Campbell shrugged, his gray eyes penetrating the nearby covert for possible movement. The overbrush hiding the covert provided perfect protection for a fox. "Beaufort's been known to waylay a few of the little beasts. Let's follow him, shall we?"

At the ring of musket, Campbell dug his heels and left the judge behind in a flurry of moist, scattered earth. Fortner considered rejoicing that he had been left alone. But the shame of reporting he had abandoned the hunt was too strong for his manhood to bear. So he pointed his thoroughbred toward the baying of the hounds and thundered into the glade.

In the distance, Fortner spied the young aristocrat charging toward a red flash of tail. The little fox had broken for a clearing in search of the confines of a hole, a serious miscalculation on the part of the furry animal. The duke's eldest son sped like the wind, riding wildly, yet keeping a grain of caution for the fences. Behind him rode the other hunters, scarlet-coated most of them and thirsty for the kill.

If I circle the fence and come around for the ambush, I could bag the beast myself and foil the young upstart. A gleam of pleasure lit the judge's ice blue eyes, and he galloped into the chase.

After only a short time, Fortner could feel his limbs growing weary and his right knee throbbing. He had circled the gate successfully, finding a length of fence downed from a recent storm. But worry nagged his mind that his frothing steed might sense his frustration at the sport, and he feared he would transfer his confusion accordingly.

The rustle of leaves and the pounding of hooves alerted Fortner to the nearing of the hounds and the lad. He admired the young man's tenacity and his killer instinct. *Sink me! The lad would sooner be a master of hounds than be Lord Mayor! He has a spark of pluck about him, that one!*

Seeing the hedgerow ahead, Fortner's eyes twinkled at the solitary flash of red that disappeared through the foliage. Holding his words as any seasoned hunter knew to do, Fortner charged toward the hedge and reached for his musket.

Rumbling close behind, the hunters drew near, and one called out that the judge had galloped ahead.

The beast is mine! Fortner swung the crop furiously, sending his steed barreling toward the wall of foliage.

A nervous foreboding crept through Fortner's senses when his eyes fastened on the hedge, which seemed taller than his horse's limbs. *Turn back, man!* But being too late to follow his own advice, he locked onto the sleek saddle and prepared for the hurdle.

The judge could feel the ground curve downward. The rainfall had collected from days past, saturating the earth in a muddy mire. The thoroughbred was fast to respond to the tricky vault, but Fortner, his senses swimming, pulled back on the reins, sending his animal into a flurry of confusion.

Hind legs slid into the mud, scattering wet silt onto the judge's buff-tinted breeches. Stumbling over a tree root, horse and rider catapulted toward the base of the hedge, and Fortner hurled headfirst into the mire.

The other hunters came fast upon them, and young Beaufort, in the lead, leaped gracefully without so much as a glance toward the hedge. One by one they all followed the lad and were gone, leaving the downed Fortner alone. The hunter's rule—every man for himself—made no exceptions, not even for a judge.

Recovering more quickly than its master, the thoroughbred stiffened its limbs to stand, circled quickly, then made a leap for the row and charged fast behind the others.

Fortner, his head pounding from the blow, peered weakly

above the hedge, expletives punctuating the air around him. His crop still firm in his grasp, he sliced the brush with its tip when he spied his horse halfway across the field, driven by the scent of the hunt. "Traitor!" he shouted as the hunters and the riderless thoroughbred disappeared into another glade. The sound of gunfire thundered in multiple report and then fell silent.

Fortner dragged himself to the base of a tree and leaned wearily against the trunk. Pulling a silver flask from his coat pocket, he tipped it vertically and determined before a minute had passed that he would drink the whole of it. *Before chasing after my blasted ride*, he reasoned, *I'll need some of this to keep my senses about me!*

Closing his eyes, the bruised and battered magistrate paused to rest for a few moments. Then opening his eyes slowly, he jolted at the appearance of the shadow of a man on foot leading a steed. "By Jove!" he bellowed, startling the disheveled man and his nag.

"Beggin' yer pardon, yer honor, sir!" The man tipped a ragged tricorn hat, swinging his arm around in a simian gesture. "Didn't mean to frighten ye, yer judgeship."

Blinking his eyes, Fortner strained to focus on the commoner. Studying the unshaven face and the unkempt strands of hair hanging in tendrils around the man's shoulders, he soon recognized the face. "Dugan?"

"Me in the flesh, sir." Dugan grinned, revealing two missing front teeth.

"Blast it all!" Fortner hurled his empty flask to the ground. "Haven't I threatened you enough about meeting me in public places?"

Dugan scanned the quiet countryside. "Wi' all due respect, this is as unpublic a place as I know of, Judge Fortner, sir."

"What in blazes do you want, man?" Fortner lowered his voice and scanned the glade for observers.

"You told me to warn ye about that pretty step-niece o' yers if she ever were to return, didn't you?"

"My step-niece?" Sitting upright, Fortner's brow furrowed worriedly. "Impossible! She couldn't have survived in that hellish colony."

"Survive she did at that, sir. I stole the papers meself offa that Portsmouth paymaster's desk—"

"What? Are you a bigger fool than I realized? What if you were caught?"

"Ol' Dugan don't never get caught"—Dugan jerked a stubby thumb toward his chest—"but if 'e did, 'e wouldn't say a word about yer honor, sir. Loyal down deep to me 'eart, that's wot."

"Your *black* heart, Dugan." Uneasiness etched Fortner's face. "You're about as trustworthy as a jackal. Now tell me, idiot—what does the paper say?"

Dugan studied the air in front of him as his hands wandered through his pockets. "Now, let's see. What *does* that paper 'ave on it. . . ?" He stalled for a moment, observing the anxious gaze that rose in Fortner's face. "I might find it sooner if'n a little coin were passed me way."

Fortner grew angry at the ex-felon's game. Suddenly his eye fell upon his musket a few feet from him.

Following the judge's gaze, the con was seized with fear and made fast for his flea-bitten nag, where he had left his own pistol.

"Halt!" The judge ordered, lifting his musket toward the lag.

"Don't shoot, sir!" Dugan pleaded. "I wasn't goin' nowhere, really!"

"Quiet, fool!" Meditating on his options, Fortner offered, "I'll pay you for your troubles. But I never want to see you again out here in the hunting glades. Understood?"

Dugan nodded, his palms still facing out and trembling.

Extracting a small purse from his vest pocket, Fortner tossed it at Dugan's muddy feet. "Now give me the paper or I'll be forced to report a regretful hunting accident."

"Got it right 'ere, sir!" Dugan fished the document from his ragged coat. His back bent at the waist, he extended the report cautiously from his grimy, trembling fingertips.

Fortner shook his head as Dugan, free of the evidence, ran to clamber for his horse. Mounting hurriedly, he disappeared into the forest.

"Coward!" Fortner laughed. Pulling himself wearily to his

feet, the judge straightened the crumpled release roster, which documented the transportees who would be paroled in the coming year. Perusing the list, he spotted the name he had all but erased from his aging memory. "No, no, can't be." Drawing his face closer to the page, his brow arched in disapproval. "Betsy Brady!" he said contemptously, rage tremoring through him. "If that barrister brother-in-law of yours interferes now, his life could become most unpleasant." A plan seething through his thoughts, he predicted, "Little wench, you'll not see the light of day, once you step through those prison gates!" The roster crumpled instantly in his taut grasp. "Not one day!"

Port Sydney

"Tea's ready, Katy. Caleb, you want a spot o' tea?"

Caleb nodded politely. "Yes, please."

Helen Muncy held the chipped yellow teapot with the same caution she would use for fine china. Personal household goods were scarce in New South Wales. Tipping the pot over the cup she had set out for Katy, she poured the steaming brew through the side of a small strainer. "Straight from England, this is."

"Smells lovely, Mrs. Muncy. Thank you for your hospitality." Katy ran her fingers down the sides of the hot cup. Ever since she was twelve, she hadn't been partial to tea, but the lady's charity at so late an hour necessitated a grateful response. "I must look a fright."

"Oh, posh! You look perfectly fine. I just hope George and Amelia aren't worried." Mrs. Muncy took a seat at the table after shooing her youngest daughter back to bed. "Sissy, you'll get a switching if you climb off your mat again!"

"How many children do you have, Mrs. Muncy?" Katy asked politely.

"Eight, all told. Quinn and I love a big family."

"I hope if I marry I have lots of children. Mum was never blessed in such a way."

"*If* you marry is right!" Caleb retorted. "Peevish girls never marry."

"Oh, hush you!" Katy chuckled at Caleb, who quickly found pleasure in sneaking one of Mrs. Muncy's cakes into his lap.

"I just want to know why in heaven's name you would be deliverin' a letter to Macarthur's office at this late hour, pray tell?"

"It's a letter of protest, Mrs. Muncy. Papa feels Macarthur's measures of delegating land and convict labor are somewhat out of balance. At the rate Macarthur's going, there'll be no landowners anywhere unless they're military officers."

"Sounds more like you'll be the cause o' your family losin' what little they do have, Katy Prentice!" Mrs. Muncy grew stern in a matronly way. "The gov'ment stores is what's keepin' me family alive."

"But you do agree we should stop relying upon the stores as soon as possible?" She defended her father's position to a certain degree.

"Well—how's your papa's crop farin' this year, by the way?" Mrs. Muncy lifted her chin, casting her eyes obliquely at the two.

Katy grew quiet, not knowing how to answer. "Eaten by pests, Mrs. Muncy—a miserable crop this year."

"Bitin' the hand that feeds you, like I said."

Pursing her lips, Katy blew across the top of her cup, eyes narrowed. Anger battled the feeling of helplessness in her mind. Setting the teacup firmly on the table, a resolution formed in her mind. "I don't want the tea, Mrs. Muncy."

"What?"

"I don't like tea."

Growing indignant, Mrs. Muncy blustered, "Well, you should've told me."

"I realize that now. I do it a lot, I'm afraid—force myself to drink of the cup that's handed to me. I'm weary of it."

"You're a confused girl, you are, Katy Prentice!" Helen Muncy shook her head, bewildered by the young woman's behavior. "Now, don't be silly. Drink your tea!"

"I *don't like tea*, Mrs. Muncy!" Katy felt a renewed valiancy swell inside of her, much akin to rebellion, but stimulating. "I'll not drink it."

She stood at once and walked out on the squeaky front landing. *I swear there's no right or wrong in this colony. Just slaves and slavemasters. I'll make my own way if I have to. Whatever it takes.*

The laugh of the kookaburra sounded from a distant tree—a mocking cry that echoed through the inky black Australian night.

A woman's scream rang from the clay-packed roadway, terror filling the senses of the midnight victim, Rachel Langley.

A blazing torch glowed against rigid aborigine faces, revealing white painted designs around their mouths and noses and surrounding their onyx eyes—piercing eyes that fixed on the terrified woman.

Rachel screamed again when the native who had lifted her from the horse freed her. The natives paid little heed to her cry, and no echo of it returned from the bush. Rachel fearfully held her breath, then released it in confusion and surprise when she realized the natives were making no effort to confine her. Seeing the men had unhanded her, she backed away, all the while watching the tribal party inspect the stallion. Running their hands from the steed's neck down to its fetlocks, they voiced their approval with nods and hand gestures. *Mr. Macarthur's stallion! I've got to get it out of here!*

A torch blazed suddenly behind them, sending the natives scurrying for their spears. Drawing back their weapons in readiness, they abruptly relaxed upon hearing a familiar voice.

"What are you doing, Kapirigi? Scaring helpless women?"

Rachel grew rigid, not knowing whether to flee away or run toward the English voice. The man who spoke calmly and disarmingly was escorting two convicts, both of whom Rachel recognized.

Kapirigi grinned, his white teeth flashing under the torch's glow. "Whit-ley!" He strode merrily toward the white men.

Heath Whitley patted the aborigine on the shoulder before directing sympathetic eyes toward the frightened girl. "I hope Kapirigi didn't frighten you, miss. He's absolutely harmless. Probably much more interested in your horse than in you."

"I suppose I'm grateful for that, sir." Rachel could still feel her heart beating against her chest.

"He can't understand a trifle of English, though." A bright smile creased Whitley's broad face. "You're sure you're all right, then, Miss—?"

"Pardon the hurry, but I must be on my way, sir. I've a sick friend to tend to at the colony."

"So sorry to hear. I'd accompany you"—Whitley sounded apologetic—"but as you can see, I'm without a horse until I can find one to purchase. I'm afraid I'd slow you down."

Rachel smiled at the handsome man. His sincere eyes sparkled like the evening's stars. Perhaps he could be trusted after all. "You've helped enough, sir. I appreciate your assistance." Approaching the stallion warily, she added, "It's nice to meet with a little kindness in this Godforsaken settlement. God bless you."

"Thank you. And He's blessed me greatly."

Feeling there was more to this mysterious Englishman than she could decipher, Rachel wished she had more time for polite chat. But Betsy could be dead by now. She must hurry to her. "Foot up, please?" she requested politely.

"Certainly." Heath Whitley stiffened his arm and cupped his large hand to hoist Rachel into the saddle. "Nice animal, miss."

Rachel slid into the saddle expertly. "Thank you, sir. I really must be going." She whipped the crop toward the stallion's flank and was off, leaving the men staring curiously after her.

"Keep her in your hand, Lord," Whitley whispered.

The road and sky became one black blanket before Rachel's eyes. Raw from gripping the horse so tightly, her legs weakened, and she felt herself surrendering to fatigue. *Oh, Betsy, I hope you're praying for me, as well!*

After twenty minutes had passed, a glow caught Rachel's

gaze and she realized the torches of the prison colony burned just over the next ridge. Renewed energy burst within her. "Almost there! Thank you, sweet Jesus!" In an instant, she saw the guard post just ahead.

Upon hearing the approaching rider, a sluggish guard roused himself from his resting place against the front gate. "Who goes there?"

Undaunted, Rachel pulled the handwritten note from inside her skirt pocket. "A messenger from Mrs. John Macarthur!" She handed the letter to the suspicious guard.

After studying the familiar handwriting, he nodded, signaling Rachel to enter through the gate. "Farnsworth!" he shouted to a sailor bundled in a dirty blanket. "Escort this woman to the contagion cell."

Tying the steed to a tree, Rachel began to run toward the ward. She ran past the young guard, who looked no older than fifteen, and paid no heed when he swore and muttered under his breath. "Excuse me, but I'm in a hurry." She attempted to sound polite.

"Blamed if I cares."

Rachel found the stone building alit with two lanterns on either side of the door. She waited impatiently for the young guard to catch up to her and fumble about with his keys, oblivious to her growing frustration. When he finally got the door unlocked, he turned without a word and trudged back to another night of fitful dreams. Placing her hand on the latch, Rachel hesitated and closed her eyes before pushing the door open. Her prayers had been continual since she first departed the prison. "Lord, keep your hand on my dearest Betsy."

Hoarse, deep coughing emanated from the barred windows, but none sounded familiar to Rachel. Peering inside, she strained her eyes to adjust to the faint yellow light that followed her into the room. "Betsy?" Her voice a whisper, Rachel swallowed and tried to speak again. "Betsy?"

"Dead."

Rachel trembled at the dreaded answer that came from a corner of the room. "Who's there?"

"All are dead. I'm dead."

"Who are you, woman?" Fear brought boldness to Rachel's tone.

"A corpse."

Rachel persisted. "Let me help you. I can get you some—"

"Go away!" the woman demanded, anger rising in her voice.

A softer, feminine voice whimpered, "Rachel?"

A faint smile lit Rachel's face. Recognition caught her ear and she turned toward the sound. "Who's that—Betsy? Please say it's you!"

"Rachel . . . i-it's me."

"You're alive!" Rachel rushed to Betsy's cot. "I missed you so, my friend!"

"Don't get . . . too close, Rachel. I don't want to make you sick. You're . . . too good to die."

"Hush, you silly girl." Rachel could vaguely see Betsy's face, a pallid shade in the lantern light, and brushed her hair from her cheeks. "You're not dying. I've prayed too hard for God to spare you."

"Well, He'd best put me back on my feet . . . o-or take me now. I can't stand another day in this black cell."

"You'll be on your feet before you know it, Betsy. I promise you."

Betsy grew quiet for a moment, then reaching up with trembling hands, she clasped Rachel's hand. "I love you so, Rachel."

Rachel felt tears rim her eyes. Her friendship with Betsy had grown immensely since they first met as prison mates aboard the First Fleet from England. But no one had ever uttered that phrase before to Rachel—and meant it. "I love you too, Betsy. The Lord is with us." Rachel stood to fetch fresh water for Betsy. "I'll be right back."

Rachel stepped out into the night, a renewed strength surging up within her. She felt she had witnessed a miracle at finding Betsy alive. Sprinting toward the well, she smiled in spite of the darkness.

5

Dreams of Tea and Roses

"Step it up! Move along, now. We ain't got all day!"

A gray silence pervaded the group of male and female convicts standing rigidly just inside the main gate of the prison colony. Their eyes, void of emotion, darted from the naval officers who stood in front of them to the marine who slouched in a weathered wooden chair marking off their names with weighty finality.

Shoving wire spectacles up the bridge of his nose, a plump officer remarked aloofly, "For those lucky devils who're leavin' this fine establishment . . ." His gravelly voice droned on, parlaying threats masked in sarcasm. A list of model prisoners had been composed by the Royal Marine authorities. Those on the list would be set free early, while those remaining behind would be forced to fulfill their seven-year sentence.

The wary prisoners remained motionless, refusing to show any emotion that would bring perverse satisfaction to their insidious keepers. Five years and eight months had passed since the First Fleet from England had landed on Australian soil. A slavelike education in servility had been forced on the inmates and had served a few of them well in avoiding contention.

"Any complaint from a settler about the likes of you could return you to our *respected* institution with your back raked at the cat. . . ."

A surly Irish convict stood with arms crossed, facing away from the officer, his penetrating eyes focused on a grim past. In the distance, brown mounds of coarse dirt and the sight of many prisoners still in shackles served as a reminder of the two alternatives offered in Sydney Cove—live or die. Thousands of prisoners lay buried six to eight feet deep in unmarked pits—the "fortunate ones" in the estimation of most. The humbled convict survivors of the starvation years, corpselike in appearance, now waited like lost souls on Judgment Day to hear the words that would release them as unwelcome citizens into the foundling colony. Two fears drummed through the convicts' minds, beating their emotions into staid numbness—*What if I'm denied release?* and, *How will I survive on the outside?*

A soft voice lilted through the breeze, drawing the line of bleak eyes back momentarily and then returning them to the front gate. "It's almost over, Rachel." Betsy extended her slender fingers to grasp the hand of her friend.

Rachel nodded, an ardent smile revealing a restored faith in her future. The last eight months since Betsy's illness had been difficult ones, and at times, nearly hopeless. Managing her assignment after moving to the Macarthurs' new Parrametta homestead and begging for visits to the colony to care for Betsy, had created more tension than she had realized. Returning Betsy's gentle squeeze and mindful of the activity ahead, Rachel watched the officers with a firm expectancy.

"Betsy Brady!" The strident voice rang over the heads of the poised inmate group.

Her breath taken for a moment, Betsy paused, then turned reservedly to Rachel and placed a kiss of assurance upon the young woman's pale cheek. "I'll wait out front for you, my friend." Reaching to scoop up her bundle of decaying belongings and squeezing quickly past those who remained, Betsy stepped fearlessly through the shadow of the aged gallows. She strode majestically through the front gate as though a coronation awaited her.

Rachel had courageously nodded in response to Betsy's assuring words, attempting to return an expression of confidence. But her trembling lips could form no reply, for dread had seized her, though she fought hard to stifle the feeling. *Good behavior—I've had my share of infractions. Betsy's the perfect one*. Wrapping her arms about herself, she stood gripped with anxiety, eyes cast down and limbs trembling. *At least you're no Macarthur slave, Betsy*. Gripping her pale pink cotton sleeves, she pursed her dry lips and waited.

Five more convicts were released . . . sixteen . . . then twenty more paraded through the front gateway without a backward glance toward those few who remained.

Rachel closed her eyes and whispered a quiet prayer. "I'm in your hands no matter the outcome, my Lord."

"Rachel . . ." The officer squinted and yanked the spectacles from his bulbous nose.

Slowly opening her eyes, Rachel held her breath. An eternity seemed to pass before the naval officer finished polishing his glasses, squinted to refocus his eyes, and returned his gaze to the list.

"Rachel Langley!" he belted, his lips puckering while he continued to peruse the register.

Elation and relief swept through Rachel, and a small tear glistened from the corner of her eye. She could see Betsy waiting for her in the tattered green skirt that had been begrudgingly handed her by the callous warden. The faded fabric blew softly in the wind, furling around Betsy's feet in quiet celebration. Rachel's eyes locked on Betsy's deep brown ones, and broad smiles reciprocated their elation. A new emotion emerged within Rachel's breast. She wanted to laugh aloud with joy, but instead she turned to gaze in compassion at those who remained. *I will return,* she promised herself.

All but running toward the front gate to meet Rachel, Betsy briefly considered turning to gaze charitably upon those who remained. But the memory of a certain passage of

Scripture seized her with worry, and she quickly clasped Rachel's hand. "Let's go, Rachel!" Turning away, she quickened her gait and left behind the dispirited captives who stood upon the red soil like pillars of salt.

"Load up quickly, men. The stores are near empty an' the colonists are blasted impatient!"

Heavy-footed marines tromped back and forth across the salt-soaked dock, hoisting new supplies into junta wagons while darting their eyes guardedly about. For when the merchant sails could be seen off the Heads, a cry rang from one side of the cove to the other, signaling a new shipment of goods had arrived and would soon be docked at port. The deluge of hungry settlers and emancipists confounded and sometimes ignited the military officials, who held to their goods with jealous possessiveness.

The rowdy jargon of the crewmen could be heard in the harbor as the land-hungry sailors, confined to the *Prince of Wales* for the last eight months, spilled onto dry land like a closet full of cockroaches.

"Ahoy, mates!" a grisly whaler hailed from a nearby whaling vessel to the disembarking crew. "Bring us wretched beasts some rum, will ye? I'll pay a half-dozen crowns for English rum!" Inflated prices drew sealers, whalers, and merchantmen by the droves, greedy delight filling their coffers with the three- and four-thousand percent markup charged for ordinary goods.

"Rum's over 'ere!" Wagging a large bottle overhead, a sailor shouted over the crowd and sloshed grog on the deck from the pannikin held tightly in his other hand. At his feet lay an open crate containing overpriced bottles of the amber elixir coveted by most of the colonists. "Half-dozen crowns'll buy you a crate!"

"It's robbery!" chided a disgruntled farmer sitting atop a wagon while his neighbors joined in the protest.

"Let's 'ang the louts for their thievin'!"

Eyes wide, the sailor protectively drew the costly bottle to his side. Mistrustful of the locals, he backed away warily. "If it's the stores yer a-waitin' on, they'll be openin' their doors in an hour, I vow."

One by one the wagons pulled away from the dock and pointed their horses toward the military stores located south of the harbor. The wagon riders paid no heed to the figure who stepped last from the merchantman's plank—a man austere in appearance, dressed in the attire of a low-ranking officer. Arriving with the merchant ship, the stocky marine stood with towering height and possessed a stern face, browned and weathered by the Pacific sun. His deep-set blue eyes, severe and almost fierce, afforded him a staring glare capable of disquieting the casual observer. Stretched taut over high Nordic cheekbones, his rugged, manly skin foretold of an outdoor life and granted him a goodly opportunity with many a careless lady.

The officer scanned the harbor with emotionless eyes. His quick steps scarcely scraped the weathered surface of the dock as he strode toward the pebbled landing. Spying a young sealer who had just settled against a post to whittle a bone, he approached the youth with a deliberate step. "You there. Which way is the office of the paymaster?" His voice held a deep, rumbling quality that disarmed the startled young man.

Gazing up at the imposing, somber figure, the sealer tried to squint past the sunlight that pinged off the surface of the brine, stinging his reddened eyes. "Yonder's the way." He gestured to the right, indicating the rutted road that disappeared between two edifices and meandered past the mud structures of the borough. "Follow it 'til the road veers left. You'll find John Macarthur's office just a mile past the bend."

The man offered no reply but stared with a rancorous glare past the sealer, his mouth drawn calculatingly.

Ready to be rid of the stranger, the youth shifted restlessly, his brows meeting in a flagrant scowl. "G'day, then!" He tipped his cap in a less than genteel fashion.

"Where's the prison colony?" The man pressed the sealer further, civility lacking in his tone.

"What do I look like, now—a crawler?" The young man

clenched his fists, sensing a quarrel brewing. A spark of anticipation glinted in his eyes.

"I'll ask once more, then." The man drew his lips together and thrust his bottom lip forward. "Where's the prison?" His enormous hands were poised at his waist, and his blackened thumbs flicked impatiently against his thick leather belt.

"Hmph! Figger it out fer yerself, why don't you—"Stopping short, the sealer's eyes widened in alarm when a pistol was suddenly pressed hard to his forehead. "Look out! Wot's 'appened to you, mate? Lost yer bloomin' mind?"

"The directions, idiot!" The menacing intruder stooped slowly in front of the sealer, his pistol—a brass-handled blunderbuss—firm in his grasp. With his mouth curved in a humorless smile, he yanked the knife from the youth's trembling hand.

Clattering to the dock, the unfinished carving spun at the sealer's feet. Drawing fearful eyes to his malefactor, he stuttered, "I-it's not but ten miles, mate . . . really! Y-you'll need a horse or somethin' to get there!" His tense voice rose in nervous tones, vexation causing him to stiffen. "I've no horse, but fer a shillin' or two an ex-lag'll get you there, I vow. A-ask about in the borough yonder."

His cheek pinched in a crooked half-smile, the surly brute gazed darkly at the sealer. "Thank 'e, scum." Chuckling with a hostile edge to his tone, he grasped the sealer's blade and stood slowly. Without taking his eyes from the anxious young man, he flicked his arm back and hurled the knife into a harbor post. It stuck soundly, dead center in the cured wood, quivering like a well-aimed arrow. A smirk challenged the sealer to take a gamble and retrieve the blade at his own imperilment. Concealing the pistol inside his waistband, he stalked determinedly from the dock.

Within the hour, the surly newcomer to Sydney Cove had secured a bay mare. Loping toward the office of the paymaster, he slowed to scan the faces of the women scrubbing laundry in front of a mud hut. His memory of a young girl sentenced to hang years ago loomed full in his mind. *Will the wench have changed very much after so many years?* he wondered.

Snapping back the reins, the rider halted the bay and proceeded to check for ammunition. Finding his supply to be satisfactory, he slapped the horse's flanks with leather and galloped into the borough. An accomplished assassin, he had seasoned his timing to perfection. Once he blended in with the locals, he would be able to mark his prey and complete the assignment handed to him in Portsmouth, England. He entered the red square of the government property to the sound of the lash and the torturous cries of embittered men.

Slithering noiselessly through the stream, a flat, diamond-shaped reptilian head projected above the water's surface and scanned the banks. Detecting intruders ahead, the green snake serpentined gracefully, its long, lithe body quickening its movements and skulking into a green array of water plants. Hiding ghostlike in the reeds, the reptile flickered a crimson tongue, stilled its water promenade, and lay still as though dead. Preparing for ambush, the snake submerged cold, lifeless eyes beneath the surface to observe the thin human fingers that dipped lazily into the current.

The smell of distant rain rode in on the wings of the salty Pacific wind as it blew through the long hair of Rachel and Betsy while they rested upon a sandy shoal.

Scooping cool spring water into her hands, Rachel watched the water trickle down her arms, making streams as it went. She stopped, her arms relaxing as a thought struck her mind. "I scarcely realized, Betsy . . . it's so hard to believe, isn't it? We're free!"

Betsy lifted herself up from a seated position and pressed her bare feet toward the water, allowing the current to wash across her weary toes. She pursed her lips when the cool stream sent a chill through her. She shuddered, squinting up toward the sparkling glimmers of sunlight filtering through the dense Australian foliage. "You're right, Rachel. I waited so many years in that dreadful place that now freedom seems unreal."

A shoal of sand arced out to the left of Rachel, trapping

water and creating a small pond. Rachel stretched out, her slender frame resting on the palms of her hands. She stared into the smooth surface that mirrored her face. No longer a sixteen-year-old convict girl, she felt as though her reflection was that of a sullen-eyed stranger. "I still *feel* like a convict, Betsy. How will I ever convince myself otherwise?"

"Let God take care of that problem, Rachel. Fill your mind with other things. Do you ever dream?"

Rachel sat up with a startled expression. Somewhere in the hazy recesses of her memory, another person had asked that question. It was too long ago to remember, but she licked her lips, still moist from the drink at the stream, and replied quietly, "Tea and roses."

"What's that?" Rachel's reply caught Betsy's interest.

"You asked me if I dreamed. That's my answer. A lovely, cozy little home, with a great large front porch . . ."

Betsy laughed, her eyes alight with Rachel's fantasy.

"And in the front yard, surrounded by all my lovely children and a dashing yet adoring husband, we're sipping English tea and enjoying our rose garden."

"And how does this dashing, adoring man keep you so well?"

Rachel hesitated, biting her lip while she formulated a reply. "He labors from sunup 'til sundown, of course! How about a farmer?"

Wrinkling her nose, Betsy shook her head and shot back, "I grew up on a farm. Too boring."

"Farmers are good husbands!" Rachel feigned defensively. "How about—a tailor?"

"No, no, not right for you, Lady Rachel." Betsy shook her head vigorously.

"What then?" Rachel absentmindedly began folding the clothing Betsy had brought with her. "You choose for me, then."

"I know! Just what you need, Rachel—a minister!"

A disparaging frown clouded Rachel's face while her brows grew taut. "Now what preacher would have anything to do with the likes of me?" Rachel wagged her head in an exaggerated fashion, her animated response bringing a laugh from Betsy. "*You're* more the type to be a minister's wife, Betsy."

"And one day, perhaps I shall." Betsy's tone grew definitive. "But, first . . ."

"What? You want to be Australia's first duchess?"

"No . . ." Growing quieter, Betsy turned to stop Rachel from her chore. Clasping her hand gently, she announced, ". . . I must return to England, Rachel."

Rachel sat in stunned silence, bereft of words.

"I'm sorry I didn't inform you sooner." Betsy's eyes grew misty. "You are the one reason I have for staying in Sydney Cove, Rachel. But a few months ago . . . do you remember when I heard from my sister in England?"

"The one that is married?"

"Alice, yes. Grace was the one who . . ."

" . . . died of pneumonia," Rachel completed the thought. "Yes, I remember you telling me."

Betsy nodded, "Yes, that's right." Sighing deeply, she continued, although the strain in her voice revealed her worry. "Uncle Cornelius has frittered away our small inheritance. Alice saw no other alternative but to wed a barrister—a man who is a great deal her senior, I'm afraid."

"But why must *you* leave, Betsy?" Rachel pleaded. "Without you I shall waste away!"

"No, you shan't—we ought always to pray and not to faint," Betsy chided gently. "I've no choice but to right the wrong that has nearly destroyed my family. Cornelius Fortner must be thrown behind bars."

" 'Vengeance is mine,' saith the Lord." Rachel cast a verse Betsy's way in a weak effort to quench her zeal.

Breaking into a broad smile, Betsy nudged Rachel lightly. "Touché! Have you no shame, using the Word of God against your own friend?"

Her shallow plot unmasked, Rachel clenched her fists. "I'm desperate! I don't want you to go, Betsy! Besides, how can you afford passage?"

Reaching for the bundle of clothes she had tucked neatly inside an old dress, Betsy slipped her hand into the pocket and drew out a small cloth-covered book. "You thought my sister sent me all these clothes to wear, didn't you?"

Rachel nodded. "Why else?"

"Alice used the clothes to hide this small journal." Betsy flipped open the pages.

"The one you write in every night."

"Yes, but my sister had a more practical motive." Turning the book upside down, Betsy shook the journal, and gold crowns scattered to the ground. "Alice sent enough money for my passage back to England. Her barrister husband has his own connections, but he can do nothing until I return as an eyewitness to Uncle Cornelius's crimes."

"But Cornelius is the one who had you sentenced to the gallows! If you return, he'll kill you for certain, Betsy!" Rachel gripped Betsy's arm possessively. "I am not letting you leave!"

"What else can I do, Rachel?"

"Let's get in touch with—Judge David Collins." Rachel grasped plaintively at pathetic straws. "He'll know what to do!"

"Judge Collins cares little about emancipists. I'm afraid he's no use to me anyway, this far from England's shores."

"What'll I do without my dearest friend?" Rachel held Betsy at arm's length, surrendering woefully to the inevitable.

"You have your faith. You'll keep growing in the strength of the Lord and . . ." Betsy's eyes grew large. Her mouth gaped wide in fright, and she gasped at the sight of the poisonous reptile coiled near Rachel's heel. "Look out! Dear God, Rachel, run!"

Coiling to strike, the glistening snake hissed and bared white fangs at the shoreline intruders, then eyed the pale pink flesh of Rachel's heel.

In an instant, Rachel leaped sideways just as the snake struck forward. Whirling to grab a small, fallen tree limb that lay beside her, Rachel lunged blindly at the predator. Thrusting downward and unsparingly upon the snake's venomous head, she pinned the reptile to the ground with the heavy end of the limb. "Quick Betsy! Do something!"

"Do something?" Betsy shrieked. "What shall I do but run?" The color drained from her face.

"No! Don't leave me! Look there!" Rachel pointed frantically. "Grab that small branch by the water!" she ordered as the snake's body rose vehemently, six feet of writhing anger struggling to free itself and plant its fangs upon the offender.

Trembling uncontrollably, Betsy raced numbly to grab the sharp stick from the water's edge. "Got it!" she screamed, terror rising in her throat.

"Come spear the beast—right behind his head!"

With white knuckles, Betsy gripped the stick in front of her and shrieked again. "No! I can't! I hate them!"

"Do it! You can do it, Betsy!" The limb shook in Rachel's grip. Too blunt-ended to bring damage to the snake's head, the branch slipped sideways and the snake shook violently, reacting to the smell of liberation.

Clenching her teeth, Betsy leaped toward the snake with wild abandon, her muscles taut. With all her strength, she plunged the stick toward the coiling monster. The long emerald tail lunged upward, sending repulsion through Betsy as the last bit of fight drained from the venomous snake. "I think I shall faint." Betsy collapsed upon the ground while Rachel vainly bludgeoned the dead remains.

The screams jolted the assassin, jerking him abruptly forward in his saddle. Hours of riding had left him edgy, and he was anxious to locate the convict Betsy Brady.

"What's that, now?" He halted the mare.

Passing in and out of the prison complex as an officer had been simple enough. Lethargy was evident among all the ranks, and he had easily acquired the parolee roster as it lay open in the guard's chair. He was disgruntled to discover that he had missed the girl's official moment of parole by possibly only an hour.

Fiercely he furrowed his brow, and his pernicious eyes penetrated the dense foliage that hid the quarry from view. "Sounds like a damsel in distress. We'll just have a look-see." Pulling a black hood from the saddlebag, he clutched it menacingly in his hand. He spurred the chestnut bay cruelly and rode a little farther down the road in search of a clearing.

"A little work, but first . . . a little amusement."

6
SHATTERED DESTINY

"I believe we've got the makin's of a crop, Katy!" George held out the slender stalk of pale yellow flax. Plucking the blue flowers from a yellow-gray stem, he handed the small bouquet to his daughter. "We might just be the first family to be off the gov'ment stores."

"I knew we could do it, Papa!" Katy smiled jubilantly. "Now if the Corps will send us enough laborers to help at the mill, this crop'll make the first sailcloth in New South Wales."

"Will we be rich?" Caleb sounded hopeful.

"We'll certainly give it a try, son." George's face reflected a spark of hope. "But our mill has much to be desired."

Katy, musing over the harvest, sensed a stirring in her mother. With shoulders stooped, Amelia stood a few feet from them, loosening the soil around the plants. The last few years under transportation had aged her beyond her forty-four years. But today, her rapid pace suggested a renewed energy. "A little meat in the soup's me only prayer."

Grasping George's hands, Katy said decidedly, "We'll make it work, Papa! I'll ride to the paymaster's and request more convict labor for the harvest next week."

George stuffed a handkerchief in his trousers pocket and planted his hands on his waist. "You'll do no such thing. I'll take Caleb an' pay the man a visit meself. It's time I met this Lieutenant Macarthur face-to-face."

Katy listened only partially, her attention drawn to the field of gray-yellow flax crowned with blue blossoms. To her, it may as well have been a field of gold. She had prayed so intently for this crop to produce. Crossing her arms contentedly at her waist, she breathed a grateful prayer.

"It's a grand crop, farmer Prentice!" An unfamiliar voice invaded her thoughts.

Katy turned abruptly. A man appearing to be in his early twenties sat atop a roan quarter horse.

"Hello, sir," George called cordially.

The young gentleman tipped his felt hat with a firm hand and sincerely greeted each of them. His gold-flecked green eyes sparkled with interest and revealed the jovial nature of the man. "Good day to you. My name is Dwight Farrell."

"I'm George Prentice. This is me wife, Amelia, and our children, Katy and Caleb."

Dwight smiled politely at both siblings, although he appeared to be somewhat taken by the beauty of the blond-haired Prentice girl. Turning back to George, he spoke informatively. "I heard your flax crop was producing, and I had to see it for myself." Lifting his hat with long, sinewy hands, he ran his fingers through the sandy hair that draped from a boyish cowlick over his bronze forehead. A firm jawline gravitated down to a small cleft chin, adding a masculine charm to his youthful face. "A farm on Norfolk Island is yielding wheat and maize."

"I heard about that farm just yesterday, Mr. Farrell." George nodded knowingly. "An' the man's an emancipist, at that."

"*That's* the miracle! My acre is only producing a small amount of flax," Dwight lamented. "Soil's too sandy for one thing. But, had I been able to buy more grain and seed, I would've made a better crop. The officer's land next to mine is flourishing, but his seed was ten times cheaper."

"Pity," George agreed. "We've sent letters to Parliament, but it takes years to gain a response. My daughter Katy, here, visited the paymaster's office a few months ago and hand-delivered a letter." George gazed resignedly at his daughter. "But she never got a response."

Dwight clenched a leather-gloved fist. "By heaven, we've got to stop the junta from ruining us all—if the rum doesn't destroy the whole settlement first. Did you hear the officers are buying up the emancipists' farms for little or nothing?"

"Why do the farmers allow it?"

"Most of them are so rum-drunk they have no idea what they're doing."

"That's their own fault, then. I've no pity for a drunkard." George lifted his tool and shoved it into the ground.

Pressing his lips together, Dwight Farrell deliberated, "If I have to travel all the way back to England, I'll find a solution. Someone has to listen to us emancipists!" he resolved purposefully.

"I agree, Mr. Farrell," George resounded. "I've fought Macarthur's junta alone for so long I've all but lost hope. If we can find more dissidents like us, I'm certain we can defeat them. But we must acquire our own governor again."

"We'll have to sober up the whole settlement, I'm afraid. The emancipists are sitting ducks, just waiting for the officers to pick them off one by one." Dwight's brow knit together in frustration.

Katy admired the pluck and reasonableness of this Dwight Farrell. She blinked and directed her eyes to the field again when she realized he was looking intently at her.

"Well, Mr. Prentice, if I come up with any solutions, I'll let you know . . . and you as well, Miss Prentice."

Katy nodded, slightly embarrassed at herself for blushing. "Yes, you do that, Mr. Farrell." Drawing herself up, she addressed him in a more watchful manner. "But keep in mind that we should make every effort to work together with the Corps. After all, they are not the enemy." She walked slowly toward the border of the flax field, still holding the blue flowers in her grasp.

His brows knit, Dwight nodded diplomatically at the young woman, but then turned his gaze upon Prentice. "If I decide to return to England, I may need to sell my land. Would you be interested, Mr. Prentice?" he offered.

Upon hearing Dwight's words, Katy hesitated, but didn't turn again to look at the handsome young man.

"Who knows but what I might, Mr. Farrell. Let me know your price if you do decide to leave. Perhaps we can work a deal."

"I'd be grateful, sir, and thank you. I'll be leaving now." Dwight tipped his hat. "Miss Prentice?" he asserted in a deep, mellow voice.

Composing her face with strong reserve, Katy turned gracefully to reply. "Yes, Mr. Farrell?"

"It's an honor to meet you. I wish you success with the Corps. If anyone can deter them, I'm certain you can." Dwight smiled broadly, handsome creases lighting his eyes.

Katy did her utmost to appear indifferent as she lifted her face to acknowledge his politeness. "Thank you, Mr. Farrell. I wish you the same success. Perhaps we can both—in our own way, of course—make a difference in the colonists' lives."

Dwight's brow arched ruefully. "I've no doubt, *you'll* do well, Miss Prentice."

Biting her lip, Katy chose not to return the compliment, thinking the man rather forward. "Good day, sir." The finality in her tone brought an end to the conversation.

Still astride his horse, Dwight Farrell rode away. But Katy stole a few glimpses before his brown coat became a distant image on the long dirt road. The sunset painted the sky ahead of Dwight Farrell in outback shades of red and yellow and mineral blue. Squinting obliquely, Katy stole a final glimpse, allowing her eyes to linger over the strong line of his shoulders and the firm, confident way he gaited the steed.

"Perhaps we should pay Mr. Farrell a visit soon," Amelia offered, a mischievous smile curving her weathered face. "A neighborly gesture . . . George, you and Katy could take the man some o' me good bread."

Katy's brow arched, quick to discern her mother's scheme. "Papa can take him the bread. Caleb, you'll go with him, won't you?"

"Yes, Papa, let me go instead," the lad volunteered eagerly.

Amelia shook her head, annoyed by the stubborn daughter she had reared. She watched Katy stride artlessly toward the shack, mincing her steps like a cat teasing a dog as she carelessly sprinkled the blue petals along the pathway.

If any man can snare that headstrong daughter o' mine, he'll have to be a determined one. Amelia gazed resolutely toward the rider who disappeared at the turn in the road. "Good luck to you, mister."

George gazed after his wife with a quizzical stare as she turned to trudge toward the cottage.

"Let's stay in that abandoned hut we saw downstream." Rachel pulled Betsy to her feet. "It'll soon be dark, and we'll never make it to the borough."

"Do you think it's safe?" Betsy glanced worriedly downstream. "Perhaps we should head farther down the road."

"I don't think any place is safe in Sydney Cove, Betsy. But we need to rest. Tomorrow we can try to catch a ride into town in a farmer's wagon. We'll have to rise early, though."

Betsy collected the bundle of clothing and hid the coins again inside her journal. "All my worldly goods in one pathetic armload. What a pauper I am."

"No less of one than Jesus, Betsy." Rachel reached for some of the clothing. "I'll help you with your bundle, but you keep the diary."

Betsy followed Rachel apprehensively, closing her eyes tightly when her eyes fell for the last time upon the bludgeoned snake.

The women stepped cautiously over the stone-covered bank and followed the curving billabong back to the abandoned mud structure. They immediately set about searching for dry twigs to build a small campfire. While storing the twigs inside the shelter, Rachel discovered an old iron pan and rinsed it carefully in the stream while Betsy gathered wild spinach and a licorice-flavored creeper called "sweet tea."

"I found a whole bed of sweet tea, Rachel!" Betsy called from the thicket.

"Just bring enough for tonight. It's growing too dark to linger," Rachel replied, narrowing her eyes toward the thick foliage that hid Betsy from view.

Betsy reached for a few more vines of the creeper, stuffing them into her skirt. "I'm famished," she muttered to herself.

"Betsy Brady in the flesh!" a raspy voice whispered.

"Who're you?" Betsy jerked her face up, startled by the interruption.

"Save a little somethin' for me, pretty lass?"

Betsy was alarmed to find a hooded man towering over her. She could hear a horse nicker distantly and realized he had tied up the animal downstream in order to steal up quietly. "Go away!" She dropped the creeper onto the ground, the fear in her eyes a living thing.

Aiming his pistol toward the girl, the assassin grinned menacingly from a torn opening in the black hood. "Come quietly, wench, or your red-haired friend is dead!"

Only a few feet away, but unable to hear the man's whispered threats to her friend, Rachel placed the iron skillet over the campfire, watching sleepily while the moisture popped and sizzled on the surface. Stretching out her arms, she yawned and watched the sun dance its brilliant finale upon the hazy mountainscape. Crossing her arms, she settled against a large, smooth rock, feeling the first chill of dusk begin to penetrate her skin.

Realizing she saw no movement in the foliage, Rachel sat up and stared into the thicket Betsy had disappeared into. "I'm starving!" she called lightheartedly, though her eyes narrowed to search the spaces between the slender trees.

When the foliage didn't stir, Rachel frowned worriedly. Standing at once, she strode toward the thicket, her pace quickening with each anxious step. "Betsy?" Finding the clearing, Rachel saw straightaway a small mound of sweet tea creeper dumped upon the ground. Then she froze when the sound of gunfire pealed through the wooden glen. "Betsy!" Terror rose in her throat.

A small scrap of pale green cloth fluttered from a bush, the familiar fabric that Betsy had worn that day. Rachel jerked the piece from the thorny bramble and ran blindly into the woods, her heart pounding wildly. No pathway was in sight, only the sound of the rushing stream to guide her. The branches tore at her skin and clothing, impeding her chase but not stopping her. She remembered the gold coins inside the diary and worried that a robber had been observing them all along. "I should have been the one to keep them for you, Betsy!" Rachel chided herself, despising her decision.

Betsy raised herself up where she had fallen onto a large, flat rock. The front of her dress was soaked with blood, and her face and body were bruised by the blows from her assailant when she had tried to escape. She shook her head as her insides began to convulse. "Why?" she asked, her eyes pleading, but the hooded man only stood facing her in an icy silence. Aiming the pistol straight toward her once more, the assassin finished the job he'd been hired to do, and the sound of gunfire exploded through the air.

Stopping short, Rachel trembled at the sound of a pitiful wail emanating from the woods ahead. "Betsy!" she screamed.

The gunshot echoed across the stream and through the dense valley, startling a terrified Rachel. No longer fearing for herself, Rachel leaped to cross the stream, her heavy skirt soaking up water as she went. Stumbling to the bank she dragged herself through a tall stand of shrubbery. Her first instinct led her to a clearing, where she startled a small wallaby. Fearing herself lost, she turned and ran in the opposite direction. Forcing her way through a mangle of branches and bush, she staggered out into a clearing and fell headlong down a mossy embankment. Lifting her face in agony, she felt numbness paralyze her as her eyes froze upon the ghastly scene in front of her.

Rachel beheld a frail clump curled atop a large rock and moaning woefully. Crying out, her soul was rent at the dreadful sight of Betsy lying so still, having been shot like a doe. But all she could say was *"No! Dear God! No!"* A shriek escaped her lips, but Betsy gave no reply. Lifting herself with bruised limbs, Rachel stumbled to where Betsy lay. She wept plaintively, then cried out in anguish, "What demon did this to you?" Desperation swept through Rachel, and she tried to lift her friend into her lap. But when the movement evoked a pained grimace, she gently placed Betsy against the stone.

Mumbling irrational syllables, Betsy rocked her head slowly back and forth as though reliving the nightmare. "No, Uncle!" she whispered.

A horse whinnied to the east of them, and Rachel glared vengefully when she caught sight of a bulky, hooded figure quickly disappearing into the dusk. Snapping her gaze back to Betsy, she implored, "Did you know him, Betsy? Tell me something!"

"D-don't . . . know . . ." Betsy's lashes fluttered, her bloody hands still limp upon the wounds in her upper abdomen and chest.

"Not your uncle?" Rachel was incredulous.

"No. Hooded . . ." Betsy coughed, relaxed against the stone again, and whispered, "Journ . . ."

"Journey?" Rachel struggled to decipher.

A frustrated gasp escaped Betsy's lips as her head shook slightly. "Journ . . ."

Rachel glanced frantically around the blood-soaked rock. "Your journal!" Tears stung Rachel's eyes. "You were robbed! It's my fault. I should have kept the money for you."

"No. Don't . . ." Betsy's voice faded.

"I'll get you help, Betsy! You're going to be just fine," Rachel assured hopelessly. Pulling her blouse from her waistband, she yanked free the hemmed portion straight around and used the fabric to try to stop the bleeding. But the wound was deep and the blood pulsed red no matter how firmly she pressed.

Tears welled in Betsy's eyes, and her lids opened partly while she whispered, "I love you . . ." The loving brown eyes grew sympathetic, as though she were more sorry for Rachel than herself. Betsy weakly clasped a trembling hand upon

Rachel's blood-soaked ones. "Trust . . . God . . . Rach . . ."

"Don't leave me, Betsy!" Rachel sobbed uncontrollably.

Betsy's eyes focused upon the stars just appearing overhead, and then she seemed to disappear into them as life departed her frail body.

"No! God, please don't do this to me!" Rachel shrieked to the heavens. "Why?" She drew her fists to her chest. Suddenly, events of the past rushed through her mind—the endless, empty nights she had spent in the holds of the transport, the guilt of her former actions that had weighed on her like iron. The transportation sentence had left her hopes barren and her future dismal. She had wished for death. Then one night, the hatchway door was thrown open, and a frail young woman stood before her, innocent of all the evil charges made against her, but still steadfast in her faith. Betsy's life had permeated the void of Rachel's world like a quiet, peaceful tide. Through her encouraging words, she had left a lingering balm of hope in the hearts of all the lives she touched. Now her final words—"I love you" and "trust God"—rang like distant church bells in time of war.

Rachel sat for many hours weeping and questioning God. Why had He spared an innocent girl from the hangman's noose, and healed her of the dreaded plague, only to allow her to die at the hands of a lunatic? Futilely cleaning Betsy's wound, Rachel continued to weep and then began to pray for God to resurrect Betsy. But Betsy stirred no more, and a new concern emerged to haunt Rachel—*What if the killer returns?*

As fingers of moonlight penetrated the eerie pall of night, Rachel, drained of all emotion, bent to kiss the cold, white cheek of her dearest friend. "I love you too, Betsy. Rest with Jesus," her voice trembled weakly.

A white gull circled overhead through the black silhouettes of the eucalyptus trees, then spiraled toward the moon and vanished.

7
FAREWELL, MY FRIEND

The parishioners of Sydney Cove gathered in front of the tiny chapel and complained amongst themselves about the cost of goods while their children played in the low limbs of the eucalyptus trees, wearing their Sunday best.

"Good day, brethren, sisters, and God go with you!" Reverend Whitley, dressed in the customary white surplice over a long black cassock, called cordially to the few devout who lingered.

The morning service had been rendered with the minister's usual ardor, but little had been returned in the way of the "flock's" response. "If I weren't called . . ." he murmured to himself.

If it hadn't been for "the call," Heath Whitley would have gone back to England months ago. Had he not believed that he was guided by God's hand, he would have been sorely disappointed in his slow progress pioneering a church among the pagans. Thus he referred to his tenacity and burden for

Sydney Cove as "the call" from God.

After six months, the minister found he had two "churches"—one for the aborigines and one for the colonists.

The aborigines had been a difficult people to reach with the gospel. Not because of their lack of clothing or because of the difference in language, but rather because white man had brought many ill habits that disrupted and often destroyed their lives. Therefore, the native Australians assumed the Englishman's religion must also be evil.

Heath had spent many evenings with his friend Kapirigi, trading languages and trying to absorb and understand aborigine culture. Thinking he had come to change their pagan habits, he soon found to his surprise that his own heart had begun to change more than had the tribesmen's.

But always faithful to his own people, every Sunday the minister unlatched the windows and opened the doors of his makeshift wattle-and-daub chapel and conducted a service for the few colonists who attended. The singing, though many times off-key, drifted through the myrtle trees and down to the billabong where natives often stopped their spearfishing to listen and sometimes nod their heads to white man's strange rhythms.

Lo! He comes, with clouds descending,
Once for favored sinners slain;
Thousand, thousand saints attending
Swell the triumph of His train.
Hallelujah! Hallelujah!
God appears on earth to reign.

Neither tribe—black or white—considered dropping their cultural differences, joining hands under the tent of blue sky, and worshiping the Creator of both their worlds. To Reverend Whitley, however, a dream burgeoned in his mind that someday . . . *perhaps when the lion lies down with the lamb* . . . but eventually he reconciled the thought in his mind as being impossible. *Only heaven would understand*.

Heath Whitley picked up his Bible and strode between the wooden chairs and out the doorway. The sun had brought the midday heat to a sweltering temperature, so he chose to take a longer, albeit more shady, route to his shack.

Straddling the gray mule he had purchased from a struggling farmer, he secured his wide-brimmed hat and set out down the pathway, the last hymn still playing through his mind.

The lyrebirds sang a song of courtship along the road, the males spreading their colorful tails in a showy lyre-shaped display to the female bird. The minister enjoyed this route, although he had to take his caution, for "crocs" prowled along the stream bed. His jaeger rifle, always loaded and at the ready, swung casually from a woven linen sling that hung from his shoulder. As a man of the cloth, he would have suffered much criticism for toting a rifle in England. But settling in the Australian wilds without a weapon would be much akin to martyrdom.

Drawing near his shanty, he narrowed his eyes. *Nothing out of place, but something's wrong*. He stopped the mule at the edge of the clearing and decided to investigate on foot. Tying the contrary beast to a tree limb, he proceeded toward the hut, his blue-gray eyes roaming the landscape. Finding his front door partly shoved open, he crouched at the small front landing made of stones. Pulling a stone free, he bent his wrist and flicked the stone through the doorway, listening intently but hearing only the rock skittering across the wooden floor.

Pushing the door boldly with one large hand, he gripped the rifle with the other and leaped into the room. "Who's there?" His voice, loud and commanding, masked the tinge of fear that followed him into the room. His buckled shoes landed beneath him soundly and a small dust cloud powdered his feet. Heath's fear was replaced with shock at the sight before him. The light shining through the only window in the dwelling directed his eyes toward the sleeping figure on his bed. Walking quietly toward the young woman, tenderness overtook him, and he suddenly felt foolish for his brash behavior. The girl did not stir, nor did she make any movement, but lay stilly, as though a spell had overtaken her.

Studying her soft features, Heath shook his head in wonderment—*the girl looks familiar*. He placed the rifle upon a wooden rack he had carved with his own hands, and then turned to seat himself at the young woman's side. She breathed heavily, and though her skin and garments lacked cleanliness, her beauty proved evident. He watched over the lass like a sentry, sensing her fragility. Time passed slowly, so Heath busied himself with changing his garments, brewing tea, and boiling a pot of soup. But he returned frequently to the girl's bedside. At times she slept fitfully as though routing an invisible foe. At other times, she slept peacefully, her limbs relaxing beneath the coverlet he had gently draped round her delicate frame.

Heath stood and gazed with a melancholy stare out his front portal, his muscular build taking up the whole of the doorway. "Who is she, Lord?" He was never one to stand on ceremony but spoke forthrightly to God—mostly out of necessity.

He sipped a spoonful of homemade soup as the afternoon shadows began stretching like gray monoliths across the front of his homestead. Turning, his eye caught movement from inside the room. The girl was stirring. He watched as she clenched her fingers and drew them to her chest. When her lids fluttered, Heath cautiously placed his bowl of broth beside him on an aged three-corner table and walked to the foot of the bed. He spoke gently, composing kind eyes to welcome the stranger back to reality.

Opening her lids slowly, Rachel squinted through hurting, red eyes. Her first thought was of Betsy, and she hoped she would wake next to her dear friend in the little shack by the stream. *It was just a nightmare...* Denial rang through the chambers of her fears. She blinked at the man towering over her. Although his face yielded no threat, she grew rigid at the sight of the gun that hung on the wall behind him. *No!* She shuddered and sat upright, drawing her feet toward herself. Her wide eyes searched the room for an exit and found one just behind him. Tearing away the coverlet, Rachel sprang from the bed, but paused as grogginess clouded her senses.

"Miss?"

The man held out a firm hand to her, but she escaped his reach and staggered into the old table, sending the bowl of hot broth tumbling to the floor. She felt her body go limp, and the man's stout arms carried her once again to the bed.

"Please . . . don't kill me!" she whispered, overcome by her helplessness.

"You're going to be just fine, miss. Let me help you." Heath placed her head gently against the feather pillow. "You're in no condition to go anywhere."

Rachel lay quietly for the next hour, allowing the benevolent stranger to pour small amounts of broth and tea through her dry, cracked lips. His kindness touched her, and after a time her eyes grew misty. "Who . . . are you?" she asked nervously.

"Heath Whitley. I came home to find you asleep in my bed." He regarded her sympathetically. "You . . . look as though you've had a rough time of it."

Whitley? Do I know you? Rachel stared straight ahead not knowing what to say. "I'm sorry if I've disrupted your day, Mr. Whitley. I won't stay long, I vow."

"I don't feel disrupted at all. Besides, where will you go?"

"I . . . I have friends."

"I'll take you wherever you need to go, miss. What is your name?" His eyes were lit with concern.

"Rachel . . . Langley. But no need to bother with me. I've caused you enough worry as it is." Rachel closed her eyes, her head beginning to hurt.

"I'm a stubborn ol' bachelor—set in my ways—if you know what I mean? I'll be hard set to be convinced of anything until I know you're well enough to travel. You may as well relax and give yourself a day or so to mend—Miss Rachel."

Rachel smiled faintly. Heath Whitley's gentle demeanor filled her with relief. When he smiled at her, she felt a warmth stir her trust. *God, I believe you must have sent me here.* Mustering courage, she finally acknowledged desperately, "I need help, Mr. Whitley!"

"So I figured."

"I don't understand, Lieutenant Macarthur, why you lend preference to officers over emancipists." Glaring reproachfully at the shrewd officer who feigned busyness at his large desk, Dwight Farrell persisted, though his patience from the last hour was running thin. "It's a mystery to me how officers can fare so well with supplies, while the rest of the colony bleeds through the nose for their lot. Can you explain all this to me, sir, so that I, too, may understand?" Sarcasm colored the emancipist's words.

Macarthur sighed heavily. He was not prepared for such a morning, nor did he appreciate being approached before his morning shot of rum. "Ye can prove such accusations, Mr. Farrell?"

"I know what *I* pay for grain and what the officer down the road pays for it. It's a blasted crime the way you military gentry control the stores. You're nothing but bloomin' elitists!"

"What's that?" Macarthur's face grew red and his fist curled around the paper in his hand. "Elitists!"

"*I'm* certain of it. The whole colony knows, and soon England will know. I will see to it!" Farrell turned and stormed from the room in protest. He had had his fill of the choleric paymaster and realized now his only recourse. *I'll find one who will listen!*

Macarthur crumpled the paper that curled beneath his fingers. "When a rebel ram raises his head, you butt 'im back in his rightful place!" he blustered while clearing off his desk. "Henderson!" he shrieked. "In here at once!"

Hearing the anger in Macarthur's tone, the private rushed into the room. "Aye, aye, sir!" He snapped a quick salute.

"I want a list of all the emancipists in the colony—*and* all their holdings! At once!"

"It'll take a bit o' time, sir—"

"At once!" As the infantryman dashed from the room, Macarthur turned and peered warily through the hairline opening in his curtains. Watching the emancipist Dwight Farrell gallop away, he muttered silent oaths under his breath. "Young upstart!" The task before him loomed apparent. In order to keep the emancipists in line, stronger pressures would need to be applied. "We'll render the crawlers a little more—spiritless, shall we say." Rancor smoldered in his gaze.

Entering the room with boxes of documents balanced

carefully in his arms, the infantryman placed them beside the paymaster's desk. "As you wish, sir."

"Find some o' the more productive plots o' land. We're aboot to do a little horse trading, Private."

"Aye, aye, sir."

Rising to retrieve his glass, Macarthur sipped his drink slowly, keeping watch upon the private, who sifted nervously through the documents.

"What sort of property do you wish to trade, sir?"

"Oh, the worst fer the best, Private, o' course!"

"Aye, aye, sir." The military attendant trained his eyes on his work and kept his thoughts to himself.

Heath used the backside of the rusted shovel to smooth the dirt, making the mound more uniform. "Ashes to ashes . . ."

The wearisome task of burying the murdered friend of Rachel Langley had taken all day. Soliciting the aid of a few parishioners to "stand in" on behalf of the deceased stranger, the minister had gone from house to house searching for sympathetic hearts—a rarity in Sydney Cove.

"We gather to mourn the death of an innocent child of God. Like a bloom cut from the flower before her time . . ."

The minister had tried to solicit an investigation into the murder, spending most of the afternoon with military officials who viewed the matter apathetically. The only official available on a Sunday afternoon had little motivation to pursue an inquiry into the death of a former convict, and so the matter had been closed with no known suspects.

"In the name of the Lord we commit our dear sister, Betsy Brady, forever into the arms of Jesus."

Rachel placed a bouquet of bright Australian flowers upon Betsy's fresh grave. Cupping her fingers to her lips, she sobbed openly, refusing the comfort offered by an emancipist's wife. She knelt in overwhelming grief at the head of the grave until the dutiful parishioners, anxious to return to their homes, one by one departed quietly.

Rachel stood slowly and turned to regard the minister.

"My heart still denies she's gone, Reverend Whitley." Her tears poured freely, her words shaded with confusion.

Heath nodded, reaching to gently grip her shoulder in a display of condolence.

"I'm indebted to you for all you've done. I can never begin to repay your kindness."

"Repayment isn't necessary, Rachel." Heath's words came carefully, as though raising his voice would shatter the girl.

Rachel stooped once more, this time brushing a stone from the grave. "If you could have known Betsy . . . she was a woman of great faith, a faith much stronger than my own." Slowly, she placed both palms against the fresh earth as more tears streaked down her face, and curling her fingers she scooped up some earth. Bringing her hands together, Rachel cradled the dirt next to her heart, then ceremoniously allowed it to sift back down on the grave. Shaking her head, she whispered through halting sobs, "I . . . miss you . . . Betsy."

Heath nodded sympathetically, Rachel's grief tearing at his own soul. "She sounds as though she was a woman of great courage." He paused, his eyes reflecting a commiserating anguish. "And so are you. You've been through a lot today, Rachel. I would like you to stay in my hut for a few days. I will bide with a family from my church. They insisted, and so must I."

Rachel's eyes gazed up through moist lashes. "I cannot impose." Guilt tinged her words.

"You aren't." Heath smiled warmly. He had heard enough of Rachel's plight to realize she truly had no place to go. Besides, living alone drove him to distraction at times. Rachel had added a new element to his life in the last twenty-four hours. The young woman needed him.

In hopes he could turn her thoughts to other matters, Heath affirmed, "I will show you where to draw your water and how to prepare meals." He accompanied Rachel to his wattle-and-daub hut. He noticed the distance she kept from him, not so much a physical distance, but rather an emotional one. She spoke earnestly of Betsy Brady's past, but said nothing of her own. Rachel recounted to him memories of her friend with the zeal of an evangelist and likened Betsy to a saint, but discounted herself as a poor comparison.

Opening the door with an air of chivalry, Heath allowed Rachel to walk past, her worn skirts swishing against the door. Making his way toward the small table where he had quietly sipped coffee just yesterday, he turned and with a slight hesitation asked, "What about *you*, Rachel? What brought you to the settlement?" He pulled a chair toward Rachel, offering her a place to rest.

Rachel took the seat guardedly. Inside the prison colony she had never tried to conceal her past, for everyone in the compound had a past. But having a minister for an audience suddenly left her feeling awkward, and worse yet, unclean. "I was arrested in England for stealing some goods," she eventually admitted. "I needed the money it would bring. But only because I was hungry."

"The blasted system is so corrupt." Heath's remonstrance was controlled, but anger sparked his words. "You couldn't have been more than a child back then."

"I was fifteen. My mum turned my sister and me out—she couldn't feed us all." Rachel saw no need to fill in all the sordid details.

"I'm sorry, Rachel. So you stole to survive and were arrested?"

Rachel hesitated, her eyes locked on the minister's. The righteous indignation in his tone would have been a comforting defense if she had revealed all her past. But she couldn't bear to tell it all—her months as a prostitute in a brothel would most certainly taint her image in his eyes. Nor could she admit she had burned the place-of-ill-repute to the ground and had barely escaped alive. "You see . . ." Biting her lip, she gazed at the man who listened to her words with such kindly interest. Her life appeared to fascinate him. Perhaps he even liked her in a friendly sort of way. But a man of his worth and integrity would not understand how she could sell herself for a warm place to sleep and a bowl of gruel. *Hold your tongue, Rachel.* "I'm feeling tired, Reverend. Would you consider me rude if—"

Heath shook his head. He wanted to hear more about this lovely young woman, but providence dictated differently.

Hiding his disappointment, he responded sympathetically, "Not at all, Rachel. I should have been more sensitive to your condition. Eat all you want and then get some sleep." He arose in a gentlemanly fashion and reached to retrieve his hat. "I'll see you first thing in the morning. Perhaps you can attend me on my rounds—that is, if you're up to it, of course."

Rachel smiled broadly for the first time that day. That someone actually desired her company warmed her heart. "I would be happy to go along, although I doubt I can be of much help."

"Nonsense. I have a difficult time communicating with some of these families. The presence of a gentle woman like yourself would be a welcome relief to them. Besides, I'm always in need of a benevolent assistant."

"All right, then. I'll see you in the morning. Will breakfast at sunup be soon enough, Reverend Whitley?"

Heath held up a hand of protest. "Not necessary—"

"No, I insist. My biscuits are some of the best, or so they say." Rachel looked almost childlike standing with fingers nervously intertwined, waiting eagerly for the minister's verdict. "It would help to occupy my thoughts, I feel."

With his brows arched in firm approval, Heath conceded. "It's true I tire of my own cooking. Thank you for the offer, Rachel. I'll return shortly after sunup for biscuits."

Following the minister to the door, Rachel began mentally planning the morning's meal. "Good-night, then."

"Good-night, Rachel." Heath tipped his hat and with a flash of a smile was gone.

After Reverend Whitley's departure, Rachel put the teakettle and a pot of soup on the stove and settled herself on the meager landing. Although the minister had been more than cordial in extending his hospitality to her, she felt uneasiness seeping into her thoughts once again. The parsonage would be a welcome respite for a day or so, but she couldn't stay indefinitely. "Not proper at all." But where to go next presented a dilemma she couldn't solve at the moment. *I'm too tired to think*. She rested her weary face in her hands.

Rising, she resigned herself to putting the matter off for another day. Perhaps Reverend Whitley would offer guidance.

"No, Rachel," she chided herself. "Learn to trust in God." She remembered Betsy's final words. Although they stung her emotions, she recounted them carefully.

Closing the door and bringing down the latch, Rachel strode to the small window and gazed upward. She knew Betsy rested in heaven. But sorrow pervaded her thoughts upon remembering Betsy's dream of returning to England. That dream now lay shattered deep inside a cold grave. *What would you say to me, Betsy? My heart wants revenge. But the thought of your saintly life haunts me, and I know you would say "forgive."* Walking to where the soup had spilled, she bent to absorb the broth with a towel.

Rachel lifted a brightly burning lantern and transferred it to the bedside table. She walked slowly to the stove, lifted the steaming kettle and poured herself a cup of tea, then ladled soup into a bowl. "It's myself I can't forgive, Betsy," she whispered. "I should have died, not you. Your life had purpose."

Bearing the tea and soup to the table, Rachel walked past the worn Bible the minister had left on the washstand. Her grief now impeded any search for answers in the Scriptures. Perhaps when the sun began to dawn, and a night's rest had bolstered her mind, Rachel would begin to trust again.

8
Rachel's Balm

"I can't allow you to go off an' work for the Corps, Katy!" George, holding his breakfast knife in the air, shot a warning glance at his only daughter. "Do you respect your father's words or don't you?"

Katy, standing erect in a light blue dress with a dark blue mantelet draped around her arms, responded in frustration, "It's too late, Papa! I've lived on my own for years now, and it makes no sense for you to try to run my life now—does it?"

George Prentice felt a twinge of pain upon hearing his daughter's words. In his own mind, he felt he could never measure up to Katy's respected standing in the colony. For the first three years as a convict, he had lived with remorse and guilt that his own daughter had been reared by the housemaid of the Governor of New South Wales.

"I can't answer that!" George's eyes smoldered. Even after he was released from prison, Katy continued to serve Governor Phillip until the day the aging head of state returned to

England. His attempt to make up for lost years only served to drive a wedge between Katy and himself and had become a harsh lesson in futility. "I've lost you, Katy—haven't I?"

Katy stood over the kitchen table, her arms crossed rigidly. "I'll always be your daughter—nothing will change that fact. But try to remember I'm grown now. I've made my own decisions for years. What makes you think I would suddenly wake up one day and begin to live my life differently than I've done for the last five years?"

George cast his eyes downward, pulling uncomfortably on his frowzy shirttail. "I'm tryin' to accept the fact you're grown, Katy. But how can any God-fearin' Christian tarnish their life with the affairs of the junta? It *ain't* Christian, I tell you!"

Katy felt her face grow red, her passion kindled. "Since when does the Bible say we're to sit back passively and starve to death? Aren't we to pray for our leaders? And what is so sinful about the New South Wales Corps?"

"It ain't the Corps, it's the man that's leadin' it. Macarthur's out to prosper only one man—'isself!"

"We obviously disagree, Papa!" Katy turned away, her frustration with her father reaching the boiling point. *He'll never understand! Our principles are worlds apart*.

"Me stomach's not takin' this feudin' so well this morning." Bustling in with the aroma of fresh air, Amelia carried in an old tablecloth she had dried in the sun. Popping it overhead to relax the stiffness, she sighed. "Just remember, both o' you, that Judas Iscariot was a zealot! I've a good mind to put you both outside to settle your differences!" She pulled a chair from under the table. "And do you have to go at it every day o' the week, now? It seems we can't have a single breakfast without John Macarthur and the blasted junta commandin' all our attention!" Smoothing away the wrinkles in the tablecloth, Amelia shot a warning glance at both of them. "Now I've invited a guest for tea. Can we settle this matter or not?"

Katy pulled two more chairs away from the table and prepared to assist Amelia. Lifting her father's empty bowl and half-eaten plate of biscuits, her brow furrowed in frustration, although her eyes softened. "I apologize, Mum. I'm sorry if we've disturbed you." Then her words became direct. "But

Papa still thinks of me as a child."

"Now, don't start with such things, Katherine Mercy Prentice!" George grew more defensive. "As a matter o' fact, I wash me hands o' the whole matter! Go on in to work for Macarthur, an' see if I care! If he takes away what little we Prentices have, then so be it!"

"I can't take any more, I tell you!" Amelia's voice reflected the high-pitched tone that warned she was on the verge of tears.

Katy drew to Amelia's side, humility brimming in her face. "I'm sorry, Mum." Turning regretfully to George, she conceded, although her tone was resistive, "Papa, I do apologize. It's all my fault. I'll stay until you've found proper help. Let's drop our disagreement, shall we?"

George heaved a heavy sigh. "No, it ain't *all* your fault—just part of it." A rueful grin broke the hardness from his gaze.

The bray of a mule brought their attention quickly toward the door.

"It's the parson arrivin' and here we all are in the middle of a quarrel!" Amelia hastened to spread the cloth over the table.

George snatched one last biscuit from the plate. "Can't a man finish 'is grub in 'is own place nowadays?"

"Go wash up, George," Amelia fussed, pulling the napkin from George's collar. "Katy, please fetch the teacups!" She rushed to restore order to her meager kitchen.

Katy laughed at Amelia's new bustling demeanor. "The parson knows we fuss among ourselves, surely, Mum!"

"No need to air our contrary ways, Katy Prentice!" Amelia's tone grew indignant. "Lord knows we've enough to contend with in this colony, just bein' emancipists!" Sliding the chairs neatly into place, Amelia snapped off her apron just as a firm rap vibrated against the front door. "Please go and check the tarts in the stove, Katy," she whispered.

Katy sighed, melancholy swirling through her. Although she had great respect for Reverend Heath Whitley, thoughts of planning a meeting with Lieutenant Macarthur weighed heavily on her mind, and she longed to be about her own affairs. She had no patience for chitchat today. She crossed the blue mantelet across her bodice, tucking it into her waist sash in the fashion of a fichu. "Another uneventful day," she muttered under her breath while Amelia ran to answer the door.

Although no blood ran from his hands, the man dressed as a corporal scrubbed his fingers raw over the bucket of water. He had killed many men for profit, but taking the life of the young wench had left a disturbing, bitter taste in his mouth. *Finished wot shoulda been done long ago,* he reasoned.

Glancing around suspiciously, he contemplated his next strategy. Another ship would not depart for Portsmouth for many days. He could easily discard his military guise and leave for Spain this afternoon if he chose such a course. But realizing his thinking remained muddled, he opted to lay low for a few days, or even weeks, until he regained his bearings. To panic could land him a turn at the gallows.

After carefully inspecting the horse's hooves, he returned the animal to its owner in the borough and strode away from the harbor, where he sensed that military investigators may be waiting to apprehend an escaping assassin.

On this day, he decided to assume the guise of a young corporal returning from a night with his lady friend. His ploy intact, he hitched a ride on a passing farm wagon. Napping in the warmth of the wagon bed's straw, he slept peacefully for a few moments until a nightmare overtook him. The contorted face of the screaming young Brady woman rose up before him and so frightened him that he sat up in a startled stupor and kicked his boot against a pail of yellow paint, spattering pigment across his boot. He cared not for supernatural beliefs, but at that moment, he would have wagered a farthing that a ghost had haunted his mind. *Bah! She's no different than any other mark!* He shook the foolishness from his mind and rested himself against the golden brown pile of straw while the wagon made its way toward the military stores.

He recalled the events of the previous evening in a more calculating manner. He wanted to be certain he had left no trails behind his work. Waiting for the Brady woman to be alone in the woods at twilight found its reward in a swift fate having been exercised upon the victim. He would've had his way with the wench, but the threat of her red-haired friend discovering them urged him to make short work of the job. The woman had seen him, of that he was certain, but the hood had flawlessly concealed his identity. However, his hasty departure from the scene had left him troubled because he heard the sound of the woman's scream. He hadn't looked back, and he was sure she could not identify him. But the worry there was a witness afoot who could destroy his plans nagged at his intellect. *Keep alert, man!* he chastened himself.

There was another element also to be resolved in his mind. The final half of the reward would be his when he returned to England with proof of Betsy Brady's death. He had taken the girl's diary at first, but then fearing the victim's possession would be found on his person, he discarded it farther down the stream. *No, a death certificate is the only proof.* Being an expert conspirator, he could easily find his way into the military records over the next few weeks. A stolen certificate would be quickly forgotten, and he would be far from Sydney Cove before suspicions would be raised his way.

The wagon stopped in front of the government building, another temporary structure built by convict hands.

"Here's your gettin'-off place, mate!" the farmer called.

"Thank you kindly, sir." He jumped from the wagon, straightening his rumpled uniform. Using the forged papers handed him in Portsmouth, the false corporal easily slipped through the barrage of military guards and into the safely secured role of a corpsman.

"Reporting for duty, sir." He saluted the officer in charge in an amiable manner.

The officer regarded the new corporal critically, noting his disheveled appearance and the straw hanging from his trousers. "You're a day late. Spent a night with the rest o' that drunken lot, I assume!"

The assassin winked artfully, his glee masked by skilled theatrics. "Not drunk so much as charmed by the beauty o' one o' Sydney Cove's fine women in the borough."

"Don't tell me any more, Corporal. I only wish to see you

on time in the future. Honesty is better saved for more important matters. Is that point clear?"

Nodding agreeably, the new implant in the government stores extended his hand in atonement. "Clear as glass, sir. An' no need to worry about me; I'm as honest as they come."

Katy nearly dropped the pan of hot pastries when Amelia's shriek rang through the hut.

The cry startling Katy, she flagged her father from the open window. Leaving the pan on the windowsill to cool, she scurried to the front door. "What is it, Mum? Whatever is the matter?" Pushing the door open wider, Katy gazed in curiosity.

Reverend Heath Whitley stood outside the door with arms crossed. He glanced first at Rachel and then at Amelia Prentice, who stood gaping in shock. "Have I missed something?" he asked, his face reflecting a puzzled stare.

Rachel Langley, poised next to the minister, stepped closer to the doorway, concern over the woman's response filling her with a mixture of anxiety and apprehension. She and Reverend Whitley were making their fourth stop and had not discussed the family they would be visiting next. Therefore, she had not considered encountering a face from the past. "Do I know you?" she asked somewhat shyly.

"Do you know me? Why, Rachel, how could you forget your old friend Amelia Prentice?" Amelia threw open her arms, her sunbaked face beaming.

"Amelia Prentice?" The name evoked feelings of warmth, but Rachel could not place the weathered green eyes and drawn mouth. "I . . . oh, can it be?" The memory of a midnight escape through London's rookeries flashed forth from a nearly forgotten past, the memory of a homeless woman and her frightened little girl. "I do remember! Amelia!" Rachel embraced Amelia, gladdened at the sight of her.

Mystified by the presence of the lovely titian-haired woman, impatient Katy stepped into the morning light that flooded the doorway. "Rachel . . ."

"I can't believe it!" Rachel moved eagerly toward Katy, her eyes finding recognition. "Little Katy Prentice!"

" . . . Langley?" Katy spoke quietly, viewing Rachel from several angles until her eyes widened in recognition. "Rachel Langley!"

"After all these years . . ." Amelia's eyes glistened warmly.

"Well, I see that I'm apt to be interrupting a reunion of sorts," Heath finally interjected jovially. "Not to be a bother! Perhaps I should leave you here, Rachel, and return to visit at a later time."

"Oh no, please, Reverend Whitley." Amelia's eyes sparked with sincerity. "Come in and take a seat at our kitchen table." She grasped the minister's large, rugged hands. "We've got the kettle on for you."

"We insist, Reverend Whitley," Katy added politely. "Do come in."

Although the familiar faces brought cheeriness to the moment, Rachel felt a sudden uneasiness. Her dishonorable past, intermeshed with Amelia's, would not be a pleasant matter to discuss with the minister over tea. Taking the seat Amelia offered, she smiled faintly but kept her eyes on Heath Whitley, whose curiosity would likely control the conversation for the next few moments.

"I can't believe it's you, Rachel. God has looked after you, I trust?" Amelia's brow arched, aware of Rachel's red-rimmed eyes and weary gaze.

Rachel leaned over the steaming cup of tea that Katy poured for her, inhaling the pungent aroma of English tea leaves swirling through the hot liquid. "God's grace is unbelievable at times"—her tone grew dark—"but mysterious."

Amelia leaned toward Rachel, her interest piqued at the worried frown that creased Rachel's temple. "Mysterious? How so?"

"You remember Betsy?"

Amelia nodded while Katy took a seat next to her.

"She was . . ." Rachel bit her lip. "Betsy was murdered."

"Murdered?" Katy's brows lifted in dismay.

"Why, who would do such a thing?" Consternation filled Amelia's face.

Rachel gazed toward Heath, the concentrated look upon her face suddenly weakening with tears. Her parted lips could form no reply.

"It's all right," Heath comfortingly patted Rachel's slender hand. Turning to Amelia and Katy he explained in sensitive tones, "Yesterday, before Miss Brady's interment, I tried to enlist the help of the junta. But forming a manhunt in this colony is like trying to rout the American rebels—it's downright impossible."

"The *junta* again!" George entered the room, drying his hands upon an old cloth. His lips pursed, he eyed Katy obliquely but held his commentary.

"Hello, Mr. Prentice," Heath remarked politely. "Thank you for inviting me today." He stood to shake George's hand.

"Please, call me George, Reverend." George nodded and extended one work-toiled hand while stuffing the cloth inside his trousers pocket with the other. Gingerly, he picked up a wooden chair that rested against the wall and squeezed it between Amelia's and Katy's.

"I'm sure we'll have a new governor before long," Heath offered diplomatically. "I doubt England can ignore our situation forever."

"*If* England's aware," George interjected. "One emancipist told us he may travel to England soon to speak to Parliament in person. I'm beginning to think he's got the right idea."

"Young Dwight Farrell." Amelia kept her eyes on her cup, although her smug grin and the lilt in her tone betrayed her intent. "He's bold, that one. Got a lot of pluck about him, I vow."

Ignoring her mother's implications, Katy returned her gaze to Rachel. "I've thought about you so often. You and Betsy were two of the bravest women in the prison colony." She shook her head. "Poor Betsy."

"I don't feel so brave, Katy. Some days I feel I can scarcely put one foot in front of the other."

Katy tried to reassure her. "You'll feel better soon. Mum was back to her old self after a week or two, weren't you, Mum?"

Amelia hesitated as though the remembrance ushered

forth pain, then nodded in agreement. "The good Lord is gracious. I'm certainly grateful to be out here and not in there. What a horrible place!" She shuddered.

"What happened to . . ." Rachel hesitated, almost afraid to ask. ". . . to Baby Caleb?"

Amelia regarded Katy and George knowingly as the sound of a musket rang from beyond the shack. "He's not a baby now, that's for certain! He's already had his sixth birthday."

Katy rested her chin on her hands. "He's a hard boy to keep down. He's out shooting targets."

"So tell me. How did you all meet?" Heath smiled, regarding the group.

Their gazes grave, the emancipists appeared to communicate a silent oath, as though privy to an ancient secret.

"Amelia and I met in London on Turnmill Street," Rachel determined to speak first. "Amelia and Katy, being homeless, came to the place where I . . . was employed."

"You worked?" Heath asked with great interest.

Nodding slowly, Rachel squirmed restlessly in her chair. "I was a . . ."

"Our rescuer," Katy interjected. "She saved our lives."

"Yes, we would've met an ill fate for certain if Rachel Langley hadn't saved us." Allaying the dread in Rachel's eyes, Amelia suddenly lit up. "Let's eat those tarts, shall we?" She bustled to retrieve the pan from the windowsill.

The conversation turned easily, and Rachel felt relief flood her mind as Katy and Amelia chatted with Heath Whitley about more pleasant matters than the subject of her past.

Before the day escaped them, Heath pardoned himself from the group. "It's best to head back before the sun sets."

"Oh, Rachel, please stay with us!" Katy insisted.

"Yes, do," Amelia added, clearing the saucers from the table. "Our work at the mill is hard and a downright struggle at times, but we can put you to work right away, if you've a mind to."

Glancing toward Heath Whitley, Rachel felt a slight twinge of remorse, for she had grown to enjoy the minister's company. "I suppose staying here would be for the best. I can't keep Reverend Whitley out of his home forever."

"I haven't minded at all." Heath pulled on his lightweight brown coat. "But I would be relieved to know you're in such fine company."

"All right, then." Rachel beamed. "I'll stay!"

"Good!" Katy followed George to the sink with the empty teacups.

"But I'll be back to check on you." Heath pointed his finger at Rachel. "I'll still be counting on you to assist me with those uncivilized colonists. The Farnsworths were grateful for the biscuits and butter you took them this morning."

Rachel felt a warmth upon hearing Reverend Whitley's words. "They have a lot of children, don't they?"

"Indeed." Heath smiled, his brows arched in an animated fashion.

Rachel could hear respect in his tone when he addressed her. His firm yet gentle mannerisms had a calming effect upon her. "I'm glad to help."

"Please drop by anytime, Reverend," George nodded.

"Yes, come back often." Amelia smiled. "We'll always have the kettle on for you, Reverend." She nodded at George, who came and stood next to her.

"That's right. God's man is always welcome at the Prentice home!" George placed his arm around Amelia's waist.

"I hope you don't mind. I like to ask a blessing on each household when I take my leave. The Lord knows we all need it here in Sydney Cove." Then placing his hands ceremoniously upon George's and Amelia's shoulders, Heath gazed upward.

Amelia and George bowed their heads and joined hands while Katy and Rachel grew respectfully quiet. The sound of Caleb's musket ringing again from the vale brought smiles to their faces, and then they grew still.

"Dear Lord, keep your hands on the Prentice family. Prosper their toil and repay them good for the evil their lives have suffered. And may your peace rest on Rachel's mind tonight as she sleeps, knowing that the past is washed away by your atoning blood."

Rachel shifted uncomfortably at the words, and Katy wrapped her arm around Rachel's shoulders.

"In the name of Jesus Christ. Amen."

A resounding "amen" rose corporately in a confident vow for the future that lay before them.

Rachel breathed a quick good-by to Heath Whitley and with a curious glance turned and followed Katy through the doorway.

"Where are we going?"

"I want you to see how Caleb's grown."

"It's so hard to believe he's not a baby anymore."

"Hmph!" Katy grunted indignantly. "Far from it. He's a hard one to tame." She turned to look at Rachel again, her eyes gazing at the frayed seams in Rachel's blouse.

"I look a fright, I'm sure." Rachel followed the direction of Katy's eyes.

"Oh, Rachel. Please don't say such things. You're as lovely as always."

"I don't feel so lovely."

Detecting the sorrow return to Rachel's eyes, Katy spoke up brightly. "We must get you out of these old hand-me-downs. Let me give you one of my dresses," she offered. "It's a bright blue frock that drapes slightly off the shoulders."

Rachel raised an eyebrow. "Sounds too daring for me."

"It will set off your lovely hair nicely. But first, come with me to fetch Caleb, will you?"

"I can't wait to see him."

Once out of earshot of the others, Katy stopped to grasp Rachel's hands and whispered, "I won't be able to stay around here much longer."

"Why not?"

"It's Papa and me. We aren't getting along so well and it's upsetting Mum more than I can bear."

"But where will you go, Katy?"

"On my own. I plan to raise enough money to run my own farm. When I worked for Governor Phillip, I learned the politics of this colony."

"But don't you feel you should help your parents first?"

"They won't allow it. I have to prove to them that the Corps is our way out of poverty."

Rachel felt sorrow grip her emotions. "But, Katy, think

about what you're saying. I've been where your papa's been. I don't trust the Corps any farther than I could throw one of them. George is right. New South Wales needs a new governor to straighten out the corruption. The military's gaining too much power."

"Rachel, don't you see? Most of the emancipists are throwing away a golden opportunity. We could all be rich—no more worry of starvation."

"Who says any of us needs to be rich? Your mum seems content just having a roof over her head."

"She's never known a better life, Rachel. I'm weary of the struggle. If Papa won't provide better things for Mum, then I'll do it. They'll see my way is better eventually."

Rachel crossed her arms at her waist. "What about your personal faith? Are you still trusting God?"

Katy sighed uncomfortably. "Of course." Walking farther she chose her words, being careful to sound sensible. "But I can't be foolish. Papa's choices in life have always landed him in the streets." Katy's face searched the brush for Caleb.

"You're still blaming George for everything, aren't you?" Rachel stopped and her eyes met Katy's penetratingly.

"Not everything. A lot of people fell on hard times in England. But now we can determine to change all that."

"I don't think you can change the Corps. They're a greedy lot."

"They hold the purse strings, but if we cooperate, they'll reward us in kind. Think of what someone like Reverend Whitley could accomplish with more capital."

"Reverend Whitley doesn't need money, Katy." Rachel felt a wave of disappointment sweep through her. "I've never met a more content person than that one."

"I apologize." Katy beheld Rachel's disturbed demeanor. "I've no right to be spouting my own causes. You've been through so much. I—"

"No need to apologize." Rachel shook her head. "Look. Is *that* Caleb? He's such a stout lad! Chasing poor defenseless beasts, I vow." A genuine spark of warmth shone from Rachel's eyes.

Sensing Rachel's show of comradery, Katy looked to see

her brother running wildly ahead of them into a thicket, his musket at the ready. The two young women ran into the wooded glen laughing but keeping a watchful eye for reptiles underfoot.

On the road a distance away, Rachel spotted the silhouette of the minister atop his mule, his wide-brimmed hat tilted boyishly. Watching as he disappeared down the dust-coated path with the melon-colored sky rising before him, Rachel felt a pang of guilt. Working beside the minister all morning had left her with a sense of worth and strong satisfaction. They had visited three families before arriving at the home of the Prentices. Each family had received them hospitably, offering food and beverage and their overwhelming appreciation to Rachel for her limited supply of medicinals. But seeing Amelia and Katy again had brought back a rush of bittersweet memories that Rachel wasn't prepared to confront.

Guilt nagged at her senses. She was unworthy to work beside a man like Heath Whitley. *It should be you here, Betsy, not me.*

Seeing particles of brown earth still lingering around her thumbnail in spite of the scrubbing she had given her hands after the funeral, Rachel despaired. *I'll never be clean again.*

She turned and followed Katy into the woods, vexed at the balm Betsy had passed on to her—a balm that, though life-changing, had not brought her peace. She still felt tarnished by a past she couldn't wash away.

9
THE RUM CORPS

"Thar's a vessel off the heads, Lieutenant Macarthur!" The ruddy ship's boy, curled around the mainmast of the merchantman, slid to safety from his perch high above the patrons who milled noisily on shore.

Macarthur waited atop his wagon, filling his hearty appetite by feasting on one of Elizabeth's tarts. "Weel enough! Tell me when she's portside." The unpleasant news he had received moments earlier from Norfolk Island would soon filter through the working-class colonists, sending some into panic and others into deeper despair. Turning to the corporal seated next to him, he remarked coolly, "Let's keep our wits and we'll be the better off for it."

The docks, groaning from the throng of farmers and sailors, had scarcely room left for one more harbor frequenter. The harvesting of flax was the talk of the harbor, and hopes swelled high that the flax trade would be the lifesaver of the colony. Finally, it was assumed, England could replace Russia's costly flax with convict- and emancipist-spun Pacific flax.

Ships' captains had waited impatiently for weeks to hear word of production at the ill-equipped mill. Lust for the trade of Australia's first sailcloth stirred within the insatiable merchantmen, and they sat with unloaded ships, waiting.

The captain of the approaching American vessel stood aft the merchantship *Hope*, his hard, flat face gleaming red under the sweltering, unrelenting sun. "Bring 'er about! Make ready!" he shouted into the mild draft that tousled his gray, windswept hair.

Calling his shipsmate to his side, the American skipper barked, "Not a sack of flour or even a nail is to leave this ship until I've made arrangements to sell the whole load of rum—is that clear, Fowler?"

"The whole load, Captain?" the short, round sailor queried, his thick lip jutting out.

"We're leaving the whole cargo here and heading back to America. I'll bet my eyeteeth these colonists are desperate enough to buy us out lock, stock, and barrel."

"And if they don't, sir?"

"Then we'll sit on the entire lot. They'll not get a stitch of cloth from me. I'll dock here until the food stores rot in the bilge!"

Rachel glanced around the musty room that housed the government stores. The shelves had grown sparse and offered little in the way of tasteful food. She and Katy perused the rows of produce, unhappily inspecting a pile of rotting onions. "Another exciting day at the Sydney Cove market," she brooded disdainfully.

"Let's take a look at the dry goods. A new piece of fabric will cheer you up. Can you sew well?" Katy Prentice elected for optimism.

Nodding affirmatively, Rachel crossed her arms and arched her brow doubtfully. "Yes, but how shall we afford it?"

"Oh, posh! Always throwing up obstacles, Rachel Langley.

We'll wheedle it out of them if we have to!" A mischievous light sparked in Katy's eyes.

The two women meandered through large piles of burlap sacks and came upon a small table of fabrics that had been rifled through by hurried women in search of a bargain. Katy lifted a blue piece of cloth, allowing the folds to relax so she could study the length. "Not large enough to sew anything of worth," she remarked somberly. Inspecting several pieces, she soon found most to be nothing but scraps. "Look at that one over there, Rachel—there—the emerald green piece."

Rachel scanned the small stacks of cloth, noting that most of the remnants were printed in dreary browns and grays. "Where? I don't see emerald green." Then her gaze fell upon a beautiful green fabric, which appeared to be a generous amount of silk. "Oh, Katy, it's simply gorgeous!" Her eyes glistened.

Suddenly a hand gloved in ecru lace reached between them both and lifted out the bolt of silk material.

Rachel's brow furrowed at the impertinent young woman who had snatched the material. "Excuse me, miss, but we were considering that piece of fabric for ourselves." Rachel's brows pinched together in an irritated frown when the young woman lifted her chin arrogantly.

Her fair complexion, set off by pale rose cheeks and large violet eyes, would have seemed lovely to Rachel if her face hadn't borne such haughtiness.

The young woman peered from beneath a stylish lavender bonnet and regarded Rachel impatiently. "The silk was on the table in plain sight of all and fair game for anyone"—she allowed her eyes to run from Rachel's face down to her fraying dress and worn-out shoes—"anyone who could afford it, that is!" She gently tucked a strand of shiny raven hair back into her bonnet.

A spark smoldered in Katy's eyes, and she gripped her fingers tightly at her sides. "Who do you think you are, Felicity Thompson, taking on such airs? We can pay for the silk as well as anyone else!"

"I never said you couldn't," Felicity retorted coolly. "I intended to pick up the fabric half an hour ago, but my father ran late from his meetings."

"Is there a problem, Miss Thompson?" A marine private acting as clerk sauntered up, cautiously keeping a suspicious eye on the emancipists. "These two givin' ye a fit, are they?"

Felicity's full lips drew to the side in a malevolent smirk. "I don't know, Private. Let me ask them. Do either of you take issue with my buying this silk?"

Seeing the anger in Katy's face, Rachel squeezed her arm and admonished her easily provoked friend. "They'll send me back, Katy. Don't . . ." she whispered.

Enjoying the fear in Rachel's eyes, Felicity returned her attention to the store clerk and turned her back on the accusing glare of Katy Prentice. "I'm ready to make my purchase, Private. Any idea when the stores are going to be restocked?"

"Any day, Miss Thompson. You'll be the first to know."

Rachel and Katy watched silently as the fashionable young woman made her purchase, departed the stores, and was assisted into a covered carriage.

"Why didn't you let me confront that snob, Rachel?" Katy stood with her slender arms akimbo, her eyes demanding answers.

"I couldn't do it, Katy." Rachel struggled with her own defense. "If we emancipists cause any problems with the settlers, they'll drag us back to the flogging post and throw us back in one of those horrible lockups. Besides, it's only a piece of fabric."

"It's a crime against humanity, Rachel! But I *know* you well. You aren't one to cower."

"I'd love to give that Thompson woman a piece of my mind, but I can't. The military's threats are intended to keep us in line. It's their way of using us as their chattel."

"Using you as slaves, to be more accurate. Drat!" Katy kicked a rotting potato across the floor. "One day—this is my solemn vow—emancipists will rule!"

"I don't have to rule, Katy. I just want back a little self-respect, that's all." Rachel sighed heavily as another thought struck her mind. "How do you know the Thompson woman, anyway?"

"Her father's a high-ranking officer in the regiment. I met her from time to time when I was employed by Governor Phillip. She's spoiled and selfish. It's all I can do not to hate the girl."

The front door flew open and George Prentice came blustering through. "Katy! Rachel! You'd better come with me quickly!"

Running to meet her father, Katy's brow furrowed in a troubled frown. "What now, Papa?"

"The word's out—it's the Norfolk Island flax mills. They aren't weavin' enough sailcloth to outfit one single ship. The talk is that we're in for another year of starvation if we don't stock our home stores."

"But the government stores are empty, George." Rachel turned at once and began to search the shelves for wheat grain. "I'll see what I can find for us today." She rambled quickly through the burlap bags again, intent on finding fresh foods.

Out of breath, George continued speaking to Katy, keeping his voice low. "There's an American ship docked at the harbor. The skipper won't allow any goods to leave his vessel until all his rum is bought. If we emancipists can pool our funds, we can buy out the whole shipment and establish our own stores."

"Let's do it, George!" Rachel lifted her empty bag from the dirt floor.

"We'll have to hurry if we're going to organize ourselves. I've sent word to the farmers who live near us to meet at the Muncys' home."

Katy crossed her arms and shook her head. "Not the Muncys, Papa. They'll oppose you for certain."

George held up a defensive hand. "I had a long talk with Mr. Muncy. I believe he listened to me, Katy. Have faith."

"Look here," Rachel called anxiously, dragging a heavy bag of grain toward them. "I found this under a pile of empty sacks. It's good wheat grain. Can we buy it?"

George shook his head. "Let's save our money. We'll soon have our own stores with prices we can afford."

Katy laughed, "In this colony? Impossible!"

Rachel gazed down at the sack of grain, wishing she had enough of her own funds to make the purchase. "But just to take some caution, shouldn't we—"

"No time to waste, ladies!" George gestured anxiously.

Rachel ran quickly after George, but Katy stood with furrowed brows, staring disdainfully after her father. *Always the dreamer*. She sighed and followed him out of the near-empty government stores.

"We'll maintain control o' the trade if we can buy out that American merchant." Macarthur paced in front of a small gathering of New South Wales Corps officers who met privately in the back room of the town pub. "If England is to retain charge of this colony, we must restrict the trade." He veiled his words carefully. "All goods must pass through our hands until a new governor is dispatched from England. By keeping commerce under the control of the New South Wales Corps, we'll maintain stricter control of Sydney Harbor's trade."

"Sounds more like another monopoly to me, Lieutenant Macarthur." An older lieutenant with piercing blue eyes shifted uncomfortably in his wooden chair and placed his pannikin of rum against the hard-topped table. "The only benefactor of such an endeavor would be the corps members. Must we always be gouging the colonists? They're disgruntled enough as it is."

"I would say it's the merchant skippers who are gouging us!" Macarthur retorted, his brow arched in a disgruntled manner. "If we pay inflated prices, we've no alternative except to pass it on to the settlers. But remember, there's a reward for all the hardships you've suffered in the past seven years. Your membership in this purchase will bring part of the profits to you and your needy families." The devious officer played upon their sympathies.

The prospect of more income tickled the ears of a number of the officers, while one or two others appeared uncomfortable with Macarthur's proposal. "Is this . . . er . . . legal, sir?"

A young corporal asked, suspicion clouding his blue eyes. The others waited for Macarthur's response like calculating vultures.

"Of course, Corporal. Shrewd perhaps, but shrewd times call for shrewd measures."

"Who will back our purchase, Lieutenant? Where will we derive the funds?" The older lieutenant reached to take a deep draw on his rum. "The skipper of the *Hope* is asking outlandish prices for his goods, you know. The vessel's stock includes *seventy-five hundred gallons* of rum!" He queried again worriedly, "Where will we find the capital?"

"I'm working on that situation at the present. As regimental paymaster, you all know that England backs my word. If you're all ready to come to a decision, I can fix the I.O.U.'s against your regimental pay. I'll see to the paperwork personally."

One by one, the officers nodded their agreement, except for one disgruntled lieutenant who got up and strode angrily from the room. "Opportunists!" he muttered and then was gone.

"Weel enough. We have a majority willing to join in the purchase. I'll arrange the capital. Jones, I'll be in need o' your assistance to prepare the proper documents."

"Yes, sir." Jones rose from his chair and turned to retrieve the proper legal seals that would authorize Macarthur's I.O.U.'s against the regiment's funds in England.

"McKinley, you fetch my driver. If we're to make the first bid on the goods, we'll need to leave within the hour."

"Yes, sir."

Turning jovially back to the remaining officers, Macarthur saluted his comrades. "Consider yourselves adjourned, gentlemen. And good day."

"Godspeed to you, Lieutenant." The officers bid polite farewells while Macarthur strode ceremoniously behind Jones to prepare his I.O.U.'s for the *Hope*'s skipper. "How'll we use all that rum, Lieutenant?" Jones spoke quietly from the side of his thin mouth.

"Rum is as good as cash in this settlement. A rum-hungry farmer'll sell his own children for a good supply o' the brew."

A surreptitious smile faintly curved his face as he strode out the door of the tavern.

The neighboring farmers sat around the front room of the Muncy cottage, swilling their tipple as though it were water. Prentice paced through the men, raising his voice in frustration. "We *must* buy that cargo, mates. Once we do, then we can establish our own stores. Competition will lower the prices in the settlement, an' the benefit will be to *all* us colonists."

Muncy, a rotund reproduction of his wife, lolled back in his seat, guzzling warm beer. "Yes, Prentice, but fixin' the debt against our own farms is a bit much to ask—we could lose everythin'."

"But our profit share in the goods'll more than repay the debt. Don't you all see? The venture 'as more gain than risk, I vow."

"It sounds risky to me too, Prentice." Emancipist Varnes joined Muncy's rebuttal. "Me and the missus 'ave worked our fingers raw to hack our fields into tillage. After years o' starvin' to death in Sydney Cove, we want to hang on to what little we *do* have. Is that too much to ask?" Varnes held out his stocky, weather-beaten hands in a show of affirmation to the other farmers who soon joined him with their nodding heads and frustrated mutterings.

"But listen to me, Varnes!" Prentice pleaded, his voice strained from the debate. "What about that missus o' yours? Wouldn't you like to be able to afford more laborers and some help for her in the kitchen so she can spend more time bein' your wife and not your hired hand?" Prentice hesitated as Varnes pursed his lips to one side and glanced toward the front porch, where the women had gathered. "And you, Muncy, of all people, should be wantin' better means o' support. Your farm yielded the poorest showin' out o' all our crops this year. Why, with a little common sense, you could take the profits from this cargo and buy some o' that prime land around the Hawkesbury River. Now, *that's* security, if ever I seen it, mate!"

Rachel stood in the doorway listening intently but having little hope that the farmers would find unity. With their minds already preoccupied with the day-to-day struggle of survival and groggy from the local tranquilizer of rum, the farmers could see only the barriers and none of the solutions. Rachel turned to listen to the chatter of the women.

"It's a sin, I tell ye—a sin against God to buy that demon rum cargo!" Mrs. Muncy's words flew as quickly as the knitting needles poised in her grasp. "Why, all's we women need is more rum to bring the ruination o' all our men in this God-forsaken settlement!"

"Well, I could use a little extry rum meself for all me misery." Gertrude Varnes rubbed her backside. Glancing sideways she noticed the shocked expressions of the other neighbor ladies. "Rheumatism," she added sheepishly.

"But the rum *must* be bought with the cargo," Katy Prentice argued. "The American skipper won't sell the cargo any other way." A thought came to mind as she grappled for solutions. "But if *we* buy the cargo, what's to stop us from pouring the rum out in the billabong?"

The women guffawed, and Gertrude retorted, "I could see me own Frederick pourin' out good rum for the crocs to swill down!"

"Oh, what's the use?" Katy muttered and walked away from the cackling knitters and seated herself on the edge of the porch next to Rachel.

"It isn't easy bringing folks together, is it?" Rachel asked quietly, her feet swinging back and forth in the tall grass framing the porch.

"You'd think their misery would be enough motivation, but I doubt this lot'll ever get together on any issue. They're all caught up in their own troubles. If everyone was willing to give up just a little, they'd all come out ahead."

"We're talking about ex-convicts, Katy. Their pasts chase after them like demons. They aren't driven by reason *or* by God. It's fear that pushes them." Rachel considered her own past.

Katy grew still for a moment, trying to maintain control of her anger. "What about you, Rachel? What are your demons?" she asked reflectively.

"I wish I could say I had none. But perhaps I always will have them, Katy. I'm not certain I could name them, though."

"I'm in the same situation. I know I feel angry quite often," Katy agreed, feeling anxiety rise in her chest.

"Angry and purposeless, that's me." Rachel aimed a finger at her own face. "Betsy always had a plan, so it was easy to follow along after her. Without her, I feel lost at times. Me . . . I'm useless . . . to myself and to God."

Wrapping her arms around Rachel's shoulders, Katy eyed her in a patronly fashion. "Now, how many times have you said that God can do anything?"

"Yes, as long as I stay out of His way." Rachel, realizing the pity rising in her tone, refrained for a moment. Then turning, she found a coy smile lighting Katy's face. At once, the two young women laughed at all their foolish chatter. "I talk such nonsense." Rachel blushed.

"No you don't!" Katy argued defensively. "You're the most normal person I know."

Pushing open the door slowly and deliberately, George sauntered out onto the porch, defeat etching his face.

Katy glanced up, reading his thoughts. "Let's go, Rachel. I'll get the wagon, Papa."

The ride down the road was quiet except for the sound of gulls overhead. "Let's head for home," George commented quietly.

Handing her father the reins, Katy climbed around the seat and joined Rachel in the rear of the wagon. Their gazes revealed grave disappointment.

Rachel clutched her friend's hand and tried to offer an assuring smile, but bitterness seethed from Katy's countenance. "Perhaps Mrs. Muncy was right, Katy. Maybe buying the rum cargo wouldn't be the right solution, anyway."

"What *is* right and wrong in this place, Rachel?" Katy shot back. "Is it right to see my family slowly starve to death?"

Rachel said no more, realizing Katy would need more time to settle her mood.

Puffing out a cloud of smoke, the skipper of the *Hope* stood rigidly at the bow. The choleric Lieutenant Macarthur paced on the sternside of him, bellowing out his complaint. "No cargo is worth the price ye're askin'! The markup is robbery!"

The American skipper stood with his feet planted and his arms crossed, a cunning stare marking his gaze. He gave no reply but waited as the lieutenant fumed and billowed like a chimney stack.

"England'll say we're all mad! These officers are raising this money against their future pay. It's hard come by, man! Surely you're heedful to realize they all have mouths to feed?"

Smugly grinning, the skipper took another draw on his long-stemmed pipe, allowing the smoke to issue from his lips in gossamer streams.

Swearing loudly, Macarthur stomped the deck violently. "You can choke on your blasted cargo! I'll not be robbed!"

Allowing Macarthur to distance himself by a few feet, the skipper turned and called in a calm tone, his gravelly voice a singsong. "Lieutenant?"

Macarthur glared back, his red-rimmed eyes threatening. "What, swindler? Have a change o' yer cold heart?"

"Not at all. I just thought it would interest you to know that a group of emancipists are meeting at this moment to discuss their bid for the entire cargo. They aim to open their own stores."

"Who organized such a venture?"

"Prentice—George Prentice and 'is neighbor, Miller."

His thoughts transparent, Macarthur clenched his fists and stood for a long moment ruminating upon the consequences of such a possibility. Two officers stood on the dock gazing up at him, their expressions gravid.

"I'll take the cargo—lock, stock, and barrel!" he conceded with contempt sharp in his voice.

"All hands on deck!" the skipper shouted, and his crew rose from under the riggings like newly hatched spiders. "Let's get these goods on shore at once. On your feet, ye lazy . . ."

Macarthur trudged down the gangplank and toward his wagon as the *Hope*'s cargo and seventy-five hundred gallons of rum were conveyed to shore. However much it had cost him, Sydney Cove was now his budding empire. "King John Macarthur . . ." he chuckled to himself, ". . . the rum king. Nice ring to it." A new demeanor settled over the new "rum king" as privates scrambled to assist him into the wagon.

10
The Future Dims

The first evidence of smoke filtered into Rachel's dream, clouding her imagination with formless enemies and turning her peaceful slumber into a nightmare. An acrid haze wrapped around her nose and throat, stinging her membranes with a dark cloud that absorbed all breathable air. She shot up from her makeshift bed on the floor, gasping for breath. "What's wrong?" Thoughts jumbled around in her groggy mind like a child in a runaway wagon. She coughed uncontrollably and strained her eyes to see through the dense vapor that filled the cottage with blackness.

"Oh, God, no! Fire! Everyone up! Fire!" Rachel shouted to the slumbering Prentices.

Standing quickly, Rachel found the upper air more poisonous to her breathing, so she stumbled to the floor in a dizzying stupor. At once, she could hear Caleb coughing from his mat next to George and Amelia's bed in the rear room of the shack.

"Papa!" Caleb's voice cried through the haze.

"Stay close to the floor, Caleb!" Rachel shouted. "I'm coming to get you!"

"Rachel!" Amelia called from the haze. "George is on the floor! He can't get up!"

"I'm coming, Amelia!" Tears began to sting Rachel's cheeks, coursing down her face in black rivulets.

"Fi-ire!" Katy's voice suddenly pierced the air. Awakening from her bed in the kitchen, she stumbled into the front room in confusion.

Rachel could see Katy's bare feet ambling ahead awkwardly, her bewilderment propelled by the cloud that filled the cottage. "Get low to the floor, Katy!" Rachel shrieked. "I'm just ahead of you!"

"Which way, Rachel? I can't see!" Katy coughed and staggered against a chair.

"On your face, Katy! I see you!" Rachel hastened her crawl across the floor but grew dismayed when Katy's body slumped onto the frayed rug and then grew still.

Rising slowly toward the open window, Rachel looked in horror at the sight before her. The stubble of the flax fields burned intensely. But the wheat, primed this week for harvest, rose in a blazing arena of fire. The window to the cottage, left open to allow in the nightly breezes, had become a vacuum for the poisonous fumes that filled the night air outside the dwelling. Rachel lunged for the window frame, struggling to slam it shut while the black smoke continued to engulf her.

"Rachel, w-where's Caleb?" Katy moaned softly. "Have to find him—" Seized with another fit of coughing, Katy drew herself up on the rug, pressing her face into the folds of her nightgown.

Abandoning the window, Rachel lunged back toward the floor where Katy lay. Grasping her hand, Rachel tugged on the girl. "This way, Katy . . . follow me." Rachel pulled her toward the front doorway but found the shortness of her breath weakened her endeavors. Upon opening the front door, the two women were engulfed with thick smoke that fanned across the front of the property like great coiling braids. Rachel stared anxiously at the fiery debris blowing threateningly close to the home. "Go outside, Katy. Take the horse and wagon and get the neighbors!"

"No." Katy struggled to pull herself to her feet. "Caleb!" she cried, her face wrenched with distress. Yanking her arm away from Rachel, Katy dragged herself farther back into the smoke-filled shack.

Terror seized Rachel as she saw Katy disappear into a wall of smoke. With a bare foot, Rachel shoved the door closed again to keep out the smoke from the field. The task of finding the others now grew paramount. The fire would soon reach the flimsy shack and they would all be trapped for certain if she didn't hurry. Making her way past the rickety chairs, she dragged herself into the rear room, where she found Amelia trying to pull George to his feet. George's pale face winced, his eyes were closed, and his hands grasped loosely at Amelia's gown.

"Help me, Rachel!" Amelia cried. "We've got to get George outdoors to some fresh air!"

"Where's Caleb?" Rachel searched the tiny room with her weary eyes.

"Gone out the window. He's safe now and running out to the road for help."

"Katy too?" Rachel looked all around.

"No," Amelia's voice rose in a question. "She's not with you?"

Rachel shook her head vigorously, her eyes planted on Amelia, pleading. "But, she came back here. I—" Turning one way and then the other, Rachel searched through the haze for signs of the young woman. The sound of crashing wood seized her with new terror. "The rear porch! It's caved in!"

"Katy!" Amelia shrieked. "No, dear God!"

At the roar of the field's inferno, the women turned their eyes fearfully toward the front room.

"The yard's ablaze, Amelia. We've got to hurry!" Rachel warned. "Perhaps Katy's gone out already with Caleb."

"No! She's still in here—I know she is—*Katy!*" Amelia called out in a panic.

"Amelia!" Rachel snapped. "I can't lift George by myself. You've got to keep your wits!"

Fighting the impulse to rush toward the caved-in porch, Amelia turned piteous eyes toward Rachel as sobs choked her words. "We've got to hurry!"

Pulling George's arms around their necks, the two women managed to heft George to his feet but found he could offer little assistance. Amelia stumbled under the weight, losing her footing, but then managed to right herself and brace her shoulder against the wall.

"No time to lose! Let's take him through the window, Amelia!" Rachel cautiously pivoted George's frame back toward the inside of the room. Bracing herself to bear the bulk of George's weight, Rachel directed, "You go out first, Amelia!"

Amelia froze for a moment, her mind captured by a ghost from the past. "No, Rachel." A strange smile curved her face. "Ladies first."

Rachel hesitated, her brows pinching her forehead into a perplexed expression. The haze that framed Amelia's aging face brought forth an image in Rachel's mind—the flight from the burning brothel she and Amelia had shared years ago. "Don't be ridiculous, Amelia! I need you outside to help me with George."

"I can manage from inside better anyway, Rachel. Out the window with you." She smiled knowingly and pulled George's weight against her own frame.

Sighing exasperatedly, Rachel relinquished her share of George to Amelia and reluctantly squeezed herself through the small window frame. Catching her fall with her hands, she moaned when a sharp pain twisted through one of her wrists. Her instincts told her to lie still, but her mind roiled with the fear that Katy lay trapped inside the shack. Rolling onto the dusty ground, she breathed in the smoke-filled air and then slowly stood to her feet. "Hurry, Amelia!" She winced. "I'm waiting for you." As she extended her one good hand toward the window, her gaze was caught by a ring of fire whipping around the corners of the property and beginning to surround the shack.

Gaining a bead on his target, John Macarthur squeezed off a round of musket and found his aim to be slightly off-center. The musket ball whizzed past the old brown bottle that he had balanced along his fence post. Waiting for Elizabeth to fall asleep, he had arisen and donned a pair of brown trousers and a cotton shirt and tramped to the edge of one of his fields. His growing sheep herd could be seen in the distance, their white fleece illumined by the moon.

The sound of hoofbeats on the road didn't surprise him, and he took careful aim again and squeezed the trigger. This time the bottle exploded into a hundred tiny shards.

"Lieutenant Macarthur, sir!" The stout rider called quietly from his mount while reining the steed to a halt. "Glad to find you awake. We've a problem in the colony, sir. Bushrangers are stealin' livestock and settin' fires. There's two farms blazin' out o' control now, sir!"

"Which ones, Corporal?"

"The Prentice farm and the Miller farm—both fairly near you."

Without so much as a blink, Macarthur replied calmly, "Have the neighbors been alerted?"

"They're on their way now with buckets, sir. But we need someone to open up the stores—we need all the containers we can muster."

"No time to reach the stores! Fetch Private Harris from the laborers' cabin over yonder." Macarthur pointed to the dwelling where a military private lived as sentry to his convict laborers. "He can get containers from my barn. Have him send a couple o' wagonloads o' convict laborers with the buckets. We can at least try an' stop the blaze from spreading."

"Yes, sir!"

"I suppose I should head out to the farms myself and offer a helping hand."

"That's awful kind o' you, sir," the red-faced private commented in surprise.

" 'Tis the neighborly thing to do, Private."

Macarthur watched the private gallop toward the farm laborers' quarters. Turning, he headed toward his immaculate stable to retrieve and saddle his own mount.

Riding down the pathway that led from his house, he encountered another rider waiting in the center of the road. Pausing for a moment, Macarthur rode toward the man, thinking he recognized him. "State your name, sir," he called out somewhat nervously.

The man on horseback sat silently, the faint glow of the predawn raising a lavender sky on the horizon.

Sliding his hand down the tip of his musket, Macarthur grew vexed when the rider reined his mount farther into the shadows. "Speak up, man! In the name o' the Crown!"

"No need to get yerself all flustered," the man whispered. "I just came to let you know the job's finished. Where's me pay?"

"I told you to hide the livestock—did you?"

"It's gone for good, but where's me bag o' lolly?"

"You can't expect pay out here in the middle o' the night like this!" Macarthur blustered. "There's a convict wagon comin' right behind me with two military men. Meet me later and you'll get your pay," he ordered, his voice rising nervously.

"I'd better—or I'll squawk like a parrot!"

"Don't threaten me, fool!"

The rider turned his steed into the woods and disappeared as the sound of wagons and hoofbeats rose behind Lieutenant John Macarthur.

"Hurry!" Caleb shouted from the driver's seat to the farmers clambering aboard his wagon. His fists firmly gripping the reins, he batted back the tears that threatened his manhood. Then fixing his eyes on the road ahead, he awaited the "go ahead" signal from the bucket-laden farmers.

Sitting atop his horse, Dwight Farrell swung his arm around and tossed an extra stack of metal pails to the men in the wagon. "Let's go, men!" Slapping his horse with the reins, the emancipist charged ahead of the Prentice wagon, leaving behind a red dust cloud.

Ahead of him, Farrell recognized the minister riding down the road leading to the Prentice farm. His mule trotted vigorously, kicking up its hooves and braying in protest as the husky minister dug his heels into its stubborn flanks. Riding up alongside Whitley, Farrell called out breathlessly, "I saw the smoke! It's the Prentice farm!"

Nodding anxiously, Heath Whitley glanced toward Farrell with a worried frown. "Yes! Is anyone hurt—do you know?"

"We don't know yet."

Whitley shouted above the sound of the wagons that rattled behind them. "Forward all!" He sighed in exasperation, his anxiety rising. "Why don't you ride on ahead, Farrell? Your mount is faster than the rest. I'll lead the wagons."

Amelia Prentice stood staring at the front room from the bedroom doorway. The walls were ablaze; the fire consumed the wattle-and-daub framework as though it were paper. As shock crowded out common sense and numbed her thinking, Amelia stood fixed in stunned horror. Rachel's pleas to her after she had seen George safely through the window could not penetrate her reasoning. She walked dazedly into the smoky room, which popped and crackled overhead from the heat of the blaze. The ceiling above the old cookstove was nothing but a fiery rubble. "It's the fire!" she mumbled.

Numbly, she cradled the blanket in which she had often rocked Caleb those long nights inside the prison compound. The blanket, now dingy and smelling of sulpher, was the only possession that seemed important, and her only thought now was to find her daughter. "Katy!" she shouted again, determination flooding her senses. *Have to get 'er out!*

A faint whisper, soft like the sigh of an infant, drifted out of the rubble toward her. Lurching blindly toward the blazing kitchen, Amelia could see no signs of life but stumbled on toward the whispered cry. "It's Mum, Katy! Where are ye?"

Throwing the baby blanket over her shoulder, she picked her way through the doorway. The heat from the smoke and flames nearly overtook her, but she steadied her teetering frame and held her breath, her eyes burning and tearing profusely. *There's bad men here! Want to hurt my little girl!* In her confused mind, she searched for the fair face of a twelve-year-old girl in a burning brothel.

Rachel began to panic when Amelia failed to appear at the window. With great frustration, she struggled to lift George's sinewy frame but could not move him more than an inch at a time. The thick smoke had turned from gray to black and Rachel began to cough uncontrollably. Nausea swept through her and she doubled over in painful convulsions.

"Rachel!" Dwight Farrell shouted from his mount. Seeing the young woman struggling with George's limp body, he leapt from his saddle. "I'll take George!" Running promptly to her side, he scooped up the emancipist in his arms effortlessly. Hefting George close to his chest, he turned swiftly and carried him away toward the safety of the approaching wagons. "Where are the others?" He turned his face at once but found that Rachel was nowhere to be found. *Dear God!*

"Amelia! Katy!" Rachel stumbled onto the floor from the window, her swollen wrist throbbing. Crawling with the aid of her one good hand, she hastened into the front room. Her eyes were drawn at once to the figure kneeling in the doorway of the kitchen. Her brows knit together at the strange sight of Amelia swaying back and forth, repeating over and over, "We're free now—we're free now."

Struggling toward Amelia with slow, painful progress, Rachel called to her but Amelia did not reply. "What is it, Amelia? What've you found?" Taking her place quickly beside the woman, Rachel gasped when she beheld the long flaxen locks and the colorless face that Amelia sat stroking so lovingly. "It's Katy!" She shook her head in disbelief. With her eyes closed and her motionless body nearly hidden beneath the fallen roof, Katy looked like a child again. "Is she alive, Amelia?" Grabbing Amelia by the shoulder with her one good hand, Rachel began to shake her, attempting to rouse her from her stupor. Panic and terror gripped her mind. "Listen to me! You've got to listen to me, Amelia!"

More debris began to fall from above and Rachel realized she had to force Amelia from the room. "George needs you! He's sick! He's outside waiting. You've got to go to him—*now!*"

Amelia struggled to form words, but confusion wrapped her speech in a strange lilt. "George?" She stared ahead, her eyes lifeless. "He's not here. He's in prison. Must save me little girl."

"No! George is out now, Amelia." Rachel felt her lips trembling. "He needs you. Please—go to him now." She reached and began to pull the aged wood from Katy's chest. She saw no sign that the girl was breathing. "*Now*, Amelia!"

"George n-needs me?"

"He's—waiting—" Rachel broke into sobs, the frustration of the moment crashing in on her sensibilities. Reaching to feel for Katy's pulse at her throat, Rachel was seized with more convulsive coughing.

"Rachel!" Heath Whitley's voice came from the bedroom window.

"In here—near the kitchen! Hurry!" Rachel called in anguish.

Within moments, Whitley and Farrell were in the room, and Farrell scooped a shrieking Amelia into his arms. "We've no time—out you go, Mrs. Prentice!" He fled back into the bedroom with Amelia fighting him furiously.

Rachel felt herself yanked away as another piece of roofing crashed in front of her. Struggling from the minister's grasp, she pleaded, "Reverend Whitley—i-it's Katy! She's—"

Whitley was fast to feel for the girl's pulse. "She's alive!" Lunging toward Katy, he kicked away the loose burning lumber and quickly examined her chest and limbs. "Her legs are burned and her hands—but the girl's alive!" He lifted her gently into his arms and crouching low ran into the bedroom. Rachel followed haltingly behind him.

As several men assisted with Katy's rescue through the window, Farrell's voice could be heard above the tumult. "You men over there! Man the buckets!"

The wagonload of buckets and men came to a halt. The farmers jumped to the ground and began to form a brigade from the well to the field.

Farrell spotted Amelia. Her eyes were trancelike as she was lifted carefully into a wagon, an old blanket snugged beneath her arm. Then his eyes fell on the limp body of a young woman being lifted to the window. Speeding toward the site of the rescue, Farrell stretched out his arms to assist. Hoisting

Katy through the window, he pulled her free from the smoke-filled room while the roof creaked and groaned overhead. Cradling the unconscious woman in his arms, Farrell rushed her away from the smoke and the throng of smoke-blackened men and laid her gently down near the road. A group of farmers' wives came to her side at once.

Stroking her hair from her face, Farrell shouted, "See to her!" He turned and fled back to George who lay on the ground where he had left him, his breathing labored. Looking up, he saw Rachel being lifted through the window, with Reverend Whitley emerging directly behind her. Looking down at George, Farrell saw the man's partly opened eyes regarding him with faint appreciation.

"I'll take you to your wife." Farrell lifted George with one movement and ducked his head as debris from the roof swirled violently around them.

The crashing sound of walls caving in behind them brought a scream from Rachel, but she ran close to Whitley's side and did not look back. "We're safe!" she cried with elation.

The farmers, whose numbers continued to grow well into the night, managed to create a sodden ring around the borders of the fields, preventing the fire from spreading to the next farm. But the Prentice fields and the Miller pasture continued to burn for another day, while the Prentice shanty lay in ruins, a smoldering, ashy pile.

For days and then for weeks, Rachel and George kept vigil at Katy's side in the home of a neighbor. Nearby, Amelia sat and rocked methodically, not speaking a word. Occasionally Dwight Farrell came by to offer his aid, but he was always disappointed to find the Prentice girl had not stirred. And then one day, as the fresh scent of wild flowers sifted in through the window, Rachel watched as Katy's hand moved slightly. Holding her breath, Rachel sat forward. She had slept beside Katy every evening, hoping to be present when she awoke. "George," she whispered.

Still moving slowly because of his smoke-damaged lungs, George set aside the dish he was drying and shuffled painstakingly toward the bed where Katy lay. Without a word, he knelt beside her.

Reaching to stroke a blond strand from Katy's cheek, Rachel spoke gently, "Katy. Are you awake? Katy?"

Lashes fluttered, and then stilled. Soon a pale tint of rose colored Katy's cheeks. Then, lids opening slowly, blue eyes gazed up in confusion at Rachel. Parting her lips, she emitted a hoarse whisper, "W-where's Mum?"

George's eyes clouded with joyous tears, and his weathered face broke into a broad grin. "You've given 'er back to me again, Lord!"

"Your mum is here, Katy." Rachel composed her face somberly. "She's been waiting all along."

Turning her face slowly, Katy curved her mouth into a faint smile as she searched the room for her mother. But seeing the weary-looking Amelia rocking back and forth without expression brought a puzzled frown to her brow. "Mum?" She cleared her throat and tried to call out again. "Mum?"

"She's—" George placed his hands gently on top of Katy's heavily bandaged ones. "She's alive but not with us, love."

Katy shook her head slowly. "I don't believe you. She's just waiting for me—that's all. Mum, it's me, Katy. Speak to me!" Anxiety marked her tone.

"Dr. White said to give 'er more time," George said gravely. "But, Katy, you're going to be well soon. I just know it. Together, we can make Mum well again."

Rachel nodded, observing the uneasiness in Katy's gaze. "Don't worry about Amelia. She always bounces back, doesn't she?"

Katy could not take her eyes away from the figure who sat rocking and muttering barely audible words. It was as though a stranger had inhabited her mother's body.

Rachel bent to kiss Katy's forehead. She watched in dismay as Katy's eyes searched down her arms to her bandaged hands. "They'll heal," she tried to assure. Swallowing hard, Katy gave no response, but continued to explore the damage done to her body. Slowly sliding her wounded hands beneath the sheet, she inspected her legs, which were also wound in bandages. Rachel helped adjust the sheet back around Katy's chest again, and their eyes met. "I'm glad we came through—God came through for us."

Taking her eyes from Rachel, Katy shook her head. "Look at me," she said hoarsely. "There's almost nothing left."

"Not true." Rachel slid over to place herself in front of Katy again. "The doctor says when your wounds heal you'll be as good as new."

"I'll be scarred. Look at me, Rachel." Katy's eyes searched Rachel's face for the truth. "It hurts! And I'm ugly. I'll never look the same again—I'll never be normal."

"You're the most beautiful woman in the colony," George disagreed heartily. "Don't talk such nonsense."

"Give yourself time, please, I beg you." Stroking Katy's arm tenderly, Rachel struggled to find the right words. She couldn't make any guarantees to Katy; she couldn't assure her that she wouldn't be scarred. But Rachel had been so elated to have Katy alive, she hadn't considered such matters before. Now, with her friend staring up at her with her pleading blue eyes, Rachel felt her voice break. "I'm so sorry."

Katy glanced over at her mother again, the creaking sound of the rocker hammering in her mind like a tolling church bell. "I need to be alone."

"No," George insisted. "You need us here—with you."

"I'll go fetch the doctor," Rachel conceded. She nodded reassuringly at George. "I love you, my friend," Rachel said sincerely as she stood to depart. "I'm so glad you came back to us."

Katy pressed her dry lips together and stared up at Rachel as though she were a stranger. No words would come forth, for she could not speak encouraging words from a graveyard of hopelessness. As Rachel tucked the sheets carefully around her again, Katy felt nothing but the numbing cold of despair—a despair that would slowly erode the tapestry of faith that knit their hearts together.

11
PARRAMETTA

A chill wind shook the myrtles, scattering their petals in a white promenade of bell-shaped blooms. Bubbling clear and cold around slick mossy rocks, a brook meandered in shallow rivulets, dividing wild forest from broken wheat fields.

Good weather had allowed the field laborers a few extra days to gather in the remains of the wheat. Rachel, her head wrapped in a printed scarf, had quickly dispensed with her allotment of sheaves and found her way to the brook for a rest. The day was still new with morning dew and she reveled in her temporary freedom. She had found the wooded abode an inviting respite, and sometimes she would nap for an hour on a sunny rock before trudging back to the bunkhouse to line up for evening grub.

"Chill in the air." She shuddered, rubbing the bumps on her arms and stiffening her shoulders. Glancing up at the white clouds that drifted in thin wisps and threaded through the azure sky like frayed silk, Rachel settled herself to enjoy the warmth of the rock.

She frowned when a shadow suddenly stretched across her resting place. The figure appeared suddenly, blocking out the sun and sending another chill through her slender frame. Fearing the consequences of an intruder, she jerked her head around. Narrowing her eyes she beheld the somber figure standing over her. "Oh, it's only you!" A relief-filled smile curved her lips.

In his grasp, Heath Whitley held a brown handwoven basket covered with worn fabric. "Mrs. Campbell fixed me up a fine lunch. There's a fresh pie and some meat. I thought you'd like to share it with me." His voice held no hesitation, but his eyes grew wide, reflecting his sincere anticipation.

"That's so kind of you, Reverend." Rachel rose, dusting away the tares that still clung to her skirt. She studied the oilskin coat covering his husky frame. The minister had begun to don the more practical wear of the settlement for everyday use. His formal dark Anglican suit was saved for Sunday mornings.

Heath Whitley offered in a friendly tone, "Perhaps you could accompany me on a ride out to view some property. Another emancipist is meeting me to assist with the inspection of the land Macarthur has offered to swap for the Prentice farm. George is still feeling poorly—his breathing's never been right since . . ."

"I know." Rachel nodded, her eyes cast sorrowfully. She crossed her arms across the plainly laced bodice that framed her shapely form and asked, "But why would Macarthur swap anything of worth for a burned-out field? I don't trust the man. Do you, Reverend Whitley?"

"I'm not certain about him, but I promised George I'd examine the land in question. Shall we go?" Whitley offered his arm in a chivalrous manner, his tanned face creased in a generous smile. He escorted Rachel through the wooded glen and led her down the pathway to the borrowed wagon.

He spied the Campbells' stout plow horse standing head down, nibbling upon the tall green blades of grass. "Up we go!" he offered jovially, extending his hand to Rachel, who stepped up effortlessly into the wagon.

Seating herself quickly, Rachel brushed away the soil from her skirt. Then smoothing the folds of the worn fabric, she gripped the seat until the wagon lurched forward. She rode quietly next to the minister for a short time. Heath Whitley had called on the Campbells and Prentices on several occasions since the fire and had always found time to speak with her. But on certain days, he had appeared to be lost deep in his thoughts, so she did not press him for conversation. Shunning her own past when they conversed, she made certain the conversation centered around the task at hand—be it tending a needy family or delivering a basket of medicinals to the boys in prison.

"You're certainly quiet today, Rachel," Heath stated with a smile.

Delaying her words, Rachel composed herself, for she felt awkward—as though he could read her worried thoughts like the pages of a worn-out book. She held her face up to the radiant sun, pretending that sunning was the only thought occupying her mind. "Just enjoying the weather."

"Well, the harvest is almost over. I suppose you're glad for that." Turning with an amicable gaze, he regarded Rachel warmly.

"Extremely glad for it." Reaching clumsily, she untied the bulky scarf and allowed her hair to fall in soft curls around her shoulders. "But I'm sad for Katy. She's walking now with the aid of a crutch, but she hardly speaks to me. She just broods about the house all day, tending to Amelia's needs."

"I saw that Amelia's no better. This morning I found her as always."

"No. It's as though she's forever reliving the horrors of that night in the—" Rachel stopped, her breath taken by her own words.

"In the—what, Rachel?" Whitley pressed for answers, glancing quickly at her before setting his concerned gaze again on the road.

"In the—boardinghouse." Rachel felt her cheeks flush, for she could not justify the lie. "You remember the story about the fire in England?"

Whitley nodded, but his eyes narrowed dubiously. "I'm not certain I've heard the entire story."

Remembering the lifeless stare of Amelia in the rocker, Rachel shrugged. "It's of no consequence now, is it? Amelia has all but left us."

Whitley pondered the thought for a moment before answering. "Think of this, Rachel. Something happened that was shared by the two of you. Perhaps recalling it all would help Amelia."

An uneasy tension rose within Rachel. She had blocked out the memory with no intention of ever recalling it. "Surely not. It seems to do such a thing would only make matters worse." Staring woodenly, she held up her chin with an air of forbearance. "Amelia's ordeal has obviously been too much for her to bear. When Katy was revived, I was sure it would bring Amelia back to us. But it didn't. What if she never comes back? We may have to face that fact."

Heath Whitley pressed his lips together, his brow pinched with concern. "George and Katy are tending to Amelia as though she were an infant. I just don't know if we should surrender her just yet. The thought nags at me that we shouldn't give up."

"What are you suggesting, sir?" Rachel asked quietly but firmly.

"What if you tried to recall for Amelia the events of the night you helped them escape from the boardinghouse fire? It couldn't do any harm, could it?"

A stinging anxiety swept through Rachel, and she felt a sickening feeling in her stomach. "What if I upset her?"

"Upsetting her would be better than having no response from her at all. Perhaps it would bring her back to the present."

Heaving a heavy sigh, Rachel stared into the distance. She started as her eyes suddenly focused upon what appeared to be a young woman walking just beyond them in the glen. The blond hair of the woman glinted enough to catch Rachel's quick eye.

Heath followed her gaze. "What do you see?"

"Perhaps nothing." Rachel shook her head. "I thought for

all the world I saw Katy Prentice walking just beyond us in that wooded area. But she wouldn't be this far from the farm without an escort." Rachel frowned and strained once again to peruse the thick stand of trees, and then she returned her gaze to the road ahead. Her thoughts had been so consumed with Katy's unsettling attitude for the past few weeks that her mind must be playing tricks on her. Turning her curiosity toward Reverend Whitley, she asked, "Will you tell me, please, why you love the ministry?"

The wagon veered right and headed for the new tract of land.

Katy crouched low behind the saltbush plants and the paperbark trees, feeling slightly foolish for hiding. She was certain Rachel hadn't spotted her, but she sat motionless until the rattle of the wagon's squeaky wheels was silenced by the distance. She had parked Papa's horse and wagon farther down the overgrown pathway. Leaning against her crutch, she untangled her skirts from a bramble of thorny weeds. Her eyes fell contemptuously upon the red streaks that scarred her legs and the burns that peeked scornfully out from her gloved hands. Wincing at the pain, she dropped the skirt with an air of disdain. Then standing weakly, she forced herself to push farther into the wild where eyes would not see. Finding a large smooth rock, she seated herself, her taut face relaxing with relief.

Katy's nerves had been a shambles since the fire. Although the Campbells had made them all feel more than welcome, Papa had never regained his cheerful morale and his health suffered worse. Rachel had stayed on with the Campbells to share in the toils of harvest and to help Katy, but Katy had built up an invisible wall of emotional protection that Rachel's warmth could not penetrate. She missed their girlish talks more than she would admit. But her worries intensified that Mum's condition would never lift.

Fingers trembling, Katy reached into the small mended purse that hung from her wrist. Opening the drawstring, she drew out a dainty flask and held it in front of her, her gaze ominous. Regarding the flask of rum disdainfully, she sighed at the self-pity she wallowed in. She dropped the bottle with disgust upon the damp forest bed. Her eyes grew moist and a solitary tear streamed down her cheek as the weight of the last several years crashed upon her emotions. "I cannot go on. There's nothing left of me," she reasoned, her voice a hoarse whisper. "I'm a worthless cripple. We've come to a treacherous and miserable land . . . who can stand?" Justification swelled in her mind as she could not think of one truly honest colonist who had succeeded. "Not one solitary hero," she whispered. Inhaling deeply, Katy stooped to retrieve the dropped flask. With the tiny cap gripped firmly in her hand, she pulled it off without hesitation. "A toast to little Katy Prentice," she said darkly. Holding the container to her lips, she tilted her head and allowed the liquor to pour like water into her mouth. Swallowing hard, her eyes teared profusely. "O-oh!" she coughed and sputtered. The rum burned her throat in a fiery bath. Taking another deep breath, Katy wrapped her lips around the flask top again, almost impassioned at her decision. After several drinks, she found the rum more pleasing, and the warm melancholy that clothed her mind assured her that a few moments of bliss was well within her rights.

Lowering herself slowly to the ground, Katy rested against the rock as a feeling of well-being replaced the anguish and the insecurity that tormented her. For at least one day, Katherine Mercy Prentice had found instant bottled peace.

"How will we know if the land near Parrametta is good?" Rachel asked as they rode by stretches of grassy land interspersed with scrub-mounded patches of red soil.

Whitley studied the land with an experienced gaze. "We'll see what grows naturally from the soil, and we'll study the lay of the land. If the drainage is poor, the property could flood. The Hawkesbury River is surrounded by good land, but it has flooded several farms. The Prentices certainly don't need that sort of problem."

"God forbid," Rachel agreed. "Heaven knows they've seen

their share of misery. Perhaps a happier future awaits them now."

"You could be right. Their situation reminds me of Jacob." Clearing his throat, Whitley continued, "He was a man in the Old Testament who had seventeen years of hardship. But then, because of his diligence, God rewarded him with seventeen years of prosperity. During the prosperous years, Jacob may have told us that his life had been wonderful."

"So you think most people surmount the wounds of hardships"—Rachel grew serious—"with the past forgotten?"

"Not everyone," Whitley shrugged. "But I believe miraculous healing is possible. Through God *all* things are possible. Why have a Savior if we can't trust Him to complete our healing?"

The words flew at Rachel like a startled bird taken to flight. Her mind was jolted, but she told herself that Whitley wasn't necessarily preaching to her. He knew nothing about her, really, except that she was an emancipist. But she meditated upon his words and pondered the concept of healing. She had become so accustomed to living with ghosts from her past, she hadn't thought of being free from them. Asking God's forgiveness and "feeling" forgiven were two separate entities. To Rachel, the latter had been out of reach. "Does healing . . . *always* . . . come for Christians?" she asked in halting tones.

"I wish that answer was always yes, Rachel. Remember the parable of the sower—" Whitley stopped as though an unseen force had spoken to him. "Do you mind my spouting on about the Bible? I don't want to bore you."

"Oh no, truly. I want to hear it." Rachel could no longer mask her anxiousness.

"Some women are bored with theological discussions."

Rachel silently mouthed the word "theological" as Whitley continued his parable of the seed and the sower. Comforted by his story, she settled into the wagon seat. She was enjoying the pleasure of his undivided attention and the smooth, deep rumblings of his voice. When he had finished, she queried further, "Do you think my life represents the good soil or the bad soil?"

"As hungry as you appear for the things of God, I'd say you

are quite fertile soil, Rachel." Satisfaction gleamed from Whitley's eyes. "I've never seen anyone strive for righteousness as wholeheartedly as you."

Rachel's brow was pinched as she contemplated his words, for she found she had difficulty receiving commendations, even from Reverend Whitley. She couldn't apply to herself the virtuous side of life no matter how hard she tried to imagine. "Do you ever feel frustrated?"

Whitley sighed. "More often than not, yes. At times, I want to give up. Working with people, Christian or not, can be a daily struggle. Then there's my own personal struggle to deepen my relationship with the Lord."

"You struggle with that too?"

"I'm still just a man."

Rachel studied the wisdom of his words and felt a hunger to know more about his work in the colony. "Oh look!" She pointed to a movement in the grass.

A small gray spiny ball ran through the grass quickly, startled by the wagon.

"Echidna. Tasty with a little stuffing," Whitley remarked. "Much like roasted goose."

"Don't tell me you eat the little things?"

"I'm sure you've eaten them too. Who knows what mysteries emerge from the cooks' pots in Sydney Cove?"

Rachel watched the small animal disappear by burrowing vertically into the ground, its prickly spines nearly camouflaged by the golden Kangaroo grass. "They're like puppies to *me*—small and adorable."

Whitley chuckled and then paused for a moment, his gaze studying Rachel with amusement.

As the wagon rumbled along, Rachel was so absorbed in conversation with the minister that she scarcely noticed the hours that passed. Even when the chill of morning no longer pricked her skin and the sun began to heat the road ahead in ghostly mirrors, Rachel did not mind nor heed the thickening of the air.

"Look now," Whitley gazed alongside the wagon. "According to the directions given me, this long stretch of property beside us is what's being offered to George Prentice."

Rachel gazed silently for a moment, her eyes fixed upon the fields colored by pink everlasting and the swaying spinefex grass. "It's lovely here."

"Let's ride further."

The wagon turned onto the field, and Rachel laughed when a flock of small green-and-yellow birds perched in a gum tree overhead fussed at the sudden intrusion. Traveling farther, she observed the horse shaking its head restlessly.

Whitley offered a comforting tone to the beast. "Easy girl." He flicked the reins to chasten the horse, but the animal drew back its head and whinnied in alarm. "Easy! Easy!" With heightened pitch, Whitley called out but was startled to see a gigantic reptile shoot from behind a saltbush plant.

The monitor lizard, brown with yellow spots, hissed at the plow horse and swung its gargantuan tail.

"It's hideous!" Rachel shrieked.

"Dear heaven! It must be ten feet long!"

The plow horse, its eyes wide, reared in fright, only angering the monitor more. The reptile lurched first to the left, then to the right. As the horse's hooves hit the ground, the excited monitor leaped onto the animal's front right limb and attached itself with its clawed feet.

"It has attacked the horse!" Rachel screamed and jumped to her feet in the wagon as the plow horse reared furiously.

Whitley turned and grabbed Rachel's arm, attempting to pull her with him. "Jump, Rachel!"

Rachel felt her body being hurriedly pulled from the wagon. She struggled to maintain her footing, all the while striving to keep her eyes on the reptile. The horse, now frenzied, struggled to throw the desert dragon from its foreleg, jerking the wagon forward and backward. Rachel was hurled to the hard ground below. Tumbling to the loam, her eyes widened at the sight of a wagon wheel lurching toward her.

"Quickly, Rachel! Grab my hands!" The minister pulled her hand as Rachel scrambled to her feet and the wheel rolled clear of them. "Stand back while I fetch my rifle!"

Seeing the rifle's leather sling hanging precariously from the wagon seat, Rachel lunged for the sling and grasped it with trembling fingertips. "I've got it!" Yanking the weapon free from the pouch, she shoved the gunstock toward the minister.

"Good girl!" Gripping it at once, Heath Whitley dashed toward the plow horse, who strained furiously to free itself from the clinging monitor.

"Don't shoot, Reverend!" Rachel screamed.

Whitley's brow furrowed as he froze upon hearing Rachel's plea. "Why not?"

"You might kill the horse!"

Whitley pressed his lips together, cutting his eyes toward Rachel and muttering under his breath. Swinging the rifle around, he grasped the tip with a gloved hand. With the other hand he grabbed the horse by the halter and pulled its head down with a yank. "Whoa!" Yanking the bit, he commanded the beast into submission. The monitor hissed, its yellow tongue drawing up like a snake's. With a single blow, Whitley caught the reptile aside its small head with the butt of the rifle. "Away, you!" His shout rose against the dry air.

The hot sun bore down, raising the high-pitched complaint of the cicadas. The monitor's head weaved slowly before the body plunged to the ground, claws digging frantically into the red earth to hasten its escape. Whitley stepped forward with one foot while drawing back the other. His boot aimed carefully, he kicked violently, sending the addled monitor scrambling for the safety of a large, densely covered gum tree.

"Easy, girl." The minister's soothing words brought comfort to the bleeding horse. Patting her gently, he ran his hand down the foreleg and examined the cuts around the fetlock. "She's shook up, but in a few days I believe she'll be good as new." He pulled a flask from inside his coat and poured the liquid on the horse's wounds.

"That was wonderful, Reverend!" Rachel strode up beside the minister. "And please forgive me. I didn't mean to interfere—"

"Now don't apologize," Whitley chastened gently. "You bore up like a soldier, considering the dragon we were faced with."

A smile lit Rachel's face. "I only wanted to say I wasn't trying to give orders, Reverend."

"I understand." He held up the rifle with a cynical gaze. "I'm an excellent shot, by the way."

The clattering of wagon wheels drew their attention back to the road.

"It's the emancipist George sent, I'm sure." Whitley shoved the flask back into his pocket.

Rachel nodded hurriedly, her eyes to the loam. "May we go now—that is, the horse . . . can it travel?"

"She's a tough old nag," Whitley assured. "She'll outlive all of us, I'm certain. But let's search for a watering hole on our way out."

Rachel nodded in agreement and then turned silently to climb back up into the wagon. She was grateful that the tension of the incident had begun to diminish, but grieved that she could not share her past with Reverend Heath Whitley. Guilt nagged at her emotions. Perhaps the minister was right—she should help Amelia in any way she could.

A bank of cottony clouds merged across the sun, bringing a slight coolness to the thick, hot air. Heath Whitley seated himself next to Rachel and acknowledged her presence with a nod and a smile of relief in knowing the horse could travel. As they neared the man in the wagon, Whitley glanced toward Rachel with his lips parted as though he held back an unasked question. "That boardinghouse fire—"

"Sir?" Rachel saw the perplexity of his gaze but did not venture to guess at its meaning.

Heath Whitley noted the way her eyes grew large, as though she cowered, whenever he made reference to the fire. Shaking his head, he sighed, flicked the reins, and chose to make no further inquiries. Instead, he allowed the girl to retreat back inside the walls that hid her life from his own.

12
THE ABDUCTION

A pungent, oily scent hung in the air of the makeshift kitchen. Rachel stood over a pot of boiling liquid, stirring the mixture with an old spoon. She hummed quietly to herself, shooing the flies that flitted about the kitchen. The open windows invited a host of pests that wafted in with the mingled aromas of freshly cut wheat and field grass. Lifting a rag from one of the many nails pounded into the wood-slatted walls, she wiped the sweat that poured down her forehead. Carefully lifting a small glass bottle from the stove top, she ladled some of the smelly mixture through the container's opening. "All set, Katy."

Katy lay still on the kitchen floor, a rumpled blanket her bed. She gazed up at Rachel in bewilderment, her face swollen and her limbs covered in fretful red sores. "Please hurry. I must have some relief."

Rachel tried to mask her amusement as she beheld the young woman lying in agony on the floor. Katy looked once again like the mischievous twelve-year-old that once battled London's bullies, rather than a mature woman of nineteen. She almost enjoyed the attention Katy was forced to allow her to administer. But she was sorry for the pain her friend suffered. "However did this happen to you?"

Katy closed her eyes as Rachel approached with the antidote. "Don't say anything, please, just get this over with!" Pride and embarrassment taunted Katy, filling her with anxiety. The insects that reigned supreme in the Australian wild had managed to conquer what no human could accomplish—the abasement of Katy Prentice.

"It just seems odd that one could fall asleep in the woods—it's not normal, I would think," Rachel said suspiciously. She stooped over Katy while dipping a soft, clean cloth into the foul tree tea mixture.

Katy winced when the strong plant compound met with the tender areas she had clawed all night. "Careful, please!" she flinched. "What is that smelly ointment, anyway?"

"Just boiled tree tea leaves." Rachel tried to reflect patience. "It's an evergreen plant of sorts. Lots of colonists use it for skin diseases and such like. I decided it would cure ant bites just as well."

"I'm not certain they're ant bites." Katy ground her teeth, her voice strained. "Could be mosquitoes."

"Looks like a bit of both." Rachel examined the bites, noticing the white spots in the center of each swollen area. "More than likely those blasted jumper ants, though." She studied Katy's swollen face. "How in the world could you sleep through all this?" Rachel persisted.

Katy opened her eyes. She was sorry for her drunkenness but too ashamed to confess. "I'd been feeling so cooped up. I took a walk and went too far," she lied. The rum had lulled her to sleep, serving to free her mind of the circumstances but rendering her helpless to predators. *How stupid I was!* she tortured herself. *I should've hid in the Campbell barn!*

"Anyone home?" a male voice called from the rear doorway.

"Don't let anyone come in, Rachel!" Katy pleaded in an all but threatening tone. "Let me get out of here first!"

"Don't be so vain, Katy!" Rachel laughed. "You lie still and let me finish with you, now."

Finding the door wide open, the gentleman stepped in, pulling his large brown hat from his head. He turned and looked with shock at Katy. "I . . . I'm sorry," he apologized. "I'll come back later!"

"Dwight Farrell?" Katy whispered, her worst fears confirmed. She felt the same embarrassment imposed on a saint caught in the worst of iniquities. "No need to leave now, Mr. Farrell," Rachel offered quietly. "Not likely she's contagious."

"I won't be but a moment. I was passing this way and was asked to relay the message that they could use your help at the prison colony. It's the fever again."

Sighing heavily, Rachel shook her head. "Poor souls. I'll head out as soon as I finish with this one." She smiled down at Katy sympathetically.

Katy cast her eyes sideways at Rachel, assured her ruin was evident. Swallowing hard, she decided to make the most of the miserable situation. "It's not as bad as it looks, Mr. Farrell. Just a few insect bites, that's all."

Dwight stepped toward the girl, amazed by the sight of her. "You had to have been pretty drunk to endure such an experience!" he said jokingly.

Rachel bit her lip, stifling a chuckle.

Katy felt her anger kindled, wondering if the man enjoyed making sport of her miserable situation. Pursing her lips, she pretended not to notice Farrell's poor attempt at humor. "Have some tea, won't you? Rachel just made it fresh there on the cookstove." Katy pointed with her eyes to the pot of tea simmering on the back of the kitchen stove.

Dwight strode toward the stove, lifting a teacup from one of the nails. "Don't mind if I do," he answered amicably.

"Been down to the market lately, Miss Langley?"

"Not in a fortnight," Rachel answered, working her way down Katy's swollen arms.

"Lots of talk about the rum monopoly Macarthur's maneuvered. I'd venture to say, he'll soon be the richest man in New South Wales."

"Not rich by my standards!" Rachel was quick to hasten

her opinion. "The Word of God says in Habakkuk that those who use drunkenness for their own gain and another's loss will be covered with violence."

Katy watched in mild surprise as an unwitting Dwight reached for the ladle in the pot of boiled tree tea leaves. Holding her words, she closed her eyes and braced for the inevitable.

"I'd be tempted myself to have a share in those gains," Dwight confessed, filling his cup with the steaming mixture, oblivious to the odor. "But I suppose you're right, Miss Langley. The man will surely come to no good end." Tipping the cup toward his lips, he drew in the topical solution. At first, he appeared confused. Expecting the robust taste of English tea, his taste buds found no recognition.

Rachel chatted on, applying the finishing touches to Katy's fingertips. "Even when it seems the outlaws are in charge, give it a little time, I always say, and soon—"

"A-agh!" Dwight spewed the brown medicine from his mouth.

Katy kept her eyes closed, but a faint smile curved her face.

"What on earth?" Rachel stood at once, screwing the lid quickly down on the ointment. Seeing the man's expression, she moved quickly toward him. "You didn't drink from the front pot, did you?"

"Afraid so!" Dwight wiped his mouth with the old rag and then ran to the pail of water that sat on the table. Lifting the metal ladle to his lips, he filled his mouth and ran to the doorway to spew out the foul tang.

Rachel lifted the teacup and sniffed the contents before turning her eyes upon Katy. Detecting the amusement in her friend's eyes, she shook her head. "You're hopeless!" she mouthed silently as Dwight gargled from the back stoop.

Beyond the shanty, George Prentice walked slowly, assisted by Reverend Whitley. Finding his way to an old chair left beneath a spreading wattle tree, he seated himself. "What did you find yesterday, Reverend—a worthless piece of land, I vow?"

"Not at all, Mr. Prentice." Heath Whitley bent down on one knee and looked up just in time to see Rachel emerge from the house. "Greetings, Rachel," he called jovially.

Rachel carried with her the basket of ointments. Walking up to face George she said with concern, "I'm needed out at the prison colony—the Irish boys. Do you think you'll be all right without me for the day?"

"Stop frettin' about us, lass. I'm growin' stronger by the day. Soon me an' Amelia'll be back fussin' like the old days." He glanced toward his wife, who sat at the edge of the field rocking in the old chair. "She walked with me all the way out here. She's gettin' better. I know she is."

Seeing the color had come back to his cheeks, Rachel noted, "You *are* looking fine today, George." She hoped to be an encouragement, but she wasn't inventing empty flattery on George's behalf. She *had* noticed a marked improvement this morning in his stamina and found solace in realizing that George might possibly regain his health.

"Why not let me drive you, Rachel?" Whitley offered, the brightness of his gaze cheering her.

She shook her head. "Thank you kindly, Reverend Whitley." Her tone was formal, being heedful of the fact that keeping her distance would lower the risk of Whitley's attempts to question her. "But today is market day for most. I've caught rides with the neighbors on many occasions. I know them all. Not to worry." She smiled confidently. "Besides, today is too lovely. I'd enjoy a short walk down the path to the main road."

"Be stubborn about it, then. But after my rounds, I'll be headed your way anyway. I insist upon bringing you back home."

Rachel contemplated the matter. She would be weary after a day in the contagion ward. "Very well. I'll return just before the convicts' evening meal. I suppose you can watch for me along the Masons' farm road. It's between here and the prison colony. I always stop and fill my water jug at the Masons'."

"I'll see you around the five o'clock hour, then?"

Rachel nodded. Pulling her old scarf from the basket, she fashioned it attractively to make a colorful binding for her hair and allow her neck to cool. Arranging her hair to one side, she draped the curly locks around one shoulder. Then taking George's wide-brimmed hat from his head, she winked. "Think I'll steal this today, sir, if you don't mind. They certainly don't make practical hats for ladies these days." Placing the hat straight on her head, she turned to make her farewells. "Good day, Reverend. Would you mind informing Mrs. Campbell I'll return this evening for supper? Oh, and don't eat all the kangaroo, now, George!" she scolded, aware of George's growing aversion for the meat.

"Bah! You can *have* all the blasted kangaroo, for all I care!"

Rachel walked along with a calculated lilt in her steps, wondering if her departure was being observed by Heath Whitley. She feared he had begun to wonder almost too much about the brothel fire. However much she enjoyed their conversations, the less time she spent with him, the better.

Tramping onto the main road, Rachel peered down the dusty route that wound around the front of the Campbell property. She saw no immediate traffic and so began on her way toward the prison. Her recollection of the sad Irish boys in the oppressive contagion ward drew her back to her early beginnings. It would be difficult to return, she realized. But even her painful memories of Betsy couldn't keep her away forever. "I miss you so badly, my dear friend," she whispered, but continued forth determinedly.

Beyond offering medical aid to those forgotten wards, she longed to share the truth of the gospel that she had found through Betsy's life—a gospel not rightly received among the citizenry of Sydney Cove. Once granted freedom, Rachel had found herself in a spiritual wilderness of sorts. She had soon realized the settlers were resistive and hard about matters of religion, and their faith in God appeared to be at low ebb. Perhaps reaching the boys before manhood would prove to be a greater accomplishment. *Surely good soil will be found in children.*

Spotting the winding road ahead, Rachel decided to cut through the woods and shorten her path. The sunlight streaming down through the trees offered an invitation not to be resisted. Venturing away from the road might be foolhardy later in the day, but the brightness of morning filled her soul with peace. Keeping her sights on the road, Rachel pushed through a bramble of shrubs and into a wooded glen. "I'll get to the prison much quicker now." Feeling the pull of an incline, she braced herself for a short run down an embankment. Startling a large red kangaroo burdened with her joey, Rachel veered away from the disturbed mother.

The sight of a shallow brook drew her for a drink, and she knelt immediately to partake of the cool, fresh water. She had brought along a canteen in her basket, but this stream provided a welcome refreshment and allowed her to save the canteen for later. As her lips touched the water cupped in her hands, she sat up and listened intently to a distant rumbling. "Wagon wheels!" The sound became distinct. Rachel quickly gathered her belongings and turned to head back toward the road. But she stopped suddenly and realized she had strayed so far from the road that it was hidden from view. Following the sound of the wagon, she ran quickly but realized the woods ahead of her were unfamiliar. "No! This way, Rachel," she chided herself and turned to run in the opposite direction. Stopping again, anxiety marked her gaze when the sound of the wagon wheels grew distant. "Don't panic!" she told herself. "I couldn't have gone far!"

Within moments, the woods grew silent except for the monotonous and continual cheep of zebra finches fighting over seeds. Rachel felt confused and turned to trudge away from the stream bed. She thought she remembered the stream to be opposite the road—perhaps running parallel to her route.

After what seemed like an hour or so, Rachel felt the weariness of worry start to beleaguer her mind and body. Finding the gnarled, dark gray trunk of an ancient coolibah tree, she sat and rested at the base, her stomach twinging from hunger. She had packed a lunch of corn cakes and dried meat and decided upon her only recourse—consume a quick meal and then make short work of locating the road.

The longer Rachel sat and ate, the more her fears grew that she was lost. Collecting her dish into the frayed basket, she stood and trekked away from the coolibah. She soon found her pace quickening, right along with her heartbeat. The woods around her grew sparse and the grass more thinly scattered. The sun's sweltering heat bore down hotter than any day she could remember, and she longed for the comfort of the cool stream bed again.

Racing blindly into the outback, Rachel's mind quickly returned to thoughts of Reverend Whitley. Had she accepted his cordial ride into the prison settlement, she would not be lost. *Pride.* She chastened herself for such foolhardy reasoning. Her soul was pricked at the thought of his honest nature.

Rachel stopped along the lonely ledge of a rocky outcrop and stared blankly at a single, pillared mesa. "Please get me back home, Lord . . . and forgive my dishonesty." Anxiously scanning the distance, Rachel spotted a tiny curve in a clearing on the edge of a wooded glen that indicated a road was present. Breathing a relief-filled sigh, she stooped to retrieve the basket. Whether the road proved to be the route on which she had started was insignificant. All roads were cattle paths that led back to the borough.

Turning abruptly, Rachel was jolted by the sight of an intruder. An aborigine man stood before her, painted with the white symbols of his paganism. He was slightly taller than Rachel and in his hand he carried a spear. He appeared to study her features with marked interest, and his gaze reflected anger at her intrusion of his territory.

But Rachel found herself more unnerved by the fact he wore no clothes. Turning to glance behind her, she realized she had nowhere to run unless she chose to leap from the ledge and risk her life. "Speak English?" Her jaw rigid, she tried to appear friendly, although the fear in her eyes betrayed her alarm.

Swinging his spear horizontally, the native aimed its chiseled tip at Rachel's heart. With a wave of his arm, he signaled the tribe that waited behind the rock pillars, and suddenly the land behind him filled with the loud cries of his naked clansmen as they encircled their leader, keeping a wary watch on the white woman. "What do I do, Lord?" Rachel whispered, but no reply returned from the heavens.

The aborigine motioned with his spear, indicating Rachel was to begin walking, but where, she wasn't certain. Taking a deep breath, she held the basket close to herself and fell into line behind the women who were following submissively behind the men. Another hour passed and Rachel found herself being forced deeper and deeper into the Australian outback. She wasn't jostled or shoved about, but she knew that if she tried to escape, she would be instantly speared.

The temperature soared in the desert sun. Rachel wondered if the dizziness she felt would make her faint, but she kept plodding forward, placing one foot in front of the other. Her mouth was dry, and her fear that drawing out a canteen would turn them all on her grew insignificant. Her thirst demanded that she take her chances. Pulling out the small bottle she had packed for herself, she quickly twisted free the top, and tilting the canteen toward her dry lips, she felt the cool relief of water wash down her throat. Beside her, a group of matted-haired women shouted out their complaints. One rushed toward Rachel with childish malice marking her gaze, her arms extended.

"I share!" Rachel held up the canteen in a friendly gesture.

The aborigine female stopped immediately and stared back at her companions, a triumph imminent. Reaching quickly for the canteen, she held it over her head and turned it upside down. Warm water rushed over her head and she laughed giddily.

The sight of the woman dousing her head amused Rachel and she began to laugh. The other females, spotting Rachel's amusement, began to laugh in kind. Angered, the woman stopped at once and tossed down the canteen with a contemptuous glare.

Turning about abruptly, the man who first abducted Rachel stared crossly at the women, his dark eyes peering out from ink black skin. Shouting angrily, he waved his arm and the women scurried to catch up with their male counterparts, prodding Rachel as they went.

Rachel felt the land around her spin crazily and her senses fade from the heat. She tottered to the red earth as her basket dropped to the ground and George's hat fell into the dust.

Their journey interrupted, the men trudged back to Rachel where she lay in a clump. One kicked her with a mud-encrusted foot while another poked at her with the blunt end of his spear. Realizing their hostile attempts to rouse their captive proved futile, two of the men picked up their red-haired prize by her slender limbs. Lifting cries to their Earth gods, they carried her away into the bush as the sun bid farewell to the misty Blue Mountains.

13
Rescue From the Bush

The breeze wafted through the rear door as the aroma of bean soup filled the air with a salty tang. But the Prentice kitchen held a cloud that no wind could muster.

Katy collected her cherished belongings—a rag doll, an old book, and three silver spoons—and placed them all into a cloth bag. These items had all been given to her as a youth when she worked for Governor Arthur Phillip. The doll had been made for her by the cook; the book and spoons were given to her by a lovely maid named Daphne. She slid the possessions snugly between her garments and closed the top with a snap.

Looking up from the kitchen table, Katy found Amelia staring toward her through clouded eyes. Although her Mum had not spoken since the fire, accusations targeted Katy's thoughts nonetheless. "It has to be this way, Mum." Her voice grew defensive, as though an argument would be offered.

Amelia's fingers curled around the arm of the old rocker,

and her lids sagged over pale green eyes in an almost pleading manner. Her fingers trembled, and then stopped at once as her gaze wandered from Katy's face down to the floor.

Katy barricaded her own tears with a hardness she had learned in the settlement. "You'll have Caleb to look after things. He's a big boy now and capable of a lot more good than I can offer." She propped the ragged crutch under one arm and steadied herself as she placed two jars of canned vegetables into her bag. "I'm more of a burden to Papa now than a help. With me out of the way, who knows, perhaps he can help you get well." She reasoned more for herself than for a mother who appeared to hear nothing. "Caleb and I have talked it over, Mum. He knows I'll be in the borough. My job with the government stores should benefit us all. I hope to be sending money to you soon."

Turning toward the simmering pot, Katy was fast to remove it from the fire before the soup boiled over. "I'll feed you your meal before I go." Once she had ladled the bean soup into a chipped bowl, Katy turned and was surprised to find a tear glistening on Amelia's cheek. "What's this?" A faint, hopeful smile graced her lips. Balancing the bowl with one hand she reached out with the other to wipe the tear.

Amelia's gaze showed no sign of recognition but instead reflected the same melancholy stare of the past few weeks.

Sighing, Katy shook her head. "Poor Mum. Probably just the steam causing your eye to tear like that. This kitchen's hotter than an oven." Katy tucked a cloth into Amelia's collar. "Time to eat, love." She looked directly into her eyes as she fed her, hoping for a glimmer of emotion. Once she felt satisfied her mother was properly fed, she rinsed the dish in a wash basin and then hefted her bag from the table. Rachel would be home soon and she could help Mum to bed.

Turning to glance at her mother one last time, she found she had trouble taking her gaze from her. She wanted to remember her in another way, not like this. Recalling livelier moments, she decided to remember Mum the way she was when they were struggling to make ends meet. Amelia was unstoppable in those days and her faith unwavering. With one glance, Mum had been able to look into Katy's soul and know in an instant what she was thinking.

Glancing out the window, Katy could see Papa standing along the Campbells' field as the twilight descended around him. He was happy, she knew, about the prospects of pioneering their new piece of land in Parrametta. But until he was stronger, he would have to stay on with the Campbells. *Don't ever stop dreaming, Papa.* Katy felt a tear well in her own eye. *Like I've done.* The sound of the military wagon pulling up caused her to quicken her pace. The surly guard assigned to give her a ride into the borough would not have much patience with the daughter of an emancipist. Gathering up her belongings, she limped out the back steps and toward the field to bid farewell to her papa, never realizing her dearest friend, Rachel, would not return.

Dew sparkled along the grass tops, dripping like liquid diamonds upon the webs engineered by nocturnal spiders. The dawn whispered its early pink veils across the firmament.

Wrapped in a faded patchwork quilt, Heath Whitley leaned wearily against the post that held the small overhang in front of the Campbell shanty. He had posted himself at the front of their property long after the household had retired. Not wishing to worry the Campbells or the Prentices, he had nearly decided to head back to the comfort of his own bed. But an urgency bade him remain, and he finally found himself camped out on the Campbells' front porch. His head had rested uncomfortably the entire night, jerking up occasionally when a sudden sound partly roused him. His red-rimmed eyes gazed with a worried stare toward the snaking pathway as he waited for Rachel to return. Then the misery of restless slumber again overtook him, and he slept another hour until the sound of a roaming echidna or a kangaroo rat taunted him with their nightly maneuvers.

The warmth that began to glow behind the distant blue ridges touched Whitley's face in a gentle kiss. His lids fluttered and he wiped his stinging eyes. Looking straight ahead, he could see the pathway beyond him was void of sight or sound. Behind him, the sound of kitchen noises drew him into the house. But Rachel's bedding remained rolled up and unused in the corner of the room. Mrs. Campbell could be seen bustling around the kitchen, muttering to herself. The harsh reality of Rachel's absence rushed at him all at once and he began to fear harm had come to her. *Where could she be?* he wondered vainly. Standing like a lone soldier, he turned to trudge into the kitchen, where Mrs. Campbell stood kneading bread dough. "Rachel didn't return—or did you know?"

Whirling around, Mrs. Campbell held her hand to her breast. "Wha'? You gave me a fright, Reverend!"

Tipping his hat, Whitley apologized. "Forgive me. But I had promised to give Rachel a ride home from the prison colony. I waited for her all evening. She never returned."

Bustling past, Mrs. Campbell was fast to search for Rachel's bedroll. "And here I thought she'd gotten up with the chickens. What's come of the girl?"

"Perhaps Katy knows something. Has she awakened yet?"

Sadly shaking her head, Mrs. Campbell replied, "Katy's gone. Broke her Papa's heart—takin' that government job and all. Left late yesterday afternoon. Like you, she figured Rachel'd be home before now."

"I'd better head back toward the convict colony. I'll be needing a faster horse, Mrs. Campbell." Whitley's request was hurried, and anxiety shot from his gaze. The Irishwoman, a short, heavy Protestant, stared up at the minister, worry creasing her forehead. "Not like 'er at all! Somethin's wrong, I say."

Whitley nodded his head and turned to splash water on his face from the wash basin. "I think I should arrange a search party. I never should've allowed her to leave unescorted. Do you think there's a chance she's stayed the night with a family in the borough?"

Pushing a wiry strand of hair from her face, Mrs. Campbell shook her head. "Not likely. She promised to be home for supper." The old woman's gray head nodded to affirm her worries and then she spilled her thoughts. "I think you *should* arrange a search party, Reverend. It's not like Rachel to stay gone this long."

Whitley replaced his large, brimmed hat and strode quickly for the kitchen exit. Borrowing the Campbell horse, he headed toward the convict camp, stopping every passerby along the way. As each neighbor shook their head and offered no clues to Rachel's whereabouts, Whitley prayed and then chastened himself again for not insisting upon the ride to the colony. Riding toward the convict colony, the worried minister searched the pathway Rachel would have followed.

After an hour had passed, he circled the prison one last time and resolved to query every man who was on duty the night before. He was informed that Rachel had never arrived at the convict camp, so a search party of marines was gathered on her behalf. Two expert marksmen were called from the stores. Leading the marines was a finely outfitted lieutenant. Before noon, Whitley led the military procession away from the borough and down the hard-packed road. The two marksmen rode up to join the others, both marine corporals. One muttered aloud to his partner, "What's the quarry?" He was a hard-faced Englishman with steely blue eyes who stooped to dust one of his boots. Hearing the marine, Whitley answered, "A lost colonist—a female named Rachel Langley. Follow me, men!" he called out hurriedly. Lieutenant Cornel Thompson rode alongside him as did the officer's pretty daughter, Felicity.

"Thank you for allowing me to accompany you, Reverend." The young woman smiled demurely. "I'll not get in the way, I can assure you of that, sir."

"Felicity's quite the horsewoman, if I do say so myself," Cornel Thompson boasted. "She was fox hunting before most boys."

Whitley nodded politely, keeping his eyes to the bush in hopes of spotting signs of Rachel. "Surely, Miss Thompson." He smiled politely at Felicity's words but didn't look up to see the admiration in her gaze.

Her eyes studying the comely face and rugged build of the minister, Felicity grew curious about the man. "You're Anglican, correct, sir?"

"Yes I am."

Felicity pressed further. "There's another Anglican minister in the borough who's founding a church. Are you working with him?"

"In the sense that we're all working for God's kingdom, yes. But that minister has his hands full with the convicts and settlers. I'm interested in the emancipists on the outskirts of the colony—and the aborigines."

"Posh!" Thompson admonished. "You'll need a miracle for that work. The emancipists are all drunkards and the blasted natives are nothing short of beasts!"

Whitley felt his anger aroused but held his words.

"Now, Father . . ." Felicity quickly assessed the minister's sensitivity. "All men have a right to hear the gospel—don't they, Reverend Whitley?"

Whitley relaxed upon hearing the wisdom of her words. "Thank you, yes. I've been teaching English to a clansman named Kapirigi. He's picked up the King's English quite well, and I believe I'm winning his trust."

Thompson sighed and shook his head. "Savages can't be trusted, Reverend. I don't care how much they're educated."

"Time will tell, Lieutenant. But education is only a small part of the answer. If God changes their heart—" Seeing Thompson's doubtful gaze, Whitley decided to change the subject.

Bringing his mount to a halt, he spied a bit of fabric on a bush and determined to investigate. "What have we here?" Walking toward the scrub, he held the horse's reins in one hand while reaching to yank away the fabric with the other. "I think this fragment could be from Rachel's dress, but I'm not certain."

"This Rachel Langley must be a special young woman to have such a handsome minister searching for her." Felicity's brows lifted as anticipation lit her eyes.

Whitley didn't hear the young woman's pointed comment but continued to examine the torn fabric. "Pardon me?" he answered tautly.

Clearing her throat, Felicity repeated her remark and then asked, "Is this Rachel Langley your lady-friend?"

Whitley turned to look at the woman, his brow furrowed. "No, nothing like that really. My friendship with the young woman is nothing beyond any parishioner's."

"I see." Felicity smiled winningly, her eyes gleaming with approval.

"Let's search these woods, shall we?" Whitley lifted his foot into the stirrup and mounted the horse again.

The search party fanned out into the woods until a shout arose from beyond an embankment. "Over here! Footprints!"

Whitley charged toward the private who had called out, encouragement rising in his thoughts. Pulling his horse up alongside the hill, he studied the small footprints, noting how they turned away from a stream bed and then entered into the woods. "Please let them be Rachel Langley's," he whispered.

Within an hour of tracking the human prints, the party reached a clearing where a rocky outcrop drew their eyes. The presence of many footprints stamped in the soft, dusty soil before them confirmed their fears that Rachel had been abducted.

"Barefoot . . . aborigines!" a marine called out as he stooped over the tracks.

Whitley felt a sinking in his soul as though a little part of his spirit had died. He dismounted and walked to stand beside the small shoe print that followed the rest. "Let's follow them!" he ordered as he ran back to jump astride his steed. The thought of Rachel being harmed urged him to bring his whip to flank, and he galloped across the arid landscape, followed closely by the military and Felicity Thompson.

Rachel had slept soundly inside a cave with her captors, despite her worry of what the Campbells must be thinking by now. Her stomach rumbled, reminding her of the previous evening's fare. The clan had stopped to hunt the night before and the young boys in the group spearfished. Rachel had consumed her roasted portion in a ravenous fashion, picking the tender meat clean from the bones. She watched with guarded interest as the meat remaining from a giant kangaroo had been divided up evenly and passed out in communal fashion to each tribesman.

The men each carried their own hand-hewn spear and carefully removed the weapons from the prey, being certain the spear was returned to the rightful owner. They called the spears *woomera* and swung them fiercely during an evening dance ritual called the *corraboree*.

One of the boys had dragged out a hollow wooden pole that was double his height. Sitting cross-legged next to Rachel, the boy pointed a thin finger at the wooden object. *"Didgeredoo!"* He smiled at Rachel, hungry for the lovely stranger's approval. Surprised at the docile nature of the clansmen, Rachel repeated, *"Didgeredoo."* She pointed to the lad and asked, "Who are you?" The boy's confusion spilled from his lips in an abundance of syllables while he tossed his moppish black hair from side to side.

Sighing, Rachel pointed to herself. "Rachel."

"Rach-el," the lad repeated. Then, as suddenly as he had repeated her name, his eyes lit with understanding. "Ah-h! Rachel!" Indicating himself again, he carefully responded, *"Wadjiri!"*

"Wadjiri!" Rachel smiled broadly. The fact that the child understood created a desire in her to tell him more—*but how, Lord?* Lifting two twigs, she fashioned a small crucifix in her hands and then held it out to Wadjiri. The boy stared at the sticks, twiddling the cross between two fingers. Then tossing it aside, he picked up his didgeredoo and resumed his playing.

Rachel sat in silence as the child droned out a haunting melody on the crude instrument while his elders sang and beat the sticks in an impish rhythm.

Kunamanda-manda
Kunamanda-manda
Kunamanda-manda
Bira bira Oi! Oi!

The music carried the clan into the night until the last tribesman curled next to his mate and fell sound asleep. The sound of the dingoes and the fear of silent crocodiles skulking from their water holes kept Rachel from escaping into the endless black stretches of the bush. And so she had slept on a mat next to two small children who cuddled next to her, gently twisting and braiding her red hair until her eyelids succumbed to slumber.

At dawn, thinking she was the first to awaken, Rachel sat up abruptly and carefully lifted one of the sleeping little girls from her side. Finding her basket atop a large rock, she realized the medicinals had been removed and saw they were lined in a perfect row next to the cave wall. The colored glass had been an oddity to the primitive people. Thinking the bottles to be a talisman or magical charm they formed a straight row with them beneath their tribal art that adorned the cave walls. Rachel quietly collected the bottles, placing them carefully inside the tattered cloth that lined the basket. Then whisking George's hat from a sleeping boy's head, she placed it atop her own.

Without a sound, she crept from the cave and climbed up the sides to find a quick lookout point. Her worn brown shoes, slick from wear, slid beneath her as she struggled to maintain a hold on the sharp rocks. As one shoe tumbled to the mouth of the cave, she lifted her other foot and allowed that shoe to drop as well. Pulling herself around a large boulder above the cave, she groaned and rested against the side. Her eyes were drawn to a smoky haze, and she could see a man in the distance dancing, surrounded by a sooty cloud. In each hand, he waved a leafy branch. Rachel recognized the man as one of the older men in the tribe. "Witch doctor." Her face reflected worry and fear for the boy who lay on the ground at his feet. The child appeared to writhe in pain.

The native witch doctor had strapped around his bony hips a feathered belt and nothing more. Dancing wildly in the smoke he hovered around the fragile-looking boy, who lay motionless on the ground. Knowing she should flee, Rachel felt an odd compulsion to investigate the matter. Climbing quickly down from her perch on the rocks, she lost her footing when the sound of the tribesmen awakening below startled her. Sliding awkwardly to earth, her fingers raked the sharp rocks all the way down until her feet hit the hard ground. The muttering from inside the cave faded behind her as she ran toward the smoke.

Cautiously she approached the bizarre ritual and watched

from behind a drooping gum tree. The boy on the ground looked to be about eight years old. The smoke curled from underneath his body, wrapping around his frame in a thick vapor. He made no complaint but lay still, a servile composure anticipating some unseen force.

The witch doctor's body twirled while he chanted, and his head gyrated in time with his flailing limbs. "*Coolamon,*" he muttered. Cautiously, as though performing surgery, he stooped over the boy and lifted a primitive dish made with paperbark. Scooping up white clay from the *coolamon*, he stroked a thin layer of the mixture over the sick boy's perspiring skin.

Rachel bowed her head and began to pray.

At once, the witch doctor leaped in the air, finished his rite, and ran off to join the clan.

Rachel cautiously stepped out from hiding and made her way to the boy. Upon seeing his face, she recognized him at once. "Wadjiri!" she whispered and then crouched low beside him.

Opening his eyes slowly, Wadjiri gazed through the cloud at the strange but lovely woman. Managing a faint smile, he responded weakly, "Rachel."

Rachel checked the boy's head and wrist as she had seen Surgeon White do on many occasions. "Fever, that's for certain." She coughed at the smoke and studied the wet blanket. "What have they laid you on?" She lifted the old gray blanket, recognizing it as having belonged to the marines. The sand beneath the blanket was steaming from smoldering embers buried just below the blanket. "Dear God, they're roasting you, child!"

Rachel slid her arms under Wadjiri and stood to lift him. The clan could be heard in the distance, beating their sticks and chanting. She prayed the witch doctor would not return for a while. Carrying the boy into the cool shade of a wattle tree, Rachel cushioned his head in a mound of soft spinefax grass. Needing a great deal of water, she made several trips to the shallow billabong near the camp. She sat about at once administering medicines and applying cold cloths to his head. "You'll be fine, Wadjiri." Rachel used soothing tones to speak to the child. *God, you've got to help me—I feel helpless! Increase my faith!* Remembering the faith of the apostles, she closed her eyes and mentally surrendered her doubts. "For your glory, Lord." Extending her hands to lay on Wadjiri's chest, she prayed aloud, "God, heal Wadjiri—in Christ's name."

Wadjiri stopped his chanting and closed his eyes, whispering, "God . . . heal . . . Wadjiri."

A multitude of gunshots in the distance brought Rachel to her feet, and instinct warned she should run. But instead, she mustered the courage to remain beside Wadjiri and comfort him. The terror-filled laments of his elders frightened him, and trying to pull himself erect, he began to cry.

"Please stay down!" Rachel begged, gesturing accordingly.

Gazing up with timorous dark eyes, Wadjiri clasped his hands at his chin as a solitary tear streaked across his cheek.

Rachel peered out from behind the tree and saw the military men riding her way. *Surely, they wouldn't shoot at me, an Englishwoman!* Her throat ached from the dry air, but she knew she had to distract them from the clan. Anxiety rose in her throat as she shouted, "Over here!"

"Lieutenant Thompson!" a private yelled. "We found 'er!"

At once, a sharply attired officer rounded the large mound of rocks that hid the cave opening. His thoroughbred neighed as a screaming native woman charged after them on foot. "*Gudjiwa! Gudjiwa!*" she cried, her fury at the man evident.

Turning to glance back at the woman, Thompson circled his horse and aimed his pistol at her.

"No!" Rachel shrieked.

The gun aimed squarely, Thompson shot off a round of musket. Exploding into the woman's chest, the musket ball tore through her heart, causing her to scream in agony before crumpling to the ground.

"No, God!" Rachel cried as Wadjiri sat up and began screaming, "*Budarindja! Budarindja!*"

The child, holding his stomach, limped toward the dead woman and then fell weeping across her still body. Riding up next to Rachel, Thompson extended his hand, thinking he had fulfilled justice, and shouted, "Jump up, miss. We'll get you out of here!"

From around the corner, Rachel could see Heath Whitley galloping toward them, elation sweeping his face as he held Rachel's slippers firmly in his grasp. "Whitley!" she cried, her eyes engraved with agony. "They've killed the boy's mother!"

Whitley, seeing the anguish in Rachel's face, drew his steed to a halt and sighed heavily. Instead of riding in as Rachel's rescuer, he had only brought blood on his hands. "I'm truly sorry" were all the words he could muster before turning to restrain the military from proceeding with their bloody duty.

14

Felicity's Trophy

The marine dropped Katy off near the town borough, his mind set on sampling the brew at the pub on the harbor. Leaning on her crutch, Katy walked down through the borough, dust collecting around her brown and ivory skirts as she went. Her newly claimed independence, she realized, would offer some inconveniences, but no more than living with her family had imposed. The two young women with whom she would live, Mary Bitters and Lorna Steed, were emancipists and as determined as she to carve out a future for themselves. One of them desired to raise enough income for living expenses and then return to England.

The shack where the women would live was located in the center of the colony, only a couple of miles from the harbor. Katy stood in front of the dwelling, biting the inside of her cheek. The house was a dismal wattle-and-daub with the windows covered by wood slats. "No worry," she decided at once.

"I can have the windows reopened and the glass replaced later."

A wave of anxiety swept through her as she rapped on the door, and it came as no surprise when a voice cautiously called out, "Who's there?"

"I'm Katy Prentice—your new boarder." Her words were forced and sounded clumsy to her. Taking the crutch from under her arm, she hid it behind herself. She waited, almost hoping that she had arrived at the incorrect address.

A short, frail-looking girl with her hair pulled up in a dingy bonnet cracked the door slightly and peered through with suspicious brown eyes. "Katy Prentice? Who are you, an' who told you we is takin' in boarders?"

"Why, a woman named Mary Bitters. I met her at the government stores only last week." Katy blinked and then drew back her face at the unclean odor that wafted from inside the house.

"Mary told you?"

Katy nodded. "Yes."

The door opened and a faint smiled curved the girl's face. "Please don't think me impolite, miss. I'm Lorna Steed. But I was expectin' a Cockney girl like meself—not a girl like you. Your finery made me think you were here to collect on a small loan I been tryin' to pay off. It's taught me never to borrow anythin', that's fer certain."

Katy glanced down at her attire uneasily. She had worn a brown cotton dress that was adorned with ivory piping around the waist and up the bodice. She and her mother had sewn the frock years ago before Governor Phillip had departed. With fabric hard to come by, Katy cared meticulously for her clothing. Seeing the girl's envious gaze she offered in an apologetic tone, "It's an old dress, miss. My mum taught me to sew and I make most of my clothing from remnants."

"It's a thing no one ever taught me to do." Lorna studied the dress with envy.

Seeing the desire in the girl's eyes, Katy offered, "I can teach you to sew, Miss Steed. Sewing isn't difficult at all, really."

"Miss Steed?" Lorna laughed easily without inhibition.

"Lorna's all anyone ever calls me. Why don't you come inside, Katy, and 'ave a look-see."

After a short trip through the two-room dwelling, Lorna pointed to an old bed. "That one was given to us from the government. Kind o' worn out, but it's a bed."

Katy eyed the splintered oak frame with feigned interest. "Actually, I've been sleeping on the floor of my mum's kitchen. However old it is, a bed would be quite nice." She smiled, still holding the heavy bag in her hands.

Lorna stood with her hands clasped and studied Katy as if she were a piece of fine china. Her eyes falling upon the bag, she said suddenly, "Where's me manners? You can place your things over 'ere." She referred to the small bureau that had been shoved up against the boarded-up window. "You're the one wot's got that good job wif the gov'ment, ain't you?"

"I suppose it's a good job. I'll know for certain tomorrow."

Suddenly the door flew open and in blustered a tall, lanky woman. Katy recognized her at once as being Mary Bitters whom she had met last week. Mary's face was flushed and her hands gestured wildly. "It's Bill Wilders!" she shouted excitedly. "He's up an' asked me to be 'is wife, 'e 'as, Lorna! By this Saturday, no less!"

Lorna grabbed the girl by the shoulders and laughed, "The ol' bloke! It's about time 'e popped the question!"

Katy stood quietly observing the revelry of the two women.

"Oh, 'ello, lass!" Mary called out to Katy. "I see you finally made it to town. Welcome to our castle!"

It was Katy who laughed now. "Thank you. But I think I should be congratulating young Mr. Wilders for his wise decision."

Lorna and Mary stared at Katy with humor lighting their gaze. Then glancing back at each other, they chuckled secretively.

"Whatever is so funny?" Katy's brow arched in question.

"Well, it's just that . . . Mr. Wilders ain't such a young man. Quite old, actually," Mary offered sheepishly.

Lorna added, "More like decrepit, the poor ol' coot."

Seeing the confusion in Katy's face, Mary explained, "I been carin' fer the old man's 'ouse since right after 'is wife died from the fever. Mr. Wilders was so lonely that I felt sorry fer 'im an' took to chattin' wif 'im every day after me chores was done."

"And . . . you fell in love with him?" Perplexity filled Katy's eyes.

"Oh no!" Mary laughed.

Lorna slapped Mary's backside crudely. "Fell in love wif the old fool's money is more like!"

"Now don't be sayin' such foolishness, Lorna!" Agitation rose in Mary's tone. "I took up wif the man an' now we're gettin' married—that's all, an' I don't want yer gossipin' tongue castin' no aspersions round about me and the good Mr. Wilders!"

Katy dusted her gloves and peeled them from her hands. "Why do you feel you have to marry the man?"

"It's the only way out o' this place! I ain't got no good job like yerself." Mary lifted her skirts in mock dignity. "As the new Mrs. Wilders, I'll get another poor soul to do the cleanin'," she boasted. "Save me 'ands fer the finer things in life." She winked at Lorna.

"I'll be jealous as a cat, Mary Bitters!" Lorna crossed her arms wistfully. "Per'aps if Mr. Wilders 'as an old coot friend, you kin send 'im me way."

Katy shook her head. "None for me, thanks."

Her arms akimbo, Mary admonished, "No wonder! Pretty lass like yerself should've been snatched up long ago. Why ain't you married yet, Katy?" She tossed her threadbare shawl atop the bureau.

"Is it a sin to be unmarried?" Katy grew slightly defensive. "Perhaps I'll be an old rich spinster with men begging after me like dogs." She seated herself on the old oak bed and tried the springs.

"Ah, some 'andsome knave'll come along and sweep you off yer feet. You'll give in like the rest of us."

Katy chuckled and spoke defiantly, "If I do, it'll not be until I'm good and ready." Scanning the room, she licked lightly at her dry lips. "I think your news calls for a small celebration. May I trouble you?"

Lorna retrieved a bottle of rum from an old ammunitions box she used for a cabinet. "A little rum'll 'it the spot. She poured the drink into a metal pannikin. "Sorry, we don't 'ave any wine or tea to offer."

Breathing deeply, Katy nodded resignedly, although she truly had a taste for the rum. "If that's all you have, then I certainly appreciate your hospitality. Thank you kindly, Lorna." Lifting her pannikin, she offered a toast. "To the new Mrs. Wilders—may your house be filled with the sounds of love and laughter . . . and the patter of tiny feet." She smiled as Lorna filled two more pannikins.

Mary agreed, but with a flatness to her tone. "To me an' Bill. To us." Her eyes held no sparkle.

Lorna guzzled the liquor, grimacing at the taste. "And to a new bottle o' rum—this'n's bitter as sin."

Katy sipped the rum slowly, allowing it to dampen her dry throat. "Permit me, please, to buy the next bottle. I know a supplier who imports from France."

As Lorna and Mary launched into simple wedding plans for Saturday morning, Katy strode to the doorway of the shack and gazed out at the men and women who sat around their front entryways guzzling down the colony sedative. Some were already drunk, and most would eventually collapse in a numb stupor. *Worthless creatures,* she thought with pity. *Thank God, I'm not like them.* Swallowing the last bitter drop of colony rum, Katy turned to busy herself with tidying up her new home.

The cicadas energized the air with their droning as they sat atop the long drooping ends of spinefax that lay trampled down by military horsemen who galloped carelessly through.

Rachel had been given a chestnut mare that was saddled with worn leather and a thin blanket. In the event that she was found, the horse had been brought along by the scouts who attended Lieutenant Thompson. She rode astride the horse, keeping her eyes straight ahead on the privates who led the way across the desert and into the bush. Still reeling from the shock of the slaughtered tribesmen, Rachel suddenly realized she had scarcely taken the time to thank Reverend Whitley. Turning to speak, she found the minister's attention was occupied by the lieutenant's daughter, so Rachel held her words.

Felicity chattered endlessly to Whitley about her travels and her family's voyage from England. Still holding firmly to the laced parasol, Felicity admired the minister with her violet eyes. "You're such a brave man, Reverend Whitley—fighting in the Revolution and all that business. Most ministers hide within the confines of the church."

"My father reared me to be a military man. 'Raise high the banner for England,' he would always say to me and my brothers." Whitley cocked back his hat and wiped his sweating brow. "It was to his dismay that I became a minister after I recuperated from an injury." He indicated the scar beside his ear.

"Don't tell me you were *frightened* into the ministry?" Felicity laughed in her soft feminine way, her tones controlled and delightful to the men who turned occasionally and smiled at the lovely young woman.

Whitley's brow pinched soberly. "Frightened? I should've been. Too young and foolish to consider my own mortality. I had sought contentment in many things—hunting, women, fencing, war."

"Not *you*, sir?" Intrigue lit Felicity's face.

"But to what purpose did it serve? Empty accomplishments. Vanity—just as King Solomon once said."

Rachel felt a tug at her heart. She had never bothered to ask about Heath Whitley's past. Spending so much time avoiding her own past, she hadn't thought to delve into his. But seeing the Thompson woman dragging the information from him made her uncomfortable. *The girl is too forward.* Rachel's respect for him would not allow her to take such liberties.

She turned her thoughts to more paramount issues. The events of the last hour raced through her mind in horrid, haunting images—the three bloody bodies strewn around the cave entrance, the ground saturated in crimson, the memory of Wadjiri's mournful cries, and the way his tender brown eyes accused her when she departed willingly with his mother's murderers. The surviving clansmen had fled into the depths of the cave, and Rachel prayed the boy would be cared for by the others. It was customary for tribal families to care for one another like relatives, with aunts and uncles exercising parental authority. Yet, the grief and guilt robbed her of any comfort. *If only I had been the first to notice the search party, I could have prevented the slaughter. Why, Lord?*

Her eyes wandered toward the Thompson woman who rode side-saddle, her red riding habit bright in the heat of the day. The slaughter had scarcely bothered Felicity at all. In fact she almost seemed to delight in it, keeping her distance from the violence, yet positioning herself just so she could witness the massacre. In Rachel's estimation, her riding gloves remained unsoiled, but her selfishness spoiled her countenance. Felicity held firmly to the parasol, holding it up with one hand while the other skillfully directed the steed. Her noble profile was set off by a stylishly plumed hat, but her features held a familiarness that Rachel could not determine. As her eyes followed the tailored lines of the dress, remembrance flooded Rachel's mind—*the woman in the stores! Felicity Thompson!*

Felicity did not notice the change in Rachel's expression, but rather leaned toward the minister in anticipation of his words. "Why, Reverend Whitley, I can't believe our paths have never crossed. . . ." She appeared enchanted by the handsome minister.

Rachel's eyes narrowed disdainfully upon remembering the uncomfortable clash between her and Felicity that day in the government stores. But she realized Felicity did not remember her and knew that to bring up such a matter would only serve to embarrass them both. Noticing the manner in which Reverend Whitley returned Felicity's smiles caused an uneasiness to rise in Rachel. Surely a man of his caliber could see through this woman's shallow ramblings. Rachel's brow pinched as she observed the grace and poise of the young woman. Her own social skills paled in contrast to Felicity's.

Rachel lowered her face, realizing comparisons only served to bring out more of her insecurities.

"Reverend Whitley . . ." Her words came haltingly. It was not her wish to interrupt, but expressing gratitude to the minister was in order. "I . . . I want to thank you for organizing the search party on my behalf." Her eyes glanced back at Felicity, whose lips pursed impatiently at the interruption. Rachel allowed her gaze to return to Whitley.

"This colony could never do without you, Rachel. And it's the least I could do for all the help you've offered to the colony families we've visited."

Whitley's brow lifted as Felicity set about at once drawing his attention back to her.

"So you make regular visits to the families?"

"Along with Rachel."

"I'd love to join you sometime. I'm quite good with medicinals."

Rachel's brow arched and a faint smile creased her cheek. This Thompson woman was under the impression that she was in some sort of competition for Heath Whitley's attention. Once she had rested for a few days, she could find all the time in the world to converse with the man if she so desired. Withdrawing from the conversation, Rachel steadied her mount and then lifted her arm to flick her reins across the mare's flanks.

"I think I'll suggest we stop soon, Reverend. Miss Thompson looks as though she needs a rest."

Upon hearing Rachel, Felicity gazed obliquely toward her and lifted her chin arrogantly. "Don't I know you?" Her tone being suspicious, her brows furrowed speculatively.

The hesitation and the silence grew awkward as Rachel wondered how she should reply. Not wanting to appear paltry or shallow to Whitley, she considered simply telling Felicity that their paths had never crossed. But such a lie could unfold as another embarrassment if Felicity remembered otherwise.

"Perhaps we've met in the borough," she answered tactfully and then saw the recognition rise in Felicity's face.

"I remember now"—Felicity's face grew taut, the composure draining from her words—"*you're* the one . . ." She stopped, a smug reflection of her contempt curving her lips in a scornful smile. "You're an emancipist!" she finally declared, not wishing to divulge the uncomfortable memory she and Rachel shared.

Rachel cringed at the word as though Felicity had said "crawler" or "tramp" or one of the many other things she had been labeled in the transportation system. She turned away with the memory of Heath Whitley's piteous gaze etched in her mind.

The air grew thick with silence as the muted riders made their way toward the familiar road where their journey had first commenced. Weary and saddle-sore, the military scouts stopped at a stream bed and assisted the women from their mounts. Felicity was quick to find a place next to Heath Whitley and asked him to fill her flask for her. Heath responded in a gentlemanly fashion while a young corporal assisted Rachel.

"Thank you for your kindness." Rachel expressed her gratitude for his attention.

"You're welcome, miss." The man smiled. "I'm Corporal Bryce Holmes at your service." His deep voice reflected the sympathy he held for the girl. "This 'ere's me partner, Corporal Nolan McGrath."

McGrath, one of the marksmen, adjusted the wad of tobacco in his cheek. Reaching out with his hand, he grasped a strand of Rachel's hair. "Red." He grinned.

Rachel drew back, yanking her hair from the man's hand. "Don't!"

"McGrath, you idiot!" Holmes whirled around, his fist raised defensively.

"I-it's all right. Please—" Rachel's eyes were wide. The malicious scowl that rose in McGrath's face unsettled her. "I'm sure the corporal meant no harm."

Holmes relaxed his hostile glare. Shaking his head at his partner, he said in a surly tone, "Let's allow the lady a little room 'ere, shall we?" Turning back, Holmes towered above Rachel and smiled down at her like a gentle giant.

"What was your name, Corporal?"

"Bryce Holmes. And I just wanted to tell you 'ow 'appy I

am that you're safe and sound from those savages."

"Oh, that," Rachel's voiced reflected regret. "I honestly never felt as threatened as you might think I would have been."

"Truly?" Holmes brows met speculatively.

"It's the truth. You see, the natives, I believe, are curious about the whites, but unless threatened, they're quite harmless."

"They looked pretty fierce to us today."

Rachel shook her head. "I'm sure you frightened them, Corporal. That little boy—Wadjiri—his mother was killed right in front of him. If strangers came riding into your homestead with weapons and shouting, wouldn't you fight to protect your family?"

"I see what you mean, Miss Langley, but actually I 'ave no family. Or, if I do, I'm not certain where they've gone."

Rachel nodded. "I'm from a similar background. I've had no family for years."

His eyes lighting with agreement, Bryce added, "Well, we've something in common then, don't we?"

"I suppose so," Rachel shrugged.

"Load up!" the lieutenant shouted. The marines finished filling their containers, and the military party was soon on its way. As they ascended a hillside, the landscape suddenly became familiar to Rachel.

"Thank goodness!" Felicity's voice rose in excitement. "We're almost home!"

Rachel felt relief sweep through her upon seeing the road ahead of them. "Home." She spoke mostly to herself for she wasn't certain now where she truly belonged. She could admit only to herself that she had found more "belonging to" within Wadjiri's tribe than she'd found at the Campbell farm.

As the sound of hooves hitting the road broke the silence, Felicity turned eagerly to her father. "Father, we simply *must* invite our courageous minister friend for dinner this evening!"

Whitley shook his head, the weariness of the trip draining him of any desire to socialize. "No, it's not necessary, miss. No need to be a bother."

"On the contrary, my dear fellow, we insist!" Lieutenant Thompson was fast to agree with his daughter. "If it hadn't been for your keen tracking capabilities, Reverend, we would've never located our lost little sheep."

Rachel kept her eyes to the ground as the military party dispersed around her.

"But I should really be the one to see Miss Langley to the Campbell farm," Whitley offered.

Suddenly Bryce Holmes volunteered, "I can take Miss Langley home. Another private and myself will see that she's returned safely."

Rubbing his palms in anticipation, Cornel Thompson decided, "Splendid! The matter's settled. Reverend Whitley, you shall dine with the Thompsons this night and we'll have our servants prepare you a room for the evening. You *must* be exhausted."

"Oh, Father, you're wonderful!" Felicity beamed.

Rachel could no longer hide her fatigue and emotional disappointment from the last few days. Felicity's smile was decidedly targeting her, and she felt the need to hasten her journey before she weakened any further and burst into tears in front of the entire search party.

"Well . . ." Whitley turned his gaze to Rachel, his patronly responsibility weighing heavily. "If Miss Langley prefers that I escort her . . ."

"No. Thank you kindly, Reverend Whitley." Rachel shook her head. "Corporal Holmes will see me home." She managed a smile and nodded appreciatively at the corporal. "Thank you so much, Corporal. You're quite the gentleman."

A spark kindled in Bryce's gaze as he beheld the lovely young red-haired woman. "I'm honored, Rachel." He smiled warmly.

Turning her horse quickly toward the Campbell home, Rachel didn't see the hesitation in Heath Whitley's face, nor could she know the frustration he felt for the decisions that had just been made on his behalf.

"Please take me home, Corporal Holmes. I'm so tired," Rachel said weakly, the defeat in her voice evident.

As the search party split to proceed in opposite directions,

Whitley couldn't help but watch the beaten-down Rachel plodding away, her head lowered. *Poor child.*

"Coming, Reverend?" Felicity noticed Whitley's hesitancy and drew immediately on her skills with men. "Can't keep cook waiting. She's a terror if her meals are kept too long."

"Hmm? Oh, certainly." Heath reined his steed around and tapped his heels to the flanks. "I'm famished, Miss Thompson, and looking forward to the evening. Thank you for your hospitality." His voice held a weary tone.

Felicity shook her head, her sought-after trophy now riding satisfactorily at her side. "No, *I* should be the one to thank *you*. This settlement can be such a dreary place at times. I'm grateful for your companionship."

As the young woman chattered on about her life in England, Whitley turned once more to find the road behind him void of riders.

15
The Gentle Officer

A soft rain wet the newly plowed fields of Parrametta. The ground had been broken with great difficulty, but eventually it yielded to the crude hand tools, and a field had begun to emerge. The soil was not as giving as the Prentices' first plot of land, and the regret of swapping hung like a black cloud over the new acreage. Rachel had followed the Prentice family to assist with the new farm and was relieved when George hired a field hand, William, to help with the heavier chores.

Rachel stood under the cover of a small lean-to built near the field. Small droplets of early spring rain collected along the strands of her hair, and with raw fingers she brushed them away. "Rose Hill," her voice spoke the name as though it held a poetic meaning. The name had been given to the Prentice farm by Katy before she had departed. *You're not a bad place, really. Somewhat lovely.* Rachel pulled a shawl about her shoulders. *But why don't I belong?*

A few settlers had moved more inland to Parrametta, but

not many. Loneliness pervaded the new settlement, for they had fewer visitors here than when they had lived near Sydney Cove. Two months had passed since her rescue from the bush, and Rachel hadn't seen Heath Whitley since the day the search party had split their paths. Perhaps Felicity was assisting him after all, and he had no need of her. But her greatest worry was in regard to Wadjiri and his tribesmen. In the short time she had been with the aborigines, a burden for the natives had grown in her heart, and she worried that more tribesmen would be slaughtered as the Europeans settled farther inland. Retaliation from the tribe would bring more bloodshed among the military and perhaps even the colonists. Often, she spent her early mornings praying, beseeching God to care for Wadjiri and his tribal family. But she hadn't shared her fears with her white peers, for the Aborigines had been classified as a clan not to be trusted among the English settlers. Rachel wearied of being misunderstood, so she kept her fears to herself.

"Looks as though you might be needin' an escort, madam."

Rachel turned toward the friendly voice and found a tall man standing with a cloak tenting his head. "Oh, hello, Corporal Holmes. Another escort?" She laughed, remembering the day he had escorted her to the Campbell farm.

Corporal Bryce Holmes had offered friendly company on that day, but Rachel scarcely remembered their conversation for her thoughts had been consumed with her worries.

"It *is* raining, madam, and I thought perhaps you'd be needin' me services again." Holmes lifted the cloak, a water-repellant oilskin, and spread it with his arms, proving there was leeway for two.

"All right," Rachel concealed her slight discomfort, for the officer's interest in her had been evident upon their first encounter. "But I still have much to do today, Corporal Holmes. I'm patching up the winter quilts for the Prentices. George needs me."

"Sounds like a big job to me." Bryce's eyes grew wide, his senses detecting Rachel's sham. "But I already spoke to George Prentice and he said he could spare you for the afternoon"—he hesitated, his lips protruding boyishly—"or the evening. That is, if you'd consider a lout such as meself worthy o' your company." His rugged countenance appeared to tame at her presence.

Rachel couldn't help but smile at the stocky man's sincerity. "But it's raining, Corporal."

"The rain's no hindrance. I've brought a military wagon from the stores—it's covered. Not a drop of wicked rain will touch your regal head."

"But where are we going?"

"A party—at an officer's farm. It's here in Parrametta. But only for us elite, you understand." His smile revealed his amusement.

Rachel glanced down at her work clothes, soiled from the morning's chores. "I'm a terrible mess. I'll need some time."

"No need to hurry. I'll busy meself with ol' George Prentice. The party's not until later tonight."

Sighing resignedly, Rachel laughed. "Oh, why not?" she said more to herself than Holmes. "I've been so taken with this farm I'm bound to turn into a vegetable myself."

The afternoon passed quickly as Rachel bathed in the nearby stream, while far from sight, Bryce Holmes chatted with George Prentice in the shade of the shanty's front porch.

When at last Rachel emerged from inside the house, the worn-out frock had been replaced with the bright blue dress given to her earlier by Katy, and she had pinned up her hair in an elegant style. Her titian tresses shone in smooth sweeps that met in a cluster of soft curls around the crown of her head. Shorter curls fell around the back of her neck, framing the blue fabric that hung slightly off her shoulders. Woven intricately through the cloth, strands of golden thread glistened whenever Rachel turned her head.

"I'm sorry to keep you waiting so long, Corporal Holmes, but I'm ready at last." With blue eyes sparkling, her smile gave away the fact that she felt as stunning as she appeared.

Corporal Holmes sat dazed for a moment as he beheld the angelic vision in blue.

"Look at *you!*" George whistled and clapped in approval while Rachel blushed.

Rachel tapped George atop the head with a gentle finger.

"Stop it, George. You're embarrassing me."

"You look beautiful, Rachel." Standing in a courtly gesture, Holmes echoed George's sentiments. "Where did you find such a lovely dress?"

"Katy gave it to me." Rachel adjusted the small purse on her wrist.

Holmes extended his arm. "Shall we go then, madam?"

"Why not?"

The spring shower had subsided, and the sky cleared to allow the final golden rays of late afternoon sun to warm the air.

Rachel felt as though she had been cloistered away for years and had at last been let out. "I want to thank you again, Corporal, for inviting me. We live so far from the harbor now I've all but turned into a hermit."

"It's a shame to find a lass as pretty as yourself toilin' away at Parrametta." Bryce reached and lifted one of Rachel's lye-parched hands. "Your hands need to be saved for more womanly things." He gently rubbed her fingers with his own.

Rachel sensed a certain desire about the man when he touched her, and not wanting to mislead him, she quickly slipped her hand away from his. Pulling loose the purse string, she hastened to cover her chapped hands with a pair of gloves she had tucked inside her purse. "Parrametta will draw more settlers soon. And I don't mind the work at all. I've seen the women in this colony come to much worse ends than my own lot. What if I had ended up at Norfolk Island? Those women are nothing short of slaves."

Holmes shrugged, "Pity to see it happen, but some o' those females 'ave asked for their lot in life."

"I don't believe anyone deserves Norfolk Island, Corporal." Rachel cautiously held her words not wanting to appear defensive, yet she was quick to indicate her convictions. "Slavery is like the symptom of a deeper problem in our society—sin."

Holmes yawned and settled his husky frame against the back of the seat. The fresh air and sunlight lulled him into a relaxed stupor. "So, you're a religious woman?"

"I'm a Christian woman, if that's what you mean. I follow

the teachings of Jesus Christ. I believe He died and rose again and is the Son of God."

"Like I said—you're a religious woman," Holmes nodded. "You Catholic or Anglican?"

Rachel hesitated, unsure of her answer. "I attend the services with the Anglicans. Would that make me Anglican?"

"I'm no judge." Holmes laughed. "I wouldn't know a catechism if it bit me."

"I only know what I read in God's Word." Rachel smiled. "Do you ever read the Bible?"

Holmes shook his head, his lips pursed as he studied the road ahead.

Not wanting to force her faith upon the man, Rachel waited and decided to change the subject altogether.

As the wagon winded through the pioneer paths of Parrametta and found its way closer to the farms, Rachel found herself enjoying the company of the corporal. Although his hulking presence would intimidate most, he had a gentle way about him that put her at ease. She found herself laughing at his humor as the first star sparkled on the horizon. Being caught up in one of his many stories, she didn't notice the hunter that watched them from the forest glade.

Reverend Heath Whitley had taken the day to hunt, hunger for fresh meat whetting his appetite for a bit of roasted game. His prey, a large red kangaroo, had been startled by the wagon and the sound of human voices. The beast disappeared without a trace. Heath crouched, realizing that his stirring could cause a traveler to point his weapon into the secluded glade and shoot blindly.

Recognizing the wagon as a military vehicle, he rested against a gum tree and waited. The driver was dressed as a marine, and the wagon was pulled along briskly by a matched set of stout Welsh mares. Heath sat forward, his eyes narrowing at the sight of the lovely young woman seated next to the officer. She was dressed in fine attire, her red hair fashioned attractively atop her head. He blinked, thinking his eyes played tricks on him, but then at once he knew the girl to be Rachel Langley. A mischievous grin crossed his face as a thought struck his mind. Crouching low behind a thicket, he waited for the wagon to pass directly in front of him. Cupping his hands to his mouth, Whitley blew out a low guttural sound like that of a wild animal.

Swallowing hard, Rachel turned quickly toward the wooded glen but could see nothing but the stillness of the foliage. "What was that noise, Corporal?"

Drawing his lips together speculatively, Holmes slowed the team and stared toward the woods. "I didn't hear anything"

Chuckling quietly to himself, Whitley drew up his hands and made the growling sound again.

"There! You had to have heard it that time!" Rachel pointed into the woods.

"I did at that!" Holmes brows lifted in alarm. "I'll get out me musket an' blow the beast to bits, that's wot!"

Rachel's mouth parted, and she reached to grasp the corporal's hands before he could reach the musket. "No, Corporal, please! Don't shoot the poor thing. We've invaded its territory, I'm sure. Let's be on our way and leave it alone."

Shrugging indifferently, Holmes whipped the team but kept a wary eye on the thickly wooded area.

Whitley smiled, a gleam of admiration in his eye for Rachel and her warm response. He turned and tramped back into the woods to hunt for his sought-after game. He stole one last glance toward the wagon and disappeared down an embankment.

The large plantation home bustled with guests, dialects from Scotland and England abundant. The housemaids, all convict women, tripped through the house wearing their new black linen garments, complemented by fine white stockings and under-the-chin caps. "Who s'is lady think she is—the Queen o' England?" a ruddy girl of sixteen remarked to her willowy companion as she trotted back to the kitchen with a punch bowl twice her size.

Casting her eyes obliquely while wiping a spill from a mahogany wine cooler, the second maid cursed and then said with a flourish, "I 'member when the mistress was a-strugglin' to feed her wee bairn off o' the stores. Now look at 'er, will you . . ." she said with disgust, ". . . velvet gown, cambric lace, clean gloves, and flappin' that fan o' hers like there's no tomorrow. She's just a proud little nobody thinkin' 'erself a gentlewoman."

Across the crowd-packed room, the officers' wives congregated in animated groups, intoxicated on the wine of new money. "Lovely party, Elizabeth." An elderly Englishwoman sipped rum punch from a crystal glass and leaned casually against a heart-back armchair. "Right sharp, these pretties. Brought them with you from England, did you?"

Elizabeth Macarthur was enjoying her first real gala affair in the settlement. Since John's promotion, the enormous home had been built for her, overrun with convict servants. John had named the plantation after her—Elizabeth Farm. "Yes, they were my grandmither's. But it's been ever so long since I could use the goblets. I certainly can't place them before those rambunctious sons of mine." She turned cordially to greet another officer and his wife.

"Elizabeth, dear. Come here and meet some guests of ours," John called from the front room.

Sighing, Elizabeth excused herself from the woman and strode toward the next room, her silk shoes keeping time to the sprightly crooning of a Scottish singer and a fiddler's strings.

O my luve is like a red, red rose,
that's newly sprung in June:
O my luve is like a melodie
that's sweetly played in tune!
As fair art thou, my bonnie lass,
so deep in luve am I;
And I will luve thee still, my dear,
till a' the seas gang dry;
Till a' the seas gang dry, my dear,
till a' the seas gang dry;
And I will luve thee still, my dear,
till a' the seas gang dry.

Lieutenant Thompson spoke with a marked change in his demeanor. "Is there a place where we can chat?" he whispered to Macarthur so his wife couldn't hear.

Turning to regard Mrs. Thompson, Macarthur assumed a jovial tone. "I'm sure your bonny wife could excuse us gents for a moment. Join me for a quid?"

Lilith nodded favorably, her rhinestones sparkling beneath the Macarthurs' candelabra.

"Sounds splendid," Thompson nodded. "I'm rather low on tobacco myself."

"Elizabeth," John acknowledged his wife who joined them, "I'd like to introduce you to Lieutenant Cornel Thompson and his good wife, Lilith." Leaning toward her guest with a proprietary gaze, Elizabeth welcomed the Thompson woman. "Pleased to meet you. But we've met before, haven't we, Mrs. Thompson?"

Lilith nodded, her thin, colorless lips smiling out from a pale complexion. "Yes, at the fish market, perhaps?"

"I can't remember for certain, but your face is quite familiar to me." Elizabeth studied the blue eyes so pale they were almost white. "Would you like to join the other ladies and myself on the veranda? Lovely starlit night to find out the latest news of the colony." Her velvet gown trailing behind her, Elizabeth extended a white-gloved hand and led Lilith through the front doorway while conversing about her new son.

Watching their wives depart, Macarthur and Thompson turned to the drawing room where the naval officers had congregated to smoke their hoarded tobacco. Pensive, Macarthur and Thompson spoke in quiet discourse.

"I'm hearing rumors, Macarthur," Thompson said gravely.

"Rumors such as?"

"Such as a paymaster having property burned to force the emancipists to trade down."

"I'll not take the blame for those devilish bushrangers!" Macarthur snapped, fumbling to light his pipe. "If tighter controls were exercised at the prison, you wouldn't have so many lags runnin' free. An' so much for guid deeds. I traded property to *save* those emancipists' hides—not ruin them."

"We officers need to be careful, Macarthur, that's all I'm saying," Thompson said tautly.

The front door knocker banged loudly again, and the convict butler, dressed in black tails, opened the door.

Rachel stood beside Holmes upon the wide portico that stretched across the front of the home. Seeing the finery of the ladies, she felt an uncomfortable pang of inadequacy—in her mind, her borrowed dress paled next to those worn by the officers' wives. Under the light of the torches that blazed around the expansive home, the lively colors, imported jewelry, and plumed headpieces sparkled gaily, and Rachel wished she hadn't come.

Holmes saw the discomfort in Rachel's gaze and said plainly, "We don't have to stay. I can take you back to the Prentice farm if you prefer, Rachel."

Swallowing the lump in her throat, Rachel shook her head, her lips pursed. "No, I need to do this, Corporal. I need to shake the past from myself." Stretching a smile across her face, she breathed deeply and turned to gaze up at the butler, who stared at them impatiently. The butler had a familiar face, and she was certain she remembered seeing him in the convict camp. *It doesn't matter*, she chided herself. *We're all who we are*.

Strolling over to greet the new arrivals, Elizabeth Macarthur poised herself in front of Rachel and Holmes. "Welcome to the Macarthur hoose," she greeted melodiously. "I'm Mrs. Macarthur." Turning to the butler she ordered, "That'll be all, Ian."

The butler slammed the door, more from lack of protocol than from displeasure.

"Pleased to meet you, ma'am. I'm Corporal Bryce Holmes an' this is Miss Rachel Langley."

Elizabeth's eyes lit at the sound of Rachel's name. "Rachel Langley? Excuse me, is it you, lass? After all this time?"

"Mrs.—?" Rachel asked hesitatingly.

"When we lived at the old hoose—you were our . . ." Elizabeth stopped to formulate a more appropriate reply.

"It's all right to say it, ma'am. Corporal, I was a housekeeper for the Macarthurs."

Holmes gripped Rachel's hand firmly and arched his brow. "An' a fine establishment you worked for, at that."

Wetting her dry lips, Rachel nodded, replying succinctly, "I left to care for my dear friend Betsy Brady."

"I remember now," Elizabeth nodded diplomatically.

"I regret to say that she passed on." Her eyes clouded, but composure galvanized her emotions. "She and I . . . we were like sisters."

"The girl died? How terrible!" Elizabeth covered her mouth with her hands. "Right after you helped deliver Ira?"

"Not long after that. She had some gold pieces, and we were without protection along the highways and the billabongs. Betsy was murdered."

Deciding the topic too dark for such a gay affair, Elizabeth changed the subject. "Have you found work yet, Rachel?"

Rachel nodded, not wishing to entangle herself again with the likes of John Macarthur. "I help a farming family here in Parrametta. I'm a . . ." Rachel hesitated and then decided she must confess the truth. "I'm a field hand."

Her brows furrowed, Elizabeth shook her head, commenting assertively, "A lassie as lovely as yourself shouldn't be toilin' an' plooin'—that's man's work!"

"It's honest work, ma'am," Rachel held her ground, her eyes trained on the small Scottish woman.

"I know a lady who could use a girl such as yourself for a ladies' maid. It'd be as honest as any job around this colony. Would such a job interest you, lass?"

"You ought to consider the offer, Rachel," Holmes nodded agreeably.

Stroking her hands, Rachel hesitated for only a moment, and then answered, "I suppose it wouldn't do any harm to inquire."

"Lilith, dear!" Elizabeth called sprightly. "I've good news for you!"

Lilith excused herself from her circle of friends, and striding quickly to Elizabeth's side, arched her brow inquisitively. "Whatever is the good news, Elizabeth?"

"I've found a wonderful maid for you. I'd like to introduce you to Miss Langley."

"It's a pleasure to meet you, Miss Langley." Talking in a whisper from the corner of her mouth, she asked, "This *lady* wants to be my maid?" Her eyes studied the beautiful young woman with interest.

"She's an *emancipist,*" Elizabeth whispered back.

Hearing the entire whispered conversation, Rachel looked away, a flicker of emotion coloring her cheeks. She would never fit into the higher rungs of society no matter how hard she tried. Even if she *had* been invited into Elizabeth's little coterie of friends all wrapped in silk and velvet, she could never hide her loathing for such a life—it was all just subterfuge anyway.

"I'll have our driver give you directions to our farm, Miss Langley." Lilith's face gleamed with gratification.

Holmes offered, "I'll get them for you, Rachel."

"All right then." Rachel grew quiet, and all present became aware of her withdrawal from the conversation.

Speaking up suddenly, Elizabeth directed her words to Holmes. "Corporal, why don't you escort your delightful friend inside for some refreshment? Dinner will be served shortly."

Lifting his brows in question, Bryce waited for Rachel's nod, and then led her inside away from the inspecting gazes of the officers' wives gathered around the front portico. Once inside, he escorted her to a quieter corner and motioned for her to join him on a mahogany settee. "I'm sorry if you've been made to feel uncomfortable, Rachel," he apologized.

"I'm quite all right, Corporal," Rachel assured, seating herself next to him. She ran her slender fingers along the soft gold brocade of the settee. "I just don't belong here, that's all."

Keeping his voice low, Holmes retorted, "Blast it, Rachel! You're as fine a woman as any crow in this room!"

"What does it matter, anyway?"

"You deserve more, that's wot! Give it time. I'll introduce you to all the right people an' you'll soon . . ."

"I'll soon what?" Rachel shook her head at Holmes. "Try to be something I'm not? It's no use."

"Let me 'elp you, Rachel. I want to take care o' you. Why

won't you let me?" Gently grasping her hands, Holmes' face filled with empathy.

Her voice reflecting frustration, Rachel replied, "I said I would take the work, didn't I?"

A strange smile dimpled Holmes cheeks as he stroked her arm. "I've pushed you too much. I'm sorry. Let me go an' fetch some punch for you."

Nodding faintly, Rachel cast her eyes to the floor as Holmes strode away. Hearing the dinner bell clanging loudly, she kept her place on the settee while the Macarthurs and their guests crowded into the dining hall. Perhaps the corporal was right after all. She needed new surroundings and new friends. "It's time to get on with your life, Rachel Langley," she chided herself.

In the twilight, a pied butcher-bird sang on a limb outside the large glass-paned windows. Turning to hear its lyrical song, Rachel was swept by a sudden rush of melancholy. She tried to shake off the gloom when the butler summoned her to enter the dining room. But her mind roiled with anxiety when she stood to take her place at Holmes' side.

"I'm really not very hungry. Would you mind, Corporal?"

"Mind?"

"I want to go back home—to Rose Hill."

16
A Bitter Affair

"Another day in the government building," Katy sighed as she prepared to depart from her shanty. Looking out through the dingy pane of glass framed by rough wood, she saw the hot sun already boring down on the settlement. A heat wave had locked onto the colony for the last few weeks. The government building offered some respite from the heat, but lethargy became the new predator of the colonists.

After two weeks of living on her own, Katy was thankful for her newly found independence, but loneliness pervaded her life. Her pay each Friday could be stretched to meet her meager needs, and she had even managed to sew herself a new dress—a frock of simple design with a smock pulled over the top. Her wounds were slowly healing and the streaks across her hands were fading. But her legs appeared to be deeply scarred, and she fought with bouts of depression. She found that even work hadn't given her the satisfaction of which she dreamed.

Tying a white bonnet underneath her chin, Katy called to Lorna, who was poking ungracefully at a seam. "Shall we go, Lorna?"

"Aw! Stuck meself again!" Lorna jabbed her finger in her mouth and then pulled it out to wag away the pain. "I'll never sew a stitch with your skill, Katy." She sighed and put aside the fabric to attend to later. Reaching for an old basket, she remarked blandly, "Mrs. Hennyson at the fish market will want me to fetch some things for her today from the stores. I suppose I should hurry. If I lose this job, I doesn't have no one to keep me like Mary does."

"Oh, I saw Mary yesterday," Katy remarked, holding a shard of mirror before her face.

"Mary? 'ow's the ol' girl farin'?"

"It's hard to tell. She didn't say a lot really, but she wore a new dress—a lovely shade of rose." Katy recalled the deadness in Mary's eyes and the weathered look of her face, but she kept the thought to herself.

"She's miserable, I vow. Waitin' for the ol' man to kick off 'as to be givin' 'er a fit."

"I wouldn't know, Lorna. I'm not sure she knows what she wants in life."

"Me neither. Nor you, if you'd ever admit it."

Katy whipped around, denial sparking her gaze. "Whatever do you mean?"

Lorna held up her thin hands defensively. "Now, don't go gettin' all upset wif me. I know life's no easier for you."

Quick to negate the girl's comment, Katy answered forthrightly, "Living in Sydney Cove isn't easy for any of us."

"Do tell. But I see you takin' those nips from the bottle from time to time. Ol' Lorna's not blind, she ain't."

Feeling her cheeks redden, Katy huffed. "You've no right meddling in my private affairs, Lorna Steed! A person has a right to privacy. Besides, what I take for pain is my own business. It's strictly medicinal."

Lorna chuckled. "Medicinal? That's a good one, miss. But you're right about me. I ain't got no business meddlin' in your life. I apologize fer that."

Her face poised, Katy answered curtly, "Apology accepted." Seeing a spark of regret in Lorna's face, she softened. "We better leave if we're to ride into town with the neighbors across the way."

While Lorna gathered her belongings, Katy left the broken mirror on the windowsill. Opening the door, she stopped abruptly, seeing a gentleman approaching her door. His hat brim was tilted, serving to hide his face, but the familiarness of his gait drew her eye. "Hello, sir," she called with an inquisitive lilt.

"Good mornin' to you!"

Once his face lifted to greet her, Katy recognized Dwight Farrell. She felt her mouth curve in an acerbic smile, but held her amusement. "I thought you had gone back to England—to fight for us colonists."

Smiling ruefully, Dwight adjusted the wide-brimmed hat, cocking it back handsomely on his head. "I decided to stay here in Sydney Cove. If I leave, I might never return."

"That would be a pity," Katy said without thought. Then seeing the light in his gaze, she added, "That is, it would be a shame for the colonists to lose one of their own to England."

Shrugging indifferently, Dwight casually remarked, "The colonists'll make it with or without me." Then his gaze grew somber as he bore his intent. "But a worse fate would be in never seeing you again, Katy Prentice." He crossed his arms at his waist, determination strengthening his stance.

Katy felt her mouth go dry. She had felt a kindred spirit with the man upon meeting him, but had dismissed him from her thoughts, believing he had sailed for England. "I . . . I don't exactly know what to say, Mr. Farrell."

"I've come to call on you." Dwight stepped toward her, reaching to clasp her hands in his own. "You may give me your answer, madam."

After a silent moment had passed between them, Lorna's voice broke the quietude. "Well, say somethin', Katy Prentice! Man's come all this way . . . least you kin do is to answer him! An' a right 'andsome man, 'e is at that!"

Katy shook her head, slightly embarrassed at Lorna's brazen words, but seeing the light of humor in Dwight's gaze, she felt relaxation sweep through her, and they both laughed. "I suppose Lorna's right, Mr. Farrell. I should answer you."

Gripping her hands firmly, Dwight awaited Katy's response, and his tough exterior assumed a conspicuous tenderness.

"I consent to your request, Mr. Farrell."

"It's a bloomin' miracle, that's wot!" Lorna shouted.

"Why are you nervous?" Corporal Holmes questioned Rachel's apprehensions. "Mrs. Thompson seems like a right nice lady." Pulling the wagon's reins to the right, he turned the dray and drove it through the open gate of the Thompson farm. It was a one-hundred-acre tract, dotted with torches pounded into the earth for the evening's affair.

"I know all that, Corporal, but I just didn't realize that Lilith Thompson was Lieutenant Cornel Thompson's wife."

"You didn't see them together at the Macarthur party?"

"Apparently not. And remember, we left early."

"What does it matter?"

Rachel drew her mouth to one side, chastening herself for her apprehensions about Felicity Thompson. Pensively, she answered, "It really doesn't matter, I suppose."

Pulling up underneath a date palm, Bryce hailed the mare to a halt. Shifting in the wagon seat, he turned to face Rachel. "I'll be back to see about you tomorrow." Leaning slowly toward her, he fixed his eyes on hers.

Rachel's brow grew pensive, and she felt the warmth of his breath. "Corporal, I . . ."

Drawing his arms slowly around her diminutive frame, Holmes whispered, "Don't speak, Rachel." His mouth was taut and his strength evident.

Rachel started to resist, but felt his lips press against hers before she could react. His kiss lay gently on her lips, but his muscular arms were immovable. Drawing back slightly, he smiled with pleasure. With one hand he cradled the back of her head, pressing her face close to his, and she saw the desire in his eyes. "Please don't," her words faltered, and she found him kissing her again.

"You're the most beautiful woman I've ever met," he spoke in quiet tones as though mere words would shatter the moment. Seeing the confusion in her gaze, he carefully released his grip and apologized. "I'm sorry if I've offended you, Rachel. Forgive me?"

Her breath quickening, Rachel pulled away. "I'm not angry with you. I . . . I'm just . . . confused." She shifted uncomfortably and gazed toward the Thompson home. "Corporal, I need more time."

"Time for what? You always question every bloomin' feelin'? I'm fallin' in love with you. What's so wrong wi' that?"

"I . . . I don't know why, Bryce." Rachel pressed her lips together, the warmth of his kiss still new, but held her words.

His dark eyes softened and a faint smile played across his lips. "I'll give you all the time you need, Rachel."

Rachel stepped from the dray, the sincerity of his words haunting her emotions. Realizing her obligation to the man, she turned her face up toward him and said apologetically, "Please forgive me of my awkward ways. I'm obliged to you for bringing me all the way out here. I don't deserve your kindness."

She stepped toward the wagon, and placing a kiss upon her fingertips, she reached upward and brushed his lips with her fingers. "Just more time." She smiled, though her green eyes belied her troubled thoughts.

Holmes did not stir until he saw that Rachel had found her way to the rear servants' exit and had disappeared into the home. Then turning the wagon, he rode away into the long afternoon shadows that stretched across the trodden road.

The sun melded with the mountaintops in orange-yellow hues, leaving Parrametta with one last bright veil upon the landscape. As a pale moon rose, a single star appeared, and together they shared the day's final hour and brightened the sky as the firmament deepened its blue. Evening was a quiet visitor, ascending from one horizon to the other until all traces of daylight succumbed to the night.

Attired in Anglican black, Heath Whitley strolled around the Thompson property, the bleating of sheep on a distant hill beckoning his attentions. He had arrived behind a group of visitors, but felt more drawn to the solitude of the pastures than to the gaiety of the evening's affair. His invitation had been delivered by a military private. Flipping over the invitation, he had found a note from Felicity scrawled on the back—*Do come, dear Reverend. I would be so bored without you. Love, Felicity.*

Finding a grassy knoll, he stepped atop its knobby crest and gazed toward the herd. He found himself questioning his motives for accepting the invitation. Felicity was a beautiful woman—and dare he admit it, desirable—and he enjoyed the rousing discussions with Cornel Thompson.

But his mind often wandered to that tranquil Sunday when first he discovered the red-haired young renegade collapsed upon his bed. *Who are you, Rachel Langley?* Upon summoning up her memory, he could smell the fresh aroma of sunshine from her hair as it fell around her shoulders in soft curls. But now her comely face became more difficult to recollect, and she slipped further from him with each passing moment, like a vision drifting back to its netherworld. *She's a precious child, Lord. Keep your hand on her.*

The violinist's strains floated through the stirring breezes, and Whitley gazed toward the portico. The flambeaus had been lit, and the home was luminous with merriment. He sighed, his gaze following the liveryman and wagon which had delivered him to the Thompson doorstep. *Perhaps I should depart as quickly as I came.*

A rear kitchen drapery stirred, and a housemaid peered out for a brief moment, then withdrew and went about her duties. "Now, don't you fill out that dress right finely." She inspected Rachel's attire with an admirable gaze. "Guests are arrivin' by the cartloads. M'lady's house'll be brimmin' wi' folks t'night from all round the settlement," she blustered while moving around two servants stirring the large pots that simmered on the cookstove.

"So tonight I'll be serving the guests, Florine?" Rachel

spoke quietly to the girl, wishing she could allay her own anxieties.

"Yes, Rachel. Tomorrow m'lady'll assign you your duties for the day. I know she likes her bath water drawn and warmed by sunup. She's a good mistress, but 'as 'er own ways, if you get m' meanin', an' it don't pay none o' us to get cheeky wi' nobody."

"I met Mrs. Thompson today," Rachel joined in agreement. "She's a lovely person, it seems to me." She recalled the gentle manner in which Lilith Thompson had greeted her personally, showing her to her quarters beneath the stairs.

"Just do exactly as yer told an' you'll find the Thompsons'll do right by ye."

Rachel gazed down at her field-calloused hands and sighed. Drawing herself up, she stretched a smile across her face. "I'm sure they will, too, Florine. When do we start serving?"

"Right when ol' Cadbury rings that bloomin' bell. Cadbury likes 'is bell an' thinks it gives 'im rule over all us." Florine winked. "But I just keeps me peace an' one day, I says to meself, I'll take that bell an' give 'im a clout with it, I will!"

Rachel laughed at the young maid from Dorset and felt the tension in her shoulders begin to relax. "I'll wager you'll do just that, Florine."

"Now take this tray out and try to get those snobs as bloomin' drunk on their feet as you can! The sooner this affair is finished, the sooner I can drag me weary bones to bed." Florine rubbed her backside.

Shaking her head, an older cook turned to chasten the maid. "Florine, mind yer tongue! Your brashness'll be the end o' ye yet!"

"Mind yer own tongue! There's none that works better'n me an' m'lady knows it!"

"Excuse me, please." Rachel took the tray and walked quietly toward the doorway, feeling the hostility between the two women as she went.

She balanced the tray of drinks and strode down a short hallway, following the voices that filled the front room. The Thompson home was not as expansive as the Macarthurs', but it held a simple beauty nonetheless. Since most of the dwellings around the cove and into Parrametta were built by emancipists who longed for England, very few permanent homes had been erected. Permanence, slow to emerge in New South Wales, found its place among the married junta officers and none other.

Several couples had begun to sway to the concert of strings, with cotton and silk skirts swirling across the wooden floor like colorful tops. Rachel stayed along the outer borders of the room, quietly offering the drinks. Taking in the beauty of the affair, Rachel stepped toward an inside wall decorated with ornate portraits and studied them with mild interest. Immediately, she detected the swish of petticoats coming from down the hallway, and glanced obliquely with narrowing eyes. As she surmised, Felicity Thompson promenaded out into the room. Her hair had been fashioned elegantly atop her head with shiny black curls that hung down and caressed her ivory neck. Rachel turned her face quickly and stepped toward three women who were quietly conversing. "Refreshment, ladies?" Her voice was low. She glanced back again and realized the stunning dress Felicity wore was fashioned of green silk. *The silk!*

A low rapping from the entrance attracted Felicity's attention and she called to the butler, "See who's come, Edgar. Quickly!"

The aging convict ambled toward the door in a worn black suit. Opening the door, he beheld the handsome Anglican minister and bowed humbly. "Welcome, parson, sir."

Whitley's face was drawn in a melancholy frown, but he managed a wooden smile. "Thank you, Edgar," he said amicably. "I trust I'm not too late. I've been admiring the livestock."

"No problem t'all, sir. Miss Felicity 'as been askin' about you an awful lot, though."

"Good Reverend!" Felicity called with a jubilant air as she strode quickly toward Whitley with arms outstretched. "I thought you'd never arrive." Her eyes sparkled, and her admiration for him proved evident in her gaze.

"So sorry, Miss Thompson. I've tarried too long in your

father's pastureland. Please forgive me."

Felicity strode up directly in front of Whitley, her violet eyes bearing a longing gaze. "Anything you ask, Reverend—is yours." She slid her slender white-gloved arm inside his and prompted him. "Father wishes to speak with you. I promised to deliver you to him personally." Not one to be dragged away by a woman, Whitley stood firm in his place until Felicity noted his resistance. She turned and her eyes held a demure but questioning look.

Whitley smiled ardently. "If I may comment, Miss Thompson, you do look beautiful."

Felicity paused, her lips pressed in a coy smile. "You certainly may comment, thank you. But, formalities dismissed, I believe it would be proper now for you to call me Felicity—don't you—Heath?"

Whitley nodded, her hypnotic perfume filling his senses. "Felicity," he repeated her name, but his tone softened. He lifted his left hand and patted her soft slender fingers which curved around his arm.

Rachel, who stood concealed behind a group of men, had watched the whole affair and hesitated, not knowing whether she should make herself known or stay hidden in the crowded room.

Lifting his eyes to scan the room, Whitley made contact with a familiar face and called out politely, "Lieutenant Thompson."

Thompson dispensed with his formalities and politely excused himself from his guests' presence. "Reverend Whitley, welcome back!" He reached out to grip the minister's hand and shook it jovially.

"Thank you, Lieutenant. I'm happy you invited me."

"Well, I've some good news I thought you'd want to hear right away."

Beaming, Felicity's innocent demeanor belied her knowledge of the news.

"Those of us in the New South Wales Corps who are concerned about the future of this colony feel that a permanent church should be built."

Whitley's lips parted and his brow furrowed. "You mean . . ."

Thompson smiled, self-satisfied. "We want to build you a new church, Reverend." He chuckled, pleased with himself.

Whitley nodded and smiled politely, but a queer feeling nagged his emotions. "Why me, sir?"

"Why not? You've a growing church. What happens in inclement weather?"

"We cancel service." Whitley shrugged, thinking of the days when the mud washed through the roof of the church's little shanty. "But there are other ministers more deserving than me."

"Such as that one over there?" Thompson spoke quietly from the corner of his mouth.

Whitley followed the man's gaze, and his eyes fell upon the astute-looking minister, bewigged and dressed as he, except for the addition of a fine expensive black coat. "Reverend Samuel Marsden," he commented quietly. "I've met him on a few occasions." Whitley remembered their meetings—always brief and leaving little impression upon him. Marsden was older than he, shorter, with heavy shoulders, and the face of a petulant ox. He had been appointed to the chaplaincy chiefly for the military and the convicts. His measures of meting out cruel punishments to the prisoners earned him quite a reputation. "The flogging parson?" Whitley whispered.

A burst of air shot from Thompson's lips. "Don't let *him* hear you say that. But he is quite the hellfire preacher, aye?" Thompson nudged Whitley with his arm. "But we believe you to be a man of vision, full of the pioneer spirit."

"And much more handsome," Felicity added with a graceful lilt to her tone as she chose to ignore her father's look of disapproval. She pressed closer to Whitley, her violet eyes fixed on no other but him.

Whitley knew he should express his gratitude, but he suspected Felicity had had a hand in the matter. He had no respect for a man who could be bought and had no intention of becoming trapped. "I'll give the subject some thought." Firmly, he shook the lieutenant's hand but looked dubiously toward Felicity.

His brows pinched, Thompson spoke candidly. "In my book, there's no thought to it, Whitley. Accept man, accept!" He vigorously patted Whitley's shoulder.

Whitley observed the smile across Thompson's face but sensed an uncomfortable pressure to surrender. He stood firmly, gazing somberly into the lieutenant's face without a word.

"You there, Rachel!" Lilith called quietly, but her tone bespoke annoyance.

Rachel had been standing in the passageway to the drawing room, painfully observing the scene before her—Felicity's arm wrapped around Reverend Whitley's as they conversed in quiet, serious tones with her father, Lieutenant Cornel Thompson. She couldn't hear their words, but the intimacy between them was apparent.

The sound of Lilith's voice jarred her to reality. "Yes, ma'am." She turned and saw the confusion in her mistress's gaze. "I'm sorry. Is there a problem?"

"Dear me, our guests! They've been waiting for you to serve their drinks." Lilith waved her hand incredulously, her eyes set on the full tray in Rachel's grasp.

Rachel quickly looked down and realized she had been so caught up in watching Felicity with Reverend Whitley that she had forgotten her duties. "My apologies, Mrs. Thompson! You must think me a dolt. I'll see to them right away." Rachel stepped toward a group of young couples.

"No, not that way, Rachel," Lilith instructed. "Over there." She pointed toward the trio that Rachel desperately wanted to avoid. "I want you to serve one of our honored guests, Reverend Heath Whitley."

Rachel bit her lip and fumbled for an excuse. "I know Reverend Whitley, ma'am. Perhaps your husband spoke of how he helped to rescue me when I lost my way in the bush?"

"*You* were the girl?"

"Yes, but I do hate to bother the man. Let me fetch Florine to finish with this tray."

"Nonsense. Florine's no server. And you've no need to be nervous. Now off with you." Lilith smiled warmly, her affection for Rachel evident. "Take the man some refreshment. I'll go to the kitchen myself to check on Florine." She gently nudged Rachel's shoulder to direct her toward the minister. "A little wine would do him good."

Rachel's face grew tensely poised as she stepped toward Whitley and Felicity. Swallowing hard, she lowered her face and circled to the rear of them. If she served from behind them, perhaps they would not notice her.

Whitley, inhaling deeply, spoke forthrightly. "I must insist on more time, Lieutenant. I'm one to give great thought to any endeavor. Many a man of God has fallen from His will with one hasty decision. To go forward without God's leading is nothing short of blind ambition."

"All right. Let me know in a fortnight." Thompson waved away Whitley's moralizing. "I'll inform the Corps at once with your decision. If you decline, there's always the 'flogging parson.' " Thompson cast a sardonic gaze toward the group of men gathered around Marsden. "His popularity *is* growing," he said distastefully.

"Wine, sir?" Rachel offered quietly.

"Yes, let's!" Thompson nodded at Whitley and Felicity. "After you, dear." He smiled at his daughter.

"Reverend?" Felicity turned to select her drink.

Whitley gestured with his hand. "None for me, thank you."

Felicity stepped toward the maid. Lifting her face, she expected to see one of her mother's usual kitchen maids. Then, drawing back her hand, she said with mock surprise, "Why, who have we here?"

Rachel felt misery sweep through her as Cornel Thompson and Heath Whitley turned to stare at her.

Whitley, nonplussed, said nothing but smiled diplomatically.

"Why, it's the young emancipist! Lilith didn't tell me *you* were the new one." Thompson, composing his words, smiled politely at Rachel.

Rachel shrugged, her face rigid. "Yes, well . . ."

Felicity didn't wait for Rachel's response but seized the moment without hesitation. "Why, I've already heard so much about you!"

Rachel looked first at Whitley, supposing him to be the

source. Drawing her gaze back to Felicity, she asked with kind interest, "Have you?"

"Why yes." Felicity's eyes narrowed, lit by a malicious spark. "The kitchen maids were all a-flutter about you today. You're the one with the handsome young corporal chasing after you."

Rachel grew taut, the crystal goblets clinking together like faint bells. She turned to Whitley, who continued to smile. "I don't think he's—"

"No need to explain." Felicity's smile was humorless. "The maids saw it all."

"Nothing to see, really, Felicity," Rachel replied in a meek tone. The room seemed to grow warmer.

"So romantic the way he wrapped you in his arms and kissed you—just this afternoon," Felicity added matter-of-factly.

His lips pressed tightly together, Whitley read the discomfort in Rachel's face. Questioning Felicity's intent, he intervened. "I . . . I think that's wonderful, Miss Langley," he artfully colored his words. "And so pleased to see you've settled into colony life. I hope the two of you will be quite happy."

Tears of embarrassment brimmed in Rachel's eyes as she glanced toward Heath Whitley. *What must he think of me?* Her head shook slowly as she watched Felicity snug closer to Whitley and smile demurely up at him.

"It's not like that at all . . ." Lowering her face, Rachel added with a note of finality, ". . . it doesn't matter." Her eyes gazed up once again at Felicity. "I need to be serving the other guests, if you'll excuse me."

"Not just yet." Felicity replaced her empty wine glass on the tray and quickly retrieved two more. Handing one glass to Whitley, she held her crystal goblet in the air. "A toast!" she shouted to the guests.

At once, the room grew quiet, and all eyes were on Felicity and the handsome minister to whom she held tightly. "To Sydney Cove's first church!"

"To Reverend Heath Whitley!" A corps officer followed jovially as the guests raised their glasses in kind—all but the Reverend Samuel Marsden, who stood glowering.

As the guests cheered, Whitley gripped his glass awkwardly. Whispering from the corner of his mouth, he said to Felicity, "Now is not the time—"

Without reply, Felicity lightly struck the rim of her glass to Whitley's as the guests toasted around the room. Drawing his glass to her lips, she sipped ceremoniously while lifting her own glass toward him. Looking with adoration into his eyes, she whispered pleadingly, "A token, Heath—for our guests!"

Whitley gazed down at the beautiful girl who held her glass toward his lips in anticipation. Turning to face the onlookers, he nodded politely, his smile wooden. "To . . . to the church," he replied quietly. Felicity lifted the wine to his lips as the guests cheered. Seeing the approval in the people's eyes, he returned a winning smile and quickly swallowed the dry-tasting wine. Then his eyes fell upon Rachel, whose gaze was all but piteous.

"Why?" Rachel mouthed silently. She shook her head, not noticing the glasses were toppling from the tray. The crystal crashed around her feet, and she lifted the tray in a fast reflex. One last goblet tumbled sideways, spilling across Felicity's green silk skirt.

"My silk formal!" Felicity gripped the skirt, angrily examining the red wine that soaked into the glistening garment. "You!"

"I'm sorry, Felicity." Rachel's brow furrowed as she beheld the hostility of the young woman's gaze.

"You wanted this silk for yourself, isn't that true?"

"No!" Rachel shook her head, feeling her cheeks flush bright red. "I swear it was an accident!"

"*She* wanted this silk from the stores, Father!" Felicity was fast to accuse. "When I bought it instead, she was furious—and jealous. *Now* look at me!"

"Felicity, are you sure about this?" Cornel Thompson attempted to reason with his infuriated daughter. "I'm sure Miss Langley's accident was not intentional."

"I've been humiliated by this servant in front of our guests. She obviously hates me." Lifting her face indignantly, Felicity looked first at her father and then pointed with her eyes at the visitors. "What are you going to do about her, Father?"

Sighing, Thompson turned to apologize to his guests, who stared motionless, appalled at the uncomfortable scene. "I'm sorry, dear guests, for the disruption." He clasped his hands in a gentlemanly fashion just as the butler's bell rang, offering an opportunity for the embarrassed host to extend a congenial invitation. "But it's time to fill our insides to overflowing. Eat—drink—and be merry!" His brow arched artfully, and his guests chuckled and turned gratefully toward the dining hall.

Running from the kitchen entrance, Lilith rushed quickly to Felicity's side, her face flushed. "Whatever is wrong, Felicity?"

Felicity glowered at Rachel, drawing her full lips into a pout. "Your new maid just humiliated me in front of our dear Reverend Whitley, that's all, Mother. Just look at my dress!"

Seeing the pain in Rachel's eyes, Whitley tried to offer polite reparation. "I assure you, I'm convinced it was all an unfortunate accident."

Lilith turned to Rachel, who stood with red cheeks, wet with tears. "Is it true, Rachel? Did you purposely embarrass our Felicity?"

Rachel looked at the girl with pained resignation. "I'm sorry to have—embarrassed you, Miss Thompson. I'll gather my things tomorrow and leave—that is," she turned to Lilith and Cornel, "if you don't mind my staying for the night."

"Well enough," Thompson lectured. "But let this be a lesson to you, young woman. A servant's loyalty must be to the entire family." He gazed at his daughter sternly. "Felicity?"

"Well, of course I accept your apology—*emancipist*," she said coolly. Smoothing her skirt with a fretful scowl, she turned her face toward Whitley. "Heath, why don't we join the others? I'm famished."

The emotion of the moment weighed heavily on Whitley's shoulders, and he began to reach sympathetically toward Rachel. Rachel, staring at the floor, lifted her eyes slowly. He wanted to comfort her, but thought better of it when he saw the disappointment in her eyes. Dropping his hand, he said nothing, but turned and walked toward the dining hall with Felicity at his side.

Rachel stood motionless, the sting of Felicity's words ringing in her ears. But even more painful was the knowledge that Reverend Heath Whitley had been bought by the Rum Corps.

Whipping around to complete his business with Rachel, Thompson asked stiffly, "You can arrange your transport, I trust?"

"Cornel, have pity on the girl. You know as well as I of Felicity's ways. . . ."

"Silence, Lilith! I'll deal with the girl in my own way!"

"It's quite all right, Mrs. Thompson," Rachel offered in an apologetic tone. "I do have someone who was coming to visit me tomorrow, anyway. But I should never have accepted the position in the first place."

"Why is that?" Thompson snapped.

Rachel paused, choosing her words. "My—*heart* wasn't in it, sir."

"Very well. Whatever the case may be, you're to adjourn to the servants' quarters on the rear of the property. The butler will have your pay for one night ready for you when you awaken. We will now consider our parting completed."

"At once, sir." Rachel curtsied respectfully and then turned to regard Lilith. She had developed a fondness for the woman in the short time she had known her. "Goodbye, Mrs. Thompson. Thank you for your kindness."

Her eyes moist, Lilith stroked Rachel's cheek. "Take care, love. God keep you in His care."

Rachel grasped Lilith's hand and placed a tender kiss upon it. "He will. I know He will."

17
Compromise of Survival

The air was tainted with the desiccated stench of barren land. Because the sky had yielded no rain for months, the fields of Parrametta had met with drought, and the emancipists who had toiled so hard for naught lived with the long-familiar fear of famine clouding their thoughts.

George Prentice sat on an old crate inside his kitchen doorway, staring blankly out across his fruitless fields. He was well-acquainted with failure, but condemnation eroded his manhood, and self-hatred tempted his faith with despair.

"George, there's a man 'ere to see you." A field hand had entered from the front entrance. "You all right, George?"

"Well as kin be expected, I suppose." George sighed, for he had no recourse except to sell the farm back to the junta. Seeing the tragic face of Amelia perched in her rocker, he thought he could detect disappointment in her countenance. *Don't fret yourself, Amelia. God always makes a way, don't He, now?*

Amelia rocked slowly, her eyes drooping and red-rimmed.

George pursed his lips, longing for the bright smile that once greeted him from his bed each morning. How he missed those gentle arms that had wrapped around him until he awoke.

Sighing, he stood and was greeted by a corporal in uniform. The man walked in slowly, his rifle in a sling at his side. "Good day, Mr. Prentice." He had a surly frown and bristly brows that shaded his eyes. He studied the room nervously.

"Good day, sir. Help you?"

"I'm Corporal Nolan McGrath." He extended a gloved hand. He lowered his voice and glanced back toward Amelia, who stared glassy-eyed. "Need to talk to you—privately. I've been sent to offer you a proposal. You're 'avin' trouble with your farm?"

"Amelia can't hear us." George nodded warily. "Who sent you?"

"Those above me." McGrath shrugged, his face petulant. "The Corps. That's all you needs to know."

"What kind o' proposal?"

Crouching next to George, McGrath yanked a straw from a broom and picked at his teeth. "One that'll save yer farm—if yer smart, that is."

"Sounds more like a threat to me." George grew defensive.

"You're not obligated. I kin up an' walk out the door as quick as I came in."

Sighing pensively, George stated, "Give me the particulars, at least."

"There's lots o' settlers in your situation, what wi' the drought an' all. Lots o' rum-hungry settlers."

"I don't touch a drop," George argued. "Not since me transportation sentencing 'ave I 'ad a drink."

"Which is why you're a proper candidate for the position."

"Oh? Why is that?"

"We need for you to assist us with the distribution of our—supplies."

"Out 'ere in Parrametta?"

"That's right. We've a monopoly on the colony's rum."

George shot back, "As well we know!"

"It's become the currency. When things go wrong, we all need a little pick-me-up. There's farmers that'll soon be so desperate out 'ere that they'll sell their land fer grog."

"Why, you're nothin' but opportunists—land-hungry sharks!" George grew incredulous.

"Don't stab your benefactor in the back, Mr. Prentice. There's a share fer you if you cooperates."

"What? Stab me own neighbors in the back is more like it! I'd be a crook!"

"You wouldn't be a crook. Just a wise businessman, that's all. Look at it as though you'd be helpin' those poor fools out from under a burden. They ain't capable o' farmin' anyway. Most are ex-thieves, lazy freeloaders barely existin' off the government stores. They deserve to lose everythin'."

"I'm an emancipist, corporal, an' your words are aimed at me as much as the next man out 'ere! I'm askin' you as politely as I know how to leave me property before I throw you off it!"

"Even if me offer would make you rich as Macarthur?"

George stopped, his breath taken. "Rich as Macarthur? You're insane!"

"Fer every deal you close on, you collect a quarter of the profits. We provide the rum—you provide the willing customer."

"Why that's . . ."

"The best deal you'll ever be offered, Mr. Prentice." He turned to stare at Amelia, who had nodded to sleep. "You owe it to the missus, at least."

The air seemed to thin, and his nerve weakened. George asked nervously, "And who collects the remainder of the profit—Macarthur?"

"A number o'—investors. They plan to make some *improvements*, shall we say, in the colony. Not all selfish gain, mind you."

"Improvements in the linin' o' their own pockets, I vow."

"On the contrary, Mr. Prentice. They've already made plans for a brand new church building."

"What sort o' minister would agree to such a thing?"

"Oh, they're all grapplin' fer the chance. One Anglican by the name o' Whitley will most likely be granted the new church."

"I don't believe you!"

"Ask the man, yerself, then." McGrath grew impatient, his weariness with Prentice evident. "You wouldn't want to accuse a man o' the cloth o' swindlin', now would you? So, do you plan to starve, or do you want a share in the deal?"

"I need more time to think!" Sweat popped out along George's brow.

"No more time, Prentice. Now or never."

"Well . . . if Reverend Whitley thinks it will help the colony. . . ."

"I thought you'd see it my way," McGrath sneered.

Rachel stood flat against the wall in the front room of the Prentice shanty. Coming in from a futile morning of searching for wild berries, she had entered quietly upon hearing the man's loud voice. Standing in shocked silence, she had listened to McGrath's entire proposal. She never would've believed that George Prentice would agree to such madness, let alone Heath Whitley. *I don't understand, Lord.* Tears coursed down her cheeks. *Have all your people gone insane?* She had developed a trust in the Prentices, and their shared faith had became a bond. Watching Katy slowly lose hope had been difficult enough. *But George and Amelia? Never would she have believed it!* She shook her head slowly. Remembering the integrity that Whitley had instilled in her, she felt sick at heart. *Are they all frauds, Lord?*

Stepping quietly to her mat in the corner, she mentally assessed how long it would take her to gather her clothing inside the roll. She could offer a weak excuse to George and depart. *Wadjiri.* Remembering the Gagudju tribe, she knew in her heart where she belonged. *I've known all along.* She entreated, "I'll live among them, Father. I'll die among them if need be. Just take me away from the deceit of your people. I can't bear the grief." Rachel slipped quietly through the front door and made her way to the field where the laborer sat taking a rest upon the ground. Composing herself, Rachel wiped her face with her apron. "William," she called. "I've some—wonderful news!"

"Whatever is it, Rachel? I could use a bit o' good news." Arising at once, William stood and dusted off his hands.

"You know how long I've prayed for the aborigines?"

William's bushy brows lifted as he crossed his arms at his waist. "You've mentioned them, among others."

"I'm taking the tribe some of our medicine."

"What? They'll murder you! George'll never stand for it!"

"I knew you'd have trouble understanding. But God has given me peace about it. I'm wanting to master their language, their customs, everything I can learn. I want to teach them God's Word."

"Alone?" William's face filled with fear.

"The Gagudjus are peaceable people."

"So peaceable they stole a farmer's cow an' killed 'is son in the process."

"But they trust me. God has given me favor with them."

William shook his head. "Talk to George. Talk to Reverend Whitley . . . o-or your friend, what's 'is name—Corporal Holmes. They'll all talk some sense into you, girl."

"I'm tired of everyone's talk." Rachel heaved a heavy sigh. "I have no use for their words. Can you understand this?" Her eyes grew misty. "I must find reality in my faith. Somewhere there has to be purity . . ." She stopped, fearing she would divulge what she knew of the corps plans.

"What's gone wrong?" William asked suspiciously.

"I have to understand what I really believe in. I have to seek God for myself and not shape my faith upon another man's hearsay."

William turned his face, looking sideways. "Rachel, somethin' 'as 'appened, I kin tell. May as well spill it all out to me."

Rachel shook her head. "It's me. I've made a grave error."

"Whatever is it?"

"I placed my faith in others instead of God. When their world was shaken, then so was mine."

"It's me an' George, ain't it? We failed you, didn't we, Rachel? Without Amelia, me an' George is poor company."

"You could never fail me, William. I've failed myself. But I have to make some changes." Rachel observed the apprehension in his eyes. "Please don't worry about me. I promise, I'll be back again—soon. It won't be long, I'm sure."

William, not knowing what to say, fixed his eyes on the young woman who had become like a sister to him. Nodding slowly, he conceded, "I'll not stand in yer way, then. My prayers go with you. May we at least send provision with you?"

Rachel smiled. "I'd be grateful. But we already have so little here."

"Wheat bread, lentils, a bit' of homemade jam an' some water, Rachel. The Lord does provide. You'll need an extra blanket sleepin' in the out o' doors like that." William's brows pinched together in worry again.

"Now, don't you start," Rachel fretted. Glancing up she saw that George emerged from the back of the shanty. His countenance could not disguise the guilt he bore in his soul.

"William, I needs to talk to you." His eyes possessed uncertainty.

Rachel, fearing her face would betray the disappointment she felt for his decision, turned to go back inside the kitchen. "I'll go and make a small basket of food for myself." Turning toward the shanty, she could hear the discussion between George and William—George calling himself a *distributor* for the Corps. His words fell upon her ears like tears of sorrow as she walked away from the only real life she had ever known to face the wilds of the outback all alone.

The middle-aged barrister from West London stood stoking the fire that blazed inside his hearth. He was a reticent gentleman of medium build and sported a handsome beard. He heaved a sigh and placed the stoker back into the iron canister. Turning to his wife, who sat sobbing upon a tapestried couch, he commented gravely, "What do you want me to do? Tell me, Alice, and I'll see that it's done."

Alice, her face streaked with tears, looked up at her husband. She was a young woman of twenty-three, slender, with flashing brown eyes that resembled those of her now-deceased sister, Betsy. Folding the letter sent to her by Betsy's emancipist friend, she spoke dubiously, "We've a duty to her,

Francis. She's been murdered, and you and I know the culprit."

Tapping his fingers to his thick bottom lip, Judge Francis Gwaltney deliberated. "But to prove such a thing is another matter altogether, my love. To begin an investigation here in England would stir the eagle's nest. He mustn't know we suspect a thing." Gwaltney pursed his lips, stroking his peppery beard. "His craftiness at such matters has proven to be vast—political connections, ties with Parliament, probably with hell itself."

"We have ties, as well, Francis."

"True. But they're honest ones—and naive compared to his den of thieves."

Tucking a strand of auburn hair inside her neat coiffure, Alice persisted. "What then? I refuse to accept defeat."

"There's another alternative. But it would take much time. . . ."

"Tell me, Francis!"

"We must travel to New South Wales. It would be, in the minds of our friends and loved ones, the proper thing to do—to visit the grave of your sister."

"I can be packed in a day!" Alice spoke ardently, a fixed determination in her gaze.

Francis, always dutiful to his profession, shook his head and contended, "Give me a week to make arrangements with the court. I'll request a temporary leave for personal reasons."

"Judge Fortner will suspect?"

"But he'll be here in London—and we'll be far away in Sydney Cove."

Alice stood, her gentility apparent, and strode to her husband's side. Sliding her arms around his waist, she smiled up with gratitude and adoration. "You're so good to me, Francis. Do I tell you enough how much I love you?"

"I never tire hearing of it. You're the brightest spot in my dreary world."

"I wish that Betsy could've known you. She would be so fond of you—somehow I know it."

"If she was half the woman you are, I'm sure she must've been a courageous young girl."

"Yes," Alice thoughtfully considered. "Betsy was courageous. But it was her faith that sustained her. Oh that I could convey my faith to others as she did. The world may never know of her existence, but time will surely reveal the lives touched by her compassion."

"We'll know how true that statement is soon enough."

"Yes," Alice smiled. "I'm certain God used Betsy's faith as a torch to light the darkness in that colony."

Francis and Alice Gwaltney gazed into the flaming hearth, their need for retribution kindled and their destiny altered by one letter from a faithful ex-convict. They never suspected that the hand of the one who penned the regretful news now faced her own unsettling future, or that she, Rachel Langley, would soon unwittingly hold the key that would solve the mystery of Betsy's murder—a key that would brand her the assassin's next target.

18
Down by the Billabong

A wind picked up, and a long-forgotten scent caressed the air—the smell of rain. The sound of a muffled distant thunder caught Rachel's ear, and a trickle of hope sparked her thoughts. "Please send the rains, Lord." She glanced toward the south. The black cloud bank rising on the horizon moved slowly, but without doubt it drew near to the bush country.

Hastening her trek along the dried-up billabong, Rachel quickly checked the fastener on her basket and decided to quicken her gait. Following the meandering stream bed, she felt she could locate the tribe again, but also realized the drought might possibly have sent the wandering nomads farther inland. She thought if she crossed the open stretch of land following the familiar monoliths, she could possibly relocate the cave before nightfall. *At least inside the cave, I'll find shelter*.

The thunder resounded, but the rains were withheld as though by nature's selfish hand. With much relief, Rachel located the parched clearing and followed the monoliths, which stood like stone guardians to the outback. Tripping in her skirt, she reached with resignation and pulled the trailing hem between her legs, and then fastened the edge in her front waistband. "No harm in this," she asserted. "There's no one around to judge fashion." The trek into the wild took most of the day, but the incoming clouds brought occasional cooling relief to the desert air.

After many hours, Rachel's soles began to wear through and the temptation to guzzle down the precious water grew immense. Spying a familiar grove of wattles and large boulders on the horizon, Rachel blew out a relief-filled sigh and trudged wearily for another hour. Nearing the outcrop at last, she stumbled toward the cave entrance and found, as she had suspected, the tribe had moved on, leaving nothing behind but a pile of animal bones. Undaunted, she prepared for her first evening in the wilds alone.

Before stepping inside the cave, Rachel saw small wisps of dust rise as the first drops of rain hit the thirsty, parched earth. She smiled faintly and, using the chiseled sticks from her basket, relit the deserted campfire with her reddened hands and made her bed beneath a tribal mural that honored ancient animal totems.

The darkened sky lit brilliantly, rousing the desert with the drum of thunder and unleashing the bowels of the pregnant skies. Within hours, the drought had abandoned its cruel vigil, having been tamed by the welcome rains that fell like veils of prayer upon the wilderness.

The dawn found Katy rummaging through the bureau drawers. She lifted each piece of her clothing, inspecting the pockets. Her share of the monthly rent had come due and was now outstanding. Her fingers trembling, she examined with great anxiety the pockets and even the lining of a wool jacket, but the search proved profitless when the pockets yielded no money. Her emotions rising with the same intensity as her pounding headache, she yanked the drawer from the bureau and dumped it upside down. Her apparel tumbled onto the weathered floor, scattering puffs of dust around her feet.

"Where is all my money?" Her voice was accusing and loud, rousing Lorna from her early morning sleep.

"What?" Lorna muttered drowsily. "What's 'at?"

Turning reproachfully toward her unsuspecting roommate, Katy charged, "I *know* I hid money in this drawer, Lorna!"

Rubbing her eyes, Lorna's brow furrowed. Her face grew cross as the reality of Katy's accusing tone stirred her sensibilities. "What are you sayin'? That Lorna would take your money?"

"You're the only one besides me who lives here."

Her temper now fully ignited, Lorna sat upright. "You've no right, Katy Prentice! I ain't a bloomin' thief!"

"I had the money in this drawer! I know—I remember!"

"How could you remember? You were so drunk last night, you didn't know your own name!" Lorna's large eyes grew moist.

"I wasn't drunk!"

"Look at your dress, Katy!" Lorna beseeched. "Just take a look at yourself!"

Katy, her trembling hands outstretched, gazed woefully down at the wrinkled cotton dress she had slept in. She had donned it only—*last night? Or had it been yesterday morning?* Her thinking muddled, she staggered to her bed and braced herself against the rickety headboard. Lowering herself carefully onto the mattress, she sat in a silent stupor as reality pounded through her senses. "I . . . I'm sorry, Lorna. I . . . I've misplaced the money for the rent. Please forgive my . . . inconsistencies. I'll get it all straight by this afternoon . . . I promise you that."

Lorna swallowed fearfully, not fearing for herself, but for the young woman she had grown to admire. "Let someone 'elp you, Katy."

"I don't need anyone's help!"

"What about Mr. Farrell? He cares so much for you. . . ."

Jerking her face toward Lorna, Katy's cheeks grew pale. "Dwight mustn't know! Do you hear me, Lorna?"

"Yes, but—"

"I promise! No more drinking for me. I'll not touch another drop." Katy stretched a mirthless smile across her face, her gaze wooden. "Rum's easy to put down. Just something I've needed for the pain in my legs. I'm getting better now." She took a step but faltered without the aid of her cane. "I've a good life. . . ." She began to sob as she fell in a heap upon her bed.

"You do, Katy. Much better'n me own. But please tell Dwight Farrell. He can help you."

"No!" Katy's anger lashed at Lorna without mercy. "And don't you interfere! I warn you, I'll deny every word. You'll be labeled a liar by all!"

"You don't mean what you're sayin', Katy." Lorna broke into tears. "You're a right fine lady I've been proud to call me friend."

"Stop it!" Lorna's words sent a wave of guilt through Katy, goading her anger. "I can't bear your sniveling assertions. Now"—she straightened herself—"I'm going to change my clothes and find a ride into town for work."

"But this is only Saturday, Katy."

"I . . . I'm well aware of what day this is. I've no alternative except to find additional work. Perhaps one of the merchants will see my plight and offer me some task for pay."

"Why not ask for an advance from the gov'ment job? They'd surely do that for you."

Katy bit her lip. For she was already behind by two advances and couldn't possibly ask for more. "I'll take care of my own matters, Lorna. But if the landlord comes by, tell him I'll drop by the first of next week to settle the matter with him. Will you do that for me, at least?"

Lorna nodded, her sad eyes revealing the pity she held for Katy.

Katy turned to retrieve her clothes. "I've made a foolish mistake, Lorna, that's all. I'll have the matter corrected before Monday." She stretched a smile across her face. "You'll see."

The sky had emptied itself of the long-awaited deluge, raining torrents for the remainder of the night. The nearby stream babbled with the new life the rains had brought, and morning cascaded through the weeping paperbarks in misty golden shades. Rachel arose early to stoke the fire and stepped stiffly outside the cave to rest herself and tend her sore feet.

Using her ragged stockings for bandages, she wound the fabric around her throbbing, blistered feet. She had applied an ointment to the sore places the evening before, but the pain had caused her to sleep restlessly upon the mat. Slipping her bandaged feet back into the worn-out shoes, she lifted the empty water container and trudged toward the billabong.

The ground was sticky, and the downpour had left the air humid, but not unpleasant. Rachel glanced warily around the tranquil surroundings, limping slightly as she went. Although at first her mind had been solely upon Wadjiri and his tribe, she now felt the loneliness of the wild closing in on her and battled the nagging impulse to return to Parrametta.

But to return to a land she had never called home seemed futile, and further, she was unable to block out George Prentice's traitorous deal with the junta or Heath Whitley's compromise of his ministry. Perhaps living in the wild offered a pardon for her troubled meditations. In time, she knew she would be able to lay those thoughts to rest as she dealt with the needs of the Gagudju.

Rachel was bewildered to realize she thought very little of Bryce Holmes, but was sorry she had not offered him a proper farewell. But she couldn't pretend to love him, and she knew when she encountered him again, she would be forced to confess the truth.

Nearing the stream, she could once again see the quiet reflections of the tree-lined waters. Rainwater covered the rocks that lined the billabong, while crystal droplets trickled melodiously from the trees and rippled the surface into a myriad of concentric rings. Suddenly a distant drumbeat pounded across the rain-drenched land, and Rachel recognized the rhythm of aborigine jubilation. She determined at once to collect sufficient water for the day and then, sore feet or not, hike farther down the shallow waterway to investigate. Kneeling at the water's edge, Rachel submerged the canteen, wishing she had brought more containers to fill. Spying a large fish drifting lazily within her grasp, she froze, calculating the distance. Not carrying a weapon, she would be forced to use her wits and bare hands to capture her breakfast. Remembering a technique used by Wadjiri's friends, she scooped a tiny fish in her grasp.

Rachel didn't notice the enormous reptile that waited in the bush beside her, for she, unlike the tribal women, wasn't disciplined in the ways of the outback. The hungry crocodile stretched out across the grassy patch, blending in with the gray-green of the landscape. The carnivore's perception that the rains brought new prey to the water hole was instinctive, and it waited with sage patience until time to strike. Ambush being the reptile's greatest strength, the crocodile did not stir or even blink as its victim sat poised within a few feet of it. It could wait for days without any movement, if necessary. Rachel hovered steadily, luring the large barramundi toward her clasped hand. The captured fingerling quivered outside her fist, the perfect lure for the large fish whose sense of smell was poor.

As the barramundi kept her attention, the crocodile began to ease toward her with soundless adroitness. The powerful jaws unhinged, exposing jagged teeth, and the crocodile narrowed the gap between the prey and the land.

A clever smile graced Rachel's lips as the barramundi targeted the squirming fingerling and opened its mouth. Pressing her lips together squeamishly as the fish prepared to swallow her hand, Rachel was unaware of the predator that crouched, poised to attack her from the flank.

Rachel felt the coldness of the gluttonous barramundi as it gulped her hand inside its wide mouth and worked its way around her wrist. With her left hand free, she snatched the slippery body while snapping her fingers inside through the gills. Lifting the startled fish out of the water, she froze when a low, guttural growl resounded behind her. The crocodile lunged for Rachel as she jerked around quickly, her mind in shock. An animalistic scream—strong, intrepid—rang across the billabong, sending a flock of pink cockatoos shrieking into the trees. *"Yak-ai! Yak-ai! Yak-ai!"* A male youth's treble-pronged spear caught the ambushed beast under a leg and penetrated to the heart. Rachel, paralyzed by the horror, could offer no sound.

The tribal youth was surrounded by frenzied boys who screamed and shrieked while lunging for the reptilian body. *"Ginga! Ginga!"* The crocodile reared its head, slashing ferociously with its gnarled tail as another lad drove his weapon into the exposed underbelly of hide. Then a third young spearman fell upon it, driving a shovelnose tip to the base of the spine. A loud snapping and grinding of bone cracked through the air, and the crocodile fell limp—a dragon slain by children.

The boys, after pulling their weapons free from their quarry, turned to look upon the dumbfounded Englishwoman who stood holding a large, wriggling barramundi in her grasp. A boy stepped forward, his eyes alight. "Ra-chel!"

Not knowing whether to laugh or cry, Rachel felt a soft laugh escape her lips while tears salted her cheeks. "Wadjiri!" Her voice trembled, but the elation was evident. "You're alive!"

Walking slowly toward her with his spear snugged loosely under his arm—a woomera dripping with blood—Wadjiri made hand gestures, and then stepped forward to grasp Rachel's hand. Her legs trembling beneath, Rachel smiled with great relief.

Wadjiri lifted her hand to touch his head and then his chest. In an effort to communicate his message, he pressed her hand over his heart and repeated the words he remembered from the woeful day on the coal bed. "God—heal—Wadjiri!"

Rachel smiled, nodding agreeably. "Yes, I believe you're right. God—heal—Wadjiri." She extended the fish to him. "For you, Wadjiri. Thank you, Wadjiri."

Eagerly taking the fish, the boy mimicked, "Thank you, Wadjiri."

While the chattering boys dragged the slaughtered crocodile aside to divide its carcass among themselves, Rachel finished the task of securing water in the canteen. She watched with interest while a younger boy waded silently into the water, his fishing spear poised above his shoulder. Although one fish bolted at his sudden appearance, he stood rigid for a long space of time and waited. Soon another fish came swimming toward him. When it nibbled at the algae around his feet he did not stir. Then as the fish turned slowly, the boy, without a word, thrust the spear into the water, piercing through the glistening black body. The jubilant boy babbled excitedly, lifting his catch over his head. Wrapping her skirts above her knees, Rachel waded out to the lad. She gestured to him, indicating that she would like to try the spear. The boy laughed and plucked the fish free. The woomera was not a woman's tool, but Rachel persisted as the other boys and Wadjiri gathered on shore to laugh at the foolish female.

Hefting the spear as she had carefully observed, Rachel lifted her fingers to her lips to quiet the boys. All was still as she stiffened her frame and prepared to strike. She spotted several black shadows gliding beneath the water's surface toward her. The boy beside her was motionless, but a critical smirk marked his gaze. Rachel resisted the urge to lunge, waiting until the cylindrical form rested in her shadow. Without a blink, she drove the spear into the water, and her feet slipped from underneath her. The fish school scattered in all directions, sending the lad next to her into a fit of hysteria. In mocking tones, he called to his comrades on the shore, obviously deriding the Englishwoman's nerve.

Her hair dripping with water, Rachel lifted herself from the pool, the spear still held tautly in her grasp. With a smile of satisfaction, she lifted the weapon over her head with both hands—an enormous barramundi flailed furiously around the sharp prong. Wadjiri, the first boy to react, leaped excitedly in the air, his favor for Rachel evident. "Ra-chel!" he cheered.

The other young males bantered back and forth in wonder at the strange occurrence. Rachel felt the confident swell of acceptance as the boys gathered around her to assist her to shore. One of the boys took the spear with the fish and danced about, waving the trophy jubilantly.

Rachel found a resting place beneath a spreading coolibah

tree near the stream. Leaning against its trunk, she wrung the water from the hem of her skirt. Her weary eyes glanced around her, determined not to be startled again by a crocodile or any other beast for that matter.

She straightened herself upright, intent on following the heroic young hunters back to their encampment. Then an object, faded blue, caught her eye. Cautiously thrusting her hands into a cassia bush, she separated the golden stalks which partially hid the object from view. Reaching gingerly, she gripped the article, finding it to be a book of some sort. "It can't be!" Her voice low, she stared with disbelief. The book's origin was unmistakable.

She glanced toward the stream, her eyes following the curving current. Brushing wet debris from the cover, she opened the small journal and squinted at the scrawled, faded writing—most of it now illegible. But she knew the handwriting as well as her own and read aloud the name still legible on the front page—"Betsy Brady," Rachel whispered. Her brow furrowed, she closed the journal as though she held a hallowed writ. Securing the diary under her arm, she turned to join the Gagudju boys on their trek toward the tribal encampment.

19
THE CONSPIRACY

Reverend Samuel Marsden, looking fine seated in his black open-topped carriage, held tightly to the reins as the matched team of black steeds strained hard to the right. Pulling onto the property, he could see the shanty ahead where the property owner, an Irish emancipist, lived with his wife and seven children. The hovel was a ramshackle affair without windows, and the front door hung precariously by one rusted hinge.

Seeing the run-down state of the house gave rise to an odd reaction—Marsden chuckled under his breath, and a gleam of pleasure shone from his eyes. As he neared the shack, two large boys who were lolling near the front entrance rose lethargically from their repose as the younger children cowered to the side of the house in apprehension of the stranger's arrival.

"Whoa," Marsden called out blandly. Placing his stout

hands upon his knees, he smiled woodenly at the two boys. "Is your father about?"

The oldest boy, a ruddy-faced duplicate of his father, crossed his arms defensively at his waist and shrugged. "Who's askin', sir?"

Lifting his chin piously, Marsden glowered down at the lad. "Reverend Samuel Marsden." A humorless smile creased his heavy jaws. "Go and fetch your father now, boy—understand?"

The boy bit the side of his cheek, his eyes narrowing at the minister's tone. He backed away from Marsden as his brother hung tightly on his arm. "I have to find him first," he whispered.

Watching the boy disappear inside the house, Marsden waited longer than anticipated and found himself growing weary of the delay. Soon a thin woman, her hair pulled back in a severe knot, appeared from inside. When the children gathered around her, she shooed them away like flies on buttermilk. "Go on, now, and give me peace," she ordered, her eyes lifeless. Peering out from the shade of her hand, she spoke coolly to Marsden in a thick Irish brogue. "State your business, sir."

"Reverend Marsden, madam. I'm looking for the owner of this property—Isaiah McNeely?"

"Mr. McNeely's out in the barn, but he's in no mood for company."

The air grew thick, but Marsden persisted. "Mood or not, I have some business with the man." When the woman offered no assistance, Marsden leaned out to brake his carriage. "Very well, then. I'll take a stroll out to the barn." Lifting his heavy frame out of the carriage, he stepped onto the moist loam. He could see, beyond an abandoned vegetable patch, a weathered structure with most of the roof slats missing. Within a few minutes he stood inside the old barn, which creaked against a mild wind. "Hello? Anyone about?"

"Hmm." A low groan emanated from a pile of straw.

Marsden strode toward the sound, his thick brows pinched speculatively. Finding a man sprawled out in the hay, he shook his head in mock pity. He spied the empty bottle next to the man, a foul odor drifting up from where he lay.

"Mr. McNeely?" His tone was patronizing.

"Wha-what's that?" McNeely's words were slurred.

"Reverend Marsden here. Sorry to . . . disturb you at this time." The light of humor marked his gaze, but his tone was somber.

"Reverend . . . Reverend . . ." McNeely continued to mutter to himself while struggling to pull himself upright.

Marsden pulled out a small purse and shook it slightly. "I'm needing to conduct some business with you, sir."

McNeely rubbed his hands up over his cheeks and then across his bloodshot eyes. Smacking his lips, he said, "I need a drink first." He turned to retrieve his bottle but found not a drop inside.

"All gone, I'm afraid." Marsden shook his head sadly, although a faint, acerbic smile underscored his meaning. Taking a deep breath, he expounded pointedly, "Awake, ye drunkards, and weep; and howl, all ye drinkers of wine, because of the new wine; for it is cut off from your mouth."

"Cut off?"

"You see, Mr. McNeely. I believe you're at the end of your rope. The price of rum shot up a thousand percent today, along with the cost of grain. I trust you've set aside a little something to care for your ever-expanding family."

"A thousand percent? It's the Corps that's robbing us blind!"

"Not all the Corps," Marsden argued. "The military's doing the best they can muster under the circumstances."

Eyeing the purse that dangled from Marsden's stodgy hand, McNeely stroked his bristly jaw. "What's that ye be bringing me?"

"It all depends upon you. I'm prepared, as an act of service to your family, to relieve you of the burden of this land."

"Sell my land?" McNeely snarled and then cursed bitterly, spitting at the ground.

"To help your family, you'd best listen to my proposition." Marsden grew stern.

Coughing weakly, McNeely gripped the post that braced the ceiling and slowly pulled himself to his feet. Eyeing the minister suspiciously, he mumbled, "Go on, then."

"Five shining crowns to relieve you of this weight around your neck."

A low guttural laugh emanated from McNeely's throat. "You've gone mad to think I'd bargain that low."

"You won't find any other offers but mine. The colony's in a frenzy to survive—some are packing up and preparing to leave for England on the next ship out."

"Says who?"

"Go into town and find out for yourself if you can't believe a man of the cloth."

McNeely's hand began to tremble, and his face grew pale. Stroking his chin, he lowered his voice. "Does the man of the cloth have a drink on 'im?"

"Six crates of England's best rum in my carriage."

"Six?"

"All yours for the asking, Mr. McNeely." Marsden locked eyes with the Irishman and waited.

Drawing his fingers across his bottom lip, McNeely wheezed and then coughed again. "You're no man of God—you're the devil 'imself!"

"Now is that any way to treat a man who's offering you the moon? Perchance I'll just take the rum and leave. I'll dump it all in the ocean and relieve the colony of the plague of liquor." Holding his words, McNeely's eyes entreated pitifully. "But that isn't *really* what you want, is it?"

His lips pressed tightly, McNeely's brown eyes grew large, and then, hesitatingly, he shook his head. "N-no, sir."

Extending his hand, Marsden smiled shrewdly. "We have a deal then, Mr. McNeely?"

Extending a limp hand, McNeely nodded and then wrapped himself around the post in remorse as the bag of coins was tossed at his feet. "Deal," he sobbed quietly.

Feeling sure of himself, Marsden marched quickly to deliver the crates of rum to the Irishman's front porch.

Seeing the minister delivering the wooden containers to her door, Mrs. McNeely grew bewildered at the sight and demanded, "What's all this?"

"I've purchased your land, madam. I must ask that you vacate the premises in two days. I'll be bringing in some men to build the new homestead."

Her face colorless, Mrs. McNeely cried, "What's Isaiah done?"

"Nothing no other man in his position wouldn't do for his family. He's only thinking of you and the little ones, madam."

Spying the rum inside the crates, the woman shouted, "What kind of minister are you?"

Scowling impatiently, Marsden responded, "The very busy kind, madam. I've much to do, so"—he tipped his wide-brimmed hat—"please forgive me for running off so quickly." He shoved the sixth crate at the woman's feet and turned to climb into his carriage. He did not look back again and so did not see the pain etched in the woman's eyes or the waifs who clustered hungrily at her feet, thinking the minister had brought them bread and meat.

Pulling away from the property, Marsden's mind moved to concentrate on more important matters, such as the need for a permanent new church building for his growing flock of parishioners, and the fastest way to acquire it.

"How many new plots secured?" The light of greed reflected from Macarthur's charcoal gray eyes. He paced around the pallets that were stacked seven high in the cramped storeroom.

"Eight in Sydney Cove. But I'm not certain of Parrametta's status, sir. The emancipist hasn't sent word that I know of." Corporal McGrath gazed nervously.

"Emancipist?"

"Prentice. He's 'avin' qualms about the whole affair, Lieutenant. Says 'e's workin' on a bloke out in Parrametta, though."

Pulling a wrinkled letter from his coat, Macarthur smacked it soundly with the back of his hand.

"What's 'at, sir?"

"News from England. A governor's been secured—a fool I'm certain'll not bide long in this desperate settlement."

"Who's the bloke?"

"Another naval governor—Captain John Hunter."

"He's returnin'?"

"Soon. Very soon."

"Grose and Paterson know?"

"Aye. They'll have to relinquish their throne," Macarthur said darkly.

McGrath bent to lift the heavy crate of rum. "I'll take this'n out to the delivery wagon, sir."

Nodding pensively, Macarthur dismissed the corporal though scarcely aware the man had departed. His mind was roiling from the changes constituted beyond his control. He had accumulated two hundred fifty acres of land, a thousand crossbred sheep, and his granaries overflowed with eighteen hundred bushels of corn. Under Grose and Paterson his progress was limitless. Hunter, former captain of the First Fleet's *Sirius*, had been a devout naval loyalist to Governor Arthur Phillip. Hunter would be a difficult man to maneuver, but he hadn't faced the power of the New South Wales Corps. In Macarthur's estimation, the colony had flourished since Phillip's departure. To place authority back in the hands of the emancipists would be to take the settlement backward. *No,* he decided. Hunter must be persuaded to maintain the iron grip on the emancipists—whether through bribery or guile was of no great significance. *I'll not relinquish a crumb to the crawlers!*

Dwight Farrell stood outside Katy's shanty waiting for her to come to the door. Upon making several visits, he had found her to be quite ill each time, and he worried that she wasn't taking care of herself as she should. Remembering her the way she was the first day he saw her saddened his heart, and he longed for carefree days when they could put the horrors of the fire behind them.

"Katy?" he called out cheerily. "Mr. Farrell at your service." He gazed down at the picnic basket held firm in his grasp. "Picnic today. Lovely day for it."

Slowly, the door opened. Katy peered from behind the

door, her face colorless. "Is that—today's the day?" her voice faltered.

Tipping back his hat, Dwight looked at her with worry pinching his brow. "You're sick again?"

Pressing her lips together, Katy nodded.

"Let me come in. I want to take care of you." Dwight reached out to grasp her thin fingers.

Shaking her head, Katy closed the door a little farther. "No." Seeing the confusion in his gaze, Katy felt guilt flood her mind. "That is—thank you for your kind offer. But the house is in such a mess. I couldn't."

"Well then." Dwight placed the basket on the steps directly in front of her. "You 'ave to eat. I'll just leave this for you." Tipping his hat politely, Dwight sighed and turned to leave.

Katy stared down at the basket. From inside protruded a bright flower. *He picked it for me.* She looked up anxiously, fighting for the words that would bring him back. But none came, and she stood with remorse sweeping through her as Dwight Farrell rode away—alone.

Stooping to retrieve the picnic basket, Katy hefted it inside and left it on the table for Lorna. She had no appetite, and the bottle of rum from the night before had left a sour taste in her mouth. Passing by the cracked mirror, she stared in shock at her own reflection. Her hair was dull and hung like tendrils around her face. Her lips were pale and her eyes stared out lifelessly. She determined at once to clean up and put on a fresh dress. "A bath. That'll do the trick," she muttered to herself.

Stumbling to the bureau, she rummaged through her clothes but was surprised to find all of them soiled. When had she last done the laundry? She shook her head. "Wasn't that just yesterday?" But the pain in her head and her legs began to grow, and she found herself staggering to the bed again. Turning her face, she began to mentally count the bottles of rum left in the crate beside her bed. "Three. Enough for the pain," she decided with relief. "Enough for the pain."

Astride his mule, Heath Whitley rode along the road from Parrametta to Sydney Cove. He had attempted to pay a visit to Rachel Langley to see if she could be persuaded to assist him on his rounds. But to his dismay, George had informed him that the young emancipist had returned to her beloved outback. *Such a danger!* He worried that she, unacquainted with the wilderness, would perish within weeks. *Go after her, Whitley!* He chastened himself for not being more attentive to Rachel's situation. *No*. He argued with himself. *She needs this time away to think*. Rachel had been through a lot. She had been absolutely humiliated by the Thompson woman. He should've been the one to escort her home. Hadn't she made herself available for service at every turn? Rocking sick infants while their mothers battled fevers of their own, Rachel had emulated all he'd ever known a real servant of God to be. *Idiot, Whitley! You're an idiot!*

"Reverend Whitley?"

Glancing up, Whitley was surprised to see a carriage pulling up beside him. He had been so engrossed in his worries that he hadn't heard its approach. Lifting his face cordially, he tipped his hat to the man who reined his black steeds to a halt.

"Samuel Marsden, here." Marsden tipped his black brimmed hat in kind.

"Oh, hello, Reverend Marsden." Whitley forced a smile. "I must've been in deep thought not to have noticed you at once. Forgive me."

"Thinking of that new church building, eh, Whitley? Not every day that a minister is handed such a prize."

Crossing his arms in hesitation, Whitley chose his words carefully. "I, as you know, haven't formally accepted the offer of the building. I'm giving the matter more thought. I need time to pray."

"Hmph!" Marsden chuckled. "You've wrangled this new building for yourself with a greater power than prayer. You and I are both too shrewd to play games, Whitley."

"I don't know what you mean, I'm sure." Whitley's brow furrowed.

"Problem is"—Marsden's brows lifted—"what to do with it

once you have it. You've little experience in the ministry. Be a shame to see you founder under the pressure. That pretty little Thompson woman wouldn't stand for it, that's for certain."

Whitley could feel his anger kindle but refused to grow defensive. "You're a confused man."

"Oh no, I see things quite clearly, actually. You marry up with the lieutenant's daughter and you'll have the first real church in Sydney Cove. But what will you do when the Corps comes to collect? You don't have the experience to know how to deal with such shrewd men. History might record later—'Heath Whitley, founder of Australia's first church to flounder.'"

"It's true, my experience is with the church itself—God's people—not with politicians or military juntas. But you can bet I'll not use the church as fodder for my own selfish ambitions."

"I'm sure your statement wasn't pointed at me, kind sir. But as a warning—give it up, Whitley. Tell the Corps you aren't ready for such a venture. The church of Sydney Cove needs a strong leader to take her forward, not a man who mixes with blacks and emancipists."

His eyes lighting with an angry fire, Whitley felt his fist curling at his side. In a moment, he could jar the man from his seat with one blow. There was a time when to do so wouldn't have been a question in his mind. But he couldn't allow himself to stoop to Marsden's pathetic level. *I rue the day, Marsden, that I allow Sydney Cove to fall into the clutches of a snake like you*. A faint smile crossed his lips. "I'll accept the offer of the church and we'll see how history records it." Whitley whipped the mule quickly on the flanks. "Good day, Reverend."

"You're a bigger fool than I thought, Whitley. You'll go down with your puny little ship!"

Marsden's words echoed in Whitley's mind until the racket made by the rattling carriage wheels had disappeared with the rantings of the angry minister. Leading his animal to a pond to drink, Whitley dismounted and strode to stand beneath the shade of a sprawling myrtle. Just this morning he had made the decision to tell the Corps that he wished to refuse the offer. Now he had allowed a master manipulator to coerce him into a decision he had no intention of making. *But I can't allow your church to fall prey to such a vulture, Lord!* He argued with the thoughts that pricked at his conscience. Seating himself at the water's edge, Heath Whitley sprawled back upon the tall grass. He stared numbly at the white clouds that drifted overhead, reflecting like cotton in the mirrorlike water. After a moment's speculation, he whispered. "What do I do now, Lord?"

20
THE LURE

Dressed in a worn calico overdress, Katy sat stiffly in Lieutenant Simons' post. She had been tardy to her work on most mornings, and the reprimands were coming more frequently. With her head throbbing and her extremities having fallen quite numb, it took an effort of will to ignore the pain and sit with quiet composure.

In the beginning, she had joined the government's work force as an assistant to a naval lieutenant, managing his correspondence and completing the written orders and reports that were shuffled around for England's welfare. Her recommendation from Governor Phillip had opened doors to her that wouldn't have transpired otherwise. But her frequent absences had eventually caused her to be demoted to the government stores—a task she loathed.

"Where were you this morning, Miss Prentice?" Simons queried gruffly, his ice blue eyes sending an unsettling pall over her senses.

"At home. I . . . I overslept." Katy's words came slowly. "I'll not allow it to happen again, I assure you of that."

"You've promised on numerous occasions to improve. I daresay you're making promises you cannot keep."

Allowing her head to rest in her hands, she grew defensive. "No, please believe me, I cannot lose this position. I'll do whatever it takes to stay on in the stores—sir." Gazing up apprehensively, Katy felt a twinge of anxiety as the man glowered down at her.

"You'll do whatever it takes?" Simons' smile held no humor, but derided her words as a spurious defense.

Katy nodded, resisting the urge to take leave of the entire situation. For she was bound by one motive—the need to survive, which forced her to take the daily beratings dealt out by the officers upon all the employees of the stores.

"I suppose you realize that the favor you've found with me is the only reason you've been allowed to remain on with the stores."

Her brow furrowed, and Katy shook her head. "No, sir. I *wasn't* aware . . ."

"It is for this reason, I am willing to strike a deal with you . . . my dear." His words grew strangely softer, although far from gentle.

Confusion marked her gaze, and her legs were beginning to throb. "What kind of—deal?"

Simons stepped toward her, his boots striking the wooden floor in deliberate sequence. He stood before the young woman with an autocratic air, his thick lip jutting out. "You were a defiant young woman when you came in here, weren't you, Miss Prentice? Thinking your connection with Phillip placed you above all others?"

Anger now rose in Katy's face and replaced her prior humility. "What is your point, Lieutenant Simons?" she retorted crossly.

"Now you grovel for the least little crumb. What has happened to you?"

"You've no right to hurl your insults, Lieutenant! I'm just a little down on my luck. If you've no work for me here, I'll find it elsewhere." Katy rose slowly in preparation to depart, leaning heavily on her cane.

"But all work is controlled by the paymaster now—or haven't you heard?"

"Not all. There are some emancipists who fend for themselves." Her gaze deliberate, she mustered a remnant of courage. "I'll not be controlled!"

"*All* the emancipists are dependent on the stores. Why even your own father is a liaison for the Corps. George Prentice trades corps rum for emancipist land. Don't tell me he didn't tell you—his own daughter?"

"Papa wouldn't do such a thing!"

"People change, Miss Prentice. You're a prime example of that. Why you'd sell your own soul right now for a bottle of rum—isn't that correct?"

Her throat tight, Katy could form no words, and braced herself with stiffened arms upon the wooden chair arms. Slowly lowering herself, she seated herself again as her emotions roiled. "No," she answered quietly, her eyes cast to the floor.

"You're lying!" Simons reached out with sinewy arms and gripped Katy roughly. "You'll do anything I ask—just for one drink." His eyes narrowed, and his intent became evident as he jerked her toward himself. "You're a drunkard! Admit it!"

"No!" Katy shrieked and then tried to pull away from him. "God help me, I'm not!"

A strange pity marked Simons' gaze and he slackened his grip but did not loose her. "If you allow, I can salvage this entire situation for you."

Lifting her face, now soaked with tears, Katy regarded Simons' smile with an air of interest, but there was something behind his gaze that shook her sensibilities. "I appreciate your offer, but I'll not be made an object of charity, Lieutenant." Her words were broken.

"No, no, my dear. Not charity." Simons gazed into her eyes and spoke quietly. "Security."

"How do you mean?"

"First of all you'll need new living arrangements. That

hovel of yours is a disgrace—what would Governor Phillip think?"

Katy glanced uncomfortably at his hands, which still maintained their grip on her upper arms. Her eyes gazed into his, full of confusion.

"You'll come to live with me, and I'll care for you in the manner in which you're accustomed. I'm a corpsman, and as my mistress, your every wish will be met at your bidding."

"No, Lieutenant!" Katy was desperate but couldn't bend to such a level—not even for security.

Loosening his grip, Simons reached slowly to stroke the back of her blond curls which fell around her shoulders. "Don't be hasty, Katy Prentice. *I* know how to care for a woman of your standing. You need certain "things" to keep you happy—true?"

"No, I do not!" Katy denied the accusation although the pressures of her financial situation weighed heavily on her.

Turning slowly, Simons reached for a carafe of gin. Pouring it carefully into a glass, he kept a watchful gaze on Katy's face. "We are the keepers of the colony. We are the rum lords." He held the glass out to Katy, allowing the fragrance to permeate her senses. "Only one sip—mustn't drink too much now."

Katy gripped her hands at her side and planted her feet as though resisting the urge to plunge off a cliff. She inhaled, and the aroma of the gin whetted her unquenchable thirst for alcohol. "I . . . I'm not thirsty," she lied.

"Now, now," Simons chastened as though he were scolding a child. "I said only one sip."

Katy, penniless for two weeks, had gone through a nightmarish withdrawal, her body begging all night for the liquor. Weary of the turmoil and deceit, Lorna had moved out. Katy had struggled alone with her self-destruction, shunning even the friendship of Dwight Farrell. And he, thinking she had lost interest, departed for the last time. Every day had become a struggle. Each step she took a reminder of her disability—both physical and mental. The headaches were frequent and her legs ached continuously. Now she could all but taste the liquor again as Simons wagged the glass beneath her nose.

One sip, she assured herself. With trembling hands, she gripped the glass on both sides. "Just one." She dared not look the man in the eye.

"That's a good girl." His strategy complete, Simons' eyes lit with the satisfaction of control. "Simons will give you everything you need."

His hair matted with sweat, Whitley shot up from his bed, the nightmare still clear in his mind. The war lived on in his subconscious, and the violence of his days as a soldier had melded with his dreams, invading his sleep. A memory still nagged at him.

During the war, the French revolutionaries had surprised his outfit, their ways of war rudimentary, but effective. An armed soldier, dressed in ragged attire and no less a boy than himself, had leaped on him with vengeful hatred. He wrestled tirelessly at first—his cunning matched against the young man's zeal. But as the match wore on, he pinned the revolutionary to the ground, snapping his enemy's own dagger from his belt to use against him. The young man did not flinch, but gazed courageously up as though dying were a privilege.

It was then that Corporal Heath Whitley hesitated too long. Perhaps he was taken in by the soldier's courage, or perhaps the young man's cause was more evident than his own. But nonetheless, the hesitation gave the lad the opportunity to retaliate. The soldier's reflexes swift, the dagger was knocked from Whitley's grasp with a blow from the right. Being caught off guard, he felt himself being thrown to the ground, and the soldier was quickly assisted by a zealous comrade. He could not overcome two soldiers. The young men, covered in the blood of Whitley's comrades, pinned him as victory rose in their throats. The bloody bayonet being plunged toward his skull, Whitley retaliated with a wild right hook as his body twisted to parry the cold steel. The hostile blade bit into his cheek, but curved as the peel of musket fire roared overhead, ending the lives of the two young revolutionaries.

For what seemed like hours, he lay next to the lifeless corpses, and a strange pity swept over him. With eyes closed, he listened to the sound of foreign cries as the French began their body count. He wasn't informed until later that his entire unit had been negated, save for himself. The soldiers lying next to him were dragged away, and he silently listened to the mourning cries over the lives of his enemy. As a good soldier, he could not pity the deaths of those who attempted to slay him, but he envied their zeal.

It was then that God had spoken to him, and he had answered silently as the enemy encamped around his wounded body. *Give me a reason to live, dear God—a zeal and purpose as fierce as that young man's.* As the stench of war and revolution enveloped his senses, the peace of God poured over his soul, and a revolution occurred in his own heart.

Resting his feet over the side of his bed, Heath remembered his vow to God. He had not promised to build a monument to God, nor to fill his own life with the security of wealth. Nor had God demanded those things from him—He only desired simple obedience. No lure of a lovely socialite wife, a new church building, or an instant congregation could deter him from his mission—to make disciples.

Reverend Heath Whitley pulled his suspenders over his shoulders and staggered to the wash basin to douse his face. To deliver the decision he purposed to make would cast a hindrance on Felicity's plans, and would render him a target of contempt among the gentry. But his conscience would be clear and his focus true—he would preach to the ears that would hear the message of Truth.

The silence of the bush had been shattered for days by the shrieks and cries of warring savages. Rachel waited pensively inside the cave with the tribal children and some of the women as nearby the Gagudju clan clashed with their hated enemies—the Mulunguwa.

Days prior, the Gagudju warriors—both men and women—had gathered at the first blush of dawn with clubs, spears, and boomerangs in hand and marched into the natural arena of bush the elders of both clans had selected for the *Banburr*—a ceremonial *corraborree* at which grudges were settled in violent free-for-all battles. The *Banburr* had continued for three days, and the cries had begun to diminish, sending a wave of anxiety through those who waited behind in the cave wondering who had survived.

As echidna meat sizzled on the fire outside the cave's entrance, Rachel leaned back against the hard cave wall perusing Betsy's diary, as she had done for months. She kept referring back to a smudged, barely legible passage that Betsy must have written years ago in England, for it made reference to her survival of the hangman's noose. It read: *A horrible man comes by my cell each day but says nothing. He only stares coldly and then smiles as though he's glad to see I'm still here. I recognize him as being one of the detestable men who work for Uncle Cornelius. I'm certain he's spying on me. His name is* . . . Rachel squinted to decipher the name letter by letter. But all she could make out were the letters from the man's surname—*M-c-G-r*.

Pain-filled wails rose up beyond the mouth of the cave, shaking Rachel from her preoccupation. She stood, realizing her time inside the cave was drawing short, for when the clansmen and elders arrived from the battle, she would return to her lean-to, a short distance from the encampment. The elder, Marbunggu, had declared her presence bad luck since the day of the white man's slaughter and had ordered her death. The first day Rachel had entered the camp, surrounded by the jubilant boys ladened with crocodile meat, the elders had stood before her. Marbunggu had glowered vengefully at her. It was Wadjiri's uncle, also an elder, who had justified the importance of her life and kept her from being killed—it was her God's magic that had saved Wadjiri. At times she noticed Marbunggu's fierce son, Gurugul, glaring threateningly at her, causing her to sleep cautiously at night. As a result, Rachel had promptly decided to keep a distance between herself and the Gagudjus in order to rebuild their trust.

Being jolted from her remembrance, Rachel watched with dread as the first bedraggled warriors arrived. Her eyes followed Wadjiri, who scrambled to his feet when the first blood-soaked victim was dragged into the cave. "Miss Rachel!" Wadjiri grabbed her arm. "You fix 'im!"

"But, Wadjiri . . ."

"Come, Miss Rachel! You fix 'im!" Wadjiri persisted, his brown eyes pleading.

Rachel hadn't been allowed to offer any medical assistance since her arrival six months ago. Tainted with Marbunggu's denunciation upon her head, she was taboo to the clan, save for a few of the women who had befriended her during the *Banburr*.

The onlookers cleared the way for the wounded. Some were carried in, and others stumbled in on their own and collapsed. Soon the cave was filled with the stench of human sweat and blood and the moans of the injured.

Rachel knelt beside a woman she knew to be Wadjiri's aunt. "Wadjiri!" Rachel called anxiously to the boy. "Run and fetch my basket. Hurry!"

Wadjiri returned from Rachel's lean-to within minutes, toting the basket that brimmed with unused bandages and medicinals.

"Rachel fix 'im!" he shouted to the others and then translated quickly for those who considered Rachel's language taboo.

A protest sounded from across the cave. Marbunggu stirred from his place on the cave floor, his head bleeding from a blow to the skull. He waved at her with a broad hand as though he were ordering her to leave, muttering weakly.

Although Rachel had come to understand the fearsome authority of the elders, the urgency of the wounded loomed paramount. "No, Marbunggu!" She pointed to Wadjiri's wounded aunt. "Please! I fix her!"

With blood seeping across his brow, Marbunggu collapsed on the cool rock floor, unconscious, and Rachel set about immediately to clean the woman's wounds. As she wrapped a bandage around her forehead, she became aware of two large feet shifting beside her. Looking up, she saw straightaway the savage face of Gurugul scowling down at her. The rancorous aborigine had a large head with a brow that protruded in a ridge over his small black eyes. He towered above the other men and was known by all to have the devil's temperament.

A gasp escaped Rachel's lips, but she stood her ground. "I fix her," she said quietly but firmly. Her face did not flinch when the native bared his yellow teeth. Rather, she stared back, dauntless green eyes unwavering as she struggled to hide her growing contempt for the man.

Wadjiri ran to Rachel's aid, his rationale evident—Rachel must be allowed to save his aunt. But with one blow from Gurugul's swinging fist, he was sent reeling to the ground.

"No, please . . ." Alarm swept through Rachel as Wadjiri gazed up helplessly, his bottom lip bleeding. *You beast!* Her brows pinched contemptuously, Rachel stiffened her lip but held her words for the lad's sake.

Gripping his spear, Gurugul drew it back, his zeal to rid his clan of the white woman and her curse apparent.

"Gurugul!" Wadjiri's uncle limped into the cave, his own body splattered with the enemies' blood. Anger sparked from his eyes as he beheld Gurugul poised with the spear's *woomera* aimed at Rachel. But whether out of his respect for the son of Marbunggu or another unknown cause, savage propriety warranted that he choose a differing strategy. Motioning cleverly, he lured Gurugul from Rachel's side, commanding his assistance to carry in an injured clansman.

Rachel completed the dressing around the woman's wounds and stood to convey her medicine basket to the next victim. She worked hurriedly, her senses keenly aware of Gurugul's watchful scowl. Glancing toward him as he placed another injured warrior at the mouth of the crowded cave, she nodded respectfully and began pressing folded bandages into the spear wound of a young clansman's side. "Lord, touch this man and bring healing to him," she prayed, scarcely above a whisper.

Kneeling next to Marbunggu, Rachel was met again with the furious protests of Gurugul. She gazed across the cave, finding his blood red eyes narrowed menacingly. So, reluctantly, she left the dying man to tend another.

Without the aid of an assistant, time wore on slowly and did nothing to calm the trouble of her thoughts. She watched with dismay as the bandages and medicine gradually dwindled. She would be forced to return to the settlement for more medical supplies. Walking to the opening, Rachel felt her strength languish under the heat, which bore down with searing malevolence. The burden of the preceding weeks in the bush now tormented her previous fascination for the savages. They weren't as docile as she had first imagined—rather, they could be vicious, especially to one another. The women were trained from childhood to be nothing short of slaves to any man's whim. Wives were loaned as sexual favors to strangers of neighboring clans simply for the asking. Understanding their rudimentary language did not unlock the mysteries of their culture as she had supposed. Instead, she felt more confused about their superstitions than when she first arrived. *I'm useless to you, Lord.*

Rachel cringed as across the cave Marbunggu fell into a fit of violent coughing, sputtering red, gasping for his final breath. She shook her head sadly when the elder drifted into eternity, his wife shrieking demonically.

Turning to face Wadjiri, Rachel tenderly stroked the boy's cheeks. "How do I reach your people, Wadjiri?" she sighed helplessly, and a tear escaped her eye.

His brow furrowed, Wadjiri smiled curiously. "With your hand, Rachel." Grasping her fingertips, he held them out toward himself, displaying his meaning.

Rachel nodded. Wadjiri's explanation was clearer than even he had imagined. "Of course. What was I thinking?" A low chuckle softly spilled from her lips as she stooped to unwind another bandage spool.

21
The Stand

"You got 'im kind-heart hand. Good hand, Miss Rachel." Wadjiri swung his arm easily as he walked along the settlement's road with Rachel. "Bring white feller magic to Wadjiri's people."

Rachel sighed as she spotted the familiar row of trees ahead just as the sun disappeared. "I've tried to explain to you, Wadjiri—I don't conjure magic. What I gave the Gagudju is called *medicine*. And I pray. My God is the healer."

"Wadjiri's people pray to goddess who is our mother and to many animal gods. Who is white feller totem?"

"No totem. He is the creator God. The Father God who made all things." Rachel pulled loose wisps of hair from around her face, straightening her hair before she arrived at the Prentice farm.

"No, Miss Rachel. All things come out of before Dreamtime. Warramurrungundji come out of sea. She create land and give birth to all people. Ginga, crocodile, make all rock country; Marrawuti, sea eagle, bring water lilies in claws and plant along land."

"But where is Warra . . . Warra . . ."

"Warramurrungundji."

"Where is your goddess now, Wadjiri?" Rachel asked respectfully.

"She great white rock in woodland. Dreaming place full of great power."

"But the great white rock, the crocodile, the sea eagle—they were all made by the Creator—God the Father."

Wadjiri shrugged. "White totem different from Gagudju."

Weariness overtook Rachel, and she was decidedly too tired to debate Wadjiri about his heathen religion. "I'll tell you more about it later, Wadjiri. Right now I'd pay half a crown for a cold biscuit. I hope George is awake." She could see the light of a lantern ahead, but it came from the small barn and not the house. "George must be checking his livestock."

Seeing signs of life invigorated Rachel, and she quickened her pace. She and Wadjiri had slept on the ground in a wooded bower the evening before, making a lean-to of sticks and brush. Curling up with a soft blanket on a mat would be a welcome change. She breathed deeply as the cicadas hummed around them. Although not moonlit, the night was pleasant—sultry and fragrant.

As they neared the weathered barn, men's voices could be heard, but Rachel did not recognize them. Strewn around the entrance she saw amber bottles, empty and noxious. She slowed her pace and gestured for Wadjiri to remain silent.

"You're a coward, George Prentice, an' a loser!" a hoarse voice rang out.

Rachel, hearing the hostility in the man's tone, ran to the darkest outer wall of the barn and hid. Wadjiri crouched beside her, his spear poised.

"You'll starve to death without the corps aid! You might as well give up an' join us!"

"Prentice is a crawler, mates. He's no good to us. I say kill 'im!"

Rachel tensed when she heard the sound of harsh blows followed by Prentice's strained voice.

"You *can't* kill me!" George's breathing sounded labored, his tone weakening. "What'll me wife do? She needs me," he rasped, "to care for her!"

"I'll take care o' the wench. I been needin' a good woman to stoke me fire."

"You don't understand, you beast. . . ."

Loud laughter filled the air inside the barn as another beating ensued.

Pursing her lips, Rachel discovered a coarse rope that was hung from a nail beside her. She looked all around, her thoughts in a panic. Lifting the coil quietly, she motioned for Wadjiri to follow her.

George Prentice gazed up, his right eye swollen and red from the beating he had just taken. Macarthur's Corps had dispatched a gang of four *persuaders* to harass him into exploiting the landholding emancipists. Their duty was clear—*sway him or do away with him*. "I won't backstab me own neighbors! It ain't Christian!"

"Is it Christian to see your *sweet* little daughter sellin' 'erself just to pay for 'er rum?" A sardonic smile creased the lieutenant's face; his eyes gleamed with gratification.

George felt the anger rising and gripped his fists.

His eyes humorless, the lieutenant taunted Prentice, "Did you bring up yer daughter to wind up in the gutter?"

Prentice staggered to his feet, swinging violently at the man. "Don't speak o' me Katy, you lyin' swine!" He delivered a right hook to the man's jaw, sending him sprawling into the hay.

"Get the crawler!" another howled.

Two corporals jumped George while another, tipsy from his shared bottle of rum, lit a roll of tobacco and stumbled out into the night air with his rifle hanging loosely from its sling. Exhaling a cloud of smoke, he squinted out into the dark and staggered forward as his worn-out boot tripped against something rigid. "Blimey!" he bellowed, then cursed when his body slammed to the ground, his rifle tumbling from his grasp.

"Don't move, or you're dead!" Rachel threatened in a whisper. She dropped the rope she had stretched across his path while Wadjiri pressed the tip of his spear onto the back of the man's head. Grabbing his rifle, Rachel aimed it squarely at his head and whispered fiercely, "To your feet—now!" She kept the rifle trained on the corpsman.

Inside the barn, the lieutenant lurched to his feet as his two cronies pinned Prentice against a post. Drawing back with a vengeance, he drove into the emancipist with full force. "I'll kill you meself, Prentice!" Just as the corpsman came at Prentice again, Prentice lifted his boot to slam into the man's groin, but the two corporals yanked him fast and he was struck again, his cheek taking the brunt of it.

"Halt or I'll fire!"

Stunned by the threat of an intruder, the officers turned swiftly about as Prentice looked up dazedly, suspended limply by the arms. "Rachel! Don't . . ." His eyes wide, he suddenly cared nothing for himself.

"Set him free!" Rachel demanded, spying the rifles that were suspended from their slings on a post.

One of the corporals laughed uneasily. "Don't pull that trigger, pretty lass. You'll 'ang fer killin' military. It's the law now." His laugh was low and guttural.

Easing toward his weapon, the lieutenant warned in unsteady tones, "Give us the rifle, miss, an' no 'arm'll come to you."

Rachel, taking fast aim, shouted, "One more step and I *will* fire!" Her eyes narrowed and Wadjiri stood soldierly at her side, his spear aimed at the corpsman.

"Wiley!" the corpsman called out to his missing comrade.

"Is that his name?" Unflinching, Rachel replied flatly, "Sorry, your Mr. Wiley is occupied for the moment."

"We tie with rope," Wadjiri grinned.

"Whatever is the matter. . . ." William rushed in and his face paled at the sight of the battered and bruised George. "George!"

"Stay where you are, William!" George warned.

"No, William, grab those rifles!" Rachel gave no regard to Prentice's admonition. "Now let the man go, or you're dead, Lieutenant!"

The lieutenant studied Rachel's eyes, and a faint smile marked his gaze. "You can't kill anyone. You're that Langley girl wot's always workin' the contagion wards." He tossed his head mockingly and said to his companions, "She's 'armless, men!"

"Don't be a fool, Lieutenant!" Rachel felt her hands tremble, but she was fast to steady her aim.

Taking a pronounced step toward Rachel, the lieutenant's stature was galvanized and he paid no heed to her threats. "Give me the weapon, wench!"

"Halt!" Rachel felt her will weakening. She had killed a man once and vowed she'd never do it again. Her eyes moistened and the officer became a blurred image hastening toward her. *I can't pull the trigger, Lord!*

William, enfolding the other two weapons next to her, backed away as one of the corporals began making his way toward him. "Rachel, pull the trigger!"

The sound of rifle fire exploded in the barn, the smoke of gunpowder billowing toward the rafters. A shriek emanated from the lieutenant's throat and he stumbled backward. "She shot me! The wench shot me!"

Rachel, bewildered, gripped the tip of her weapon—*still cold!* "I . . . I didn't . . ."

"No! Not Rachel!" Another voice called stridently from behind them, near the barn's entrance.

"Caleb!" George grew dumbfounded at his son, who stood with feet planted firmly, his rifle tip smoldering.

Rachel stared with amazement. "*You* shot him?"

The lad strode defiantly toward the lieutenant who had buckled to the ground. "You ain't shot, scum!" He reloaded his rifle with agility and skill. "I shot your bloomin' hat!" He kicked violently at the lieutenant and pointed his weapon at his head. "An' I never miss what I aims at!" Gripping the trigger, he grinned, "*Now* I'm aimed at you!"

Grappling for his hat, the officer saw at once that the boy spoke the truth—his hat smoldered from a black bullet hole. "Don't fire again!" The lieutenant saw vengeance in the boy's face. "L-let go o' Prentice, men! Now!"

As Rachel and William confidently resumed their vigil

with the confiscated rifles, Caleb and Wadjiri aimed their weapons at the lieutenant.

Prentice staggered to Rachel's side and retrieved the rifle she had secured. Kissing her cheek fondly, he turned his attentions toward the corpsmen. "I want you to take a message back to your Lieutenant Macarthur."

Indignation rose in Caleb's face, his blue eyes fierce. "Papa, you can't let them go!"

"Quiet, son!" Prentice spoke firmly. "I want Macarthur to see how decent people behave. Now, all o' you corpsmen go back and tell Macarthur that we emancipists ain't dogs. We're landholdin' citizens o' New South Wales—an' plan to stay that way. We're God-fearin' and want to raise our children the same way—not as thieves or murderers like the lot o' you."

"I agree, George," Rachel nodded anxiously.

The lieutenant gaped up at Prentice, an aborigine's blade at his throat and a Winchester rifle aimed at his brow. He shrugged agreeably, but hatred seethed from his eyes.

Prentice persisted, his eyes fired with a patron's wrath. "If you return as you did tonight, we *will* defend our families an' our land! Understood?"

The corporals nodded, tight-lipped.

His teeth gritted, Caleb repeated angrily, "Do you understand, scum?" He cocked his rifle threateningly, tossing his blond hair over one brow.

"Easy, boy." The lieutenant held up his hands palms out and indicated that he understood. Gazing cautiously back at Prentice, he forewarned, "Macarthur ain't one to strike no deals, Prentice."

"I'm makin' no demands. Just leave us alone!"

A corporal warned, "You'll all starve. . . ."

"Shut up!" Caleb yelled.

"It's all right, Caleb," Rachel spoke in a soothing tone. Although the vigilantes had shaken them, a sense of well-being stirred her emotions. She had just witnessed something she had thought long lost in this dreadful colony—a man of faith defending his integrity. "God'll keep us. Let's let them go—without their weapons."

Caleb, trying to shake off his anger, asked of the aborigine, "Who're you?"

"Wadjiri. Warrior like you."

"I'm Caleb. I ain't no warrior, though. I just hate corps scum."

Swearing and stumbling for the door, the corpsmen filed out of the barn. Arms around the boy's shoulders, Rachel smiled as she, Wadjiri, and Caleb walked side by side. She would sleep better knowing the Prentices stood in a more justifiable path. But fighting the Rum Corps would be like waging war against the devil himself. "We've taken up our cross, George."

George shook his head. "God 'elp us. We're an unlikely crew, ain't we?"

Many days would pass before the Prentices, along with Rachel and Wadjiri, would cease from their window vigil. Fear that the vigilantes would return in force haunted them day and night, and they maintained surveillance with the rigidity of an army.

"I'm tired o' standin' guard, Papa," Caleb complained. "We scared 'em off. They ain't returnin'," he reasoned, his tone marked with firm persuasion.

"I believe you're right, son," George agreed. "We're livin' like prisoners in our own home."

"It's ridiculous." Rachel poured a cup of flour into her large bowl of bread dough.

George stared pensively through the window. His watch had been unceasing since the night of the encounter, and his body begged for rest. The sight of a passing rider trotting down the pathway beyond their shanty caused instant anxiety to sweep through him, and he wearied of the vigil himself. "Put away your weapon, son. I can't live like this the rest o' me life, either."

"Our prayers are unceasing," Rachel justified. "God is with us—I'm sure of it." She turned to assist Wadjiri as he twisted yarn around his slender fingers demonstrating a cat's cradle.

"And if we die, then the better off we'll be in heaven." She scratched at her nose, streaking white across her face. "I'll not live in fear anymore."

"Anyway, I could pick off one o' the rats in an instant!" Caleb positioned his rifle upon the hand-hewn rack.

Rachel's brow furrowed with worry. "Let's pray we don't have to kill anyone." She cast her eyes dubiously toward the lad.

"I'll not stand by and allow those junta devils to threaten us! Does God want us to cower like dogs?"

Shaking his head, George replied quietly, "Not cower, Caleb. We're to show the light o' Christ—that takes more courage than a show o' violence."

Rachel sighed. "I hate politics. I feel so confused. When do I stand up for my rights, and when do I stand on God's Word?"

"You're right, you know, Rachel." George smiled, his eyes lighting prudently. "God didn't call us to war, did He?"

Rachel twisted her fist down into the bowl of dough, kneading it until it was smooth. "He called us to be obedient." Leaving Wadjiri to finish the cat's cradle, Rachel shoved her bowl aside. Standing, she lifted George's small Bible out of the windowsill. Opening the tattered pages, her eyes perused intently. "Obedient," she whispered. For the remainder of the morning, she would devour the Scriptures like a hungry scholar.

22
The Unwitting Savage

The red skies of New South Wales grew more intemperate as did the government's climate. As England dallied in their efforts to produce a governor, Macarthur, possessed with his military's zeal for monopoly, continued to seize the land holdings of the weak and the besotted, filling his coffers with the pillage of his conquests. The richer he grew, the more corrupt grew his military elite—with the emancipists sinking further into the plebeian mire of poverty and crime.

The clamor of the crowds assembled around the gallows increased, and the dissidents grew in number as more and more convicts were freed into the settlement, joining the emancipists' ranks.

With the midday heat bearing down like a blacksmith's iron, ten men and three gaunt women lined up beneath the creaking steps of the gallows. All but one were emancipists caught pilfering from the government stores. The one stood out, for his skin was black and the clothes forced upon him were ill-fitting and not his own. He glared contemptuously out at the crowd, although the masked fear in his eyes when he beheld the swinging rope did little to hide his horror.

Rachel and Wadjiri stepped down from the Prentice wagon. Their eyes were drawn to the aborigine, his face familiar to them. "Let's move in closer, Wadjiri," Rachel whispered. Followed closely by the boy, Rachel pushed through the crowd to get as close to the condemned men and women as the military guards would allow.

Standing only a few feet from the aborigine, Wadjiri called out, "Gurugul! Gurugul!"

The Gagudju elder's son turned at once, startled to hear his name called out so freely. He muttered in quiet tones to Wadjiri, his once-hard eyes now full of self-pity. His former proud-warrior posture sagged under the weight of a slave's demeanor. Lifting his shackled wrists, he spewed a hostile display of anger when his eyes focused on Rachel.

A marine guard stepped up at once, shaking a whip threateningly in the face of the Gagudju warrior. Turning toward Wadjiri the sentry waved away the boy with a blistered hand. "Off with you, boy!"

Rachel squeezed Wadjiri's shoulder as the guard glared at him suspiciously. She recognized the guard from the prison camp. "He's with me, sir. Wadjiri's with me. I'll see to him."

Wadjiri reached with long, thin arms to clasp Rachel's face. His eyes entreated her to draw close, and whispering fearfully, he informed Rachel of the circumstances. "Gurugul kill military man because military men kill many Gagudjus. It is our law that one from other tribe die for death of ours."

Sighing, Rachel answered, "Yes, I know." Still struggling to understand aborigine custom, she remembered the tribal law. It meant that even if the chosen victim was innocent of the offense, he died because he represented the murderer's clan. "Gurugul killed an officer?"

Wadjiri nodded, casting an oblique gaze toward the young man revered so highly in his tribe. "It is like your law of Moses. Eye for eye—tooth for tooth. Gagudju die so white feller must die."

Rachel remembered the slaughter of the Gagudjus, and

guilt flooded her mind again. *This is my fault*. She beheld the hatred in Gurugul's eyes. All the clansmen she had saved with her medicinals would never account for the one who was about to be hanged.

"Lieutenant?" she called out to an officer who stood near the line of the condemned.

The officer, standing with a reticent gaze, narrowed his eyes at the young woman. "What is it now?" he asked gruffly.

"That man—that aborigine—he isn't accustomed to English law. He acted out of respect for his tribal laws. Doesn't that account for something?"

"Ignorance is all it accounts for. Now don't bother us with your bleedin' heart nonsense."

"But, sir," Rachel persisted, although her tone was cautious, "how can a man live by two laws? These clansmen can't read. They've lived under their own reign for centuries."

The officer cursed, stomping a smoldering roll of tobacco underfoot. "Then they better change with the new rules or all be 'anged! Now go on wif ye! I ain't got time to be disputin' the Crown's laws wif no emancipist."

Rachel blushed when a group of officers' wives turned to stare disdainfully toward her. Drawing herself up, she disputed their accusing glares. "I'm a citizen of this settlement and expect to be treated as such!" Taking Wadjiri's hand as the women gasped around her, she made her way back to the wagon to wait for George Prentice's return from the harbor. "Perhaps we should leave in a few days, Wadjiri. We can take the news back to your tribe."

"No, Rachel." Wadjiri shook his head as though he harbored a dread secret. "Gagudju people *know* of Gurugul's hanging. Say that whites have brought curse on aborigine." Wadjiri's face grew more somber and his brown eyes softened. "Say Rachel Langley brought curse. You not allowed to be with Gagudju—forever."

"I can't go back?" Rachel shook her head. "But I want to return with you, Wadjiri."

Wadjiri confirmed her fears, shaking his head.

"But what about you, Wadjiri? I have to take you back to your tribe."

"No. Not safe. Not many days away, Dreaming will bring way for Wadjiri to go back, be with people. Dreaming always bring aborigine back to land. For now, I stay with Rachel."

"But they need our medicine. Wadjiri—they need to know of God's love."

His brows furrowed, Wadjiri gazed at Rachel as though he pitied her. "You give all to me. I take back to people."

Smiling weakly, Rachel felt a flicker of hope. "Rachel is happy you're here, Wadjiri."

Seeing the executioner slipping the noose over the native's head, Rachel's eyes began to moisten. Although the man had terrorized her, she had grown to love his people and realized he was the result of a culture who had spent too many centuries away from their own Creator.

Turning her back on the gallows' scene, Rachel cringed when a primitive scream rang out above the heads of the onlookers. Gurugul died screaming a curse down on his white slayers. The unwitting savage had fallen prey to a civilization that dared to call him inhuman.

A red-faced farmer pulled into the square. He had departed his farmhouse alone, but now his wagon was weighed down with six men who had hitched a ride along the way—all newly released from the Norfolk Island prison colony where they had been in exile for five to seven years. The men, women, and young boys who managed to survive the torturous punishments inflicted during their stay at Norfolk were often left so pitifully debilitated they could scarcely walk. Reining his wagon to a halt, the farmer waited silently as the men disembarked. Most were Irishmen dressed in tattered trousers and colorless shirts that had been given to them upon their departure. One man, overshadowing the others, limped slowly, dragging one foot, then leaned for only a brief moment on his bad leg, and braced for another belabored step. Around his head he wore a ripped piece of fabric which covered most of his face.

In a hoarse whisper he begged, "Coin fer a beggar." He solicited a group of colonists who stood gossiping in front of a tavern. "Just set free from Norfolk Island—I'm near starvation. . . ."

"Off wif ye, beggar!" one man yelled rudely while another jostled the ex-convict roughly.

Turning to glare at the perpetrator with his one good eye, the emancipist staggered backward and then grabbed a hitching post to balance himself. "Agh!" he yelled roughly, then cursed, swinging vainly at the man who shoved him. "I'll bash in yer head fer that!" he threatened, his breathing shallow.

At once the men backed away, and one shouted, "Guards! This 'un ain't ready fer civilized society yet!"

Still milling around the gallows, the military guards turned to locate the commotion. "What's yer problem?" a stocky officer in red tunic demanded.

The lumbering ex-convict bolted at once and dragged himself into a back street between two shops. Angry voices followed him, and his pace being slow, he was soon seized by the men and thrown against the stone walls in the alleyway. After being battered in the stomach and around his head, he slumped to the ground as a young fisherman tore the rag from his face. "A monster!" one shrieked, beholding the seared facial skin which appeared to melt in reddish rolls around the victim's cheeks and jawline.

"Kill 'im! Kill the monster!"

"Hang 'im!"

Retrieving a musket, a farmer with leathery skin yelled, "Back away. All o' you! I'll finish 'im off!" He aimed the rifle squarely at the felled giant, who slumped limply against the moss-coated wall.

"Halt! What's going on?"

Their heads jerked toward the sound, and a tall gentleman in clerical garb stepped toward them. The young fisherman shouted, "It's nothin', Reverend, sir. We've just caught us a monster, that's wot! One wot's traveled all a-way from Norfolk Island."

Ignoring the laughter and mockery of the man, the minister queried further. "Monster?" His eyes narrowed as he neared the man who lay at their feet. "May I examine him? I'm Reverend Heath Whitley."

"I wouldn't come near, sir. He's a dangerous lot, that one."

"Looks too battered to harm anyone, if you ask me." Heath Whitley shook his head and pushed his way through to the victim. Stooping to draw close to the man, he shook his head. "This man's been badly burned, but he's no monster."

Lifting his face, the ex-convict flinched upon finding the man so near to him. He drew up his fists and wheezed, "Go away or I . . . I'll kill ye!"

Whitley reached for the man's hands and realized they were as seared and mangled as his face.

"Look out, Reverend! We warned you!" The farmer stiffened, holding his musket ready.

Whitley waved his hand at the mob. "Everyone calm yourself." He fixed his gaze on the ex-convict and spoke kindly. "Would you come with me to my house, sir? I'll try and get some medicine for you."

His one eyelid opened and he spoke weakly. "Kin you fix me face?" Hardening his gaze, the man whispered, "Kin you work a miracle fer me?"

"I can give you a place to mend, sir. The rest is up to the Lord."

With a stream of red trickling from inside his mouth, the ex-convict keeled over.

"Get me some help!" Whitley shouted. "I'll need a wagon to take him back to my parsonage."

The men stared in a stupor as though Whitley had asked for England's crown. Backing away, the men retreated one by one, leaving Whitley alone in the alleyway with the emancipist.

Laying the ex-convict carefully upon the ground, Whitley stood at once and ran into the streets of Sydney Cove, shouting, "Help! There's a sick man here! He's wounded!"

"Reverend Whitley?"

Whitley turned and found the familiar faces of George and Caleb Prentice. "Thank the good Lord!"

"Someone's hurt, sir?" George asked worriedly.

"He's an ex-convict, George."

"So am I," George shrugged. "Where is the man?"

Rachel shifted uncomfortably. The Prentices had taken longer than she had anticipated, and the angry mob of men at the end of the square gave her cause to worry. Their shouting and waving of muskets had caused a stir that even the military couldn't quell. "What do you suppose is wrong, Wadjiri?"

Shrugging his shoulders, Wadjiri asked, "White feller have *corraborree*?"

"Not likely." Rachel sat forward and watched as two men carried another who appeared to be unconscious. "Look—over yonder. It's George! And . . ." Rachel paused, "and Heath Whitley too."

She yanked the reins, startling the Prentices' nag. "Yah!" she shouted. "Let's go!"

George glanced up and saw Rachel headed straight for them with the wagon. "Thank God!" He strained to keep hold of the heavy weight of the ex-convict's bulk.

"This way, Rachel!" Caleb called out, anxiously directing Rachel to the side of the dirt road.

Pulling back on the reins, Rachel drew the horse and wagon to a halt and stood at once. "What's happened?"

"We've a sick man here, Miss Langley." Whitley groaned under the man's weight. "We'll have need of your medicinals."

"They're in the wagon—a fresh supply." Rachel frowned in sympathy as she gazed upon the disfigured face of the man they hefted into the rear of the wagon. "Oh, Reverend Whitley," she said. "The poor man."

Wadjiri's eyes grew large. "Evil upon this man."

"Not evil, Wadjiri. Looks like a horrible accident." Rachel handed the reins to the lad. "George, why don't you drive the wagon? I'll jump in the back and see to the man. Does anyone know his name?"

Whitley shook his head. "Not yet. He passed out before I had a chance to ask."

Rachel swung her feet around, her skirt swishing against the wood. Fast to retrieve the medicine basket beneath the seat, she pulled out bandages and ointments and began applying them to the ex-convict's wounds where he had been beaten. "These other wounds appear to be much older."

"He's been victim to some sort of fire, I'd say." Whitley held the spool of bandage while Rachel unraveled a foot-long strand, cutting the length with a sharp knife. "I'm glad God brought you all here today. I would never have gotten any help from these townsfolk."

Rachel shook her head as she pressed firmly against a gash in the man's lip. "I'm not certain how to change them—the colonists, that is. Only God knows." She watched with dismay as the bandages around the man's lip turned crimson. "We'll have to find the surgeon. This man has two deep wounds—one on his lip and the other on his forearm." She wrapped the bandage around his arm after pouring an elixir over the pulsing gash.

"F-food," the man muttered barely above a whisper, and his eye rolled back under his lid. "H-hungry."

Caleb, sitting next to George, turned around to face them. "Papa can drop off Wadjiri and me near the convict colony, and we'll go for the surgeon. Then Papa can take you all out to Reverend Whitley's place. We'll meet you there as quickly as we locate Surgeon White," he offered.

"Good plan, my boy." George nodded. Rachel pressed the cloth against the man's lip. "This man is half-starved. We'll start him off with some hot broth and a cup of strong tea."

Pulling off his black coat, Whitley grabbed another spool of bandages and began tearing them off, making extra strips for Rachel's use. When their eyes met momentarily, he said quietly, "Welcome back, Rachel."

"Thank you, Reverend." Rachel smiled. "It's good to be back. That is, if I'm needed here."

Looking up astutely and then back down to tend some small wounds along the man's shoulder, Whitley nodded. "Sydney Cove needs you, Rachel Langley. They just don't realize it yet."

Katy paced in front of the room that had been her home for many months since she moved away from the shady countryside of Rose Hill. Near the doorway, the worn leather bag containing most of her belongings waited beside a wooden crate that held the remainder. She gazed around the two-room wattle-and-daub, which she had detested from the first day she had beheld it. Her first five years with Governor Phillip had been a sheltered haven compared to the last two.

"Almost time," she said nervously, gazing at the old pocket watch given to her by her papa. Hearing the clanking sound of wagon and tack, she tensed, realizing her days inside the old shack had drawn to a close. She walked around the room again, the hem of her new dress whisking against the floor as she went, scattering soft orbs of dustlike dandelion seed.

The loud, rude knock at the door pounded like a judge's gavel upon her conscience. "Coming," she called out, frustration rising in her tone. She sighed as the room around her appeared emptier than when she first arrived. The cupboard shelves were void of the beans and potatoes that Lorna once kept on them. The wine shelf held nothing now but stains and two empty bottles. Her entire savings had dwindled like the last thread on a spool of yarn.

The knock sounded again, rattling the front door in agitation.

Katy stooped to gather her bag under her arm and shoved the crate to the other side of the doorway with her foot. Opening the door slowly, she lifted her face and nodded politely at the young private, whose cheeks caved in as he sucked on a soggy roll of tobacco. "Hello, Private." Her dispirited gaze said more than the deadness in her tone.

"Are you Miss Prentice? The one wot's goin' to be livin' out at Lieutenant Simons' place?"

Biting her lip, Katy nodded. "I am."

"If you ain't some classy-lookin' dame!"

Katy despised the way the man leered at her, but refused to allow any show of emotion. "Carry my belongings?" she asked coolly.

"Right away, miss." The private was fast to collect the crate and the cloth bag from her arms.

Watching with distaste as her personal items were tossed into the rear of the military wagon like so much refuse, Katy took one last glance around the room. Noticing the soft light of midmorning sun streaming through the small window, she smiled at the radiant glow it gave the room—almost reminding her of the tenement flat she and her parents had lived in when she was a small girl in London. "It's been a good house, really," she whispered decidedly. "Actually, it just needed a little more care." She glanced at the wooden window whose weathered sill held a couple of songbirds. "Some simple curtains would've added a nice touch."

"Comin', Miss Prentice?" The private was growing impatient.

"Shortly," Katy answered absentmindedly. Walking back into the room, her mind began assessing the problems that had seemed so important yesterday and the week before. *Do you know what's happened to me, God? Can you see me? Katy Prentice has finally surrendered—after all this time—to the wrong camp*. "I can't do this. . . ." She shook her head. Pressing her lips together, she bowed her head slightly, her arms crossed at her waist. *I'm not sure how to find my way out of this—difficulty. I'll probably fail you again. But if you'll still have me—"*

"Miss Prentice!"

Marching quickly back to the door, Katy stretched a smile across her face. "I'm sorry to have bothered you, Private. But . . . I've changed my mind."

"Wot's that?"

"I said—I'm not going with you. You'll be so kind as to convey my message to the lieutenant?"

"He'll be mad as a hammer, he will at that!"

"Simons will get over it, I'm sure. I'm just not—cut out for such things."

As the private darkened the air with mariner's oaths, Katy felt a swell of relief wash through her. *What has happened to me? What brought me to this place?* She spied a dusty book in the corner of the room. It had lain on the shelf since before she came, never picked up by Lorna or herself. Reaching with a gloved hand, Katy brought the unused Bible to her lips to blow away the cobwebs and layer of dust that coated its cover.

Katy heard the sound of her bag and crate being tossed brusquely through her front door. Without so much as a glance back she called out quietly, "Thank you, Private," but kept her eyes on the Bible.

She seated herself on the floor, without a worry about the pale blue dress she wore. She couldn't recall any Scripture, but knew the answer for her trial was surely recorded inside the Writ. Page after page she turned, and the Bible stories her mum once read returned to her memory as though it were yesterday. She shuddered upon reading of the destruction that came upon God's children through their willful acts of disobedience. Gazing toward the light that shone into the empty room, she shook her head. "I know I deserve it, Lord, but don't kill me just yet. I haven't finished reading the book."

23
A Corporal's Proposal

Rachel glanced up at the moon, which shone smooth and silvery like a polished coin. She had bandaged up the ex-convict as best she could and walked out to the small stone landing in front of Heath Whitley's house. As she and the others waited for Caleb to return with the surgeon, George's pacing had begun to drive her to distraction. So she sipped the last of her hot tea and wandered out into the stillness of the night.

Although the heat of the day had left a blanket of humidity in the air, the field flowers furnished an aromatic quality that offered a decidedly pleasant evening. Spying a round, smooth rock bordering the landing, Rachel seated herself, drumming her fingers to the rhythm of the night crawlers.

"Rachel?"

Glancing up toward the doorway, Rachel smiled at the minister and noted he had changed into a more comfortable shirt. She couldn't help but admire his athletic frame, his handsome demeanor, and the strong, firm curve of his face.

But beyond his robust appearance, it was the gentility of his eyes that drew her—and his courage. After facing the colonial mob and taking charge of the volatile circumstances, Heath Whitley had immediately launched into a shepherd's role, caring for one that no one else would bother to help.

"You did a wonderful thing, Rachel. I know you didn't have much time to think, but your instincts were incredible. Our patient is awake now. He wants to meet the young woman who fostered his rescue."

Shaking her head, Rachel laughed. "It wasn't I who saved the man. It was you. . . ."

"Now, now. Up with you. You've a patient demanding to see you, Dr. Langley."

"Doctor?"

"Why not? You do everything a doctor would do."

Rachel stepped through the doorway, her shoulder brushing against his. "Make way for Doctor Langley, then." She smiled. The touch of his broad arm against hers stirred her emotions, but she gazed straight ahead, determined to keep her thoughts on the task at hand. "How are we doing?" she called to the bandaged man, whose feet stuck out and over the end of Heath Whitley's bed.

"Head feels l-like . . . i-its been blowed off. More to eat?"

"Too much food right away might do more harm than good," Rachel chided. She remembered the starved young convicts from the Second Fleet who had stuffed their stomachs at the first sight of food and fallen ill. One young man had died. "I'll give you one more cup of broth. How's that sound?"

"I'll take whatever ye gives me," the man grumbled. "But I'd kill fer a side o' beef right now." He gazed up at Rachel and his one good eye studied her critically. His brow furrowed and he made a low moaning sound.

"Something wrong, sir?"

"I . . . I know you."

"I don't believe we've met. My name is . . ." Rachel stopped for a moment, her eyes studying the man's dark hairline and the piercing eye. The rest of his face was too disfigured to distinguish any familiar characteristics. Then suddenly, as though she relived a nightmare, the fire in the brothel blazed before her. The memory was etched in her mind in red-and-black charred images—the building crumbling around her, Amelia, and little Katy. The man who threatened to molest her—*Dring!* His face now loomed in her mind's eye. *God, no! It can't be! He couldn't have lived!*

"Rachel! Caleb has returned with the surgeon!" Heath Whitley rushed to the doorway. "Dr. White!" he called hurriedly. "In here!"

Rachel backed away from the man, noticing the way he gripped and ungripped his marred fingers. "I—we haven't met."

"I still says . . ."

Rachel turned away at once, no longer able to bear the horrible truth that stretched before her. "I'm t-tired, Reverend Whitley. You have no further need of me now. I'll see if someone will drive me back to Rose Hill."

"You don't have to leave so suddenly, Rachel." Whitley's brow was pinched, his eyes questioning. "Is something wrong?"

"No. I . . . just as I said . . . I'm tired. I must get some rest." Rachel nodded politely to the minister. "Good evening to you, Reverend." She felt shame wash through her as though all the lurid details of her past had spilled out in plain sight of Heath Whitley. She knew if she didn't leave at once, that if the man was indeed who she suspected he was, it would only be a matter of time until he remembered who she was—and worse yet, *what* she was.

"Will you return tomorrow? I'll still be needing your assistance with this fellow." A faint smile curved Whitley's face.

"No . . . what I mean to say is that . . . I'll see that you get all the help you need with the man. I promise you that."

Whitley's puzzled glance followed Rachel as she all but ran through the doorway.

"Good-night—Sydney's Angel." A smile creased his cheeks.

Rachel whipped around, her cheeks flushed. "Where did you hear that?"

"I've been visiting the contagion ward. Those young lads are infatuated with you."

"Well, they're just—children. They like to play those games, you know. I'm certainly . . ." Rachel hesitated. How she so desperately wanted to be all that Reverend Heath Whitley had assumed her to be. But it was all a fantasy and worse than that—a lie. "I'm no angel, Reverend Whitley." She stood with her fingers gripped at her sides. Gazing into his gentle eyes, she whispered, "Good-night."

Hastening out into the warm night, Rachel ran straight into the tall officer who had escorted Surgeon White, Caleb, and Wadjiri from the convict colony. "Oh, excuse my clumsiness!" she apologized.

"Quite all right, missy." The corporal smiled.

Rachel backed away to get a better look at the man. "Why, Corporal Holmes. It's you."

"Me in the flesh. When I 'eard about your problem out 'ere, I decided to lend a 'and an' see what I could do."

"You could be of great assistance to me, Corporal. Could you drive me home?"

"At your service, madam." Holmes tipped his hat and turned to face the surgeon, who was quickly being handed his supplies from the wagon by Wadjiri. "Could you spare me for about an hour, sir? This young woman needs to be escorted back to her home."

Surgeon White, his silver hair glistening in the moonlight, nodded politely. "Certainly. This patient will take some time, I'm afraid."

"Thank you, Corporal Holmes." Rachel strode determinedly toward the military wagon as George walked toward her, arms laden with supplies. "George, I'm afraid I'm exhausted. And I really should rush home to check on Amelia. I hope you don't mind that the good corporal here is escorting me home?"

"Not at all, love. If Surgeon White didn't need me, I'd go with you. I'll bring the boys home, if you don't mind."

"Certainly," Rachel nodded. She and Holmes waited patiently on the wagon seat as the surgeon collected the remainder of his tools and walked briskly up to the stone landing and into the shanty.

When the night air had grown still, Holmes was the first

to speak. "I missed you, Rachel. I was saddened to hear that you had gone—and worried. You could have been killed." He flicked the reins.

"God kept me safe. I learned a lot from them, Corporal."

"How to sacrifice infants?"

"Stop it, please! You've a lot of misconceptions, as do all of us. It's true they're pagan, and their treatment of women is atrocious. But the love of God, I believe, can change the most savage of hearts. Even white man's."

"*If* you speak the language."

"Is it so impossible to learn? They aren't babbling some sort of gibberish, you know. They have their own language, their own customs."

"Don't get in such a dither, now. I didn't intend to say anything to upset you. I was tryin' to tell you how much you've been missed is all."

"I know. I'm sorry if I snapped at you. I'm just so—very tired." Rachel tensed. The thought occurred to her that Reverend Whitley might mention her name to that man. If he truly were Dring, he'd certainly remember her by her name. She drew her fingers to her lips, stroking them worriedly. *Please, God, don't let . . .*

"Whatever is on your mind?"

"Nothing. Truly nothing." Rachel gazed stoically into the darkness of the road ahead. Then deciding to change the subject, she interjected, "I do believe I've found a clue to solving Betsy's murder."

Holmes' brow arched ruefully. "How so?"

"I found her diary washed up on a stream bed."

"How could she know the man that murdered her? Probably just a bushranger."

"I don't believe that, Corporal. Betsy had an uncle who wanted her dead. She knew *something*—I'm not sure what—that would expose his corrupt political dealings."

"Did she tell you?"

"Not exactly. And her diary is mostly illegible now. But there is a name of a man who worked for Cornelius Fortner."

Holmes sat forward with interest. "And what would that be?"

"Someone whose name begins with the letters M-c-G-r. That's all I could decipher. But I intend to show it to the authorities. There is at least enough information to start an investigation back in England about Fortner."

"Rachel, I'm afraid for you. This man could be dangerous. What if he tries to kill you next?"

"How would he even know about me?"

"True. But why don't you allow me to turn in the evidence? At least then you wouldn't be implicated. I can't allow you to endanger yourself."

Rachel paused. "You would do that for me?"

"Absolutely. I'll just quietly give the information to Macarthur."

"No! Not Macarthur!" Rachel vehemently insisted. "He's as corrupt as Fortner."

"Who then?"

"What about Lieutenant Thompson? Or better yet, his wife. I trust her."

"All the better reason that I should convey the diary. Consider it done," Holmes answered jovially. "Well, I believe your momentous return calls for a celebration. There's another party in two nights at the Macarthurs' place. What say?"

Rachel shook her head. "No, I don't feel up to it, Corporal."

"You've got to allow yourself to become a part o' this colony, Rachel. Why always place yourself on the outside lookin' in?"

"It isn't like that at all, Corporal. Those people don't extend any sort of welcome to emancipists. In their eyes, we don't belong."

"That can change easily." Bryce pulled the black steed to a halt.

"What're you doing?" Rachel stared curiously at the officer.

Holmes gently clasped Rachel's hands. "Somethin' I 'ave no practice in doin'."

"What's that?"

"Proposin' to a lovely lady."

"Oh, but, Corporal . . ."

"Don't 'ave to say nothin' to hurt ol' Holmes' feelin's. Give it some time to think about it. But I could build us a home that'd put ol' Macarthur's to shame. You'd be an officer's wife. The past would be behind you."

"I don't know. We . . . don't know enough about each other. I know nothing of your past. You really know nothing of mine."

"Sydney Cove is a lonely place. Some officers is hitchin' up with the convict women as they come ashore. You and me, we knows more about one another than that lot knows. Who cares about the past, anyway?"

Rachel swallowed hard, her mind wandering to thoughts of Heath Whitley and the man he now looked after. "I wish no one did. But unfortunately they do." She shook her head, suddenly feeling uncomfortable. Turning to face him, she asserted, "I have an answer for you now. I can't marry you. It wouldn't be right. I don't love you. But I do appreciate your friendship."

"I don't give up easily," Holmes tried to smile, but there was an edge to his tone.

"Please don't be upset with me." Rachel sensed a change in the man's demeanor, but wondered if her weariness was simply heightening her sensitivities.

"I could never be upset with you. I love you, Rachel Langley."

Rachel tried to return a warm smile, but the weariness of the day had drained her of emotion. "Please, could we go now? I must get home."

Holmes whipped the horse's flank and gave the command that sent them down the road. The two rode the remainder of the way in silence, the cloud over a high moon darkening their path.

Making her bed on the floor, Katy lay atop the quilt her mother had sewn for her years ago. Believing she would be leaving the old shack, Katy had sold her few pieces of furniture for thirty shillings. That was how she came to own the new frock. But she did not fret that she was now without material furnishings. Instead, she felt a certain peacefulness envelop her. She knew she could run back to the safety of Papa's farm, but a strong determination dictated that she hack out a life for herself dependent on no one but God.

By selling the new dress that afternoon, she had been able to stock her larder with beans, some fresh produce, and brined beef. There would be no wine on her shelves, and especially no rum. Although even a vicar was prone to sip a glass of wine with his meal, Katy could not trust herself or her motives and prayed God would strengthen her will to stand strong.

Keeping her thoughts on ways to raise income from her own home, she began mentally assessing her talents. She was organized and could sew as well as Mum once did. The skills of the one tailor in town was a poor comparison to Mum's techniques. *I can start tomorrow.* She decided the extra money left from the sale of the dress could be used to purchase thread and needles. *I'll go house to house soliciting seamstress work. I can work out of this shack. Who knows but what I can have my own piece of land? Who's to stop me?*

A twig snapping outside her shanty jolted her from her thoughts and sent a shiver of fear through her limbs. She rolled over slowly so the wooden floor wouldn't creak and pushed herself toward the window using the quilt as a buffer. Her heart pounded against her chest when she heard what sounded to be a muffled voice.

Then she froze when the air overhead exploded with the sound of shattered glass. A large rock crashed through her window and landed only a foot from where she lay. *Simons!* Another rock was hurled through the upper glass in the window. Katy pulled herself into a ball, tucking her head between her legs as the shards of glass crashed around her.

"Come out, wench!" a raspy male voice shouted.

"Go away!" Katy sat up with tiny pieces of glass sparkling in her hair. "Leave me alone!"

"Not likely, wench!"

Laughter echoed all around the shanty and Katy realized she was surrounded.

"We're here to make a little proposition!"

Katy lifted her face to gaze out through the open window. "What kind of proposition?" she scowled while squinting to make out the faces of the men on horseback.

"You reneged on a promise. It'll cost you to stab a corpsman in the back, wench!"

"I've a right to realize my own mistake!" Tears brimmed in Katy's eyes. "Leave me in peace! I'll never darken Simons' door again!"

"It's too late. The deal is made. Gather up your things now!"

Katy glanced around at each shadowy figure. Every corpsman wore a dark handkerchief covering his nose and mouth. Steadying herself against the wall, she stood and shouted, "I won't do it! You'll have to kill me!"

The moon glinted off several musket barrels like silvery threads of steel. "You'll wish you were dead by the time we're finished with you." The leader threatened in angry tones, his eyes glistening dark and saturnine.

Her breath quickening, Katy jerked around, determined to escape through the rear doorway of the small kitchen. Her prayers were fast but filled with courage as she limped toward the door.

"'ave your way with 'er, men!" the leader laughed crudely.

Glancing back toward the window, Katy could see the men dismounting from their horses, hurling licentious threats as they made fast for the front entrance. *I'd rather die. . . .*

The front door rattled as the hostile mob of Rum Corps brigands tried the dilapidated handle. The shanty shook while the locked door was bludgeoned time after time, the intruders loosening the lock with each blow. Abruptly, the door flew open and the men stumbled into the room, leering and calling out their lewd remarks, the stench of rum following strong after them. Searching the room, they found it dark and empty. Bewildered, the leader speedily ran to the rear exit. Throwing open the door, he stuck out his head and called to the two men who stood watch at the rear. "Did the wench run this way?"

"We just got 'ere, sir. The Prentice woman couldn't 'ave run out that quickly. Not wif 'er bad leg an' all—could she?"

"You blasted—" The leader shook his head. "Did you let 'er escape?"

"I don't see 'ow she could, Corporal McGrath. Me mate 'ere and m'self were fast to our posts."

"Shut up, idiot!" McGrath commanded hoarsely. "Don't say me name aloud like that!" He wheeled back toward the open door. "Drat! The wench got away!" Whirling around to face the others, he shrieked, "She couldn't 'ave gotten far! Search all around. Mount your steeds! At once!"

The shanty's wooden floor thundered with the sound of pounding boots and drunken voices, and then grew silent except for the ticking of the pocket watch Katy had left on the larder shelf. In one corner the old quilt lay piled in a heap. A pale trickle of sawdust and bark sifted onto it from above as a board was shoved away from the attic rafters.

Katy, sweating from the heat of the isolated space, shoved out her face and gasped for air. She had scrambled up the larder shelves, legs throbbing, and forced a loose board from the ceiling. *Thank you, Lord, for wisdom.* She eased herself down from the rotted wood, but the board snapped and she dropped at once onto the quilt. Gazing up to inspect the rotted ceiling, she shook her head. "They could've found me easily. The ceiling could've given way and dropped me at their feet." She shuddered at the thought and reexamined her gratitude. "Thank you, Father, for small miracles."

24
Field of Desolation

The New South Wales autumn paralleled the northern world's spring, ushering in another season of harvest. In seasons past, the frequent droughts had parched the ground into a dust-ridden desert, or the monsoons had turned the valleys into mossy lakes. This fall season, Parrametta began to display early signs of fertility and the earth began to sprout at Rose Hill, promising a late but fruitful harvest.

With the sky glowing a soft cornflower blue and green shoots speckling the brown-and-gold landscape with new life, Rachel still thought often of Betsy's death. Accompanied by Wadjiri, she had frequented the graveside twice over the last weeks of summer and found wild flowers had overtaken the small mound marked by a simple, carved stone. Paying her respects, she could not shake the hope that justice would somehow reign and the murderer be found. But no amount of hope could quell the pain she felt, for she missed Betsy more than she ever had her own disjointed family.

Rachel stepped toward the new rows of vegetable tops, questioning the nagging thought that this harvest held a certain significance. The fear that the Rum Corps would retaliate hung over their heads, especially at night when the junta could lay blame for their destruction upon the escaped convicts. Worse yet, George and Amelia had received a message from Katy—she too had been threatened. But the scent of vegetation caused a buoyancy in Rachel's emotions, and she felt a certain hopefulness wash through her. "God bless this harvest," she prayed. "Use it to prosper Rose Hill."

"Garden good thing."

Wiping her palms against her checked apron, Rachel turned and found that Wadjiri had walked up behind her. "Gardens are wonderful if they're allowed to grow. It looks as though this one has finally produced." She smiled and the pleasantry of the moment gladdened her.

"We *eat* seeds. I see if we plant in ground like white feller, we have more to eat."

"I'm glad you understand. Perhaps you can share this wisdom with your elders."

"True." Wadjiri hesitated. "Your friend be planted in ground."

Rachel hesitated, not understanding Wadjiri's intent. "You mean—Betsy?"

"What will grow from her seed?"

Rachel, feeling somewhat annoyed, crossed her arms at her waist. She had been patient with the lad's lack of understanding with her culture, just as he had been patient with her. But Betsy's memory was personal to her, almost sacred. If the lad was toying with her grief, she didn't find it humorous. "People don't have seeds, Wadjiri. That is, except for when a husband and wife make children."

"We believe our ancestors become part of us when they die. We carry them inside."

"I understand that philosophy," Rachel reasoned. "Sometimes I still feel as though Betsy is here with me. But her spirit has gone to be with God."

"Did she give you something to keep from her?"

Rachel remembered the diary, but Betsy hadn't actually

given it to her. And by now it was safely in the hands of Mrs. Thompson. "I don't suppose we ever had anything of worth to exchange. Betsy certainly didn't plan to die."

Wadjiri shrugged, seemingly dissatisfied with her answer. "We not keep property of ancestor. All get old and no good. We give stories and pass down Gagudju law." He crossed his arms with an air of superiority.

Rachel nodded, although his comments raised a revelation. "How thoughtless of me," she said more to herself than to Wadjiri.

"What is thoughtless?"

Rachel chuckled. "It means I'm thinking only of myself instead of others. Betsy *did* give me a priceless gift. God forgive me if I ever forget."

"What gift?"

"She showed me the Way. I would've been lost without it."

"You mean the book of your god, Jesus Christ?"

"She gave me the Bible. But beyond that was the way she lived. No matter what difficulties life dealt out, God's love shone through Betsy. She was a beacon—like a bright light—on that dark voyage from England."

"I see love in you." Wadjiri wrapped his arms around Rachel's waist and smiled up at her.

Clasping her hands around Wadjiri's face, Rachel was stirred by his words. "Truly?"

"Cross on heart." Wadjiri made a sign across his chest with his finger. "Rachel show the Way on her heart too."

Rachel sighed and her brow furrowed. The nagging feeling of the past suddenly haunted her again. The memory of the fiery brothel flooded her thoughts with remorse. She shook the condemnation from her mind. "Let's go back to the house. If we hurry, we might get a chance to go into town with George. He's driving to the harbor to buy some fresh fish."

Wadjiri nodded agreeably and the two clasped hands as easily as a mother and child would do. Turning their backs on the field, they didn't see the movement from the far east of the garden plot. A ravenous sheep loped onto the field and began nibbling the fresh vegetable shoots, its front teeth precisely biting off the plants to the level of the soil. Then another followed. A young man, stout and quite tall in appearance, lingered behind a row of scrub with a long, thick stick. Taking the stick in his grimy hand, he prodded twenty more pilfered sheep onto the field. Then turning quickly, he mounted a military steed and galloped away, leaving the livestock to ravage the first crop at Rose Hill.

Katy paced across the elegant living room, her arms carefully holding a finished frock, expertly stitched and sewn from bright yellow fabric. She had mustered a great deal of courage to solicit the business of this family. With the tapestried rug design now etched in her memory, Katy looked up to find a plain-faced woman standing at the hallway entrance, smiling faintly.

"Hello, Mrs. Thompson. I've finished your dress, or rather, your daughter's dress." Katy unfolded the frock, allowing it to drop to its full length.

"My, it's lovely, Miss Prentice." Lilith Thompson nodded approvingly, her hands clasped gracefully in front of her. "You do lovely work. Who taught you such skills?"

"My mum. She was actually much better than I am, but she's—ill now and can no longer sew."

"Prentice. Let's see, now who are your parents?"

"George and Amelia Prentice."

"Don't believe I've met them. Colonists from England?"

Katy deliberated before answering. "From London. Yes." She glanced down at the dress, wishing to go on with other matters. "I've sewn some extra lace round the hem and the bodice. I hope your daughter likes it."

"Felicity will find it—satisfactory." Lilith gazed to her left through the tall window, her thoughts wandering. Drawing herself up, she turned back and addressed Katy. "But *I* think the dress is beautiful."

Katy had noticed Lilith Thompson's impatience with her daughter, but she kept her thoughts to herself. She and Rachel had had a taste of the girl's selfishness, but she knew that harboring resentment would only bring bitterness. "Is Felicity here so I may try it on her once more? We need to be certain of the fit."

"No. I'm afraid she's gone off with a group of her young friends. She's a busy young woman."

Nodding that she understood, Katy smoothly proffered a solution. "No bother at all, ma'am. I'll simply leave it with you for Felicity to inspect later. I'll drop by in a few days to inquire of the necessity for another fitting."

"Good enough, Miss Prentice. I do appreciate your efficiency."

Handing the garment to Lilith, Katy curtsied properly and excused herself. "I'll be going now, ma'am. Is there any more work you'll be needing?"

Lilith shook her head. "Not for now. But I believe Elizabeth Macarthur could be in need of your services. Do you know where the Macarthur farm is located?"

Katy struggled to hide her displeasure upon hearing the name. "I believe everyone knows of the Macarthur farm," she said darkly.

Elizabeth lifted her chin in an inquiring manner but commented simply, "Yes, they're quite well-known."

Nodding, Katy stared at the floor, rubbing her fingers nervously.

Lilith's brow was pinched. "Something's wrong?"

Sighing heavily, Katy shook her head. "No, ma'am."

"Lieutenant Macarthur isn't too popular among the civilians, is he?"

Katy glanced upward, her lips pursed as she ruminated upon Lilith's words. "*Especially* among the civilians."

"I'm so sorry, dear. But he does have a right to purchase land, I suppose."

"All persons do, ma'am. However, his rights are not in question, but rather his methods."

Batting her lashes, Lilith drew near to Katy, grasping her arm gently. She glanced around the room and finding no servants about asked, "Could you be seated, Miss Prentice? I wish to hear more."

"No, I can't." Katy shook her head. "I have to keep my mind on my sewing business. It's my only means of survival."

Lilith gazed into Katy's blue eyes, a calm assurance in her tone. "Please?"

Katy found herself being seated in a tufted chair. She smiled uncomfortably at Lilith, who seated herself directly across from her in a matching settee and draped the yellow dress across the back. Lilith sat quietly for a moment, her eyes narrowing somberly. "Remember my position, Miss Prentice. I have to be cautious, as well. If we speak, then let us both share in confidence."

Katy wondered if she was being set up by Simons. "I don't know what to say, Mrs. Thompson. Attacking the Corps is a dangerous undertaking. I should know—I once worked for them."

"That's why *I* have to be careful." Lilith's eyes widened as she fingered the arm of her chair. "My own husband has been duped, I believe, into joining the Corps. He felt it was his military duty. But I'm seeing some characteristics inside the cartel that are causing me some alarm."

Katy felt a measure of trust begin to grow between them. "How do you mean?"

"Most of the property being purchased is falling under the control of one man—Macarthur. If others were benefiting from this so-called military government, I wouldn't be so concerned. But Macarthur's control is growing too strong. His monopoly could soon become unstoppable if left unchecked. The man is frightening to me."

Closing her eyes and sighing, Katy nodded agreeably, feeling a wave of vindication sweep through her. "I'm so glad to hear you say that." She looked squarely at the officer's wife. "But what can be done?"

"First we pray."

Taken aback, Katy's eyes lit with relief. "You're a Christian woman?"

"Yes, and I suspected the same about you."

"How so?"

"Call it discernment, I suppose. For a few years I've found myself trusting more and more in Him to speak to me." She smiled warmly. "I had once walked without God in my life, never hearing His voice. But with His help, I'll never make that mistake again."

"Nor will I," Katy added gravely. "I nearly destroyed myself. I believe I was the most selfish person in the world."

"No worse than I. Now I know why Paul called himself the 'chiefest of sinners.' " She paused, studying the lovely features of the young woman. "How do you mean you've failed?" she asked with great interest.

Katy deliberated. "I've pondered the matter a great deal of late. But I believe I leaned too heavily on my parents' faith instead of cultivating my own. Then when faced with the lure of material gain, I chased after it without hesitation. But then it all . . . came apart. I . . . I became a drunkard."

"Poor child."

"Oh, but He's brought me so far since then," Katy was fast to reply. "I feel good again."

"God is merciful, isn't He?" Lilith's eyes appeared to escape to the past. "My parents *considered* themselves religious. But their religion was one of convenience, an issue of status that accompanied their wealth. But they had no time for a plain little daughter. I grew up feeling as though . . . that somehow . . . I was in their way."

"How sad. But you married?"

Elizabeth gazed down at her hands, seeming to trace the years of age with her weathered eyes. "Not at first. Felicity is . . ."

Katy swallowed hard, seeing the pain in Lilith's eyes. "You don't have to tell me."

Lilith pressed her lips together and again focused her attention on Katy. "You've made your confession. Now let me make mine. I believe God sent you to me."

"For some reason, so do I." Katy drew her fingers to her lips, her emotions stirred.

"Felicity is not Cornel's daughter. She was six months old when I met him. My parents had sent me away to a boardinghouse to have my *mistake* all alone. Cornel was a young private at the time and took me under his wing. He married me and made Felicity his daughter."

"He's actually a good man, then?"

"I swear it. But my parents refused to help us, and Cornel has some bitterness about the difficult years we endured financially. He saw this military corps as our security. But his loyalty to the militia has blinded him to the corruption."

"What about Felicity? She knows?"

"She knows about the adoption. I've never hidden that fact from her, but Cornel and I have spoiled her to make up for the past."

"Could Corne—Lieutenant Thompson change his mind about the Corps? If we prove the junta's dealings are illegal?"

"I'm sure of it. Cornel would never do anything illegal. He is opportunistic, but he isn't a swindler."

Katy hesitated, feeling anxiousness rising inside her. "You've given me hope. But I can't rush into this situation, Mrs. Thompson. I have to pray and seek God's direction. My willfulness can get in the way at times."

"I agree. We shall pray and ask God to reveal the truth to those who will listen. When the time is right, I have someone to introduce to you—a man who might be able to help you."

Katy agreed. "When the time is right." She stood and relief washed through her. "I can't believe I've actually found a friend."

Lilith stood as well and extended her hand. "For as long as you need me."

Katy looked down, her mind fixed upon her own divulgence. "Now I want you to know something else about me."

"Certainly. If you wish." Lilith nodded amicably.

"My parents are emancipists. I would have been separated from them in England had I not secured a position with the commander of the First Fleet."

"So you worked for . . ."

"Governor Arthur Phillip. But he's gone, and now we must all do what we can to save this colony from the Rum Corps."

"The Rum Corps?"

Katy blushed. "My apologies. That's what the emancipists call the New South Wales Corps."

"No apology needed. They *are* a Rum Corps."

Katy noticed the sky darkening through the windowpane. "I must be going now, Mrs. Thompson—Lilith." She embraced Lilith Thompson and quietly exchanged farewells with her. "I've much to think about and pray about. Surely there are colonists and emancipists in this colony who are willing to resist the junta."

"Katy Prentice . . ." Lilith smiled slyly, her head tilted.

"Yes?"

"Emancipists *are* colonists."

"So they are!" Katy nodded, her heart gladdened at Lilith's words. She left the Thompson farm as the sun slid like a gold coin into the pocket of the mountainous horizon. Darkness veiled the sister settlements of Parrametta and Sydney Cove in shades of inky blue, with all the landscape becoming one with the shadows. But a new vision for a brighter colony swelled inside the heart of Katherine Mercy Prentice.

"Out! Out!" Rachel shrieked, running across the field, her skirt catching on the plant stubs that stuck slightly above the ground. She swung a tree limb through the air, swatting a sheep against its stubborn head. "No!" she shouted as the beast grappled for one final taste of the green plant, snipping it off greedily at the ground.

Running to the far end of the pasture, she saw two strays running into the thicket. She followed them, wondering if the man herding them would be nearby.

"Drive 'em back this way, Rachel!" George yelled. "We need to keep them as evidence."

Rachel waved broadly with her hand, indicating that she understood and made her way through the thicket to head off the wandering two. "This way!" she yelled at the animals, waving them back toward the field and the rest of the herd. As the two sheep loped away bleating, Rachel's eye caught a glimmer of something shining in a clump of spinefax grass. *What's this?* She pushed away the long slender reeds and reached in cautiously to grasp the coinlike object. Lifting it with an air of curiosity, she turned the object over and noticed the small clasp at the top. "Looks like a small medallion." She rubbed her thumb over the etching in the front that portrayed a saint of some sort. Then flipping it over, she immediately realized the back was engraved with two initials—*K.M.*

Looking all around, she searched for further evidence. If the sheep had been released by a corpsman to retaliate against the Prentices, there would be footprints in the soft clay around the scrub. While the shouts of George and the boys rang across the field, she stooped low to the ground, backtracking the path of the herd. Suddenly her eyes were drawn to a set of human prints beside the sheep tracks—boot prints pointing toward the field. The man must have stood watching as the sheep loped past, for there were no signs that he had walked beyond that point.

Rachel slipped the medallion inside her pocket and walked back onto the field, her thoughts whirling. *Who is K.M.?*

"Away!" Wadjiri shrieked as Caleb ran past chasing a bleating ewe.

"I'll kill it!" Caleb threatened, his eyes red with hostility.

"Stop!" George ordered, swinging his arm vainly toward another woolly perpetrator. "It's no use."

"Why?" Caleb's mouth dropped open as Rachel and Wadjiri joined him at his side.

"The damage is done. More than half the crop is destroyed. Let's herd the beasts into the barn."

"And be accused of thievery? We'll be hanged without a trial if the sheep belong to a corpsman!" Rachel disagreed emphatically.

"I'll send out a letter to the government buildin' and ask that it be posted publicly. I'll demand that the owner of these sheep come forward and pay the damages to my crop. If they never confess, the sheep are mine!"

"Will it work, George?" Rachel stood with a proprietary look on her face. "Will they believe an emancipist?"

George shook his head. "I don't know. But I won't be run off me farm by the corps. I'll bloomin' well fight if I has to!"

Rachel watched as Caleb and Wadjiri brought the small herd into formation, shouting and clapping their hands. "If the sheep were stolen, the owner is not at fault. He'll come and take the herd and leave us without recompense."

"Why do you think the sheep were stolen?" George's brow was pinched with frustration.

"What owner would take such a loss? Besides, look, see what I have found." Rachel drew out the medallion for George to see.

"A saint's medallion." George vaguely recognized the patron saint. "It could've been dropped by anyone."

"But it wasn't covered up by the elements," Rachel reasoned. "We've had our share of storms, and the medallion's too clean, I believe, to have been lying on the ground for long. And not far from the medallion I found human tracks—over there." She pointed.

"It's the junta!" George grew angry. "They've ruined me, all right! Why the good Lord's not stoppin' them, I'll never know."

Studying the damage, Rachel wondered if her prayers had reached heaven at all. "I prayed just this morning for this crop to be the one to prosper Rose Hill." She shook her head, biting her lip to hold back the urge to cry. "I don't understand either."

"Let's don't blame God." George placed his arm around Rachel's shoulders. "He must 'ave a different plan."

"Maybe to go back to England." Caleb's words grew definitive as a hopelessness darkened his gaze. "You was brought 'ere against your will in the first place."

Wadjiri asked plainly, "Is England home, George?"

George stared pensively, the last ray of sunlight outlining his face in a waxen yellow. "I don't rightly know anymore. Where is me 'ome?"

Rachel gazed back to see the clouds forming hot yellow streaks of light that melted in vertical bands above the horizon. The final glow was a stunning finale before fading into night. "Let's go inside, shall we? The damage is done. Tomorrow we'll be rested and more apt to work out a solution." She tried to sound confident, but her words were taut and the strain of their plight was evident in her tone.

Her prayer lay cold and silent in the pit of her stomach—*Dear God, where is home?*

25
FACE FROM THE PAST

Katy poured herself a glass of water from a crystal pitcher that sat atop Lilith Thompson's mahogany serving table. The table sat in the center of the parlor, accenting a simply decorated room. She could hear the quick muffled succession of feet walking toward the room, so she sipped quickly from her glass and took her seat on a dainty chair with cabriole legs. Having taken several days to deliberate, Katy had finally agreed to meet with Lilith's *friend* to try to set in motion a plan to weaken the power of the junta. She had grown curious about the nature of the meeting, since Lilith had divulged no information about who the person might be. And so she poised herself, hoping the man to be a leader of sorts—perhaps a politician from England or a nobleman.

"Katy?" Lilith called, standing next to a large oil painting that accented the wide open doorway.

"Yes?"

"I've someone for you to meet."

Katy stood at once, a certain anxiousness seizing her. "It's nice to meet you, sir. I . . ." She stood with her hand delicately outstretched, a perplexed gaze upon her face.

"And it's a pleasure to meet you as well, Miss Prentice!" Dwight Farrell extended his hand jovially, his charm set off by the handsome smile revealing a slight gap between his two front teeth.

"You're the . . ."

"Indeed. I was just as surprised myself. Lilith is quite the concealer o' secrets." Dwight winked at Lilith.

Lilith's pale skin flushed pink around her cheeks. "Actually I'm quite the novice when it comes to—spying."

"Is that what we are?" Katy stared first at one and then the other. "Spies?"

"I'll never tell." Dwight crossed his arms across his chest, his eyes flashing conspiratorially. "Are you sure we're alone, Lilith?"

"Quite. The servants are all out picking vegetables from the garden. They'll be all day preparing them." She placed one palm inside the other. "Take your seats while I check the hallways." Lilith stepped quickly from the room.

Katy found a chair but shifted uncomfortably in it. "Mr. Farrell—Dwight." She swallowed hard, her eyes searching his.

"Yes, Katy."

"Before we go on, I feel I owe you an apology. I've made some mistakes."

"And so have I. I shouldn't have abandoned you."

"You didn't abandon me. I practically ran you off." Clasping her hands, Katy lifted her face, her eyes tinged with regret. "I've been a fool."

"Don't say such things. We've only met today."

Her brow furrowed, Katy's tone was one of curiosity. "Today?"

"Just now. My name is Dwight Farrell." He introduced himself ceremoniously, bowing his head in a gentlemanly fashion.

Katy felt a tear surface and allowed it to spill onto her cheek. "Pleased to meet you, Mr. Farrell. I'm Katy Prentice."

"And I'm the Queen of England!" Lilith reentered the room, her eyes lit with confusion.

Dwight laughed first, followed by Katy. "It's a . . . bit hard to explain," he said to Lilith.

"No need to bother." Lilith seated herself. "Well, we're all clear for the meeting. If you're ready to commence."

"What have you found out so far about Macarthur?" Katy asked Dwight.

"Macarthur's a difficult man to pin down. He's got his hands in every pot in the settlement. Finding a witness to accuse Macarthur of wrongdoing is like trying to find someone to testify against the king—near impossible!"

"Lilith?" Katy's gaze reflected caution. "What about your husband?"

"Cornel? He's not been party to anything illegal, not to my knowledge, anyway. Macarthur is careful about who he divulges information to. I suspect most of his dirty work is carried out by unscrupulous ex-convicts—ones who aren't worried about their reputation."

"Has anyone heard from England?" Katy leaned forward with her hands planted firmly against her knees. "From Pitt?"

"I received a reply to a letter I sent a year ago." Dwight smacked the back of his hand against the letter. "Nothing but a lot of polite talk saying how a new governor will be sent as soon as possible. They didn't bother to address our grievances."

"We *are* still an English colony, are we not?" Lilith pursed her lips.

"More like an English orphan!" Katy's voice grew terse. "I do wish Macarthur would make one mistake."

"I'm sure he has. We simply haven't been able to unearth it yet," Dwight reasoned.

"What about the emancipist settlers?" Lilith poured out a cup of steaming hot tea.

"They're so busy surviving they haven't the time to organize a revolt."

Katy clenched her fists. "I hate that word—*revolt*. There has to be a better way. Something without bloodshed. What we need is—"

"A bloodless revolution!" Lilith waved her finger in the air.

Dwight stared as though a thought smoldered in his mind. "Then we'll have to hit them where it hurts—right in their greedy little pockets." He slapped his trousers pocket.

"But how?" Lilith asked. "We would need support—colonists with money."

Katy tapped a finger across her bottom lip. "I know none that would help us. What about you, Lilith?"

"All the wealthy are members of the New South Wales Corps." Lilith shook her head. "Even my own husband. Who among them is willing to give up one shred of their wealth?"

"Who says they have to lose anything?" Dwight drew closer to the two women. "We'll earn their trust. They'll tell us what they know without realizing it."

"Now *that* I can do!" A faint smile creased Lilith's cheeks.

Dwight's eyes reflected quiet concern for Lilith. "It'll be risky. If Macarthur finds out—"

"He won't." Lilith crossed her arms at her waist. "If I'm to be a spy, then a good one I'll be."

"Should we keep meeting here?" Katy grew somber. "We don't want to draw suspicion."

"No. In two weeks, let's meet in Parrametta." Dwight took charge. "At Rose Hill."

Katy felt a renewed energy. "I feel alive again. I never realized how oppressed I was working for the Corps."

Dwight's face reflected worry. "But are you safe now?"

Heaving a sigh, Katy shrugged. "I'm not certain. Simons sent his men after me one evening. I've stayed with a family in town ever since."

Dwight nodded agreeably, but his eyes grew concerned. "Should you move back to Rose Hill?"

Katy hesitated, hoping to be certain of her answer. "I'm not ready, Dwight. When I go back to Rose Hill, I want to be a different person—I have to be."

"I think you're a wonderful young lady." Lilith clasped Katy's hand. "I'd be proud to call you my daughter."

"Thank you, Lilith." Katy reflected upon how proud her parents had always been of her. "I've made some mistakes I regret."

"We all have, dear." Lilith nodded, her lips pressed together. "That is why God invented His grace."

"But there is something else He invented for which I've learned I must strive." Katy felt humbled at the thought.

"What's that?" Dwight asked.

"His righteousness. I'll never take its importance for granted again."

Dwight shifted in his seat. "Listen to you two acting as though you've murdered someone. You both must think I'm the worst of sinners."

"Oh no." Katy shook her head, acknowledging Lilith's broad smile. "That title belongs to us."

Hastening toward the government building, Rachel walked briskly with the letter from George rolled up and snugged underneath her arm. She knew she must make haste to declare the damage done to the property before the owner reported the missing animals stolen, leaving George suspect. She was also troubled about the medallion and the initials engraved on the back. It was remotely possible that the initials matched the name of the man in Betsy's diary. *But why would Betsy's murderer want to harm George Prentice? Nothing makes sense!* The thought nagged at her that she needed to recheck Betsy's diary. The man whose surname began with *M-c-G-r* might still be a suspect in Betsy's death, and if he were, the lieutenant-governor should set up an investigation even if the medallion meant nothing. *What if the man's running free in the colony?* Rachel determined to have another look at the diary to see if the man's name matched the initials. "I've got to find Holmes."

"There she is—pretty lass." The voice was a low whisper, almost unnoticed by Rachel.

She jerked her face around, her brows pinched. She gasped at the scarred face in front of her and backed away, her eyes wide. "No!" She felt the large blistered hands grip her arms and wanted to scream, but no sound escaped her lips.

"Is it?" The man loomed over her. The bad eye was now

patched, but the rest of his face was scarred beyond recognition—part of his flesh pink and part a colorless gray. Pulling her into the alleyway between two stone structures, he placed his face close to Rachel and studied her much as a poacher studies the contents of his trap. He inhaled deeply, the sound of his breathing hissing. "It's you, ain't it, now?" he leered.

"Who?" Rachel felt the pent-up anger begin to release. "Who do you think I am?" she demanded to know.

"You're all growed up. I almost didn't know you. 'cept for the—" He flipped a ringlet of her hair. "Red. You're the one wot tried to kill me—ain't you—*Rachel Langley?*" His grip tightened.

"It *is* you, Dring!"

"Wot's left o' me. You thought you got away, eh? But ol' Dring, 'e's like a ghost, now ain't 'e?"

"Let me go!" Rachel's eyes were threatening.

"You still got the fight 'n you, I see." Dring laughed bitterly. "But I saw how you 'ad that minister fella believin' you're a good girl now." Dring's eye narrowed and his voice grew more threatening. "He knows better now."

The words fell upon Rachel's ears like the stones of a mob. "You *are* a beast! You're a monster!"

"Shut up!" Dring hoisted Rachel above the ground, her feet lifted just inches above his own. "Don't you call me that!" he demanded, his defensiveness now outweighing his hostility.

Rachel saw humiliation cloud his gaze and a feeling of pity swept through her. "I'm sorry, Dring. But you don't know me now! You didn't know me then!"

"Once a whore, always—"

"Not true!"

His teeth clenched, Dring pulled her closer. "You tried to kill me!"

"I tried to save a woman and her little girl—from a horrible fate! Is that so wrong?"

"You ruined me!"

"You were supposed to run out—with the others!" Tears coursed down Rachel's cheeks. "I didn't want to kill anyone—not even you." Her words broke into sobs.

Lowering Rachel, he pinned her to the stone wall. "I've prayed for death many a night. Death would've been a better fate."

"I'm sorry for you, Dring. But God can give you strength now—"

"Bah! God! God laughs at ol' Dring. Look at me! I'm a beast—there's no soul left inside here!" He pounded his chest with one hand. "It's gone to hell an' waitin' fer me."

Rachel shook her head. "No—"

"What's this?"

Rachel turned quickly toward the sound of the voice. "Corporal Holmes!"

Dring glared at the corporal, his bottom lip protruding fiercely. "Off wif you!" he sneered.

Holmes was fast to aim his musket. "Unhand the girl!" he demanded.

"Don't shoot, Bryce! Please!" Rachel placed herself between Holmes and Dring.

His eyes narrowed, Holmes spoke in a steady but low tone, "Walk toward me, Rachel."

"He's not armed! Don't shoot!" Rachel pleaded.

Dring jerked Rachel close to him again, his arm tight against her throat. "That's where you're wrong, Red." He pulled out a long, tarnished blade. "One move, soldier-boy, and I cut the wench's throat!"

"No, Dring!" Rachel shouted, more out of remorse for the ex-convict than fear for herself.

"You'll hang for this, crawler!" Holmes' jaw was set as he gazed around the buildings for reinforcements. "There's not a marine around here that'll let you pass through with a hostage."

"I'll die with the girl, then!" He pressed the tip toward Rachel's throat.

Seeing the man was without conscience, Holmes appealed to his sense of bargaining. "Well enough! I'll help you escape. But then you'll let the girl go!"

"In me own time—me own way." Dring's sense of control was restored and his voice reflected a sick confidence. He staggered back, limping and pulling Rachel with him.

Holmes slowly took one step toward them.

"Back, you!" Dring threatened.

Holmes, shouldering his musket, held both palms out. "You're safe wi' me, brute! I ain't followin' you!"

Dring staggered to the rear of the boardinghouse, still holding Rachel around her throat. Bracing his shoulders against the doorway, he shoved with his body while twisting the latch with his free hand.

"You'll be trapped if you go inside," Rachel whispered.

Tightening his grip, Dring breathed out, "Why do you care, wench?"

Rachel did not answer but instead prayed silently for the man.

Stopping to eye the corporal, Dring ordered in a callous tone, "Drop your weapon an' turn around, soldier."

"But you'll kill 'er!"

"I said drop it an' turn around!" Dring leveled the tip against Rachel's throat. "Now!"

Holmes cut his eyes to Rachel.

"It's all right, Bryce. Just do as he says." Rachel nodded woodenly.

Holmes gripped the musket by the tip, placing it cautiously against the wall. Then, turning his back, he yelled, "I've done what you asked, crawler! Now let the woman go!" He stood for a silent moment with no sound coming from the alley.

Rachel whispered a few feet from behind him, "He's gone."

Holmes whirled around, snatching up his weapon. "Which way did he run?"

"I'm not certain." Rachel gazed up wearily. She was stooped with her face to the wall. "He forced me to look away." Her shoulders shook with soft sobs. "He said he'd come back for me."

Holmes saw the open door to the shop and laughed. "I'll trap 'im now!" Whistling to two of his marine buddies, he shouted, "Guard the front!" as he tore through the rear entrance, his musket loaded.

Rachel straightened her clothes, her hands trembling. She strode to the rear of the alleyway and peered down the squalid back street where small children played games in the foul mudholes. A tawdry woman from an upstairs room drew out her head and dumped a pail of dirty water onto the avenue below. Beyond the buildings, she watched a lumbering man in tattered raiment amble around the corner and disappear. Even knowing the man might return to kill her, she pitied him. She quietly withdrew from the scene and made her way to the front of the boardinghouse to wait for the corporal, knowing he would emerge without his quarry.

The front door flew open, and Rachel determined from Holmes' scowl that he was furious. He barked to his comrades, "Did he come this way?"

The two men shook their heads, indicating they hadn't seen Dring.

"The lout's long gone, I vow," one private said, wanting to quit the chase.

"Bryce, I'm not harmed, truly. Why don't we forget about Dring? He's not going to have too many places to hide." Rachel tried to sound reasonable.

Holmes studied Rachel's face, perplexity etching his gaze. "He could've killed you."

"I know. But he didn't. He's just a man full of much pain."

"He's a dog!"

"No. Just bitter."

Holmes dismissed the two privates with a nod and stepped from underneath the boardinghouse portico. The heat of the day caused him to wipe his brow and gave rise to a surly frown across his face. "How do you know the man?" He fixed the musket underneath his arm with the barrel pointed downward.

"I knew him in England." Rachel kept her answer brief, wishing to change the subject altogether.

Holmes stopped beneath the shade of a tavern portico. His eyes narrowed and his mouth was twisted as he scrutinized the girl's words. "What if I told you I stood there listenin' to you two fer longer than I'd intended?"

Rachel could not evade his questions forever. With a sigh, she asked one of her own. "If that's true, then why are you asking me anything at all?"

"I want you to tell me for yourself. What did you do back in England?"

"I—" She felt the blood rush to her head, pounding against her conscience. "I can't say!"

Holmes shouldered the weapon and gripped Rachel's arms. "Why won't you trust me?"

"I don't know!"

"I told you, I 'ave a past as well."

Rachel pulled away, feeling cornered. "Why must we discuss it?"

"Because I care for you. Is that so blasted wrong?"

Wiping the moistness from her eyes, Rachel shook her head. "I'm so sorry, Bryce. But in England I was a child with few choices in life. And I don't wish to linger over a foolish past. Is *that* so wrong?"

Holmes pressed his lips together, a slight trace of frustration lingering in his gaze. But he held his words and nodded accordingly. He studied Rachel's face and the frustration drained from his eyes. Then he noticed the roll of parchment she had snugged beneath her arm. "What is that?"

Her brow furrowed, Rachel looked obliquely and remembered the letter. "Oh, the letter. I'd completely forgotten. I've got to take it to the government building for George. Someone herded a flock of sheep into his field and nearly destroyed the entire crop."

"What will he do now?"

"He hasn't decided, but he wants the owner to pay retribution."

"Rachel, you can't take that letter in."

"Why not?"

"Because George is an emancipist. They'll not take his word over a colonist's. He could be accused of stealing those animals. The farmer of that stolen flock was most likely the man I heard rantin' and ravin' in the government buildin' this morning. He'll have George hanged!"

"That's what I feared."

Holmes held out his hand. "Let me see the letter." He unrolled the correspondence and studied it quickly. "The only way George can return those sheep is to bring them to me. I'll see they're returned."

Her voice tense, Rachel retorted, "But what about his retribution?"

"He'll have to forget about it."

"No!"

"Rachel, you must listen to me. The Corps is powerful. The Prentices have stood up against them, and they won't relent until George Prentice is ruined!"

"Then I'll take the matter to Parliament if I have to—along with Betsy's case."

"What do you mean?"

"That's another matter. I need you to return the diary to me. I found a medallion near where the flock was released. I believe the name of the man in Betsy's diary could bear the same initials as what I saw engraved on the medallion."

"Where is this—medallion?"

"George is keeping it for me. We're going to insist that the military properly investigate both cases."

"Rachel, Betsy's murderer is long gone. When will you accept that fact? And the man—or men—who did this to George, I'm certain has connections with the Corps."

"I have to know for myself, Bryce. Please, just give me back the diary."

"But you asked me to give it to Lilith Thompson."

"I've changed my mind. I'll go and get it myself."

Holmes sighed, exasperation rising in his voice. "You don't have to do that. I'll go to Lilith Thompson myself. Can you at least give me a few days?"

Rachel felt a twinge of guilt when she saw how frustrated he was. "I apologize for my fickle ways. But no one cares that a gentle young woman was murdered without cause. No one cares that an emancipist family is being destroyed by a corrupt system. If I don't do something, Bryce, then neither will anyone else."

"I understand. But you won't be any good to the Prentices if you're dead. Let me help you."

"How?"

Holmes studied the matter for a moment. "I believe the

owner o' that flock lives on a piece o' land near Botany Bay. I'll draw a map for you to take to George before you head back this afternoon. Tell George to meet me with the flock shortly after sunset in two nights. I'll see that they're returned—an' if I can find out anythin' at all about the persons who did this to 'im"—he resolved the matter in his mind—"I'll work on the retribution."

"Oh, Bryce, that would be wonderful!"

"No promises, mind you."

"I understand." Rachel felt relief sweep through her.

"But if the matter's to be properly addressed, I'll need to ask around about the medallion. Ask George to bring it with him in two nights. I'll give him back the diary so he can bring it to you. I'm not altogether sure who I can trust about any o' this situation."

"It's so good to find an honest man in this settlement." Rachel crossed her arms at her waist. "It seems honesty is a rare commodity these days."

"No need to worry about me," Bryce assured. "I'm as honest as they come."

26
River Voyage

"What have you found out, Lilith?" Katy seated herself in the wooden chair in her parents' kitchen. She passed around a plate of fresh hot-sliced bread and a small bowl of homemade jam.

Lilith sat primly, her pale pink dress starched crisply—a stark contrast to the drab kitchen. "I've found out very little about the men who threatened George. But one of my servants chats frequently with a Macarthur servant. They suspect one of the men might possibly be an officer in the Corps—perhaps a corporal. His name is McGrath."

"It seems I've heard of the man." Katy dusted the crumbs from her fingers. "He's Irish?"

"Probably. He's worked under Cornel but appears to have more dealings with Macarthur. I can try to find out where he was the night of the assault. If George can identify the man, I'm certain he'll not wish to shoulder the blame alone." Lilith poured a drop of cream into her cup.

"Good work!" Dwight sipped strong black tea from an old metal cup. "If we can find one weak link, Macarthur will be more vulnerable to confrontation. Katy, is your father around today?" He wiped his mouth with the back of his hand.

"No. He's taking the flock downriver to Botany Bay. Rachel and Caleb are seeing him to the end of the road. Here's the note I found." She handed Rachel's quickly scribbled note to Dwight. "Another corporal, a friend of Rachel's, is meeting him. He's promised to see the flock is returned without involving Papa."

"Very good. George doesn't need a theft charge hanging over his head. The man's trustworthy?" Dwight's brows arched dubiously.

"Rachel's known him for quite some time."

"Good enough, then." Dwight arranged the tin cup next to the slice of bread with his brawny hand, slowly twisting the cup while he thought. "I'll need to have a talk with George when he returns home. We'll need to keep our suspicions to ourselves until we have us some better evidence."

"I've found some information." Katy smiled broadly. "Something I'm certain has Macarthur frothing at the bit."

"What's that?" Dwight cocked his head to one side.

"New South Wales will soon have a new governor—sent from England. He'll be commissioned within days."

Lilith's mouth opened with astonishment. "A new governor? Cornel never told me?"

"The militia hasn't been informed yet by the lieutenant-governor. Because of my connections with Governor Phillip, I was granted a brief audience with Grose early this morning." Katy recalled her days aboard the First Fleet. "The governor-to-be was once captain of the *Sirius*—John Hunter."

"What do we know of him?" Dwight cut his eyes suspiciously.

"He's loyal to England. He was a good ship's captain. That's all I remember about the man." Katy shrugged indifferently.

"Surely, he wouldn't approve of this military monopoly." Lilith shook her graying head.

"I'll know soon enough." Katy poured more tea for the two

of them. "He's granted an appointment with me within two weeks. I left behind a list of our grievances as colonists as well as emancipists. Grose's assistant promised that he would hand deliver it to Governor Hunter personally."

"Things could change in this settlement—an' soon!" Dwight's voice reflected encouragement. He smiled warmly at Katy as she filled his tin cup and placed another slice of hot bread in front of him. "I thank you." He reached to take the cup but instead found his hand wrapping around Katy's. "Pardon me." He nodded diplomatically but quietly enjoyed the soft touch of her skin.

"Not to worry." Katy returned his smile. She was glad to be working side by side with Dwight Farrell, however long it had taken for such a thing to happen.

"Hello? Mrs. Thompson?" Rachel breezed through the rear entrance of the kitchen clad in a pale pink dress. She wore a thin gold chain around her neck, which hung inside the bodice of her dress. "And Katy! Oh, I've missed you so!" She ran to greet Katy with a kiss on her cheek.

"And I you, Rachel. I've much to share with you." Although she smiled, Katy's gaze was darkened with a hint of melancholy. "I found your note this morning. I'm sorry I missed Papa and Caleb."

"He's well on his way with the flock. And good riddance to the beasts." Rachel seated herself at once, her head dropping back in exhaustion as she lifted her thick damp hair off her neck.

Wadjiri tripped through the doorway, his arms brimming with potatoes. "Here's the last of them. I'll—hello?" He almost dropped the load.

"Oh, let me help." Katy was insistent, running to help with the potatoes and leading him to a small worktable where they spread the dirt-covered tubers. "You look exhausted, child. Please take my chair."

"His name is Wadjiri. He's from a tribal clan in the outback." Rachel patted his back fondly. "Wadjiri, this is George's daughter, Katy."

"Pleased to meet you, Katy. I'll wash up outside, then take fast run to fishing pond. Save me large piece of bread."

Katy smiled as each person around the table waved goodbye.

"His English is excellent." She looked eagerly out through the doorway. "He's adorable."

Following Katy's gaze, Rachel offered, "He's quite the fisherman. And your brother Caleb is quite the sheepherder. George is following along on horseback while Caleb guides the leader sheep up front. It's quite a sight to behold! Once they're rid of the flock, they plan to sleep overnight along the roadway. So many newcomers with campfires set up now at night, they should find plenty of company." Rachel laughed heartily. "They'll just have to have their tea on the billy!"

"I carry mine with me!" Dwight lifted his tin cup, black around the bottom from his many nights spent in the wild. "It's the way with all us mates now."

"Mrs. Thompson," Rachel began. "It was so nice of you to come all the way out here."

Lilith waved her palm. "It was no bother. The meetings with Dwight and Katy are important to me." Rachel's brow furrowed slightly. "Oh, I see. So you're helping the emancipists?" Her eyes narrowed speculatively but lit with humor.

Lilith held a finger to her lips. "Watch you don't spread it around now. I'm a spy."

They all laughed but then Rachel grew somber. "So you didn't come out here to deliver the diary?"

"Diary?"

Seeing the confusion in Lilith's face stirred a bit of anxiety in Rachel, but she proceeded with her story. "Yes. Corporal Bryce Holmes told me he delivered Betsy's diary to you—for your husband to investigate."

"I remember you speaking of your friend Betsy." Lilith appeared to be thinking deeply, trying to recall for Rachel's sake. "But Corporal Holmes has not been out to the farm but once this year and that was to deliver some papers to Cornel regarding his transfer from England."

"Oh?" Rachel began to feel apprehensive.

"Something about a mixup. He needed Cornel's signature as proof of his arrival, or something to that effect. The matter was settled quickly, I recall." Lilith noticed the perplexity in

Rachel's face. "Is there something wrong?"

"I'm not certain. Corporal Holmes promised he would retrieve the diary from you. He swore he had already delivered it to you himself."

Dwight sat forward, still fingering the crust of bread. "What was in this diary, Rachel?"

"It could all be nothing." She looked at each, her eyes wide. "Or it could be the one thing that tells us who murdered Betsy."

"What did it say, dear?" Now Lilith's face reflected concern.

"She wrote at great length of a man who was watching her—a man hired by her uncle to watch her until she was hanged back in England. I believe his initials were K. M.—the same initials that were on the medallion. The last name begins with M-c-G-r."

Lilith's face grew flushed. "As in McGrath?"

"It couldn't be the same person." Dwight shook his head. "McGrath is from Ireland—isn't he?"

"We don't know anything about him, really," Lilith asserted.

"Bryce Holmes mentioned a Corporal McGrath. They're fellow marksmen in the Corps. But what about Bryce?" Rachel grew more worried as she recalled the corporal's words to her. "Why would *he* lie to me? Why would he keep Betsy's diary from me?"

"Is there anything else you can recall, Rachel?" Dwight persisted, his face earnest. "Anything?"

"There was one more matter." Rachel pursed her lips to draw in a sip of tea. "Bryce seemed concerned about the medallion. He wanted George to bring it to him"—her brows furrowed—"tonight."

"We've got to intercept George." Dwight sat up at once.

"This is my fault," Rachel whispered, staring down at the floor.

"Rachel, how could you have known?" Katy reached to stroke her friend's arm. "And we don't know anything at all, actually. None of this may mean anything. What if Corporal Holmes merely forgot to deliver the diary?"

"He . . . no, Katy. I remember all he said to me. He didn't forget. He lied to me."

"Where have they gone?" Dwight stood up, shoving his hands back into his gloves.

"I gave the map to George, but I remember it distinctly." Rachel's voice was assured. "I can draw another for you—but I'm going with you."

"Too dangerous, Rachel." Dwight cocked his hat with a thick finger. "What if Holmes is connected with this murderer, as you say? He could be trying to get to you. Remember, you were nearby when Betsy was murdered."

Rachel shook her head. "I can't imagine Bryce being involved with this murderer—but then, I never would've believed he would lie, either." She felt a sickening pain twist through her stomach. *Bryce would never kill Betsy. But perhaps he knows who did.*

"Dwight, before you head for Botany Bay, would you consider involving Cornel? I so want him to see the truth." Lilith's pale eyes were pleading.

Crossing his arms at his waist, Dwight sighed. "What if your husband won't cooperate? What if he runs to Macarthur with all our information?"

Lilith lifted her chin as though she fought against an enormous weight. "I've prayed so long for Cornelius to see the truth. There has to come a time when I trust him with it. Can you understand that?"

"Yes. But we've little time if we're goin' to reach George before he arrives at Botany Bay," Dwight argued.

"It's right on the way. Cornel's at the convict settlement today. He can ride ahead with you. I'll bring Katy and Rachel in my wagon."

Rachel turned hurriedly to sketch the map on a scrap of paper.

"I can agree to that. Let's go, then!" Dwight stood and whirled around, his boots pounding the floor.

"You all . . . go on without me. I need some time . . . I . . ." Rachel stood with tears brimming her eyes and handed the map to Dwight.

"You don't have to explain." Katy gathered up the plates

and saucers and dumped them all in a large pan to soak. "I understand."

"Be careful." Rachel's voice was quiet but controlled. She watched as the three of them disappeared. Walking into the next room she found Amelia staring out a window from the rocking chair. *Poor thing. God keep her safe.* "I'll see that William stays with you," she assured mostly herself. Then her conscience roiled as Heath Whitley's words found their way through her worried mind. "Amelia," she hesitated. Seeing Amelia gave no response, she shook her head. "This is all so silly." Then seating herself in front of Amelia, she spoke softly. "Do you remember the fire?"

Amelia's face trembled and her eyes widened.

Seeing the fear in her face, Rachel backed away. "I . . . I'm sorry. I shouldn't have said that!"

Amelia settled into her chair and rocked more steadily, turning her gaze toward the window.

Standing with a melancholy sadness sweeping through her, Rachel sighed. Glancing out through the doorway again, she saw the dust of the horses and the wagon as the trio sped away. "Godspeed, but you'll never make it on time," she whispered. "George is hours ahead."

"Fish for supper table!" Wadjiri called from behind her.

"So soon!" Rachel spun around and found herself smiling at the sight of Wadjiri standing in the kitchen doorway. He had run all the way across the front room with the dripping wet fish—at least a dozen large barramundi on a string. Beneath him on the floor was a widening puddle, and the trousers she had sewn for him were soaked.

"You couldn't have caught them so quickly."

"No. We caught them and left them on string early this morning. See?" Wadjiri pointed to the saturated clothing. "White feller clothes no good for fishing."

Rachel smacked her lips and then laughed. "Most people don't dive in to catch their fish! Now here, look at you. You're making a terrible mess! Lay all the fish in this pan." She lifted the pan from a hook. "We'll soak them in salt water until we return."

"Where we going?" Wadjiri complied with Rachel's request.

"You remember the map I gave to George this morning? It showed him the way to a farm near Botany Bay."

"Yes, I remember."

"What would be the fastest way to get there? Do you know a better way?"

"Wadjiri always know a better way."

"I imagined as such." Rachel placed her hand aside her face.

"White feller always go long way. Gagudju take swift way—on *wanbiribiri.*"

"You can take me there—now?"

"Yes. We must go now to the river. Yes. Good river—good fish. Sometime crocodile wait for dumb feller to come along and he eat 'im!"

Rachel sighed in exasperation. "Don't give me any more details. May we go now?"

"Follow Wadjiri. Wind spirits will take us."

"No, God will be with us," Rachel corrected. "First let's get William to look after Amelia."

Rachel and Wadjiri ran through the rear doorway and toward the barn to prepare the old steed for the ride.

Katy, Dwight, and Lilith raced toward the convict settlement, with Dwight breaking ahead once his eye caught sight of the encampment. With a haze wrapping the afternoon sun, the atmosphere hung like a stagnant wall. The sound of the barreling steeds and the wagon wheels disturbed the stillness of the countryside.

Lilith gripped the reins, pulling the two-horse team to a slower pace. "Let's wait over here, beneath this tree." She pulled the reins to the right. "I'm exhausted."

"Would you prefer to wait at the convict settlement?" Katy asked. "One of the privates could drive you home before nightfall."

Lilith frowned. "I *am* getting old, aren't I?"

Katy pressed her lips together in amusement. "Now, I didn't say that. You just look a bit pale."

"You wouldn't mind?"

"Not at all. As a matter of fact, if I secure a mount inside, we could make faster time," Katy was quick to assess.

Lilith resolved, "That's a much better plan." She had been watching a man riding toward them. Leaving the settlement, he had waved broadly at Dwight as he rode in. "Who is that?"

Katy looked in the direction where Lilith pointed. She saw the familiar dark Anglican silhouette and the gait of the mule. "Hello!" she called anxiously. "Reverend Whitley!"

Whitley kicked his mule, and it galloped steadily toward them, swirling up dust behind them. "Afternoon, ladies!" He drew fast upon them. "Whoa!" he called out firmly.

Katy sat forward, glancing toward the prison entrance and then back at Whitley. "Did Dwight speak to you?" Her voice was grave, and a glimmer of valiancy lit her gaze.

"All he said was that George was in trouble. May I help?"

"I'm sure we could use your help," Katy nodded. "Rachel just told us that Corporal Holmes could possibly be setting up George for an arrest."

"Holmes? The man she's been—"

"Yes, he's the one." Katy evaded the subject of their relationship. "He took Betsy's diary from Rachel, and it appears the man's been trying to conceal some evidence from the authorities surrounding Betsy's death." Katy felt a surge of anger rise from within. "When I think of how he charmed us all. . . . Holmes could be dangerous, that's for certain."

"Where is Rachel?" Whitley looked anxious.

"She stayed with Amelia. She's quite upset."

"I'll ride with you, then."

Katy saw the anxiety in his face. Turning to face Lilith, she asked suddenly, "Would you like to ride into the prison settlement now? Remember, I need to borrow a horse?"

Lilith nodded. "We should hurry."

"We're riding almost to Botany Bay," Katy informed Whitley. "George is supposed to meet Holmes just after dark with that stolen flock of sheep."

Lilith gripped the reins.

"I'm ready, if you are." Heath tipped his black hat, and the mule beneath him turned around with the squeeze of his legs.

The yellow haze of the day darkened so vaguely that the change of sky went unnoticed. Threads of gray clouds meandered into the haze, blending in from a far west horizon like the wing tips of a carrion. Then, like a silver needle bent by force, a far streak of lightning zagged down through the stratosphere and placated the gaunt outside world with a sudden illumination.

"*This* is your *wanbiribiri?*" Rachel stood on the river's shores, staring at the raft made of sticks, paperbark, and vine. She bit her lip, her gaze skeptical.

Wadjiri nodded proudly. He had hidden the homemade craft in the thick, brambling recesses of some thorny shrubbery. "It's a fine boat."

"It's not a boat. It's a—raft," Rachel said uneasily.

Detecting the skepticism of her stare, Wadjiri grew defensive. "Fast way to Botany Bay. Want 'im?" He crossed his arms, his eyes gazing up from a sullen face. "Or not?"

"I'm not criticizing your craft," Rachel said apologetically. "You're sure it will float?"

"Best of all *wanbiribiris*. Let's push to water." Wadjiri bent over, his trousers still damp from his fishing excursion. He lifted one end of the heavy raft with strong, sinewy arms.

Rachel was fast to his side, gripping a corner as they wheeled around the crude raft and dragged it backward to the embankment. The incline gave them better leverage, so they repositioned themselves and ran to the other side of the raft. Rachel groaned as she shoved against the outer frame and then felt the ease as the raft slid onto the surface of the water. Wadjiri lifted the long shaven limb he had hidden with his craft and stopped the raft at the edge.

"Jump, Rachel!" He leaped onto it with ease and perfect balance, his other hand firmly gripping his spear.

"Oh my!" Rachel wrapped her skirt around herself and jumped as the raft pulled away from the bank, drawn slowly by the current. She spilled onto the rough surface, her hands smacking against the hard limbs. Securing her balance, she slowly lifted her face, her red locks tumbling across her forehead. "It *seems* this *wanbiribiri* can hold us," she said more for her own assurance.

"Fine boat." Wadjiri sprawled forward against the vine-wrapped branches and dipped the pole down into the water's depths. With one hard shove the raft floated down the river and away from Parrametta. Rachel watched with discomfiture as the darkening sky lit with spidery threads of lightning.

27
The Sniper

"We're passing by Mulunguwa land." Wadjiri crouched low on the raft and silently pulled the pole from the water. "Mulunguwa is Gagudjus' worst enemy." His keen eye had detected the change in the territory.

Rachel heard the tautened nature of Wadjiri's voice. The sky had deepened from gray to black with no sunset hues to console the landscape. The thunder rumbled like an approaching stampede of cattle.

Staring up at the sky and back at Rachel, Wadjiri's eyes were wide, and he took great pains to stretch himself flat on the raft. "Please lie down, Rachel," he pleaded in a cautious tone. "Mulunguwa will find us."

"Mulunguwa." Rachel tried to recall the meaning of the word while she complied quickly and lay quietly beside the boy. "Isn't that the name of another tribe?"

"Killer tribe. They slaughter our people one by one while we sleep."

"How horrible. Your men can't stop them?"

"Their killer come and burn bones or human fat outside our hut, which makes Gagudju fall into deep sleep. Person who is sung does not know what is happening to him."

"Sung?"

"You call it a trance. While Gagudju sleeps, Mulunguwa takes his knife and opens very small cut in belly so he can reach in with his fingers and cut out kidney fat."

Rachel squinted and then frowned. "They leave them to die like that?"

"No. First they stuff some soiled cloth in wound and then seal up cut with string and wax to make invisible. In a few days, person who is sung becomes ill and drops over dead. Hard to prove who sung Gagudju." A cloud parted, revealing the moon and outlining his face in a blue cast.

Rachel tensed when a distant howl drifted over a crest and down across the river. "Aborigines have frightening enemies."

"So do white feller."

A row of reeds stirred near the shallow embankment, their tops making black mirrors that swayed to the movement of a platypus that scurried from the human scent. "I hope we arrive soon. It's too dark for my liking."

"Look!" Wadjiri's voice filled with panic. "Gulla-gulla!" He pointed to a black tree, dead and leafless. The silhouette of the tree with the moon partially glowing behind it, gave the tree an uncanny glow as though inhabited by spirits.

"Wadjiri, no!" Rachel clasped his hand. "It's only a tree."

Wadjiri persisted. "No! See where *Lorrkun* has been fulfilled." He indicated again with his thin finger, pointing to what looked to be a platform of sorts in the tree.

Seeing the platform of sticks, which looked similar to a gargantuan eagle's nest, Rachel nodded slowly. "I see it now." She remembered the aborigines' ritual of burying the dead in the bough of the gulla-gulla.

"We about to go under dead man's Shade."

"We won't be harmed, Wadjiri." Rachel felt a queer anxiousness seize her, although she did not believe in ghosts.

"*Djumdjum* is spirit of the killer Mulunguwa who killed the Gagudju. We cannot cross his Shade." Wadjiri took the pole and thrust it into the water to slow the raft against the current.

"Wadjiri! We can't stop!" Rachel yelled. "We've got to find George. We're almost out of time!"

"Shade will find us!"

"No! God will protect us!"

The sound of the current rushed past them and their glances locked in a silent exchange. Wadjiri resolutely lifted the pole from the water.

As the raft began to drift again with the current, Wadjiri dropped the pole at his side and threw himself down flat. Flinging his arms over his head, he shouted, "Rachel's God—keep Shade from us!"

"Quiet!" she whispered. "What if someone hears you?" She held a finger to her lips.

For the first time, Wadjiri prayed silently, his face against the wet wood. Rachel closed her eyes, the rock and sway of the water lulling her to drowsiness. The current began to pull the raft along at a swifter pace. She did not see the light that flickered along the ridge and then disappeared in the density of the brush. Nor did she notice that the raft had begun to take on more water.

Passing under the shadow of the gulla-gulla, the crude vessel floated silently past the Mulunguwa corpse, which was wrapped in paperbark and stringybark to prevent defilement from the black carrion crows that circled overhead. Wadjiri would not lift his face until they had traveled miles away from the burial site.

Wadjiri drew himself up and gazed to his left beyond the embankment. "Someone is watching."

Seeing nothing but black forest, Rachel narrowed her eyes and searched the land for movement. "I see nothing. You're still afraid of ghosts?"

"No. Ghost not carry light."

Rachel looked again and then saw what Wadjiri had seen. A light flashed through the distant trees and disappeared. It was moving at a swift pace but was too far away to decipher. "What do you make of it?"

"Someone watching us."

"Who would know we're here?" Uneasiness pricked at Rachel's emotions. "Perhaps it's George. Are we close to the meeting place?"

"We are close." The sound of musket fire rang down through the woods. The musket ball tore through the water just beyond the craft.

Rachel jerked and grabbed Wadjiri, pulling him down flat against the surface.

"It's Shade! We turn back now!" Wadjiri snapped as he grappled for the pole. Thrusting it back into the water, he struggled with the guide stick when it found no bottom.

"It's no ghost! Someone's trying to kill us!" Rachel pulled the boy down again. "Stay down!"

The rifle fired another time, hitting the side of the raft and splintering a limb. Wood shattered all around them and the raft took on more water.

Rachel screamed as the disintegrating raft rounded a corner of the meandering river. The sound of the current rose, and the speed of the craft upset their balance. Wadjiri tumbled to the side and was nearly swept away, but he gripped the outside frame with both hands. "Rachel!" he shouted. At once, the thunderclouds released with a sickening deluge of rain. "Where are you?"

"I'm here!" she cried, her face barely visible above the rocking craft's side. Her hair was matted around her face and her fingers trembled to cling to the splintered wood as the rain spilled down with a force.

Wadjiri mustered all the strength he could and pulled himself back onto the raft, his spear still in his grasp. Swooping with both hands, he stretched himself across the loosening limbs and gripped Rachel's hands. "Hold to me!" Fear rose in his throat as the rapids and the rain pounded against both of them.

Feeling the boy's strong hands grab hers, Rachel could see nothing except the occasional white froth that slapped across her face, stinging her eyes and blinding her. Although the sniper had most likely lost sight of them, the pounding current now clawed at her, tiring her body and her will. "Wadjiri!" she felt the raft swirl through a torrent. "I see something ahead! What is it?" She shouted above the roar.

Wadjiri turned to behold the water disappearing into a black pit as they neared a great falls. "It's end of world, Rachel! Your Jesus come soon."

"Oh, Wadjiri," Rachel cried and strained to see through salty tears. "I wish that He were." She began to sob. "Come quickly, Lord! Save us!"

Wadjiri closed his eyes tightly and braced himself for the inevitable plunge that would soon swallow up their lives.

Rachel felt a hard jolt that threw her solidly against the raft. She was stunned when the current began to fly past them. "We've stopped!" She stared across the wood pieces that slowly began drifting away. "Wadjiri! Look!"

Opening his eyes, Wadjiri held up his hand at the spray that hit him in the face as he struggled to pull himself from the current's flow. "Rachel!" He beheld the enormous tree that had collapsed at the edge of the embankment. "Your Jesus—He saved us!"

Rachel climbed out, struggling to hold to the slippery trunk of the fallen tree. She straddled the felled wattle tree's broad base and reached down to grasp Wadjiri's hand. "Grab hold!"

Straining against the current, which splintered the craft to pieces, Wadjiri held to the outer limbs of the tree. "I can't—reach you."

"Let go of your spear! Grab my hand!"

"I can't!" Wadjiri's woeful brown eyes looked up at Rachel. "Gagudju man cannot lose his spear."

"You can make another! It's not worth your life!" Rachel edged as far forward as she could without falling headlong into the foam. "Wadjiri!"

Wadjiri was swept quickly out into the current, his one hand still clinging to a soggy branch.

"Not to worry." Tears welled in his eyes. "Dreaming take me back to land." His tone was faltering.

"Please, Wadjiri!" Rachel cried as the lad slipped from her reach. "Don't leave me!" she shouted in horror as Wadjiri was whipped into the blackness of the falls. "No!" her cries rose up in a wailing remonstrance. "Not the boy!" she pled. Her eyes beseeched the heavens. "Take me instead. I'm the wretch!"

The roaring blackness returned no cry, but inhaled the river's contents like a wide, gaping throat. Rachel lay curled around the trunk for the space of a few minutes, her hair drenched and clinging to her face and arms. She breathed deeply in an effort to stifle the uncontrollable weeping as remorse swept through her. Then a distant bleating caused her to pause and sit slowly up. "George," she whispered feebly. "I've got to warn him!"

After pulling herself around and back up to the gnarled roots that protruded from the earth, Rachel staggered to the muddy ground. The rain was subsiding but the pain in her heart was insufferable. "Why, God?" she cried out. *Was there a chance I might be too happy in this world? Betsy first? Now Wadjiri?*

Trudging up the steep slope, Rachel used her hands to assure her steps. Her fingers were soon clay-caked with the red mud of the river basin. Pulling herself up and across the ridge, she lay for a moment catching her breath. She could see a faint light ahead, and the sound of the bleating sheep grew louder. The pale pink dress she had donned that morning now clung to her like heavy burlap, streaked with the red soil. She pulled up the hem and squeezed out as much of the water as she could and then shook the fabric, allowing it to drop sticky and wet against her weary frame.

Staggering from one tree to the next, Rachel fought the urge to stop and rest. She soon spotted a clearing ahead. The rain had ceased but dripped from tall, bending conifers, dampening her crown again. But she was only aware of the sight before her. She hid behind twin pines and held her breath as her heart pounded in her ears.

"Where is Corporal Bryce Holmes?" George lay flat against the ground, face down with Caleb next to him. "What 'ave ye done wif 'im?"

The tall, churlish man who stood over them with a musket pointed at their heads would not answer. He only reached up from time to time to secure the dark hood that covered his head. Rachel peered from around the tree and gasped at the sight of the hood. *Betsy's killer!*

His deep-set blue eyes stared out cold and lifeless from the small holes cut in the fabric. Reaching to search their empty pockets for money, he muttered about the worthlessness of an emancipist.

"Why are you doin' this?" George questioned adamantly.

Drawing back a heavy boot, the assassin kicked George ruthlessly in his side. As George doubled over, his head tucked to his chest, the man stormed toward the wagon and yanked Caleb's leather pouch from the seat. The sheep scattered in alarm and moved away from the darkly dressed man. Whirling around in a hostile fashion, he spewed, "Where is it?"

"Where is wot?" Caleb's scowl was just as hostile.

"The medallion! Where have you hidden it?"

"It's in the bloomin' bag! Look again!" Caleb retorted angrily. "Just take it an' leave us be!"

Rifling through the bag again, he thundered, "It ain't in 'ere!" He hurled the bag to the ground and stormed toward the two on the ground. "Give it to me—*now!*"

George lifted his face wearily. "The boy's tellin' the truth! The girl, Rachel, put it in the bag 'erself!"

"You give it to me or I'll blow yer 'ead off—the boy goes first!"

George staggered to his feet, his stomach roiling. *"No! Not me boy!"* He rushed at the man, his face full of fury.

Whipping around to face Prentice, the assassin placed his finger on the trigger. "You're dead, Prentice!"

"Stop!" Rachel shrieked. She tore from around the trees and raced toward the assassin. "The medallion's right here!"

The musket exploded and Prentice crumpled to the ground. "Papa!" Caleb cried, terror rising in his eyes.

"Dear God!" Rachel screamed while the assassin was fast to reload. "You beast! I forgot to put it in the bag!" she wept openly, angry tears streaking her face. "I'm wearing it around my neck!"

"Hold it right there, missy!" he threatened. "You got it, then give it 'ere!"

Rachel lifted the long chain that hung around her neck and down into her bodice. From the end twirled the silver-sainted medallion. "Who are you? McGrath?"

The hooded man laughed hoarsely. "Never you mind." He reached for the necklace and yanked it viciously from Rachel's grasp.

"Got you!" Caleb yelled as he leaped, wrapping his arms around the man's legs.

As the assassin spun around to combat the lad, Rachel, in a frenzy, snatched fiercely at the black hood, yanking it triumphantly from his head.

The man, furious, jerked around, stepping back to aim his weapon at them both. Seeing the hood fly from his face, his eyes narrowed. "You're more stupid than I thought!"

Beholding the assassin's face, Rachel cried out, "Bryce!" Disappointment flooded her countenance. "Why?"

"No, wench. Not Bryce."

"Who then?"

Bowing his face slightly in mock servility, he answered slowly, his eyes fixed on hers, "Kelly McGruder, at your service."

"You're an imposter! You killed Betsy, didn't you?" Rachel's eyes were accusing. "Did Cornelius Fortner send you?"

"You know too much."

"But why did you come after me! Why ask *me* to marry you?"

McGruder, alias Holmes, began his confession, the inevitable working its way through his thinking. "I caught a glimpse o' you right after I finished off the Brady girl. I knew that if I could convince you, I could put up the perfect front. Who would suspect Rachel Langley's fiancé o' killin' 'er best friend?"

"You're loathsome! Betsy was innocent!"

"An eyewitness to 'er uncle's, shall we say, *indiscretions*. Besides, Fortner 'ad too much on me. Returnin' to England would o' landed me a turn at the gallows."

"But why involve the Prentices?"

"You wouldn't come to me as long as you 'ad them to take you in. I knew I 'ad to sink your little ship."

"How unfair! I wouldn't have come to you anyway! I never loved you!"

"Nobody says no to McGruder." He glared menacingly, drawing his musket to the side of his face. "An' all good witnesses go to heaven. Say goodbye first, Rachel Langley. Then the Prentice brat'll follow close behind."

Caleb backed away, shaking his head. "You'll hang, McGruder!"

Rachel shook her head. "You can't kill me. I know you won't." Her brow furrowed and she stepped backward from the man, her eyes fixed on his.

Staring back, his gaze soulless, McGruder laughed. "You ain't never met the devil 'isself." He curled his finger around the trigger and locked his sights on Rachel.

His head snapping back in alarm and his eyes wild, McGruder wheezed out a silent oath. Then his eyes were cast down and fixed at once on the spear that quivered from his chest. "Agh!" He muttered unintelligible phrases before slumping to the ground as a stream of red trickled from his mouth. Rachel's hands flew to her lips and she turned at once to see the small, slender boy who stood between the twin pines.

"Wadjiri! I thought you were—"

"See? Gagudju man cannot lose his spear."

Elation swept through Rachel as she ran toward the dripping wet lad. Not knowing whether to laugh or cry, Rachel threw her arms around him and shouted, "Praise be to God!"

"He saved me, and I saved you," Wadjiri said smugly.

Caleb ran to throw himself on his papa. George stirred at once, his eyes fluttering. "You—made it, m'boy!"

Caleb gaped at George as though he beheld a ghost. "You ain't dead?"

"Got me in the shoulder, all right"—George smiled faintly, favoring his right shoulder—"but I'll live. I banged me bloomin' head, though, when I fell."

"I'm so glad you're alive, George!" Rachel promised, "I'll fix you right up. When I get you home, that is."

She turned slowly to gaze upon the man she had known as Corporal Bryce Holmes. *I never knew you*. She glanced toward the black hood and then back at the face she had trusted with her life. Dropping her head, Rachel wept bitterly.

Wadjiri placed his arm around Rachel's waist and pressed his face into her side.

"We found them! Look!" Katy shrieked from horseback as she emerged from a stand of pines.

"Katy, me love, it's about time!" George tried to pull himself up, but winced at the pain.

"We had to take shelter from the storm in an old shack." Katy emerged toward the lantern, which still glowed from the stump. Behind her galloped Dwight Farrell, Lieutenant Cornel Thompson, and a small battalion of his mounted militia.

"Get this man medical attention at once!" Thompson barked. He threw his leg around and jumped to the ground to attend to George. "My apologies at the corps indiscretions, Mr. Prentice." Walking toward them, he spotted the corporal's body. "It was as you suspected?" He was incredulous.

Rachel nodded. "He tried to kill all of us, sir." She wiped the moistness from her eyes. "And he's not Holmes—he's Kelly McGruder. He's the man who killed Betsy Brady."

"You're a brave young woman, Miss Langley." Thompson walked over to inspect the body, crouching cautiously beside McGruder, feeling for pulse. "He's dead." He scrutinized the spear that protruded from a blood-saturated military shirt.

"My spear." Wadjiri was fast to reclaim his possession.

"Papa, you're hurt!" Katy followed closely behind Thompson, tossing her reins to a private. She seated herself abjectly at his side and clasped his hands in her own. "We found the man who threatened you in the barn. McGrath!"

"So he did confess?" Rachel asked anxiously.

"Not fully, I'm afraid," Thompson shook his head. "My dear wife insists the man has ties to Macarthur, but we've yet to have any witnesses implicate the paymaster. Give us a few days."

Two of the privates parted to allow past the last rider.

"Where is she?" the man's deep voice asked anxiously.

Rachel gazed up, her heart quickening at the familiar voice. "Heath Whitley," she smiled broadly.

"I couldn't believe it when I heard you speak, Rachel. I thought you were home." His eyes softened upon seeing her. "I would've been worried sick had I known." He pulled his wide-brimmed hat from his head and shook the rain from it. Then stepping slowly toward her, he clasped her hand. "How did you arrive ahead of us?"

Rachel cast her eyes obliquely at the lad who stood beside her. "With a little help from Wadjiri—and the Lord."

"Fine boat," Wadjiri nodded. "Eaten by river, though."

Dwight Farrell crouched next to Katy and placed his hand atop hers. His eyes regarded her warmly. "We'll get us that Macarthur yet, won't we, love?"

Sighing wearily, Katy nodded hesitatingly. "After I've had some rest. But yes," she agreed wholeheartedly. "Let's not give up this time."

"Rachel," Whitley spoke quietly but firmly. "I'll drive the Prentices home in their wagon tonight. You and I will use the time to talk. You'll ride with me?"

Rachel nodded, and then turned to eye the dead corporal who lay on the ground. "Yes. I have much to tell you—once and for all."

"I know."

28
Sydney's Chapel

"Amelia," Rachel whispered. "I want to talk to you." She glanced nervously toward Heath Whitley, who sat quietly on the edge of George and Amelia's bed.

Whitley nodded confidently. "Go on. It's all right."

"I want to talk about the fire. Remember?"

Amelia whimpered, but her eyes remained glassy.

Rachel had tried for several evenings to gain a response from Amelia. Each night, she felt she saw glimpses of a breakthrough, but then Amelia would retreat back into her protective shell. "It wasn't a boardinghouse, was it? Remember the brothel where we all met?"

George crouched anxiously in the doorway. His head was bowed in silent prayer.

Feeling a lump in her throat, Rachel forced herself to go on. "You helped save me, Amelia. I know you thought the fire was a bad thing."

A single tear glistened in the corner of Amelia's eye.

"But it was actually a good thing. You and Katy got away. Katy's fine now. She's well."

Her lip trembling, Amelia whispered, "Ka—"

Rachel turned to look anxiously at George. Pressing her lips together, she continued with a firm determination. "Look at me, Amelia." Rachel clasped Amelia's face in her hands and looked deeply into her green eyes. "I'm Rachel. Your friend. The fire is gone. We're all safe now."

Amelia shook her head, her hands flying up to push Rachel away. "No!" she whimpered.

Rachel felt her emotions surface but held her composure. "Come back to us, Amelia. George needs you. Rose Hill needs you—all of us do."

The muscles in Amelia's face began to spasm, and her hands trembled almost violently.

"Per'aps we should stop now." George looked worried.

"Please," Heath Whitley tried to offer comfort, "we should at least try."

Wiping one of his eyes, George nodded. "Go on, then."

"Remember the young girl who helped you escape the fire?" Rachel began again. "It was me. I was a—" She glanced toward the minister.

"A sinner like me," Whitley said softly.

"A prostitute." Rachel felt her breath quicken. "But I found the Lord—just like you prayed I would." Rachel felt the pain and remorse well up within her. Her head dropping in Amelia's lap, she cried without inhibition. "Please come back to me. I need you." She shook her head. "You're the only mother—I know." She sobbed, feeling her tears soaking the blue fabric of Amelia's dress. She cried for a short time and then heard George whisper something to Heath Whitley.

Feeling a gentle finger stroke her hair, she heard a quiet, feeble voice speak. "D-don't cry, love. Mum's here."

Rachel gazed upward while Amelia placed her trembling fingers behind her head, cradling her red hair around her neck. "Mum's here." A faint smile creased Amelia's cheeks for the first time in months.

"Glory be!" George cried as he ran to his wife.

"Amelia!" Whitley stood to his feet.

"Please say you hear me!" Rachel grasped her hands around Amelia's frail wrists.

"Of course I 'ear you, dearie. You're sittin' right in front o' me," Amelia laughed softly, her eyes focused lovingly on Rachel. "George?"

Rachel threw her arms around the woman who had truly been a mother to her, and wept tears of joy. "Amelia's come back to us, George!"

"Lovely day for a wedding." Rachel smiled at the crisp blue sky that blanketed the day with warmth. A pleasant breeze stirred the trees left standing around the newly erected chapel in Sydney Cove.

"Yes, and such a beautiful bride," Amelia beamed. She had grown stronger over the last few months and had even begun to cook. She battled occasionally with bouts of fear, but George was always at her side holding her hand. Together with Caleb, they began raising their own flock of sheep.

The two women clasped hands and strolled beneath a spreading wattle that filled the air with a fragrant aroma from its bountiful clusters of golden blooms.

Rachel watched with anticipation as wagonloads of families began to arrive. The emancipists' wives were all dressed in their Sunday best, twirling gay parasols over their freshly coiffed hairstyles.

"Look, Amelia. Even the Thompsons are coming."

"Lilith said she wouldn't miss it for the world," Amelia said knowingly.

"I'll go and speak to her." Rachel laid the fresh bouquet of nosegays on the small wooden bench where they sat.

"I'll come shortly," Amelia waved her on. "I'm enjoying this shade."

Rachel walked quickly to greet Lilith, her eyes growing misty.

Lilith stepped gracefully from the carriage, her hair decorated with colored plumes and flowers. "Oh my, Rachel. Just look at you! That dress is simply lovely."

Rachel held out the skirt. "Katy and Amelia helped me make it. It's silk—can you believe—me in silk?"

"Why yes." Lilith turned to observe her daughter, who stepped haughtily from the wagon. "We all can imagine, can't we, Felicity dear?"

"Yes, of course, Mother," Felicity answered curtly. Popping open her parasol with a snap, she hid quickly behind it and strolled past both of them, her steps brisk.

"Well, look at *you*." Rachel referred to Lilith's uncharacteristic choice of attire—a bright pink dress with matching adornments in her hair.

Lilith winked. "Katy's taught me to be more of an adventurer."

"I could use a little less of it myself. But I'm so glad you came." Rachel lifted her chin buoyantly.

"I was so afraid we would be late." Lilith's brow was pinched with worry.

Rachel followed her gaze, and they both observed Thompson walking hastily to greet Heath Whitley. "What's wrong?"

Leaning forward to express confidentiality, Lilith answered quietly, "Trouble at the convict settlement. The Irish convicts are brewing about their treatment, but their demands are impossible to meet. It could mean bloodshed."

"How dreadful. Lieutenant Thompson's all right?"

"He quelled a feud this morning, but there's something frightening about all of it. Rumor is that the Irish are planning an uprising to overthrow the Corps."

"Well, is it any wonder?" Rachel stared off in the distance, her mind recalling the small Irish boys in the contagion ward. "The abuses are rampant inside those prison walls, Lilith. Heath and I are determined to make a difference for the lads. And I'm certain the Catholics are none too happy about being forced to attend Reverend Marsden's services—they hate him as it is."

"Yes. Such a shame your Reverend Whitley wasn't awarded the new chapel. It's all beyond our control. Cornel can't get Macarthur to listen, so the Corps is growing each day by leaps and bounds. It's a dangerous world."

Rachel lowered her voice. "Our new governor is a disappointment, isn't he?"

Lilith's eyes searched for listening ears who might overhear. Finding no one nearby, she whispered, "A dismal disappointment." She composed herself, her face brightening. "Here I am rambling about the end of the world—we've a wedding to attend. I see Reverend Whitley's arrived."

"Yes. We were able to secure the chapel in spite of Marsden."

Rachel turned blithely, the sound of violins and a pianoforte sounding forth the harmony that heralded the day with hope.

"Run along now. You'd better get in place," Lilith scolded affectionately. "Where's Katy?"

"Probably waiting for me." Rachel turned at once, lifting her silk skirt and petticoats to make haste for the rear of the chapel.

The wooden seats filled up quickly, and the excitement of the parishioners was evidenced by the sound of their gay talk and subdued laughter as they awaited the ceremony. All faces turned toward the front as Dwight Farrell and Heath Whitley stepped out from a room behind the pulpit and made their way to the front of the small sanctuary. The music swelled and the back door opened ceremonially. Escorted by Caleb, a little girl entered, scattering petals down the narrow aisle. The spectators stifled their laughter as the lad tugged uncomfortably at his collar and pulled the girl along as though they were in a three-legged race.

"He'll be a hard one to tame," one spinster remarked to her widow friend.

Then Wadjiri tripped across the front of the chapel, dressed in a stylish coat with tails. He had battled against the stubborn women but had lost, or so the women thought—until they saw he had left his shoes at the doorway. Running up barefoot beside the men, he held up a satin pillow on which rested a single golden circular band.

Rachel stepped in, her yellow skirts billowing around her as the spring breeze followed her into the room. She smiled broadly at Whitley, who beamed at the sight of her. The spinster leaned forward again. "They say the Langley girl'll be hitchin' up with the minister before long."

"What's takin' her so long?" the widow asked.

"Who knows but God Almighty? She told the man she wanted to wait. The Prentice girl knows a find when she sees 'im, though."

As Rachel found her place next to Caleb and the flower girl, the pianist glanced toward Reverend Whitley, and at his nod began to play the familiar wedding strains. The violinist joined with him and the congregation rose to their feet.

Rachel turned to watch her cherished friend step through the chapel doorway on the arm of her proud father. Katy's beaming face was covered by a filmy white veil, and her rustling bridal gown was crafted from a simple but elegant design. The three of them had spent weeks making the dresses for this day, but now the attire seemed secondary. *Katy's getting married!* Rachel burst into tears but managed a smile for the bride.

Katy and George promenaded down the aisle as though they were royalty, and Katy moved gracefully, without the trace of a limp. Stopping at the front pew, she bent to kiss Amelia's tear-streaked face. Then stepping up beside Rachel, she turned to face her waiting groom.

Dwight's green eyes twinkled with anticipation as he smiled at his bride. "I love you, Katy Prentice," he whispered. "You are my prize."

The bride and groom joined hands as Heath began the ceremony.

The doors to the chapel opened without a sound and admitted a lone figure. He staggered a bit and slowly found his way down the aisle, pausing to lean on every pew before stopping in the middle of the sanctuary.

Katy and Dwight saw the change in Whitley's face, but did not understand the whispering and gasping arising behind them. Katy turned and her hand came up to her lips. "It's Dring," she whispered, turning to gaze at Rachel. The disfigured man stood in a bent posture, his eye still covered by the patch Heath Whitley had made for him. He was dressed in the same tattered clothes given him when he was discharged from prison.

Katy released Dwight's hand and moved slowly toward the intruder. "It's all right, everyone," she tried to speak assuringly.

Rachel stepped forward and stood at Katy's side, wrapping her arm around Katy's. "Please come in and take your seat," Rachel nodded at Dring. "We've been waiting for you."

Dring shuffled awkwardly to find an empty place, but none was offered.

"Would one of you please make room for Dring?" Katy smiled. "He's our special guest."

At once, a gentleman in a tall top hat stood and bowed cordially to the man. "Please take my seat, sir."

Dring turned to nod at Rachel and Katy. "Thank ye," he muttered.

Squeezing between two women, he gestured affirmatively to the bride. "Go on, then."

Whispering so only Rachel would hear, Katy said, "He's seated himself next to Felicity." She hid a smile as she turned to clasp hands again with Dwight.

"Good," was all Rachel had time to say.

The nuptials were carried forth without incident, and Mr. and Mrs. Dwight Farrell were presented to Sydney Cove as its newest colonists.

Heath Whitley extended his arm to Rachel and escorted her through the doorway of the chapel. "They're a handsome couple, Dwight and Katy."

Rachel agreed, but the urge to cry was still strong. She smiled up at the handsome minister. "With those two together, they could conquer the world if they put their trust in God."

"I'll settle for Sydney Cove." Whitley's face grew somber.

"Lilith said there's an uprising brewing at the convict settlement."

"Yes, Cornel Thompson informed me." Whitley gazed up at the man and woman who stepped from the carriage just beyond them.

Rachel followed his gaze inquisitively. She noted the

woman was trim and dressed in expensive, tailored attire. Her auburn hair was coiffed underneath a fashionable hat.

"Hello." Rachel greeted the couple with a cordial nod of her head.

"We're trying desperately to find Rachel Langley." The woman's soft brown eyes reflected her words.

"I'm Rachel Langley. Is something wrong?"

"Rachel! You're more lovely than I imagined." She introduced herself. "I'm Grace Gwaltney. Betsy Brady's sister."

Rachel looked again into the large brown eyes and studied the soft features of the woman's face. The similarities between the two sisters were remarkable. "I can't believe it!" Rachel welcomed Grace as though she were Betsy herself. Taking the woman's hand, she felt the tears resurface, but instead of remorse, a peace enveloped her. "We've much to talk about. Many things have been settled."

"So I've heard." Grace pressed her lips together, the emotion of the moment almost overwhelming.

"I heard the confession myself—Cornelius Fortner is the perpetrator." Rachel watched as mixed emotions arose in Grace Gwaltney's face. "I will testify."

Her eyes tearing, Grace looked up at her husband.

"We have what we've come for, dear." Francis smiled with assurance.

"There's food and drink waiting at Rose Hill," Heath offered. "Mr. and Mrs. Gwaltney, we would be honored if you'd join us."

Grace affirmed the offer but could not take her eyes off Rachel. It was as if the two women had found a common link that somehow allowed them to reach out and touch the life of the young woman who had brought so much change to their worlds. Faith, hope, and love had sprung up from the seeds Betsy had sown.

Rachel took Heath's arm and allowed him to whisk her up into the carriage. "Please follow us," she instructed the Gwaltneys.

As the freshly painted carriage swayed down the road, Rachel reflected upon the past and the future all at once. Marrying Heath Whitley would bring great change to her world.

She had plenty of time to make that decision. But what about the young boys in the contagion ward—the outcasts of Sydney Cove? They still needed someone to stand on their behalf. How could this nation stand if its future wasn't nurtured?

"Do you think this colony will survive, Heath?" she asked quietly.

"Only the Lord can answer that question, Rachel. I know that I plan to sow as much of the Word of God into it as I can. I also know we can stand on a promise."

"Which is?"

" 'For as the soil makes the sprout come up, and a garden causes seeds to grow, so the Sovereign Lord will make righteousness and praise spring up before all nations.' "

"So be it," Rachel affirmed. "God bless Australia!"